P9-CLL-432

SHROUD
OF ROSES

SHROUD OF ROSES

A CORNWALL AND REDFERN MYSTERY

GLORIA FERRIS

DUNDURN
TORONTO

Copyright © Gloria Ferris, 2015

All rights reserved. No part of this publication may be reproduced, stored in a retrieval system, or transmitted in any form or by any means, electronic, mechanical, photocopying, recording, or otherwise (except for brief passages for purpose of review) without the prior permission of Dundurn Press. Permission to photocopy should be requested from Access Copyright.

All characters in this work are fictitious. Any resemblance to real persons, living or dead, is purely coincidental.

Editor: Allison Hirst   Cover design: Laura Boyle
Design: BJ Weckerle   Cover image: mauhorng/istockphoto
Printer: Webcom

Library and Archives Canada Cataloguing in Publication

Ferris, Gloria, 1947–
    Shroud of roses / Gloria Ferris.

(A Cornwall and Redfern mystery)
Issued in print and electronic formats.
ISBN 978-1-4597-3060-1 (pbk.).—ISBN 978-1-4597-3061-8 (pdf).—
ISBN 978-1-4597-3062-5 (epub)

    I. Title. II. Series: Ferris, Gloria, 1947– . Cornwall and Redfern mystery.
PS8611.E785S57 2015   C813'.6   C2014-907368-2
                                C2014-907369-0

1 2 3 4 5   19 18 17 16 15

We acknowledge the support of the **Canada Council for the Arts** and the **Ontario Arts Council** for our publishing program. We also acknowledge the financial support of the **Government of Canada** through the **Canada Book Fund** and **Livres Canada Books**, and the **Government of Ontario** through the **Ontario Book Publishing Tax Credit** and the **Ontario Media Development Corporation**.

Care has been taken to trace the ownership of copyright material used in this book. The author and the publisher welcome any information enabling them to rectify any references or credits in subsequent editions.

J. Kirk Howard, President

The publisher is not responsible for websites or their content unless they are owned by the publisher.

Printed and bound in Canada.

VISIT US AT
Dundurn.com | @dundurnpress | Facebook.com/dundurnpress | Pinterest.com/dundurnpress

Dundurn
3 Church Street, Suite 500
Toronto, Ontario, Canada
M5E 1M2

GARY PUBLIC LIBRARY
KENNEDY BRANCH LIBRARY

3 9222 03090 322 8

*This story is dedicated to my friends in
Bruce County, Ontario.
I continue to be inspired by the area's beauty
and mystery.*

BRUNSWICK
ACTIVITY BRANCH LIBRARY

CHAPTER ONE

KNEES AND ELBOWS PUMPING, the two men shot out of the building like a dragon's fiery breath was scorching their asses. As the shorter of the two reached for the door handle of a battered Ford pickup truck parked at the curb, his feet lost traction and he skidded into a snowbank. His companion leaned against the tailgate and pulled a phone from his pocket. When he saw the Cherokee bearing down on them, he ran toward it, waving his arms.

Neil Redfern slammed on the brakes and stopped his vehicle in the middle of the street. When he got out, his hand automatically went to his Glock. "What's the problem, sir?"

The man leaning on the Ford had a tall, lean build, and sported a black beard and moustache. Both men wore heavy plaid shirts with black toques pulled down low on their foreheads.

Seeing a uniformed cop, the bearded man slumped

over, inhaling lungfuls of icy air. He motioned with a flashlight at the two-storey brick structure behind him. For now, he seemed incapable of speech. Neil looked at the other man, who was sitting on a mound of snow, rocking back and forth, hands shielding his eyes. He was mumbling non-stop, but Neil couldn't make out the words.

"I'm Police Chief Neil Redfern. Is someone in danger inside?"

The two men looked at each other, then shook their heads.

"Am I in danger if I go in there?" He wasn't wearing a shoulder radio, or a vest, and didn't want to walk into a shitstorm without backup.

Vehement head shakes from both men, but Neil wasn't risking his life based on what they thought.

The lettering on the truck spelled out DAVIDSON AND CUTLER SALVAGE, and a heavy chain led from the bumper of the truck to the entrance of the building. The double entrance doors had been pulled away from the frame and lay on the ground. The words LOCKPORT H.S. 1961 were incised on a stone arch across the front of the building. The windows had been boarded up and fitted with iron bars.

The bearded man gestured to the old high school with one arm and poked himself in the chest with the other hand. "I'm … I'm Fang Davidson. That's my cousin, Larry Cutler."

"Why are the doors on the ground?"

"We bought the salvage rights for the building. It's going to be demolished next week. We have to take what we can now. Nobody gave us keys, so we had to break the doors down."

Cutler had regained coherency. "Tell him what we found, Fang."

Fang clamped his lips shut again, looking as though he was going to pass out or puke.

"Take your time," Neil told him. If one of them didn't spit it out fast, he was calling for backup. The day shift was already spread thin due to a flu bug and the Christmas parade about to start over on Main Street. He didn't have to strain his ears to hear the Salvation Army band trombones warming up with "Good King Wenceslaus." The parade was the reason he had been using the back streets to get home from the station.

Neil turned toward the curb to try his luck with Cutler. Davidson clutched at his arm. "No, I ... I have to show you."

Neil shook Davidson off and focused on Cutler. But now the man refused to meet his eyes.

He called the station on his cell. "Lavinia, I'm about to enter the abandoned high school on the corner of Brant and Chippewa Streets. Two men, Larry Cutler and Fang Davidson, requested assistance. Yes, I said Fang. If I don't call back within ten minutes, send backup."

"Okay, let's go." He led the way inside, his Glock in one hand and Davidson's flashlight in the other. Davidson and Cutler followed close behind.

Cutler crowded against Neil. "Straight down the hall. At the end, hang a right. Second door on the right — the girls' locker room."

"You won't need the gun," Davidson contributed, his voice cracking.

"Stay back," he ordered them.

A few metres inside and it was dark as a crypt. Staying close to the wall, they passed an opened door leading to the offices. Metal lockers lined both sides of the hallway. All were wide open and empty. He stepped cautiously over buckled flooring and fallen ceiling tiles. The hall ended in a T-intersection. Neil swept the weak beam of light to the left before turning the other way. About twenty metres in, he passed the closed door of the boys' locker room. Another ten metres and he faced a yawning blackness.

"In here?" Neil indicated the opening with the flashlight. The door had been propped back. Without stepping into the room, he couldn't see an identifying sign.

"Yeah," Cutler confirmed, pushing up against Neil. "In a locker."

Neil elbowed him back. "Stop breathing down my neck."

He edged into the space, back against the wall. Only the sounds of the salvagers' breathing behind him broke the silence. On the left bank of lockers, the first half-dozen doors had been flung open, some hanging loose from one hinge.

Neil swept the light inside the opened lockers. They were empty except for a few items of stained fabric and some tattered textbooks. He sniffed: mould and stale air.

He indicated the first closed locker. "This one?"

"Yes." It was Cutler's voice.

Davidson's respiration increased. Neil's skin tightened and he moved farther away from the men.

"Was it closed when you got here?" Neil positioned himself in front of the locker.

"Yes. They all were."

"So you closed it again?"

"Guess so. Must have been reflex."

Neil reached out with his left hand and grasped the handle. His right hand tightened its grip on the gun.

Davidson croaked, "It's … It's …"

Neil threw the door aside and jumped back.

He didn't expect the dry, brown heap of bones that lay on the bottom of the locker. The rib cage had settled gently onto the smaller bones and cradled the skull on top, like a pyramid-shaped Halloween decoration.

With a soft clacking sound, one long bone and a few smaller ones tumbled out onto the chipped tile floor. The rest of the skeleton shifted, releasing puffs of dust and fragments of cloth or paper. Leaning in, Neil observed a layer of dehydrated body fluids and decomposed flesh under the bone heap. Some of it had dripped out and dried in a half-metre-wide stain on the floor.

The skull tipped off the rib cage and dropped onto the edge of the metal locker, rocking twice before falling to the floor. It rolled across the tiles and stopped, the teeth resting against Neil's boot.

He flinched and backed up another step. The mandible broke away from the skull, as if the mouth had opened wide in soundless laughter.

Neil shook off his revulsion and noted the rows of flawlessly formed teeth. Then, his attention fastened on the left temple. The area near the orbital bone was a jagged black void. He reached for his phone.

The Scene of Crime team had set up lights powered by a small generator. Like an alien sun, the artificial daylight shone mercilessly on the floors and walls, reaching into every corner.

From the hallway, Neil leaned over the police tape and called to the coroner squatting in front of the locker. "Any thoughts yet, Ed?"

"Interesting," the man replied. "This is the first time I've examined skeletal remains at a crime scene."

"Same for me, Ed."

Dr. Ed Reiner took a small flashlight out of his pocket and rammed his head and shoulders into the locker, avoiding the pieces of skull and other bones on the floor. He hummed and sniffed like a bumblebee with hay fever.

Neil shoved numb fingers into his pockets. He moved back a few feet to speak to the officer who had been first to respond to his radio call.

"What's the story on this place, Bernie?" His gaze swept the room with its rows of metal compartments and scarred wooden benches.

Bernie watched the coroner for a moment. "They built a new high school in the south end of town about fifteen years ago and boarded this one up after the last graduation party. The town council tried to sell the building, but no bites until recently, when it was bought by a developer who plans to put up a seniors' residence."

Bernie Campbell was a twenty-year veteran of the Lockport Police Service. He was methodical, reliable, and marginally respectful. His ears were bright red from the cold as he watched the coroner.

When it was clear Bernie was done answering his question, Neil asked another. "What do you know about the two guys who discovered the remains?"

Bernie didn't consult his notebook. He pointed his chin at the two men standing in front of the boys' locker room. "Left to right, Larry Cutler and Fang Davidson. Cousins. They're from Dogtown. They bought the salvage rights and have a week to strip the place before the wreckers arrive. Construction for the new residence starts in the spring."

The Davidson and Cutler names meant nothing to Neil, but he knew Dogtown was a collection of house trailers and outbuildings scattered over five or six acres of countryside west of the town limits. Its residents kept to themselves, married each other, if rumours were correct, and stayed out of trouble for the most part.

"Fang?" Who gives their kid a dog's name?

Bernie consulted his notebook for this one. "His real name is Rupert. I'd rather be called Fang, myself."

Cutler and Davidson huddled together, the colours of their plaid shirts blending into a riot of conflicting patterns. Both men drew rapidly on cigarettes, expelling plumes of smoke into the frigid air of the corridor.

Under the harsh lights, Cutler seemed younger than Neil had thought, maybe late twenties, and Davidson a few years older, around Neil's own age. They didn't look much alike except for identical sets of white, even teeth.

The younger man rocked up and down on his heels, seemingly recovered from his fright and anxious to speak. In contrast, Davidson continued to stand motionless, his face drained of colour, his dark eyes red-rimmed. The cigarette shook in his fingers.

Neil asked Cutler to wait and motioned Bernie to stay with him. He drew Davidson back to stand in front of the police tape. "Please describe how you came to find the body, sir. From the beginning."

Davidson took another drag on his cigarette. "We started in the offices and took out a few things. Trouble is, most of the wood stuff has rotted and anything metal is rusty. We'll be lucky to make our money back."

During his account, Davidson's attention remained fixed on the floor of the room beyond. On the separated sections of skull. The coroner's body concealed the rest of the skeleton from view. Ed continued to hum content-edly, but he had stopped sniffing. Neil took Davidson's arm and pulled him away from the doorway.

"Go on."

"We worked our way up the main hall from the office, checking the lockers for anything we can sell. When we reached the gym wing, we went into the girls' change room first …. Well, that's when we found it." He dropped his cigarette butt and ground it into the floor.

Davidson hunched his shoulders and fingered his cigarette pack. Neil exchanged him for Cutler and heard the same story in different words. Knowing Bernie had contact information for both men, he dismissed them.

"Chief, do you need me for anything more?" Bernie kicked his toes against the wall to restore circulation.

"Yes. Stop at the station and write your report. I want to read it later this afternoon. Don't leave until

I get there." He ignored Bernie's exasperated expression and turned back to the locker room. Ed mumbled incoherently.

"What?"

"I'm stuck!" Ed's narrow shoulders hit the sides of the opening as he tried to pull his body free.

Constable Thea Vanderbloom appeared at Neil's side. At his instructions, she had photographed the rest of the school.

"You got photos of the locker and bones before Dr. Reiner arrived, didn't you?" he asked.

She nodded. "Do you want me to suit up again and take more shots inside the perimeter?"

"Yes. You can help Oliver with the evidence collection. But, here, give me the camera."

Holding it by the strap, he called to Oliver Mendez, the SOCO working beside Ed. "Give this to Dr. Reiner. Ed? Can you take some close-ups of our vic's bones while you're in there, before they're disturbed any further? Change the setting ..."

"I got it!" Half a dozen light explosions followed before the camera appeared over Ed's hooded head again.

Oliver handed the camera back to Neil, then pulled on Ed's shoulders and twisted his head until the coroner popped free. A few more bones spilled onto the floor.

"Well, shit," Ed said, "isn't this a party?" He pulled his mask down. His lips were blue from the cold, and he inspected a tear in his coveralls. "I hope my new down jacket isn't ripped, too."

Neil leaned against the door frame. "Learn anything, Ed? What did you smell in there?"

"Nothing. No odour of decomposition. A few bits of tissue are still adhering to the bones but not much is holding them together. Poor little girl."

"This is a child?"

"A female. And she's small. We'll need a forensic anthropologist to better define the age range, but she's not a prepubescent child."

Ed Reiner was an OB/GYN with a thriving practice in town, making his on-the-spot determination of sex and age range more reliable than that of the average small-town coroner.

Ed stooped for a closer look at the skull. His gloved fingers probed the splintered bones of the depression. "Pretty safe to say this is the cause of death. I'll take some more photographs at the hospital morgue." His phone rang and he stripped off his gloves before answering.

"I have to go. Patient in labour. I'm all done here, anyway."

Thea and Oliver transferred the bones into a body bag, then spent another hour collecting samples from the bottom of the locker and floor. Finally, they disappeared around a corner into the area that held the showers and toilet stalls.

Thea came out and spoke to him. "Chief, we found a discolouration on the edge of a porcelain sink. I took some swabs before spraying it with Luminol. The stain reacted, but it could be something other than blood, like fecal matter or even fossilized horseradish. Other than that, I don't see anything that matches the size and shape of the wound."

When the EMTs arrived, Neil asked them to take the body bag directly to the hospital morgue. Ed wanted to conduct a quick exam before sending them to the Provincial Forensic Pathology Unit in Toronto. The Unit would make it a priority to identify the victim. The evidence bags would be driven to the Centre of Forensic Sciences by one of his officers. Meanwhile, he needed an unofficial ID to work with.

The chill in the building seeped into his core, and he knew his team had to be feeling it, too. He planned to keep the scene secure for at least tonight, so he needed to arrange for coverage.

"Thea, where's Dwayne? He can help seal this building off while we go back to the station to write our reports and get warm."

"Dwayne's working the Christmas parade. He's driving the 4 X 4, flashing the lights and blasting the siren to give the kids a thrill."

"Call him in, please. Priority."

Leaving Thea to contact her partner, Neil opened the set of wide doors off the hallway and entered the shadowy gym. The ghostly imprints of basketball lines segmented the floor. Rims and nets hung on either end of the space. Tiers of benches sagged against the far wall, the wood splintered and rotting. A half-dozen folding tables defined the perimeter.

Metal trash cans stood beside each table and Neil looked into the nearest one. It was filled with shredded paper. He transferred the flashlight to his left hand and rummaged through the bin with his right, gloved hand.

Before the mice moved in, the can had been filled with paper plates and cups. Plastic utensils had dropped to the bottom of the container.

The beam from his flashlight swept across the ceiling and stopped when something glittered back at him. *What the hell?* Memories of his high school years rushed back. The dances in the gym. Music, streamers, banners, spotlights. Spotlights aimed at …

He laughed at himself and watched the silver disco ball sway slowly in the air current flowing through the open doors.

After the final dance, did the graduates leave behind one dead classmate?

CHAPTER TWO

MY FEET WERE FREAKIN' FREEZING, and the parade wasn't half over. I wore long johns under my elf costume and wool socks on my feet. But the soles on my curly-toed shoes were so thin and smooth that I felt every wad of gum littering the parade route. And I was losing traction as the snow accumulated on the pavement. Everyone loves snow on Christmas Parade day. Everyone except this elf.

I had no scarf because "elves don't wear scarves," according to the parade führer and my ex-cousin-in-law Glory Yates. I donned red earmuffs but Glory took them away and handed me pointed, thin felt ears which hooked on over my own. As a result, my ears were as numb as my toes.

Glory had ordered me to walk along the parade route on the left side, smile at the children, and hand them candy canes. I tried that for a while, but it was more fun to toss the candy into the crowds of sugar-high kids and let them fight over it.

Glory trotted up ahead like a thoroughbred filly in a white designer ski suit and fur-lined boots. Her red hair exploded from under a green toque with a white bobble. She looked very Christmassy. And warm.

My cousin, Dougal Seabrook, worked the right side of the street. He was dressed like The Cat in the Hat and pushed a grocery cart to collect non-perishables for the food bank. He had complained bitterly about the costume, but I would have traded in a minute. At least his costume covered most of his body and nobody could recognize him.

I shuffled over to him, trying to stifle the ringing of the bells on the tips of my shoes. "Why is Glory wearing a headset? Who's she talking to?"

Dougal snatched a can of tomatoes from a tot with a copiously running nose. The kid stuck out his tongue at Dougal, who shoved some candy at him and backed away. I heard him mutter, "Hope your teeth rot out, you snot-faced little shithead."

To me he said, "Who knows? She's probably hooked up to CSIS, identifying home-grown terrorists for them. Oh, hell, here she comes. Try to look like a home-grown patriot."

Glory cantered up. Clipboard under her elbow, she managed to clap her hands together. "No fraternizing! And don't forget the staff meeting at the greenhouse tomorrow morning."

I marched in place and felt a painful tingling in my toes. "Why do we need a post-parade debriefing on Sunday? Can't we do it another time, and another place?" Like in the summer, around her pool, with lime coolers to deaden the pain of listening to her voice.

She reached over and straightened one of my frozen ears. It was a miracle it didn't snap off. "The parade is only one item on the agenda. If you see Rae, remind her as well. Now, you two, get back to your posts. Dougal, shoulders back! You're supposed to be a role model. And, Bliss, I noticed you aren't interacting with the crowd. Move, both of you, and whip this crowd into the Christmas spirit!"

She caught sight of a group of junior baton twirlers on the brink of a collective meltdown, and darted off. Once she was out of earshot, Dougal called after his ex-wife, "Fuck you."

"Yeah, and the gas-guzzling Corvette you rode in on," I added. Our voices may not have been the whispers we were trying for, since Glory turned around and started back. Fire burned in her sea-blue eyes.

I abandoned Dougal and ran up the street past the Salvation Army marching band to the head of the parade. On the way, I passed my friend, Rae, dressed as a chipmunk. Which one? Who cared? I didn't stop to give her Glory's message about the meeting. I eased in between the police Blazer 4 X 4 and the lead convertible, and threw a handful of candy canes at some hooting teens.

Well, geez, I couldn't stay there either. The mayor and his wife, Mike and Andrea Bains, rode in the back seat of the convertible like a couple of royal poobahs. Mike, a.k.a. the Weasel, was my ex-husband, and Mrs. Weasel had been my lawyer during the divorce proceedings. It took me two years of living at poverty level before I persuaded them to hand over my fair share of the matrimonial assets. I had to use a smidge of blackmail and the resulting transaction hadn't been profitable for them. A cold war still raged.

Taking aim at the top of Andrea's faux fur hat, I winged a candy cane. Whoa, perfect shot. The hat flew into the street. His Honour the Asshole said something to his wife and they both looked around. I gave them a big elfin grin, then turned my head and smiled at all the people crazy enough to stand around on the main street on a snowy December Saturday with the temperature hovering around -12°C.

A Shriner on a miniature golf cart reached down and scooped up Andrea's hat. He presented it to her with a flourish and puttered away. Where did he come from? Lockport didn't even have an Ancient Order of Mythical Masons Temple.

A short siren wail sounded from behind me. I dropped back and tried the passenger door of the 4 X 4. It was locked. I rapped on the window and kept rapping until it lowered a half inch. "Open the door, Dwayne. I need to warm up."

"I saw what you did, Bliss. I could charge you with assault, and I would if you weren't the Chief's girlfriend."

"Well, I am, so deal with it. Unlock the door."

"No. I got orders to keep unofficial personnel out of the vehicle, especially Bliss Moonbeam Cornwall. Keep marching, elf."

"I'm in no mood for negotiations, Dwayne. I'll jump on and ride this thing like a hood ornament. If I'm not mistaken, the photographer from the *Sentinel* is standing just up ahead."

Snick. The door unlocked. I pulled myself in and cranked the heat up. The toe bells jingled merrily as I put my feet over the vents. Helping myself to a cookie from the open package lying on the console, I said to Dwayne, "Thanks, I appreciate this."

The Cat in the Hat trotted alongside. His cart was overflowing and, still, people thrust groceries at him. He motioned me to get out and help. I sent him an air kiss and took another cookie.

"You aren't supposed to be in here. Get out." Dwayne moved the cookies to his lap where I sure wasn't following them, so I nibbled at my second to make it last. The radio emitted a string of static and Dwayne pushed a button to silence it.

"No, I'm sitting out the rest of this parade right here. You can let me off at my house."

"You look hilarious in that costume, Bliss."

"Yet, here you are, a big bad cop driving four kilometres per hour, tooting your little siren once in a while to excite the tots."

"The Chief promised I don't have to do this next year. Can you say the same?"

He had me there. No doubt, Glory was already planning how to torture me in next year's parade. She was big on the local food bank, which was only fair, since she had never gone hungry a day in her life — not that I've ever seen her actually eat. She liked to remind me that I had relied on the food bank during my darkest, post-separation days when I worked five jobs to keep a trailer roof over my head. The elf costume was going to be a December must-have for the rest of my life. Unless somebody kills her first.

My cell rang. I took off my elf hat and scrunched down so Glory wouldn't spot me. It was my sister. Blyth lives in Rexdale and is blessed with two toddler sons and a husband in pursuit of a doctorate in psychology. She's a full-time librarian at the University of Toronto and gaggingly efficient at everything.

"Bliss? Hi. What's that racket I'm hearing?"

"I'm marching in a parade. I'm the head elf, in charge of all the other elves." Beside me, Dwayne snorted, and I cupped my hand over the phone.

"Oh. Good for you. I just called to ask if you'd heard from the parents lately. It's been a while and I'm a bit concerned." From the noises in the background, she should worry more about her kids fluffing George, the gerbil, in the dryer.

Dougal's stovepipe hat galloped past, pursued by Glory's white bobble. I slid onto the floor. "A couple of weeks ago, I texted Dad. The eavestrough along the front of the house is loose. He replied to get it fixed and use the maintenance fund he set up at the bank to pay for it."

"A couple of weeks ago? Okay, that makes me feel better. I haven't heard from them in at least two months. I wish they'd call once in a while."

"Yeah, or even visit. That would be nice." Our parents left three years ago to tour the West Coast in an RV and we haven't seen them since. Blyth was pregnant with her first child when they left, so they have never even seen him, or his brother born a year later.

The radio hiccupped again, and a female voice clearly stated, "Officer Rundell, pick up the damn radio."

I said to Blyth, "Got to go. Important parade stuff to do."

Dwayne fumbled the hand-piece, dropping it twice before finally speaking into it. "Sorry, Lavinia. Go ahead."

I turned my head politely before snickering. How this idiot got through Police College was a mystery.

When Lavinia finished with him, sweat ran down Dwayne's face and his lips trembled. I felt sorry for him and turned down the heat.

He rolled his eyes from side to side. "I have to get out of this parade."

"Now you're talking. Hit the siren and we'll nudge our way through the mob blocking the next exit."

"You can't come. I have a hot shot. Get out, Bliss."

Hot shot is police-speak for "get your ass over here PDQ."

"I'll wait in the car for you. Just leave the cookies."

"Please! This is serious."

"Oh, all right. Geez!" I tossed a handful of candy canes at him, then hopped out and watched him swing the 4 X 4 around the convertible and punch the siren. He leaned out the window and shouted at the crowd to get clear. Children screamed and covered their ears. Some elderly folk stumbled trying to jump out of his way. Finally, he had open pavement in front of him and the vehicle roared off.

Holy mama! The hot shot better be calling Dwayne to a murder scene or Redfern would be fielding public complaints by the shitload.

CHAPTER
THREE

NEIL AND THEA ARRIVED at the station to find Bernie tapping slowly on a keyboard, still wearing his coat. He looked up as the door opened and said, "Got my notes in the computer, Chief. Anything else?"

"Yes, get yourself a coffee and come into my office."

Neil shed his outer garments and sat down at his desk with his notebook in front of him. When Bernie arrived with his coffee — and his coat — Neil gestured at the other chair and asked, "How long have you been on the force here, Bernie?"

Bernie looked at the ceiling, then the floor. Finally, he said, "Twenty-one years?" He sipped his coffee and appeared to reconsider his answer. Then he nodded. "Yep, twenty-one years this coming May."

"Okay, you said the old high school was abandoned about fifteen years ago. What else can you tell me about the closing?"

Bernie lifted his coffee to his lips, thought better of

taking a drink, reached inside his coat to scratch something, and opened his mouth. "Well, I could be wrong, but seems to me the kids who graduated in June of 2000 came back in October — Thanksgiving weekend — for their official graduation ceremony and a dance in the old gym before it was closed up. Guess the school board didn't want any partying in the new school. It had already opened that September. September of 2000."

Neil didn't care about the new school. "So, October 2000. Party in the old building. Okay, Bernie, thanks. Just print me off a copy of your report before you go, will you?"

"Sure. No problem." Bernie left the room with more spring in his step than when he came in.

A red light blinked from Neil's phone. A text from Cornwall:

BN RBBD. ND BG BLND CP. HRY

What? She swore she used official texting acronyms but he wasn't good with missing vowels.

Thea came in and saw him frowning over the message. "Problem, Chief?"

"Here, can you make out what Cornwall is saying?"

He should have known better.

Thea squinted at the message. "'Been robbed. Need big blind cop. Hurry.' Or maybe that's 'Need big blond cop.'" She glanced at his hair. "In which case, that would be you, Chief. Sounds like you should step on it."

He snatched the phone back and willed his ears not to redden.

"Aren't you going to reply, Chief?"

"No. Do you have something for me?"

"Lavinia is arranging for the night shift to cover the crime scene. Dwayne is at the site now, helping the guys tape it off. Cutler and Davidson came back, asking when they can get in to finish their salvage operation. They only have until next Friday before the demolition crew arrives."

"They mentioned that." Neil thought for a moment. "They'll have to hold off for one more day at least. If that means the demolition is postponed, as well, then tough shit. Pull up a chair, Thea. Write this down."

He waited until Thea was settled. "Check missing person reports for the past sixteen years. Young female, that's all we know. Ask Public Works to search their records for work orders on the building going right back to the school closure. I want to know when the building was last accessed."

"Anything else?" Thea asked.

"That's all for you. Get Dwayne to help when he gets back. Tomorrow, I'll talk to Cutler and Davidson again. I want to ask if there were any indications that the building was breached before they broke through the front doors. Davidson was pretty shook up today. Maybe he'll remember more tomorrow."

"Those two live in Dogtown," Thea said from the door. "Are you going to take someone with you?"

"You think I might disappear and never be heard from again if I go there without backup?"

"Not the way you mean. Dogtown residents haven't committed any serious crimes as far as I know. But word has it the clan is always looking for new breeding stock." Thea looked Neil up and down. A brief smile flitted across her lips and disappeared so fast he wasn't sure he had really seen it. "Just kidding, Chief. Have a good evening."

Bernie tapped on the door frame. When Neil motioned him in, Bernie dropped his report on the desk and stood silently.

"Yes, Bernie?"

"I just thought of something. You might want to talk to Earl Archman. He's the high school principal now and taught math at the old building. He'll have a better handle on the dates you're interested in. Maybe."

Neil wrote the name down. "I'll talk to him, thanks, Bernie. Good night."

The red light on his cell flashed. Cornwall again:

BNG WRNT

He didn't dare ask Thea what the shorthand meant. He stepped out of the warm building that housed the municipal offices as well as the police service. The snow had tapered off, but the wind off Lake Huron cut right through him. He fastened the ear flaps on his fur-lined hat. Only four o'clock and it was almost dark.

If there was any place more desolate than Bruce County in the winter, he hadn't found it. No wonder most of the retired townspeople stampeded to Florida right after Christmas and didn't return until April. The rest kept a few cases of beer in the fridge, gassed up their snow blower and snowmobile, and waited it out. Some days, he asked himself why he didn't go back to Toronto where he wouldn't have to fight his way through mountains of snowdrifts for four months of the year.

Before taking the chief of police position in

Lockport three years earlier, he had worked the Drug Squad in Toronto, where he regularly witnessed grisly death and general mayhem. Here, he investigated stolen lawn ornaments, grow ops, highway carnage — and a few murders.

Neil decided to stop at the Chin Chin Restaurant to buy dinner before driving to Cornwall's house on Morningside Drive. It was a safe bet she wasn't cooking. While waiting for his order, he tried once more to decipher her cryptic second text message. This time his brain filled in the missing vowels. Warrant. She wanted him to bring a warrant?

He felt a sudden stirring in his groin. When the food was ready, he pushed money into the owner's hands and hurried to the Cherokee.

CHAPTER
FOUR

I TOOK A CHEESE PUFF out of the bag and let it melt on my tongue. Just as I reached for another, someone tried to open the kitchen door behind me. Fortunately, I had locked it earlier.

A heavy fist slammed against the metal. I stood up, taking my time. I ate the last two cheese puffs, savouring every morsel. The hammering continued as I licked the pseudo-cheese off my lips, folded up the empty bag, and dropped it into the trash can. Then, I went to see what all the fuss was about.

I opened the door and looked up. Yes, exactly what I ordered: one big, blond cop. A white carry-out bag from Chin Chin's dangled from a gloved finger. Perfect.

He leaned his muscular six-foot two-inch frame on the jamb and pulled on the right ear flap of his mad trapper hat. "I understand you've been robbed, ma'am."

"Yes. Yes, I have, Officer. I'm extremely traumatized." I placed back of wrist to forehead and fluttered my lashes.

"Sorry to hear that. What did the suspect take?" He cleared his throat and unbuttoned his coat.

"All my clothes are gone. As you can see, Officer, they left me nothing but this white, lacy thong." I opened my robe, flash-freezing my ta-tas and throwing my high beams on.

He blinked at the thong, go figure. "I'm sorry for your loss, ma'am. May I come in and initiate an investigation?"

I held my ground. "Do you have the warrant?"

He moved closer, forcing me to back away. "I don't need one. I suspect a crime has been committed on these premises. Please step aside and close the door, ma'am. I am officially freezing my ass off."

"In that case, I guess you can come in." I locked the door behind him. Taking the bag of food, I set it on the counter.

He dropped coat, boots, and socks on the floor, and kicked them aside.

"My goodness, Officer, you still look terribly over-dressed. Here, I'll help you out of your clothes, but leave that sexy hat on." The hat flew across the kitchen and landed on the stovetop. "No? Do you need help with the belt?" The thing had multiple safety releases, likely meant to protect a peace officer in a risky situation such as this. I could only find two of them.

He deftly pressed a clasp and sixteen pounds of equipment clattered onto the kitchen table. "Where's Rae?"

"In Owen Sound with her sister, Christmas shopping. What's this thing on your belt? Did you get a second gun?"

"It's a Taser. I'm the only one authorized to carry it."

I had always wanted to shoot a Taser. "Can I hold it?"

"No."

"I just want to see how it works."

"No"

"Just show me ..."

"No." He took off his pants and shirt and covered the belt with them.

I added my robe to the pile. "Wow. You do have a second gun, Officer. I hope you don't plan to use it on me." I ran my nails down his chest and watched the muscles contract.

With shocking haste, his Jockeys came off. "That depends. Right now I need to inspect the scene of the alleged crime."

"That would be my bedroom. It's this way. I see you're bringing that gun. Good idea. You never know what may be hiding in the closet. Or under the bed."

He gave the bedroom a perfunctory sweep with his navy-blue eyes. "Are you sure this is the right place? I don't see signs of a disturbance."

"I assure you, Officer, I don't have a stitch left." I whipped off the thong and threw it. He caught it and tossed it over his shoulder. "But, I'm so upset, I may be confused. We can look in the bathroom if you like. Perhaps the shower?"

"Later. I'll search the bed first."

He tossed the decorative cushions on the floor and threw aside the duvet. Before I could save myself, he swept me up in his arms and dropped me on the bed.

He jumped in beside me and pulled the duvet over us both. "Start at the beginning. Leave nothing out."

"Well, if you insist, Officer. I'm sure it won't take long."

Seven minutes later, we sounded like a couple of asthmatics as we sucked in air and expelled it. I could feel Redfern's heart banging against my chest.

"You sweated all over my bed. I just changed the sheets yesterday. Now I'll have to do it again."

He ran his finger between my breasts, then held it in front of my eyes. "What's this? Sweat?" His tongue traced a path from the hollow under my ear, along my collarbone. "Yes, I believe it is. The sweat of a thirty-two-year-old female; five foot two inches, one hundred and ten pounds; crazy, multi-coloured hair; deep brown eyes tilted up at the sides, with criminally long lashes that make men go weak at the knees; perfect lips that, when opened, exude words that will one day land her in jail, or find her fleeing from an angry mob of relatives and neighbours; a small cleft in the firmly-set chin.... By the way, what's your real hair colour?"

"Are you serious? What kind of a detective are you?"

Redfern pulled me closer. "That's not a given. I've seen ..."

"I don't care to hear what you've seen. I've been thinking. Can you be a fireman next time?"

He drew his head back. "No. I can rustle up a real fireman if you want one. But I refuse to watch."

"I understand. You want a *ménage à trois*. I'll get back to you on that. I'm starved. Are you?"

"I need a shower first." He checked his watch — what, was he running behind? Twenty minutes to do Bliss, including a shower? "I appear to be covered in orange finger marks. Have you been eating cheese puffs again?"

"Get over yourself, Redfern. The marks aren't *all* over you."

I looked around for my robe before remembering it was on the kitchen table. My white thong hung from the bedside lamp. Since it was used on ceremonial occasions only, and then very briefly, I stuck it back in the drawer.

Redfern pulled himself free of the tangled mess on the bed and headed for the bathroom.

After doing a few stretches to get the kinks out, I called, "I guess I should join you, just to save water, but don't get my hair wet. I just washed it this morning."

My ensuite bathroom had a small shower stall, built for one. With two of us in there, we needed to be inventive, but since Creative is my middle name, we were both clean in a couple of jiffies.

Dried and dressed, I retrieved a container of shrimp chow mein from the microwave and dropped it on the table with the other Chinese offerings. I rubbed the blond spikes on Redfern's head. "So, how was your day, dear?"

"Interesting."

We ate from the containers, passing them back and forth across the table. I waited for him to continue. When I looked up from eating around the celery pieces in the chicken chop suey, I found him watching me. I knew that look. *Can I trust her not to blab this all over town before dawn tomorrow?*

"Listen, if the Weasel called to complain that I knocked his bitch's hat off in the parade, it's a lie. The same goes for any kids who say I hit them with candy canes. Bald-faced lies. Maybe it's Dwayne? He got called to a hot shot and nearly ran over some seniors when he peeled away from the parade. Surely, someone complained about that?"

Redfern plunged his fork into a sesame ball. "Sounds like you had an interesting day, too. But mine trumped yours."

"How so?"

"Promise to keep this to yourself?"

"Look up *discretion* in the dictionary and you'll see a picture of Bliss Moonbeam Cornwall."

"Last week you told me your picture was under *flexible*. All right, I'll take a chance. Skeletal remains were discovered in the old high school."

"No way! I went to that high school!" This is what happens when you waste a day dressed like an elf, handing out candy to ungrateful kids. You miss all the good stuff.

"Tell me, Cornwall, would you happen to be a member of the last class to graduate from that old building?"

"Yes. Have you identified the body?"

"Not yet. There's not much to go on."

I shivered. "If it's female, I know who it is."

CHAPTER
FIVE

OVERNIGHT, A STORM had blown in from Lake Huron, dumping seven centimetres of fresh snow on the county. Neil didn't look forward to the barrage of multiple vehicle pile-ups on Highway 21.

When he entered the station on Sunday morning, it was deserted except for Lavinia, their civilian dispatcher. Her weekend replacement was on maternity leave, and Lavinia seemed in no hurry to line up a sub. He asked her to contact the two officers setting up radar on the highway at both ends of the town limits and tell them to pull over motorists to warn them of the hazardous driving conditions. He had another officer patrolling the residential streets, and a fourth had the unrewarding task of touring the outlying concession roads checking for God knows what because nothing ever happened out there.

Looking out his office window, Neil could just make out the flat-topped roof of the old high school, two blocks over. Snow would have blown in through the doors by now. No harm done to the crime scene. He'd take a last look around later before releasing the building to Cutler and Davidson.

Neil turned to the radio on the windowsill behind his desk. "Danny? Are you anywhere near Dogtown?"

"Just coming up to it now, Chief." Over the static, Danny sounded morose. Nobody liked the township detail, and the squad car always returned low on gas and full of snack wrappers.

"Good. Tell me what's going on."

"The gate is closed across the compound entrance. No tire tracks in the snow. Smoke coming from two or three residences and some outbuildings. Some kids and dogs playing outside."

"Thanks, Danny, that's all."

Sunday morning might be a good time to catch Cutler and Davidson at home. He wanted to talk to Earl Archman, as well. But it was 8:00 a.m. — too early to show up on anyone's doorstep.

His mind wandered back to earlier this morning, to Cornwall, barely opening one eye when he asked her if she wanted some scrambled eggs. She had stared at him through her tangled hair and blown a raspberry at him. Strange how they could communicate so well without words.

He opened the yearbook she loaned him last night and turned to the pages that showed pictures and write-ups for the graduates of year 2000. Thirteen young faces looked back at him, six boys and seven girls, including Cornwall. Even at seventeen, she was hot. Twelve years of Mike Bains, through university and a bumpy marriage, had stripped away the innocence shining from her eyes in the photo. Unfortunately, time had that effect on most people. He definitely wasn't the same kid who graduated from university and applied to Police College.

Before he could stroll too far down memory lane to the dark places in his own past, his desk phone rang.

"Hey, Neil, it's Ed Reiner. Got a minute?"

"Sure, Ed. Are you at the hospital?"

"I'm at home. I sent the bones to Toronto, but I did a quick examination before I packed them up. Anything I say isn't official, of course, but since it'll be a long wait for the lab results, maybe I can give you something to work with regarding her identification."

"Ed, I'll be grateful for whatever you can tell me. Do you want to meet for coffee?"

"Mason Jar, half an hour?"

Neil spent the wait thinking about the discussion that he and Cornwall had last night. Of the other six female graduates, Cornwall knew the whereabouts and the married names, if applicable, for all of them except one. One girl she insisted would surface in his missing person search.

He left the yearbook on his desk and went to meet Ed. The wind blew straight at him as he descended the steps to the street and walked next door to the Mason Jar. He ordered a cup of coffee and watched the swirling snow through the window until Ed burst through the door in a flurry of energy.

"I just have a few minutes, Neil. Got a patient in labour, only three centimetres dilated so far, but that doesn't mean anything with a first pregnancy." He placed his phone on the table and called to the waitress to bring him coffee and a doughnut.

Neil looked at the doughnut. When he ate one in public, he felt like a stereotype. He got out his notebook and pen.

Ed pulled off his orange toque, his scalp shining under the Tiffany-style lamp hanging over their booth. He leaned over the table, ready to bolt if his phone rang. "I mentioned yesterday that the bones are those of a young female of slight build. Okay, after a closer look, I believe she was between sixteen and twenty. Her teeth are exceptional, no cavities, straight, can't tell with superficial examination whether braces straightened them or she was born that way. I found some long, dark hairs on the skull. The skull, by the way, isn't abnormally thin, so the depression was unlikely to have been caused by a light tap. By the colour of the bones, remaining tissue, and the condition of the scraps of clothing, she's been in the locker for years. If the school has been closed for more than ten years, I'll bet she's been there that long, or close to it." He paused to bite into his doughnut.

Neil decided to play devil's advocate. "A crime occurred. No doubt about that. But this might not be murder. Could be she fell against something, which caused the fracture. Someone panicked and hid her in the locker. We're waiting for residue results from a washroom sink."

"It's possible, I guess. That's for you to determine. Most importantly, who is she? A young girl like that must have been missed by someone. What about missing person reports?"

"I have Thea working on that. But we may have a possible identification ..."

His cell vibrated in his pocket. As he listened to Lavinia's voice, Ed buttoned his coat and got up to leave. Neil stopped him with a raised hand.

"What exactly is the priority, Lavinia?" He listened for a minute. "Where? I'm on my way."

He looked up. "If your patient can spare you for a while yet, Ed, you need to come with me."

Ed pulled his cap farther down his forehead. Behind his glasses, his blue eyes gleamed. "Where are we going?"

"St. Paul's Episcopal Church. A dead priest."

CHAPTER
SIX

THE WIND OFF THE LAKE drove the snow straight at my windshield, so I stuck to the speed limit on the highway, more or less. A cop stood beside his snow-covered cruiser, but when he pointed the radar gun at me, I noticed that, for once, it wasn't Dwayne. I gave him a friendly wave as I passed.

A second squad car slipped out of the next concession road and pulled onto the highway behind me. Lights whirled but no siren shrieked, so I kept driving. A few seconds later, the siren wailed.

Thinking the cruiser was in hot pursuit of a speeder, I steered my Matrix to the shoulder to let it by. It pulled up in front of me. Dorky Dwayne stepped out wearing his stupid fur hat, ear flaps dangling.

I rolled my window down partway. "If you're collecting for the policemen's ball, Dwayne, I give at home. Frequently."

"You were picked up on radar, Bliss. Speeding."

"I was not speeding!"

"You were going eighty-eight in an eighty."

"You want to go to court on this one, Dwayne? The judge will fine *you* for wasting his time." An SUV flew by us, going at least a buck ten. And it didn't even move to the far lane as it passed.

"I'm not giving you a ticket. The Chief says we're to warn people to slow down because he doesn't want any accidents today. First snow days are always the worst."

"I know that, Dwayne. Unlike you, I've lived here all my life. Okay, consider me warned." I glanced in my rear-view mirror and screamed, "Look out!"

Dwayne flattened himself against my open window just as an eighteen-wheeler roared by, moving over at the last second. An avalanche of dirty snow and sand slammed against the side of my car. Dwayne glared after the truck's tail lights and mumbled into his radio. The backs of his coat, pants, and hat were covered in brown mush.

The idiot had a death wish. "That was a little too close, Dwayne. Maybe you shouldn't stand on the highway. I'm duly warned, so can we wrap this up?"

"I need your driver's licence and proof of insurance first."

"For what?"

"For my report."

I was going to be late for the meeting, and the Demented Duchess would be in fine voice. We tried not to make Glory screech in the greenhouse. The acres of tempered glass over our heads was stronger than regular glass, and could supposedly withstand the sound waves only dogs can hear, but we didn't want to test it.

I handed over my documents and watched Dwayne scrutinize them closely for expired dates or a fraudulent address.

"How's the investigation going this morning?"

"Which one would that be, Bliss?"

"How many bodies turned up in your jurisdiction yesterday?" *Moron.*

"Only one yesterday. Another one today." He jerked his head up and closed his lips tightly, but once uttered, you can't return words to the brain, as most of us have learned the hard way.

I stuck my head out the window. "There's another skeleton? In the high school?"

"Not at the high school, and not bones, either. Here." He dropped my licence and insurance papers in my lap and walked away. I rolled my window all the way down and called after him, "Is it anyone I know?"

"Probably," he said over his shoulder. "You know everyone in the county."

He made an illegal U-turn on the highway and zoomed off.

Just for the hell of it, I did a hundred and change on the highway and made the right turn onto Concession 10 without due care and attention. My back end slid around the corner and the Matrix did a one-eighty, forcing me to perform a U-turn to get back on track. I skidded more slowly onto River Road, but floored it again when I reached the parking lot at the greenhouse. With some fancy hand-over-hand steering and expert braking, I managed to come to a perfect landing between Glory's brand-new Land Rover (the Corvette spends winters in its own heated garage) and Dougal's almost-as-new Lexus. Rae's battered green Echo stood in lonely exile at the far edge of the lot, accumulating a layer of lake-effect snow.

The greenhouse was the Lockport Division of the Belcourt Greenhouse Corporation. It sounded much grander than it actually was, although it was the largest greenhouse structure in the tri-county area — that would be Bruce, Grey, and Huron Counties. The Belcourts assured me it was bigger than their other two greenhouses in St. Catharines and Niagara Falls. Big yawn.

When I first saw the high expanse of endless ceiling overhead, I was sure Dougal, a recovering agoraphobic, would be conducting business from under his desk, if not from home. He had whimpered relentlessly until Ivy Belcourt allowed the contractors to install a false ceiling of some light-filtering opaque glass over the office cubicles. Now, he was here every day, all day long.

I kicked my boots free of snow at the door and shed my coat in the humid anteroom. I heard the sounds of battle even before I opened the door to the foyer.

The grand foyer showcased the two monster *Titan arums*, now in dormancy, which belonged to Glory and Dougal, as well as other exotic plants in full bloom. I halted in the doorway.

Glory and Dougal faced off. Simon, Dougal's African grey parrot, was perched on a nearby table, shifting from foot to foot. On Friday, the six-inch pots on the table had been filled with flamboyant petals in off-white with pink and yellow spots. Now the pots held only green stalks and a few thick leaves. A layer

GLORIA FERRIS

of colourful petals covered the floor. Rae flattened herself against the wall and edged toward the door to the plant rooms. She caught sight of me and her expression begged me to help extricate her from ground zero.

I pulled my cell out and took a few shots, one of Glory's wide-open mouth, her face as red as her hair. She was hitting some new heights decibel-wise. If the greenhouse didn't shatter now, it could withstand anything, including the earthquakes and tidal waves that accompany a polar shift.

"You can't blame Simon for everything that happens around here." Dougal's mouth thinned into a mutinous slit.

Glory was uncharacteristically profane. "He ate the fucking alpinias!"

The Apocalypse was nigh. I captured a shot of Glory's eyeballs turning red, a sure sign the Four Horsemen were saddling up. "The *Alpinia zerumbet variegata*," she snarled, raising her red-tipped claws into attack position.

The hell with it. I engaged the video and audio features. This opportunity might never come again.

Simon showed no signs of remorse. Now perched on Dougal's shoulder, he fastened his beady eyes on Glory. If he was trying to appear innocent, he should have spit out the petal hanging from his beak. I moved the phone around the room to capture everything. Maybe this would go viral on YouTube.

"He's destroying our entire inventory." Glory used her taloned finger to prod Dougal in the chest. "I vote we take him out in the woods and leave him for the coyotes."

"That won't work." Dougal was standing up to his

ex-wife's assault pretty well, considering she scared the shit out of him. "Simon could outrun a coyote. He could probably outrun a whole *pack* of coyotes."

Even I knew that was bullshit.

"Not if his legs are tied together and he's tethered to a rock," Glory shrilled. "What's the use of trying to operate this business if that stupid bird eats the stock before we can ship it out?"

"He doesn't eat it! He likes the pretty colours of the blossoms and plays with them."

"Well then, let's feed him some pretty, toxic plants!"

It was time for a note of reason, before Glory shoved Dougal through the glass wall and the entire structure collapsed on our heads. I said, "Maybe we should call in the big gun. Phone Ivy in Arizona and talk to her about Simon."

At the mention of Ivy Belcourt, Glory's mouth upturned into an evil Grinch grin.

"Good idea, Bliss. I'll email Ivy pictures of the alpinias, and the empty spot in the shade room where the *Hoya carnosas* used to be." Ivy had fled south for the winter, but she was capable of tuning up any of the combatants by phone, including Simon.

"*I* am not pleased," Glory stated, lowering her nails an inch. "I can't work like this. If you don't take Simon home, Dougal, I'm going to sell my interest in this business. It's the bird or me. Take your pick."

Before Dougal could pick, and I'm pretty sure I knew which way he'd go, a short man with gelled black hair and agate eyes stuck his head in. "Shall I set the sandwiches out in this ... room, Miss Glory?"

A laden tray preceded him as he took a few tentative steps. He wore black cotton pants and white tunic. His tan Sorel boots reached his knees.

"Pan! What are you doing here? Are you a chauffeur now?" I had never seen him in the greenhouse before, or anywhere other than Glory's mansion, except once outside the local pot dealer's trailer. And that had nothing to do with me. At the time, I lived next door to the local pot dealer and couldn't avoid seeing his customers.

Pan was Glory's houseboy. He didn't cook, since she seldom ate, and he never did housework, since my cleaning company, Bliss This House, cleaned Glory's Tudorstyle mansion once a week. Other than answering the door, refilling her wineglass, and dodging the missiles she flung during her frequent fits, it was anybody's guess what he did with his time.

Pan's interruption sidetracked Glory's preoccupation with bird-icide. She gave a derisive snort. "Somebody has to serve the sandwiches. Pan, you can take the tray through to the prospective garden room. The meeting will start momentarily."

Pan scurried away. He had no idea where he was going, but looked happy to escape.

I was confused for a different reason. And suspicious. Glory lived on protein shakes and white wine at home, and she never brought any food to work. I opened the door to the corridor and was hit in the face by air even more humid than in the foyer.

"Hey, Pan. Wait up. Do you know what the meeting is about? And did you bring any booze?"

"It's not even noon."

"If things go bad, could you slip me some Riesling in a water glass?"

"I would if I had some. You're very amusing, Bliss. Regarding the reason for this meeting, well ..." He mimed hanging himself with a noose.

I led the way to a long room at the back, home of the future tropical garden. Plans included a waterfall and pond with accompanying bridge, and stone benches to sit on and contemplate the sodden flora. I heard talk of fish for the pond and maybe a few tropical birds as play-mates for Simon. Good times ahead.

For now, the upcoming Garden of Eden contained a long table and a half-dozen lawn chairs. We used it as our lunchroom, and it was pleasant to wear sunglasses and a T-shirt and pretend it wasn't -8°C outside. And that was back in November.

Pan pulled napkins, paper plates, and Tupperware containers of pickles and cookies from the cloth bag slung around his neck. Before I could eat more than a sandwich or two, the others came in. All were unblood-ied, even Simon.

Dougal immediately took off his shoes, socks, and shirt, and rolled up his pants. He filled a plate and sank back in a lounger. I was impressed that a former agora-phobic could sit in such a vast space, look upward at the endless ceiling, and appear so relaxed. I took a closer look at him. Yeah, tranqu'ed. Who could blame him?

Rae chose a low-slung sand chair, which left her with her knees up around her ears. She realized her mistake and attempted to get up. After several tries, she rolled off onto the floor and stayed there, legs folded lotus-style.

Pan hauled a chair to the farthest corner of the room and sat down, ready to hop up and fetch something if the Mistress of Mayhem should beckon. She rested a hip on the table and tapped a fingernail on the ever-present clipboard.

"Everyone sit down. I don't want to be here all day." She flung her titian hair back and picked up a pen from the table. I started to worry. St. Patrick's Day was less than four months off, and I sensed another parade on the horizon. Elves and leprechauns are related, aren't they?

Glory clapped her hands for order, even though the rest of us hadn't uttered a word. "Okay, everyone. First item: yesterday's parade."

We groaned. Outside, the storm picked up and hurled tiny ice pellets against the glass. Surely Ivy's architect had taken Bruce County winters into account when he drew up the greenhouse plans.

Glory's lips smiled at us. "Parade collection was a success! I had a look at our stock earlier this morning, and I believe the food bank can feed our needy families through Christmas. Seventeen grocery carts filled with food. Let's give our Cat in the Hat a hand."

Rae and I gave Dougal a round of applause. Far from looking pleased or embarrassed at the accolade, Dougal eyed the door and put on his socks. He knew something bad was coming.

"Everyone did a fabulous job yesterday." Glory turned to Rae and widened her smile fractionally. "But what happened to the other chipmunks? I only saw one."

Rae licked her lips. "I asked Dwayne Rundell and

Thea Vanderbloom to do it, but at the last minute Dwayne said he had to drive the police car in the parade and Thea got called in to work. I didn't have time to find anyone else."

"I'd have been a chipmunk," I said.

I shouldn't have opened my big mouth.

A tinge of red appeared in Glory's eyes. "We needed an elf, Bliss. And you're short. However, this might be a good time to mention that I received quite a few complaints about you. Did you throw candy canes at a group of teenaged boys?"

"They laughed at my bells."

"And did you knock Andrea Bains's hat off?"

"Lucky shot."

"Next time, you'll hand out leaflets."

"Next time, I'll kill myself first." I ate another sandwich and turned my head to stare out at the snow-covered trees. According to legend, if you looked into Glory's eyes during their crimson phase, you turned into a zombie. I never chanced it.

It seemed like a good idea to change the subject, though. "Hey, did you guys hear about the skeleton in the old high school?"

Dougal straightened up and rolled down his pant legs. "It was all over *CTV News* last night. I'll be surprised if they don't find worse things when they tear the building down. Like asbestos." He put on his boots.

"I heard it on the news this morning, too," Rae said. "I wonder if a homeless person crawled in there for warmth, and just died. It's so sad."

Redfern had made me promise not to speculate on

the identity of the skeleton, and I didn't want to mention a second body in case Dwayne had pulled that one out of his ass.

Glory slammed her clipboard against the table. Her pen flew off into a corner, missing Simon's tail feathers by a hair. The parrot shot her a look of hatred, but wisely kept his beak shut.

"It's a terrible thing, but can we get back to business? We have another item to discuss. We're going to have a Christmas open house and sale, here at the greenhouse. On December 14."

Dougal wasn't as drugged as he looked. "Not happening. That's two weeks from yesterday. We can't organize a show and sale in such a short time!" He struggled into his shirt.

Rae's round blue eyes widened even more. "But, Glory, we don't sell poinsettias or other seasonal plants."

Glory waved Rae's objections aside, and totally ignored Dougal's. "If people want seasonal plants, they can buy them at the grocery store or local flower shops. We'll sell exotics, of course. Fortunately, we have a surplus at the moment. And I've already spoken to Ivy. She thinks it's a wonderful idea. So, we're doing it."

Dougal's testosterone spiked, causing his mouth to malfunction. "Who put you in charge?"

Glory and Dougal were home-grown Lockportals. They hated each other growing up, much like now, but something extraordinary happened when they went to university to study plant science. They fell in love, or whatever that was. Personally, I believe all the pollinating — and field trips into the bush — screwed up their

hormones. It lasted long enough for them to graduate, take a European holiday with classmate Chesley
Belcourt, and get married.

Now, they were divorced and minority shareholders
in the Belcourts' Bruce County greenhouse enterprise.
That's *minority* shareholders. No reason for either of
them to show up every day. Or any day.

Glory loomed over Dougal. "Ivy did, you useless
worm. I'm in charge of this fundraiser."

"Fundraiser? Didn't we just do that?" Dougal
bounced his chair back a few feet and struggled to his
feet. "Anyway, I'm too busy to get involved with anything you're in charge of."

Dangling a preposition was a sure sign of fear, and
Glory knew it. She lifted a high-heeled boot and shoved
him in the chest. He fell back down again. "I guess you
weren't listening. The food bank will be empty before
the New Year. The admittance fee to the event will be a
food item. And cash only for plant sales, no guarantees
since most people will kill the plants before Valentine's
Day. All proceeds to the food bank. Understand?"

We did.

Unfortunately, she wasn't done. "You will all wear an
appropriate costume …"

"I'm not wearing that Cat costume again. It's too hot in
here." Dougal sat in his chair, crossed his arms, and looked
defiant. But we all knew he was as beaten as the rest of us.

Rae's lip trembled. "And Glory, I can't wear the chipmunk costume either. I'll sweat to death."

I figured it was now or never. "And I'm not dressing
like an elf. Ever again."

"Fine! You people are selfish to the core. I will leave choice of costume to your discretion. But remember, nothing frightening to children, like witches or zombies. And no stupid robots or superheroes. Got it? As the dumbass here has pointed out, we have less than two weeks to pull this together, and all of you will help. Take a copy of this list, and I don't want to hear any complaints about the work assignments. And no trading tasks either."

I didn't care if it was barely noon, I was going to have a glass of wine, maybe two, any colour, when I got home.

Rae squirmed like people do when their phone vibrates in their pants. She got up and walked to the window before pulling it out.

Dougal and I reluctantly took a list from Glory. My job didn't look too bad. I could accomplish it in one morning. Dougal glowered at his ex-wife but didn't open his mouth again. He stuffed the paper in his pocket without glancing at it and started for the door.

I heard a sound from Rae, and turned toward the glass wall. She stared at me and tried to speak. Her legs gave out and she sank heavily to the floor.

I dropped down beside her. "What's wrong, Rae? What's happened?"

She clutched at me. "It's Sophie. She's dead!"

"Sophie who?" I knew a couple of Sophies.

"Sophie Quantz. She fell from the choir loft this morning or last night. Nobody knows for sure."

Dougal postponed his dash to freedom. "She runs the Step Dancing Academy in town, right?"

"No, you're thinking of Sasha Gillhouse," I said.

Glory addressed her ex-husband. "Idiot. She used to be Sophie Wingman. You went out with her in grade twelve, remember? She was only a kid in grade ten then. Now she's an Episcopal priest at St. Paul's."

"Oh, that Sophie," he said. "I barely remember her."

"She was in my class," I said. "After graduation, she went to a university out east, then to Divinity College. I haven't spoken to her since graduation ..."

Graduation. *Well, shit.*

I pulled my phone out of my purse.

CHAPTER
SEVEN

NEIL AND ED DROVE TO St. Paul's in separate vehicles in case Ed was called back to the hospital to deliver a baby. Two empty squad cars lined the curb in front of the church. Constable Cory Angetti wound perimeter tape through the bars of the wrought-iron fencing. As they headed inside, Ed observed, "Our last body was six months ago when that deranged woman axed her husband to death. Now, two bodies in two days. It's a record for me as coroner. How about you, Neil?"

"Only since I moved here, Ed. I'd see three or four dead bodies some days in Toronto. Mostly overdoses."

Violence was seldom involved in those deaths. But dead was dead, and six years on a Toronto drug squad had hardened him, although highway crashes still knotted his stomach and put him off his food for a few days.

In the vestibule, Thea and Oliver pulled on their crime scene gear while Bernie ran police tape across the door leading into the nave. Bernie's partner, Margo

Philmore, waited near four individuals sitting on a corner bench. Three were elderly females; the fourth, a male, mid-forties. His shaggy dark hair was shot through with grey. He moaned and rocked rapidly on the bench.

Neil turned to Bernie. "You were first responder? Who have we got?"

Bernie took his hands out of his pockets as he stepped forward. He spoke in a low voice. "Reverend Sophie Quantz, age 32, married, no children. Priest of this church. Bullet hole in the forehead. Lying across a couple of pews directly below the choir loft."

He nodded his head at the foursome on the bench. "The ladies were the first into the church for morning services. One of them called us. The male is Kelly Quantz, the husband. He came in with the parishioners and saw the body. He's been incoherent since I got here."

"Did any of them go near the body? The husband?"

"One of the ladies checked for a pulse but didn't move her. They said Quantz tried to go to her, but they managed to pull him away."

Neil glanced over at the three elderly women, dressed in wool coats and knitted hats, pale but with stoic expressions. "Good thinking."

"I tried for a pulse, too. None."

"You've started the log sheet? Good." Meticulous records had to be kept on every individual entering and leaving the crime scene.

While Ed suited up, Neil stood behind the tape and looked into the nave. The woman's body was sprawled over two pews, head hanging back but face up, arms and legs flung into unnatural positions. He counted the pews. She had fallen into the eleventh and twelfth. From this location, there was no visible blood, and the blonde hair fell forward, obscuring her face.

He moved aside to let Ed slide under the tape, followed by Thea and Oliver. His two SOCOs stayed back while Ed walked slowly to the body, watching where he put his feet down.

Neil turned away and pulled Margo aside. "Do you have all you need from the ladies?"

"I think so, Chief. They were a bit early, and chatted for a few minutes out on the steps. Mr. Quantz came around the back of the church from the direction of the manse and greeted them. The front doors here were locked, which was unusual before a Sunday service. They went around and came in a back door. They saw the body as soon as they stepped into the nave. One of them unlocked the front doors to let us in."

The women were reluctant to leave Quantz, but he assured them that the new widower would be well looked after. They refused a ride in a cruiser, one of them asserting she was still fit to drive her own car home, thank you, young man. She reminded Neil of his Grandma Ida.

When the doors finally closed on the women, Neil turned to Quantz. The man seemed unaware or not to care that his supporters had deserted him. A steady keening sounded through the fingers spread across his face. His body shuddered.

Neil stood in front of him. "Mr. Quantz. I'm Chief Neil Redfern. Are you able to answer a few questions for me?"

Quantz turned his body away, toward the wall. "My Sophie. My Sophie." He rocked back and forth.

"When did you see your wife last, Mr. Quantz?"

The only answer was a series of sobs that increased in intensity until the tiny vestibule echoed with his grief. He pushed Margo away when she put her hand on his shoulder in an effort to calm him.

Ed Reiner ducked under the tape and dropped his bag. Neil stood up and watched Thea and Oliver trot down the centre aisle and set to work.

"I've called the EMTs, Chief." Margo stepped away from Quantz. "They're standing by."

Ed peeled off his gloves and coveralls. He pulled Neil away from Quantz and kept his voice low. "Another one for autopsy. She has a bullet hole above the left eyebrow. No exit wound so the bullet is still in the skull. I'll take a quick look at the hospital before sending her to London, but I can't get the bullet for you. Liver temp suggests death occurred twelve to fifteen hours ago."

Quantz moaned softly. He tried to get to his feet but fell back onto the bench and slammed the side of his head against the wall.

"So, last night between 9:00 p.m. and midnight?"

"Roughly. I'll try to confirm that before sending her away." He turned his attention to Quantz. "Husband?"

Neil nodded and watched as Ed rummaged in his bag and pulled out a hypodermic needle and a vial of liquid. He expertly administered the shot before Quantz knew what was happening.

"What is that? I need to be able to talk to him."

"It's a benzodiazepine, and you have five to twenty

minutes before it takes effect. It won't put him to sleep, just relax him. I don't know if he'll be able to answer any questions."

Neil instructed Bernie and Margo to restrain Kelly Quantz until he calmed down. The man continued to wail and thrash against the hands holding him. He was incapable of communicating where he lived or when he had last seen his wife.

Fifteen minutes later, Bernie and Margo were sweating and swearing under their breath as they continued to wrestle with Quantz to prevent him from banging his head against the wall. Ed speculated about giving him another dose, but if it came to that, it would be tomorrow before the man was fit to undergo questioning.

Finally, the fight went out of Quantz. His body went limp and his eyelids fluttered, then half closed.

"Mr. Quantz." Neil spoke loudly. "Can you tell me when you saw your wife last?"

The flaccid lips parted. "Last night?"

"When did you miss her?"

"Didn't. I'm an artist. Sometimes work all night."

"So, you worked all last night?"

"Yes. Came to church for the service. Found this." His eyes closed again, and this time they didn't reopen, although his eyeballs jumped frantically behind the lids.

Ed leaned over and took the man's pulse. "You should wait until the sedative wears off, Neil. I don't think you'll get much sense out of him now."

Neil told his officers to take Kelly Quantz home and stay with him. If this was an act, it was a good one, but he wouldn't rule out a domestic killing at this point.

He turned back to the coroner. "Ed, is there anything else you can tell me about the wound?"

"No powder or stippling marks around the entrance, so it's a distance wound, from at least three feet away. A small-calibre bullet, a .22 or .32. That's a guess, though. I haven't seen a lot of bullet wounds."

Ed's phone beeped, and when he checked the display, he said, "Here we go. Baby on the way. I'll be in touch, Neil."

Alone in the vestibule, Neil contacted Lavinia. "Send a couple more units to St. Paul's Church on Balmoral Crescent. I need both sides of the street canvassed. I'll meet them here. Thanks, Lavinia."

He paced the steps outside until the units showed up. "Hit each house, and if there's no response, make a note so you can go back. We need to know if anyone heard or saw anything near the church from six o'clock last night to six this morning."

He left them to it and returned to the vestibule. At first, he couldn't see either Oliver or Thea. Then, Oliver's head bobbed up from between two pews close to the victim's head. When he saw Neil, he pointed up. Thea was working in the choir loft.

The church grew darker by the minute. Neil looked at his watch and saw it was already four-thirty. He stuck his head into the nave and located a row of light switches. He flipped them all and watched overhead chandeliers and wall sconces light up, bathing the nave in a soft glow that was helpful for now, but would be inadequate in another half-hour.

He paced again, bone-chilled and hungry, hating that he was stuck on this side of the perimeter. If only he could charge into the crime scene like the detectives did on cop shows.

Thea appeared behind the tape. "There's no sign of disturbance up there, Chief. The lectern is upright in the middle of the loft, and stacks of hymn books are piled neatly on one of the benches. I took plenty of shots of everything." She stripped off her overalls and other gear. Her dark ponytail swung free and she shivered. "It's freaking frigid in here."

"Did you find anything at all, Thea?"

She handed over an evidence bag. A small metal cylinder lay inside. Her eyes shone. "A shell casing. I found it under a bench."

Neil held the bag up against the light. "It's too small for a .40 calibre. A casing from a .22 is thinner, so I'm thinking this could be a .32." Seemed like Ed was right.

"Good job, Thea. What about fingerprints?"

"Hundreds, as you'd expect. But I found a set of handprints, with corresponding fingerprints, on the railing. Like someone had their back to the railing and gripped it. Interesting if they turn out to be Reverend Quantz's prints."

Oliver joined them and packed his gear away. Evidence bags went into a separate case.

Neil closed his eyes and imagined a woman's body falling fifteen feet from the loft. It wasn't often he wished he had spent time in homicide.

The autopsy results could take weeks. The report

might help, might not. The chances of the bullet showing up as a match in another homicide somewhere weren't great. And guns used to kill were rarely registered, no matter where the crime occurred. From the casing Thea found, they could determine the calibre of the bullet and a list of weapons that used that calibre. Reverend Quantz met someone in the choir loft last night. He had to scrutinize her life and determine who wanted her dead. Or who *needed* her dead.

"How many other exits from the church besides this one?" he asked Oliver.

Oliver jammed his numb hands back into his coat pockets. "There's one from the back room where the … priest, or whatever, gets dressed for the service. It's the door the three ladies and Mr. Quantz found unlocked this morning. So, Reverend Quantz may have come in that way last night. And possibly her assailant. There's another door from the walk-up basement. It's locked from the outside and barred from the inside. I think it used to be an old coal cellar, but doesn't look like anyone's been down there for years."

Neil stepped aside. "You two get back to the station and start processing the evidence for transfer to the CFS in Toronto. I'm going to arrange for the church to be secured. We might have to take another run-through tomorrow."

By the time two more officers arrived, it was fully dark. "These outer doors aren't locked and we don't have the key yet. Put some tape across and make sure no one goes in."

His phone rang as he climbed into his vehicle:

63

Cornwall. Maybe she wanted him to answer another robbery call. That was going to have to wait. Sunday or not, he had two deaths to investigate.

"Hi, Cornwall. I can't talk right now. An incident …"

"I know all about it. Reverend Sophie Quantz died in her church. Do you know who she is?"

"You mean other than the priest at St. Paul's?"

"Yeah, other than that. Her maiden name is Wingman."

"I don't see…. Wait, wasn't she in your graduation class?"

"Congrats, you aren't as blond as you look, Redfern. Yesterday, you discover the body of someone who shall remain nameless for the moment, but could be a member of the last graduating class of the old Lockport High. Today, another grad dies. I believe in the occasional coincidence, but this looks more like cause and effect."

Neil thought so, too. The trouble was, Cornwall had a talent for adding two and two, getting to four, but causing a lot of trouble on the way. "Keep this theory to yourself for now, okay? We can talk as soon as I take care of a few things. Where will you be?"

"At home, waiting for you, cutie. I'll even make you dinner. Bring the yearbook."

She rang off and Neil drove to the station. His stomach lining gnawed itself and acid splashed into his throat. Cornwall's cooking was a hit-and-miss challenge. He preferred to barbecue a steak while she emptied a ready-made salad into a bowl. And if he read the signs correctly, she thought she would be helping him with the murder investigations.

He asked Lavinia to connect him with the Ontario Provincial Police headquarters in London.

CHAPTER
EIGHT

I WAS WELL INTO my second drink when Redfern finally showed up.

"Close the door, will you? You're letting all the heat out." I sucked up the cherry at the bottom of my glass and stabbed a mandarin orange slice with the point of my wee umbrella.

"Why are you wearing a bathing suit and eating a fruit salad from a margarita glass?" He hung his outer layer of clothing on a hook by the door and loosened his tie. "Christ, it's hot in here."

"This is a special, vitamin-packed margarita. I cranked the heat to twenty-five, so you better divest yourself of some more clothes. Just a suggestion, I'm not trying to be bossy." I tied the strings of my sheer black cover-up into a neat bow and padded into the kitchen to turn the broiler on.

When I returned, Redfern was fiddling with the thermostat.

"Hey, leave that alone, copper. Nachos will be ready in a couple of minutes. Sit down and I'll pour you a drink."

He eyed the pitcher of margaritas like it had committed an indictable offence and he was preparing to whip out the handcuffs. "I'd rather have a beer."

"Go get one, then. And check the nachos aren't burning while you're there. I'm going to be pretty wasted if I have to drink this whole pitcher by myself."

He came back with a tray loaded with nachos, salsa, sour cream, and a frosty bottle of Molson Canadian. His hair was standing up in sweaty spikes and he shed another layer of clothes down to his underwear, but not before closing the drapes and locking the front door. Like anybody who wanted in wouldn't go around to the kitchen door, or come through the garage.

"Where's Rae?" He sank down beside me and picked up a napkin.

"In her bedroom. She'll be out in a minute." I laughed at his expression. "Kidding. She's in Owen Sound again, staying overnight with one of her sisters."

"You didn't answer my first question. Why are we pretending it's July and listening to steel band music? Which is quite loud, by the way."

"That's two questions. But I have one answer. I'm trying to forget about the first storm of the winter, with at least four months to go until spring. I'm feeling quite depressed."

"Maybe we can take an island vacation in January or February. Would that help?"

A dollop of sour cream dripped onto my bare knee.

I leaned over and lapped it up. "Don't toy with me, Redfern."

His gaze followed my tongue back to my mouth. "We'll do it if you want, but right now I have a crime or two to solve."

I ignored the napkins he handed me and licked the salsa off my forearm. The ice was melting in the pitcher and I topped up my glass, adding more fruit and a fresh umbrella. "So. Sophie Wingman. Murder?"

"Perhaps."

I snorted. "Sure. Pull the other one, Redfern."

"If you were on the job, I might tell you that, at this time, murder is probable."

"I may not be on the job, but I bet I know more about this town and its citizens than your exclusive little club."

"I don't doubt that, Cornwall."

"What are your reservations, then, about giving me more details?"

"I can't allow a civilian to influence the investigation."

I picked up a maraschino cherry by its stem and twirled it in front of my eyes. It was so round and red and perfect. I placed it on my tongue and slid it into my mouth. *Mmmmm.* "I don't aspire to be a cop, or even a police rat. But I do have a vested interest in solving the murder of a classmate. Make that *two* classmates." I spat the stem towards my paper plate, but missed.

When he began his obligatory protests, I waved my hand in front of his face. "Yeah, yeah, I know. A teenage girl felt a heart attack coming on and crawled into her gym locker to die alone. She didn't want to bother anyone. Makes perfect sense. And another girl becomes a priest, only to be murdered in her church the day after the first girl's body is discovered."

He tipped the last of the bottle's contents down his throat. "I'm only too happy to hear what you know about your two classmates. But what you tell me has to stay between us."

"Whatever. So, it's settled. I'll give you all the deep background you need, and you keep me in the loop."

"Sure, Cornwall. You go first. But I'm going to turn off the music and lower the heat."

"You can be a real downer. I can hardly wait to get you alone on an island. You'll probably bring your own water-purifying kit."

While Redfern carried the remains of our meal to the kitchen, I emptied more fruit into my glass and opened two yearbooks to the pertinent pages. I organized my thoughts between bites.

"What are we looking at, Cornwall?"

With my shoulder touching his bare chest, it should have been a cozy prelude to a delightful interaction, but tonight was all about business. I nudged the first volume. "This one here is the book you borrowed, from the year I graduated. The other is from the following year. Most of us bought it because it had two full pages of photos of us on the official grad night that occurred the next October."

Redfern pulled it out of my fingers. "Take me through each one. Who's in it, what they were doing."

His phone rang. I sat back and watched him search frantically through the pile of clothes — shirt, pants, jacket — where was that darn phone? By the time he located it in his coat, it had stopped ringing. The sweat ran off his body in rivulets and I opened the front door and fanned it back and forth to let some of the snowstorm in.

The cold air froze the blood in my veins, so while Redfern redialed, I went to my bedroom and changed into a pair of jeans and a sweatshirt.

When I came out, Redfern was pulling his clothes on with one hand while holding his phone in the other and conducting an official-sounding conversation. Who says men can't multi-task?

"Okay. Why didn't we have a report in our files? Really? When? I wonder why Davidson didn't mention this to us. Read it to me. Okay, call me back."

I scooped more fruit from the pitcher into my glass and watched Redfern button his shirt.

Redfern in full uniform can be an intimidating sight — for some people. His hard stare made even innocent folk quake in their shoes. "What's up with you, Redfern? Got a hot tip?"

"Tell me everything you remember about your graduation night. Begin with your arrival at the high school."

"Oh, well. There are a few gaps in my memory. Keep in mind, it was a long time ago."

He sat down in the easy chair across from me until our knees were almost, but not quite, touching. "High school graduation is a highlight in everyone's life. You must remember something."

"We had all moved on, whether to university, college, jobs, whatever. The ceremony was just for our parents' benefit. They wanted to see their kids dress up in robes and stupid hats and get handed a rolled-up piece of paper that didn't matter because we all knew we had graduated the previous June."

"Point taken. The ceremony didn't matter to you kids. Any of the grads missing?"

"We were all there, except Lionel Petty, who went to the University of Victoria and refused to fly back, then or ever. His mother accepted his diploma." I pointed at Lionel's picture. He looked nerdy, but he was stubborn. It was impossible to talk him into hiding a paper bag containing a wasp's nest in the boys' locker room to get even for their sexist behaviour over the past four years …

"Forget Lionel then. Everyone else there?"

"Each and every little captive one of us."

"So the ceremony is over. You have a party in the gym?"

Vague wisps of memory were all I had from that night, most of them from before the party began. "After the ceremony, the parents left, taking the rented gowns and caps and diplomas. The few significant others weren't allowed to stay …"

"Why not?"

I shrugged. "Maybe the chaperones didn't want anyone making out in the dark corners. Then, the decorating committee — including my reluctant self — hoisted the disco ball to the rafters, set up tables and refreshments. We flipped the lights off, turned on the floodlights, and the DJ started playing tunes. And there it was. One magical evening." After that, the rest of the night was pretty much a blur.

Redfern didn't glance away from my face. "Go on."

"To tell you the truth, I believe someone may have brought a bottle of tequila, or two, and when the authority figures weren't looking, some of us may have poured a drop or two into our pop cans. You have to remember, Redfern, we didn't want to be there, our high school teachers were still trying to boss us around, and they wouldn't let us leave until we had a party to celebrate our graduation. By the time they unlocked the door — and that had to be against the fire code — we were pretty much blasted. Even the nerds were bored into imbibing."

"You paint a vivid picture, Cornwall. So, that's all you remember?"

"Pretty much. I do recollect the body jam in the door to the parking lot when they finally released us. Must have been midnight or so. But you can't go by me."

"Obviously. What next?"

"I woke up rolled in a rug in the back of Fang Davidson's pickup. In Dogtown."

"Really? Did Fang roll you up to keep you warm?"

"I think I did it myself, to prevent liberties being taken with my person. It's a trick I learned from my dad, and that night wasn't the first time I took advantage of his wisdom."

"I feel a strange compulsion to hear the end of this story."

"Well, that's about it. I unrolled myself and wandered away to find Fang. His father told me he was passed out in his bedroom and drove me home himself. My parents were still sleeping. I crawled into bed. And

I've never been able to drink tequila since. End of story."

"You just made a quart of margaritas."

"I used white rum. And Grand Marnier. It doesn't taste as good as it sounds."

He shook his head like a dog that stuck its head too far into the water dish. "And that's all you remember? You can't recall where anybody else was, or where you were for that matter?"

"Sorry, Redfern." My glass was empty of fruit and I reached for the pitcher, but Redfern picked it up and headed for the kitchen. "Don't throw out the fruit! It's expensive."

He returned with his notebook and pen in hand. Things were about to get serious. I stifled a snort at his cop face. He was so cute.

"Besides your fellow classmates, who was at the dance? Caterers, chaperones?"

"No caterers. Our moms supplied the sandwiches and desserts. Mr. Archman was there, and a couple of lady teachers whose names escape me at the moment. Mr. Archman is principal now. The others might be retired, or dead. Oh, and Kelly Quantz was the DJ."

Redfern looked up from his scribbling. "Kelly Quantz? Sophie Wingman Quantz's husband?"

"Kelly always DJed the school dances. He was a graphic artist, designing covers for books, mostly horror and fantasy. But, that doesn't pay well, so he moonlighted as a DJ at the school dances — and weddings. I think he still does."

"So, he would have known Sophie when you were in high school?"

"Everyone knew Sophie." Oops, I shouldn't have started down that road. Speaking ill of the dead isn't classy.

Redfern must have caught an inflection in my voice. "What does that mean?"

"Well, before Sophie became a priest, she was ... um ... not so priestly."

"Who was she not priestly with? Anyone in particular?"

"Pretty much everyone in particular. She nearly went through the entire senior class by spring break. There were even rumours she was involved with an older man."

His phone rang again. He did a lot of listening and a bit of grunting; so sexy. "Thanks, Bernie. If you find anything else, call me."

"What's the big news, Redfern? Does it have to do with this case?"

He pushed the yearbook with the grad photos closer to me. "First, tell me which boys were involved with Sophie."

CHAPTER
NINE

NEIL WATCHED CORNWALL as she leaned over the yearbook. Her crazily striped hair was pulled into a ponytail and her toenails glowed neon green. He meant it about taking a vacation. Somewhere warm where they could lie in the sand and coat each other with sunscreen. Margaritas would not be served, but he would find her some other tropical drink with an umbrella … and no tequila.

"I can't remember the exact order, but the only guys Sophie didn't date in senior year were these." She pointed to four young males in turn. "Nerd, gay, nerd, and this guy, Chico Leeds, who was under the thumb of his girlfriend in grade eleven. But Sophie cut a swath through the rest of the class. After spring break, though, she didn't date anyone. I only remember because it was so out of character for her. That's when the rumours started about the older man, but it could be she just got sick of the male sex, or ran out of options."

"Do you think any of Sophie's relationships were sexual?" Neil noticed that Cornwall's ex-husband, Mike Bains, was not one of the excluded males.

"At least some of them, yeah. Boys like to brag, I know, but I think some of their stories might have been true."

"Including your ex-husband's? You weren't dating then?"

"He was one of the legions of Sophie admirers. The Weasel and I didn't get together until university. Second year."

Cornwall's big, dark eyes fastened on his and he felt a sudden rage against Mike Bains for hurting her.

"As far as you know, was the relationship between Bains and Sophie a serious one?"

"I already told you, Sophie didn't have any serious hookups in senior year. Certainly none that lasted."

"What about Kelly Quantz? Anything between them back then?"

"Maybe he was the older man she was seeing, if there was one. Kelly is at least ten years older than Sophie. But there was no sign of it on grad night that I can remember. What did Bernie have to say?"

"In a minute. What about Fang Davidson? Did he harbour any resentment when Sophie broke up with him?"

"Who knows. Sophie was a slut back then. Everyone was surprised when she went to Divinity College, and even more surprised that she came back to the scene of her sinful past."

Neil replaced the yearbook with the one containing pictures of the grad party. "Let's go over these photos.

Maybe something will come back to you if you talk about them."

"I kind of doubt it, Redfern. After that night I swore off the hard stuff, and only drank an occasional glass of wine in university. Blackouts are a warning that one should limit one's alcohol intake."

"Yes, I've heard that. Just tell me who these people are and what they're doing. And don't speculate."

She pointed to the first picture. "The Weasel sucking up to Mr. Archman. Did I mention the Weasel was the high school valedictorian that year and spent a lot of time sucking up to everyone except his classmates? He showed nothing but contempt for us, and that should have been a warning to me, but I was too dumb to see it."

"Ancient history, Cornwall. He was never good enough for you. Let's move on."

"Next one: Fang and Chico either lowering or raising the disco ball." She looked up. "Is the ball still in the auditorium?"

"Still there, as well as the garbage nobody cleaned up."

"Yeah, well, that was supposed to be the last duty of the decorating committee. Chico, Fang, and I were told to come in early the next morning and remove all that stuff and pile it behind the new high school. Plus, bag up the garbage and throw it into the Dumpster behind the gym. By the time I remembered that, I was back at university the following Tuesday and didn't give a shit. It's not like the school board could revoke my diploma."

"You're a rebel, Cornwall. Who's Chico, by the way?"

"Charles Leeds. He manages the Canadian Tire store in town."

"And would Faith Davidson be Fang's sister?"

"His twin sister, yes."

Cornwall had started wearing eye makeup, making her eyes seem even bigger and darker. With sweatshirt and jeans, she looked like Cleopatra on casual Friday. She aimed those eyes at him now. "Those bones in the locker are Faith's."

Neil looked at Faith's picture. Long dark hair, slight build, perfect smile. Perfect teeth. "About the phone call, Cornwall. Bernie says that Faith Davidson was reported missing by her parents two weeks after your party at the high school."

She stood up and walked away. When she came back, she held a glass of water which she drank in one long swallow. "I knew that Faith was missing. I heard it from my parents when I came home for Christmas. I thought about her for a long time, wondering what had happened to her. We had been friends at school. But then life happened. I forgot about her. Everyone said she disappeared in Toronto where she was staying with an aunt and going to college. I can't remember which one. But the skeleton has to be Faith."

Neil said, "Until a few years ago, Dogtown was under the jurisdiction of the Owen Sound Police Service. They initiated the missing person report. A few years later, there was some sort of boundary re-alignment and now Dogtown is part of Lockport."

"Oh, sure. They even tried to amalgamate us with Blackshore to the north of us, and everything in between, and call us something else. We just ignored it."

"The Davidsons reported Faith's disappearance to

the Owen Sound force. We'll have a bulletin somewhere, but the investigation file is lean. Bernie obtained a copy of the report from Owen Sound and read me the highlights. We can't be sure at this time that we've located Faith Davidson, but it appears she was never seen after grad night."

Cornwall stared at the pictures in front of her. "Here's Faith. Standing off to the side ... alone, as usual. I think she was the only one who wasn't drinking." She looked up. "She just came back from Toronto for the evening and was taking the late bus back to the city. Did she get on that bus?"

"A witness saw a young woman waiting at the Greyhound bus stop in front of the Petro station about twelve-thirty. She was wearing a white dress. The bus driver couldn't confirm he picked anyone up at that stop on his way through Lockport. Not after two weeks. They didn't have electronic tickets back then. So we don't know if the young woman was Faith. If it was, she got on the bus and disappeared in Toronto."

"Faith's graduation dress was bright yellow. Like a buttercup. And she wouldn't have worn it on the bus. She would have changed into jeans and a jacket. I guess we know she disappeared right here. She never left the building that night."

"We can't be sure yet, Cornwall. Were you good friends with Faith?"

"Yeah. We hung around at school. Me and Faith, Fang, Chico ... a few others I haven't seen in years."

During his time on the Toronto force, Neil knew of many people who slipped off the radar and were never

GLORIA FERRIS

heard from again. There were just too many places to
hide, or hide a body. He thought a small town might
be different, but he should have known better. Big city,
small town, it was all the same. And poor communica-
tions were a major cause of screw-ups between police
jurisdictions.

He stuffed his tie in his pocket and put on his belt.
"Why don't you throw a few things in a bag and come
home with me for the night, Cornwall? I'll bring you
back first thing in the morning."

A faint smile appeared, then vanished. "It's pretty
stormy out there. Maybe you should close the highway
and just hunker down here for the night."

"The OPP decides when to close the highway. I have
a full day of interviewing ahead of me and I'll need a
fresh uniform. How about it? I don't want to leave you
here alone in case the power goes out."

"If that happens, I'll pull a blanket in here and sleep
in front of the gas fireplace. I won't freeze, or starve, but
thanks."

He leaned over and gave her a lingering kiss. Maybe
he could run home in the morning to change. Spending
the night in Bliss Moonbeam Cornwall's bed was far
more enticing than returning to his cold cabin in the
bush and sleeping alone.

Before he could change his mind, he stepped out
into the storm. The snow had turned to sleet that cut into
his face as he scraped the ice from his windshield. He sat
in the driveway for a few minutes to let the inside of
the windows defrost. Fuck. Bruce County in the winter
had to be the shittiest spot on the planet. The sun didn't

shine for days, and the snow came at you sideways — try driving in that without your stomach heaving.

He restrained himself from charging back into the house, throwing Cornwall over his shoulder, and dragging her back to his cabin. She'd kick him in the head, call him an asshole, and never speak to him again.

He knew why she didn't want to spend the night at his place, and it was his fault, no doubt about that. But he didn't know what to do about it. He backed out of the driveway and drove cautiously out of the subdivision toward the highway — which may very well be closed by morning if this weather kept up.

The sound of a revving motorcycle filled his vehicle: Cornwall's ringtone. He touched the Bluetooth button on the steering wheel. "Have you changed your mind? I'll come back for you …"

"No. Listen to me. Did you find Faith's suitcase?"

CHAPTER
TEN

I DECIDED TO SLEEP IN and hit Canadian Tire when the store opened at ten. Glory's non-negotiable list put me in charge of decorations for the food bank fundraiser and I was going to get everything done in one stop.

Monday morning's sky was more grey and desolate than Sunday's and, while the snow had tapered off during the night, the frenzied wind still blew off the lake. The parking lot of our national icon to tacky Christmas crap, as well as everything else a Canadian needs the rest of the year, was almost deserted. I planted my feet gingerly in six inches of fresh snow.

I took one step and windmilled desperately before falling to my knees. Under the snow lurked a layer of ice. I skated to the entrance and tumbled through the automatic doors.

By the time I found Chico in the paint section re-filing colour chips, I had formulated the perfect plan to separate him from some of his better-quality seasonal home decor. I explained my mission to my old high school buddy.

Chico placed the customer service desk between us and pushed back his black ringlets. His hair was even longer than in high school. He pursed his lips and aimed his pale grey eyes at the twelve-inch fake tree in front of him. He plugged it in, and tiny coloured lights blinked on, reflecting off the lenses of his black-rimmed glasses.

"I don't know, Bliss. We still have three weeks until Christmas. After our year-end inventory, I can give you some leftover merchandise, but right now, I don't know ..."

"It's not like I'm asking you to contribute decorations for my own house. This is for the food bank. Think of all the little hungry children. Think of their excitement when they see the lights and decorations at the greenhouse. Imagine the huge sign at the entrance that acknowledges the Leeds family for their generous donation."

He pulled the collar of his trademark red golf shirt away from his neck and remained mulishly unconvinced. "Well, maybe a string or two of twinkle lights."

"Do you have a chair I can sit on, Chico? I fell in your icy parking lot and feel a bit dizzy. I'm sure I'll be fine, though." I smiled and let my lower lip tremble, just a little.

After that, Chico couldn't fill up a cart fast enough.

"Try to keep up," I called over my shoulder as I wheeled the cart through the aisles. I tossed in not only indoor and outdoor twinkle lights galore, but reindeer, snowmen, elves, and every damnable Disney creature from Micky to Ariel, the red-headed mermaid with the improbable mammaries.

When one cart was full, I left it for Chico to push and nabbed a second one away from a shopper whose back was turned. Bonus. The cart already contained a few tasteful decorative items. I halted in front of the artificial Christmas tree display and contemplated a ten-foot monstrosity. Behind me, Chico made a soft mewling noise. I reached for a box, then hesitated. Glory hadn't mentioned a tree. I suspected she'd make us sacrifice a real fir. I pulled my hand back and heard a shuddery sigh from my helper. The hell with it. I reached for a pre-lit twelve-footer and laid the box over my cart. Behind me, the whimpers turned into bleats.

There. Done. Two shopping carts heaped to the tipping point with the best of Christmas cheer. I promised Chico a second sign of gratitude set up inside the greenhouse and scored a seventy-two-piece place setting of "Seasons Repast" china. What the Bitch of Christmas Present would do with that was anybody's guess, but I looked forward to the look on her face when she saw it.

Chico insisted we had to go through the checkout where he would put in some mysterious code and void the sale. Standing in line, I unzipped my parka and fanned my face with a box of tinsel. In my book, power shopping was right up there with jogging in the fitness department. And about as fascinating.

Chico sweated, too, but I'd guess not from exertion. It was more likely he was wondering if he should write this off as a charitable donation, or if it would be more advantageous to use it as an entertainment expense. If I remembered correctly, he was not great at numbers, so hopefully he had a good accountant.

The checkout lady didn't seem to care that she was checking her boss through. She scrutinized each item as I handed it to her, turning it over as though she had never seen the like before, then turned it again until the bar code could be ever so slowly scanned. I added a couple of rolls of duct tape from the rack. Duct tape always comes in handy when sticking things to walls, or trees. My phone chirped nonstop in my purse. It was bound to be Dougal wanting to know why I wasn't at the greenhouse yelling at deadbeat customers.

Chico leaned on his cart and panted like he had done all the work. "Say, Bliss, I guess you heard about the body they found in our old school. Who do you think it is?"

I stopped fanning. My fellow decorating committee member from high school could have some memories rattling around in his brain that might help me figure out this puzzle. Or might help Redfern, I should say.

I reached into my tote bag and extracted a yearbook. I opened it to the pictures of the now-infamous grad party and shoved it in front of Chico's eyes. "You took all these pictures, right?"

He took the yearbook and smiled appreciatively. "I haven't looked at my copy in ages. Hard to believe it was fifteen years ago, right, Bliss?"

"It seems like a lifetime ago to me. Especially since I can't recall anything after the ceremony. What about you?"

"I took a lot of pictures that night. Don't you

remember? I had my regular Nikon, and a Polaroid. Fang and I …"

The cash register bleeped and the cashier shrieked. She held up a box of gold balls. "Oh, my God! The register doesn't recognize the bar code." In an instant she had gone from laconic to dangerously anxious.

Behind us, the line had grown to five customers, each with a heaping shopping cart. In Lockport, that's a riot in the making. The customers muttered and glowered.

Chico tossed the offending ornaments over my head onto the pile of goods already scanned. "Never mind," he told the cashier. "Keep going. I'll call in someone to open another register."

Since our scanning lady was about to go ballistic, and while Chico was calling on the intercom for Rick to present himself at Register Four, I scooped up my remaining items and deposited them on top of the carts waiting on the far side of the war zone. My eyes met the clerk's, and we nodded. Screw the year-end inventory.

A bright red parka hung by the door and Chico put it on before helping me out with his donations. Halfway to my car, my feet lost traction. I clung to the side of the shopping cart, but Chico fell against me. The weight of his body took us both down, me on the bottom.

"Get off me!" When I raised myself to my knees, I left a red stain behind on the ground. "Ow, my nose. It better not be broken."

"Oh, my God, look at you! I'm so sorry, Bliss." Chico squawked in abject contrition as we crawled toward my Matrix, dragging the carts along by their axles.

"Although, if you wore boots with sensible soles instead of three-inch heels, you might not fall so often."

"What's your excuse?" I shot back. "Your sensible soles almost killed me."

It was a long crawl, long enough for me to formulate another clever plan. I pulled myself up and opened the hatchback. Chico had to use one hand to empty the carts while clinging to the back of my vehicle with the other. I stood by and held a wad of tissues to my nose.

"Tell me, Bliss, what else can I do for you?"

He should be trying to remember his lawyer's name.

"Two things, Chico. First, you can clear this parking lot of snow, then get your employees to crack open a tub of Ice Melt. You're losing customers." I pointed to a man twenty metres away who was flopping around on his back like a beached tuna.

He started toward the fallen customer. I stuffed the tissues into my pocket and clutched the front of his coat. He tried to pull away and my grip tightened. A few droplets of blood fell from my nose onto the red nylon of his jacket and disappeared. "Secondly, mark December 14 on your calendar. I'll send you an email with the details, and I'll expect confirmation."

"Sure, you got it, Bliss. But you do remember I'm married, don't you? I have three kids." He pulled free and speed-crawled over to the man who was beating his heels and flapping one arm, trying for enough leverage to get his fat head off the ground. Something was wrong with his other arm.

It might be fun watching Chico try to buy off this guy. I crawled after him, leaving a blood trail on the ice.

GLORIA FERRIS

Chico tried to roll the man over, and good luck with that. The guy had to weigh three hundred pounds.

"What are you doing?" I pulled Chico away. "You need to call an ambulance. You could injure his spine."

"Oh, for God's sake." The victim had a commanding voice for someone in his condition, and it seemed familiar. "Charles Leeds. And Bliss Cornwall. Good God."

I looked at the beefy face, the triple chin, and eyes enfolded in layers of flesh. "Mr. Archman?" Since I had last seen him, the man had eaten himself into obesity.

He gave me that steely glare that used to make me regret whatever I had done to land in detention.

"Chico. You've injured Mr. Archman!"

"Take it easy, Miss Cornwall, you're dripping blood all over me. I believe my left arm may be broken. Perhaps you *should* call an ambulance, Mr. Leeds."

88

CHAPTER
ELEVEN

"I DON'T KNOW WHAT I'm supposed to do now without my Sophie." Kelly Quantz was slumped in an easy chair, arms hanging, a burning cigarette dangling from one hand. He seemed unable to pull his attention from the ceiling to look at Neil. "Without her, there's nothing left for me."

Tears coursed down his face and he made no attempt to wipe them away. His eyes were swollen and red and he had clearly not shaved or showered that morning. A group of women — parishioners, undoubtedly— buzzed around in the kitchen, looking into the living room and casting worried glances at the widower.

While he waited for Quantz to compose himself, Neil scanned the room. The rectory resembled a movie set of an old-fashioned parlour. Worn, but clean and comfortable furniture, subdued area rugs dotting the hardwood floors, a few tasseled lamps — everything he'd expect in the home of an elderly priest. But Sophie Quantz was thirty-two, the same age as Bliss. The only incongruent elements sat on the small side table at Quantz's elbow. A smeared glass with an inch of amber liquid, a near-empty bottle of Canadian Club, and an ashtray overflowing with the debris of numerous cigarettes. These items seemed at odds with the carefully placed furniture and an antique mantel clock over the wood-burning fireplace. This morning, the fireplace was cold and cheerless.

A haze of tobacco smoke hung in the air, causing Neil's eyes to smart. He was tempted to open a window and let some fresh winter air in, but he didn't want to interrupt the flow of Quantz's words.

An inch-long ash fell from Quantz's cigarette. Neil planted his boot on it, smearing the ash into a black smudge on the rug.

He glanced at his watch and touched Quantz's arm to get his attention. "Can you tell me when you last saw your wife?" Quantz had told him yesterday in the church but he had been barely coherent at the time. He wasn't much better now.

The widower looked up at Neil blearily. If there had been a window of rationality between the drugs Ed Reiner gave him yesterday, and this morning's bottle of whisky, Neil had missed it.

"I saw her yesterday," Quantz said, and erupted in another flood of tears. His chest heaved and for a second Neil thought the man might vomit. He moved out of the way and removed the cigarette from Quantz's hand. He had been puked on plenty, and had learned to heed the signs. A collective murmur of dismay rose from the kitchen.

He had dispatched Bernie to keep the visitors in the kitchen, but the unflappable officer was losing the battle. Half a dozen women pressed against him in the doorway, and his outstretched arms wouldn't be effective for long. Neil stood with his back to the kitchen, shielding Quantz from their view. He addressed the man again.

"Mr. Quantz. I know this is difficult for you, but we need your help to determine what happened to your wife."

"Somebody killed her and she fell off the fuckin' choir loft, that's what happened. Now she's dead and I don't know how I can live without her." He threw himself back in the chair and sobbed.

"What time on Saturday did you last see her, sir?" Neil was damned if he'd leave without some answers.

Quantz hiccupped and reached for his glass. Neil itched to take it away and tell the man that liquor wouldn't help, but he wasn't the morality police, damn it.

"After dinner. I went to my studio to do some work. I'm a graphic artist. I must have worked until two, three in the morning. Then I crashed on the cot in there. I woke up late and had to rush to shower and change for the service. Sophie had already left for the church. That's what I thought, anyway. When I got to the church — I always go in the front entrance with everybody else, but it was locked, so me and the ladies had to go in the back. That's when we found … we found …"

He bent over in another paroxysm of grief. Neil didn't have much time. The throng of worried parishioners was going to break past Bernie any second.

"What time did you go to your studio after dinner, Mr. Quantz?"

"Don't know. Maybe seven o'clock or seven-thirty." He threw back the liquid in his glass and poured the remainder from the bottle. He drank half of that down, and his body began to shudder.

Neil took the glass from his fingers. "I'm very sorry for your loss, sir. Try to get some rest now."

In the kitchen, he asked the ladies, "Does Mr. Quantz have any family in town?"

A middle-aged woman in a navy exercise suit answered. "He only has a mother, Chief Redfern. She's in the nursing home in Blackshore. Poor Kelly is quite alone now." Assenting murmurs surrounded him, almost drowning out the sorrowful sobs from the living room.

"I'm going to call Victim Services," he said. "Someone needs to check on Mr. Quantz and help him through this."

"We'll make sure Kelly is looked after." The navy-clad woman looked around at the others for support. Everyone nodded.

"Mr. Quantz is lucky to have such good friends. However, in situations of sudden death, it's routine to ask a crisis intervention expert to look in on the victim's family." If Kelly Quantz decided to swallow a bottle of pills with his whisky, he didn't want anyone pointing a finger at his department. He stood back as the women stampeded around him to minister to Quantz.

He let Bernie get behind the wheel of the 4 X 4. "Where to, Chief?"

"Hang on a minute." Neil called the high school to

ask if Earl Archman was available.

He listened to the principal's secretary, then thanked her and rang off. "We're going to the hospital, Bernie. Earl Archman slipped on some ice and is in the emergency room."

He wasn't having much luck with interviews this morning. Kelly Quantz was drunk and seemingly grief-stricken. It remained to be seen if Earl Archman would be able to talk, let alone recall an event from so long ago.

"Do you think Reverend Quantz fell over the railing by herself after she was shot, Chief?"

"Seems that way. The autopsy will determine any pressure bruising from fingers, but I don't think anyone would bother to drop her over when she was obviously dead from the bullet to the forehead."

Bernie turned into the hospital's freshly ploughed and sanded parking lot. They parked, then stepped out of the car, a cold wind from the west, off the lake, blowing loose snow and sand into their faces.

Neil glanced up at the building. His wedding anniversary was coming up. He and Debbie had been married on December 23, thinking it romantic. She had teased him he would have a hard time forgetting a date so close to Christmas. He shook off the black memories that engulfed him. Hospitals always generated a feeling of depression in him.

Bernie stomped through the automatic emergency doors ahead of him. "Whoa." He grabbed Neil's arm and pointed.

Neil had spotted them already. Bliss sat on an orange plastic couch and held a bloody wad of tissues to her

GLORIA FERRIS

nose. A man wearing a red parka leaned over her, his arm draped across her shoulders. A mane of dark curly hair hid his face from view, but he seemed familiar.

Neil strode over to the pair. "Cornwall! What happened to you?"

The curly-haired man yanked his arm away. Glasses encircled his alarmed, round eyes. Bliss pulled the tissues away from her face. Her nose was puffy and small scratches criss-crossed her upper lip and cheeks.

"Hey, Chief. Hi, Bernie! Nice of you boys to check on me, but I just took a tumble in the parking lot at Canadian Tire. Somehow, my face got mashed into the ice. The ambulance swept me up along with another victim of Chico's safety violation. The doctor twisted my nose and said it wasn't broken. Then he threw a box of tissues at me. Apparently, I was bleeding on the floor. I'm supposed to stay here until it stops." She sounded like she had a bad cold.

Bernie blinked and opened his mouth to speak, but closed it again after catching Neil's warning glance. Bliss was slightly battered, but essentially fine. She was wearing high-heeled boots, but Neil knew better than to comment on their impracticality. Instead, he turned his attention to the guilty-looking man. "And you are?"

Bliss answered for him. "This is Chico Leeds. We went to school together. He owns Canadian Tire now."

Charles Leeds: another face from the yearbook.

"I'm married." Chico's face reddened and he shifted as far from Bliss as he could get without actually moving to another couch.

"And you have three kids. Nobody cares, Chico."

Bliss caught a drop of blood escaping from her right nostril. "Listen, Chief. The other victim is none other than Mr. Archman, our old high school math teacher. Since you're already here, this would be a perfect time to interview him about the graduation dance. I think his arm is broken, but he doesn't appear to have a concussion."

Neil's mouth opened and closed again without any words coming out. Bernie snickered under his breath and Neil whipped his head around. "Go and ask about Mr. Archman's status, Bernie."

Bernie sauntered off, still chuckling. Bliss watched him leave, then mouthed the word *sorry*. She had trouble with boundaries, and they needed to have a talk. Another one. The entire force considered him whipped, and they weren't exactly wrong.

"So, how did the interview with Sophie's husband go?" Bliss looked at him as though she really thought he was going to discuss an interview with her in front of Chico Leeds.

Before he replied, Bernie returned with the news that Earl Archman was in a treatment room having a cast applied to his broken arm. "They should be done with him soon. Do you want to wait around, Chief?"

"No. We'll catch him tomorrow. Either he'll be home resting or back at the high school. Let's go." He would find Fang Davidson and interview him this afternoon.

They were almost out the door when he heard Bliss's congested voice.

"Hey, guys." She stood up, dragging Chico by the hand. "Can you give us a ride back to Canadian Tire?"

CHAPTER
TWELVE

CHICO WATCHED REDFERN stride through the automatic doors with Bernie close on his heels.

"I thought Chief Redfern was your boyfriend or something?"

"He's something all right." I knew perfectly well that Redfern wasn't running a taxi service, but he didn't have to say it in such a snotty tone with Bernie snickering openly behind his boss's back.

I turned to Chico. "Hustle back to your parking lot and pick up your vehicle. Then come back for me." The real taxi service ran just two vehicles and both were usually busy shuttling DUI citizens to and from the liquor store.

"It's almost a kilometre. And the sidewalks haven't been plowed yet."

"I bet you're sorry now you didn't de-ice your parking lot. Quit whining and get moving. While you're gone, I'll find Mr. Archman and try to talk him out of suing you. Go on!"

Chico opened his mouth to protest. I took the tissue away from my nose and allowed a trickle of blood to run down my chin. He scurried off.

Luckily, the nursing station was vacant. My boot heels clicked on the tiled floor, so I tiptoed up the corridor, checking the examination rooms. Most were empty except for a couple of screaming toddlers in one room and a woman at the mercy of a gynecologist's speculum in another. The last room contained a mound of stomach under a white sheet. The biggest pair of pants in the world hung over a chair in the corner. I had found Mr. Archman.

I approached the head of the bed, and nearly jumped out of my skin when my former math teacher emitted a thunderous gasp and sucked in a couple of litres of air. His breaths came and went, noisy but even. Then, silence. I waited, but nothing happened. He had stopped breathing.

I ran into the corridor, but there was no help in sight. Behind me, the gasping and sucking resumed, followed by more stentorian breathing. Geez. Somebody with a forklift should roll the guy over.

The breathing stopped again. I poked his arm, the one not wrapped in plaster and bound to his chest. Silence continued. I poked him harder, this time in the folds of flesh where his neck could be. He snorted and flung out his good arm, knocking me into the chair holding his pants. His eyes flew open.

I leaped off the pants and approached the bed, keeping out of striking range. "Hi, Mr. Archman. How are you feeling?"

"Who are you? Oh, Miss Cornwall. Good God. What are you doing here?"

"I sent Chico to get his car so he can drive us both back to the Canadian Tire parking lot. Which I'm sure has now been ploughed and de-iced. I hope you won't sue him, Mr. Archman. He's a little thoughtless, but he means well."

"You haven't changed since you were seventeen, Miss Cornwall."

"Well, thank you, Mr. Archman." I tossed my hair and wet my lips. They tasted like blood.

"Always a smart aleck, I meant. Charles Leeds is still your creature. You still lead that poor boy around by the nose. Or something else."

"So not true. He's married. With three children. And I have a boyfriend of my own."

"Ah, yes. Our handsome police chief. Let's hope that relationship works out better than your marriage to our mayor and future member of Parliament. I always knew Michael Bains would make something of himself."

I narrowed my eyes and fought the urge to press a pillow over his fat face. "We'll just have to wait and see about that, won't we? Speaking of police, Chief Redfern wants to talk to you."

"I'm sure he does. But I have no intention of filing a complaint against Charles. Could you hand me that glass of water, please?"

I passed the water and waited while he slurped his

fill. "Chico will be relieved to hear that. But that's not why Redfern wants to interrogate you."

"Interrogate me? Suppose you enlighten me, Miss Cornwall, since you seem to have the *ear* of the highest level of our town's law enforcement."

This was not going as well as I'd hoped. I had forgotten how sarcastic and cutting Mr. Archman could be. It wasn't my fault I didn't get math. If I was good at it, I wouldn't have studied arts in university. I'd be a quantum physicist right now, discovering the secrets of the universe instead of running a cleaning business and kicking deadbeat ass by phone at the greenhouse.

I edged closer to the bed. "I guess you heard about the body found in the old high school. And about Sophie Wingman?"

"Of course, the news is all over town. A tragedy. It's bad enough poor Sophie is dead. I only hope the body in the high school isn't local as well."

Really? He hoped that?

"That would be too much of a coincidence, don't you think? A skeleton is discovered in the building that was boarded up hours after the last graduation dance. The next day, a grad who attended that party dies an unnatural death." I had to be careful. Redfern would be greatly pissed if I spilled any confidential information. The trouble was, I didn't quite know what he considered confidential. Everything, probably.

"Oh? I suppose you think you know who the first victim is?"

"I'm not at liberty to say. I was hoping you remembered the grad dance."

"I remember it quite well. It was the last, and most horrifying, event to take place there. I had been drafted to chaperone, a duty I took seriously until I realized most of our graduates were stinking drunk. Thereafter, I and the other chaperones did our best to find the source of the alcohol but were unsuccessful. At midnight, we unlocked the doors and you fled into the night like scalded cockroaches. We should have called the police to haul you all down to the station for drinking under-age, but we didn't want to spend the night making statements. It's a miracle you all survived."

Well, we didn't all survive, did we? Faith Davidson, wearing a white dress, reportedly got on the Toronto-bound bus after the dance and was never seen again. If the skeleton was Faith, she never got on that bus and the witness was mistaken. Or lying. I was out of my depth.

"Mrs. Czerneski was a chaperone, too, wasn't she?" The diminutive Mrs. C's dyed-black up-do bobbed in and out of my memory bank, but whether from grad night or French class, who knew?

"She was, poor soul. She passed about five years ago."

"Really? I hadn't heard. Who else?"

"Who else chaperoned? Fern Brickle. That was it. Just the three of us. Thirty wouldn't have been enough to control you."

"Come on, Mr. Archman. We weren't that bad."

"You were the wildest, most disruptive class in the history of Lockport High. And that includes both the old and present buildings. The only exception was Michael Bains, and perhaps Charles Leeds. Unfortunately, Charles wasn't adept at mathematics like someone else

I won't mention." He turned his massive head in my direction.

"Don't look at me." Here was an opportunity not to be missed. "What about Faith Davidson? She was always top of the class with grades, and very reserved."

"Ah, yes. Poor Faith. She was a nice girl. It's a shame she didn't go to university, but didn't she attend a technical college in Toronto?"

"For a month. Until she disappeared."

"Ah, yes. The cities often chew up our young. Many times I have wished I had stopped when I saw her waiting for the bus and persuaded her to let me drive her home for the night. She could have caught another bus the next day. Then, whatever evil befell her in Toronto during the night might have passed her by."

I tossed my bloody wad of tissues into the garbage can in the corner. Mr. Archman was the witness who saw Faith waiting for the bus. That was why Redfern wanted to interview him.

"Maybe the evil befalled ... be*felled* Faith right here in this idyllic little town. Maybe she didn't get on the bus at all that night." Screw Redfern. But I wouldn't mention the yellow dress.

"I understand you have an English degree, Miss Cornwall? What university might that be from? Were you absent the semester they covered verb tenses? Maybe you can drag your BA and a can of Benjamin Moore over to my house and paint my bathroom."

A short balding man wearing glasses and a white lab coat breezed into the room. He looked like the doctor who had his fist inside the woman down the hall.

And the one who twisted my nose in the waiting room. "Sorry to keep you waiting, Mr. Archman. I wanted a word before you leave. The x-ray shows ..." He caught sight of me and stopped.

I edged toward the door. "Okay, I'll just be outside, Mr. Archman. If you're being released, Chico and I will drive you home. If not, good luck."

"He'll be a while yet." The doctor scrutinized me in a way I didn't like. Actually I didn't like any doctors much, but especially gynecologists. They made me nervous.

"Okay then, take it easy, Mr. Archman."

"Wait." The doctor stepped in front of the doorway, blocking my escape. "How's the nose, Bliss? I see it's stopped bleeding, but you should put some ice on it immediately to prevent your eyes from bruising."

How did he know my name? I hadn't signed in. The triage nurse hadn't been any more interested in me than Dr. Four-Eyes here. A little late for ice now, wasn't it?

He buttoned his lab coat and straightened the ID badge clipped to his breast pocket. "I'm a friend of Neil's. He talks about you. I'm the town coroner."

"Neil who? Oh. You mean Redfern. What's he been saying about me?"

"Only positive things, Bliss, I assure you. You make a handsome couple."

A couple of twits. One twit can't commit, and the other can't broach the subject of commitment. "I don't suppose you have any news on the skeleton? Or Sophie Quantz?"

The pursed lips were the only answer I was going to get from Redfern's pal. As I passed him in the doorway,

I whispered, "He has sleep apnea." There, my conscience was clear. Then I hoofed it down the corridor before I was asked to help Mr. Archman with his pants.

In the waiting room, my "creature" was back and relieved that Mr. Archman didn't plan to sue him. But I reminded him that he wasn't out of the woods yet. I expected him to follow through on his promise to attend the food benefit on December 14. I didn't care how many children he had.

CHAPTER
THIRTEEN

NEIL TOLD BERNIE to head back to the station, and Bernie had sense enough to keep his mouth shut on the drive. Why had he snapped at Cornwall and left her without a ride back to her car? Yeah, she was a little control freak. He'd known that from the beginning, and normally it didn't bother him. If she wasn't strong-willed, she wouldn't have survived two years of poverty after her divorce, living in a rundown trailer park with drug dealers for neighbours. She not only survived, she forced her bastard ex-husband to fork over her share after he swindled her out of a fair settlement. He suspected she used blackmail on the Weasel, as she called him, sometimes to his face, but justice wasn't always legal. He never questioned how Cornwall did it. From the look in Mike Bains's eyes whenever he was forced to speak to Neil, he still harboured a grudge by association. Neil's mind flashed back to the pages of grad photos in Cornwall's yearbook. At seventeen, Bains was one of Sophie Quantz's many boyfriends.

"Hey, Chief." Bernie swung the 4 X 4 into the chief's parking spot in front of the station. "I thought we were going to Dogtown to interview Fang Davidson."

"We are, Bernie. I need to check a couple of things first. Go have your lunch and meet me back here at one."

As he entered the outer office, Thea waylaid him, holding out a sheet of paper. "Chief, the lab in Toronto just faxed this over."

He took the paper. "Already? They generally take months to get back to us."

"We sent three samples scraped from the bottom of the locker. They must have a plant enthusiast, because a technician analyzed one right away and saw the granules in the sample. Anyway, you'll find this interesting."

Neil looked at the results. "Roses? There were rose petals in the bottom of the locker?"

"*Red* rose petals."

He didn't get it at first. It took a second. To confirm, he pulled out his cell and pressed number two for Cornwall. Number one was his mother. He should reverse that order first chance he got.

She answered on the third ring. "What? I'm kind of busy looking for a new boyfriend."

A sharp pain pierced Neil's right eye. Was he too young to have a stroke? "We'll talk later, Cornwall, okay? Right now, one question. Did you grad girls carry bouquets of red roses?"

Silence, not even the sound of breathing. He figured she had hung up on him. Then, "Yes, we did. And the guys had rose boutonnieres. Red rose boutonnieres. Why?"

"Thanks. See you later."

Lavinia tugged at his arm. "The OPP investigator is in your office. He got here about a half-hour ago, so I gave him coffee and let him sit in there. Here's a cup for you. And I've ordered a couple of lunch specials from the Mason Jar. I'll bring them in shortly."

"Thanks, Lavinia. What would I do without you?"

"You'd starve." She winked at him and bustled over to her desk to silence the strident ringing of the phone.

Small towns couldn't afford to keep officers accredited in homicide investigation on payroll. Instead, they called in external expertise when needed. Neil took a deep breath and counselled himself to be polite to whichever OPP know-it-all sat in his visitor's chair. Balancing his coffee cup and the lab report in one hand, he shoved his office door open.

The know-it-all was in Neil's chair, boots on his desktop. As Neil closed the door behind him, the officer leaned back and tossed his cap with the distinctive blue band onto the desk beside his boots. The black eyes crinkled at the corners as he smirked at Neil.

"Get out of my chair, you bastard."

The man waved a limp-wristed hand. "Love your hat." He rocked back and forth a few times on the chair, then stood up. His muscular frame was wider than Neil's, but he was an inch shorter.

Neil threw his flapped hat at the top rung of the coat stand in the corner, where it landed and, with the precision of long practice, stayed put. "You'll be wishing you had one after a few hours in this town. I see you got a haircut. They must have pulled you off undercover. Permanently?"

"They gave me a choice. Come in from the dark side or hand in my badge. Since I only have twelve years to go before I can take my fuck-all pension and make some real money in private security, I came back to the fold." He ran both hands through his black hair, longer on top than regulation but buzzed short at the sides. "Did you negotiate your Toronto pension into your chief's job?"

"I did all right. What are you doing on the travelling team, Tony? Are they still trying to keep you away from the female constables at headquarters?"

"I've turned over a new leaf. I asked for this assignment. As soon as I heard there was a possible murder in Lockport, I signed up to solve the crime for my buddy." He punched Neil in the shoulder.

Neil punched him back. "I'm guessing they booted you out of the Drug Enforcement Section, and you were in such a snit, you signed up for investigative liaison duty."

"Something like that. Jerks. They forgot what went down in this town last summer or they never would have let me come back."

"They needn't worry. You don't look anything like Snake, the outlaw biker. Even if there was anybody left in Hemp Hollow from that drug ring, they wouldn't recognize you." He thought for a minute. "Although Cornwall and Rae Zaborski will make you right off. Guess that doesn't matter."

"Miss Bliss? How is she? You and she tight? Cute as a little bug, that one."

"She's fine, better than ever. Where are you staying?"

"They booked me into the Super 8. The best place in

town, I was told. Say, are you still riding that girly Gold Wing?"

"I won't be riding anything for another four or five months. But yes, I still have my Gold Wing, and I'm not trading it in for a Harley."

Neil opened his door and called Thea over. "Get hold of Fang Davidson, would you? Ask him to come in this afternoon ... as soon as possible." He was curious about Dogtown, after all he'd heard about inbreeding and moonshining, but he needed to brief Tony on the skeleton and Sophie Quantz.

Tony's eyes lingered on the door. "Nice. Who is she? Is she seeing anybody?"

"Yes, she is. Eyes front and take a seat, Tony. It'll take a few minutes to go over the crime scene reports. Both scenes." He took his own chair and waited while Tony pulled the straight-backed visitor chair over to the desk.

"Both? As in plural? I thought there was only one body. Sophie Quint."

"Sophie Quantz. I guess they didn't tell you. The day before Sophie died, we found the skeletal remains of a young woman in a locker in an abandoned high school. We think she's been there fifteen years."

Tony's eyes brightened. "You think the deaths are related?"

"Yeah, we do."

It took Neil an hour to bring Tony up to speed. Halfway through, Lavinia brought in their lunches.

Tony set his empty Greek salad container aside and closed his fingers over the last of the sweet potato fries. "What is this stuff anyway? It doesn't taste bad but not as good as regular fries. Is Lavinia trying to date you or mother you?"

"She doesn't think I eat properly, I guess. She's always stuffing me with salads."

"Doesn't Miss Bliss feed you well?"

Neil snorted. "Hah. Cooking is not one of Cornwall's interests. Or skills."

"Fascinating. That you still call her by her last name, I mean. Anyway, to recap the deaths. You think the skeleton is Faith Davidson, who never left the high school after a graduation party. The school was boarded up shortly after. Sophie Quantz was part of the same class and she died less than twenty-four hours after the discovery of Faith's remains. That about cover it?"

"Exactly. The local mayor, Mike Bains, was one of the graduates, as was the manager of our local Canadian Tire store, Charles Leeds. And Faith's twin brother, Rupert, or Fang as he is affectionately known in these parts."

When Tony opened his mouth, Neil said, "Wait. That's not all. The rest of the class is scattered all over the globe. We'll interview the locals. But there's one more little grad who can't remember much of that night because she was trashed. Guess who?"

"Not Miss Bliss?"

"You got it. And she plans to help us whether we want her to or not."

"She's lived here all her life, hasn't she? She'll be a good source of background intel."

"Remember last summer, Tony? She was in the middle of everything and nearly got herself killed."

"Come on, man. Miss Bliss is clever, as well as easy on the eyes, so I think we should let her ..."

"I hate to admit it, Tony, but she came up with something I hadn't even thought of. Faith's suitcase. She planned to take the bus directly back to Toronto after the party at the school. So where was her suitcase?"

"I'll bite. Where was it?"

"We found the suitcase against the back wall of the gym, under a tiered bench. The bag was too long to fit into a locker in the change room, so Faith must have stashed it in the gym herself. We missed it first time around. We'll show it to the family, see if they can identify the contents. But I don't think there's any doubt they belonged to Faith."

Lavinia opened the door and announced, "Fang Davidson here to see you, Chief."

CHAPTER
FOURTEEN

"CAN YOU DO SOMETHING with this?" I pulled the towel off my damp hair and stood in front of Rae in the living room.

She looked up from her anatomy textbook and set aside her pen. "Like what? I don't have time to put another colour in tonight. I have my massage therapy final in less than a month and have to cram like crazy."

Have I mentioned that Rae is a former hooker? We both used to live in trailers in Hemp Hollow, and I brought her with me when I moved into my parents' empty house. Now, she's a part-time receptionist at the greenhouse, and one day a week she works for me cleaning houses. In her spare time, she's studying to become a registered massage therapist and plans to open her own business. She's too busy to backslide into her old life, even if she's tempted. I make sure of that.

"I don't want another colour." Even Redfern was beginning to make cracks about my many-shaded tresses. "Can you style it or something so it doesn't look so striped and frizzy?"

"Sure. I'll French braid it. Oh, and then I'll make your eyes look smoky. You won't be able to keep the Chief off you."

"That's not what I'm after tonight. He's tied up with the OPP investigator, so I'm on my own. I'm going to the Wing Nut for a glass of wine and some company."

Rae doesn't do things halfway, so by the time I picked my way over the icy driveway to my Matrix — in knee-high, low-heeled boots — my person was not only French-braided and smoky-eyed, but plucked, blushed, and lip-glossed. Somebody better try to pick me up after all that.

The Wing Nut is a restaurant and bar south of the cemetery on Highway 21. In a bygone era, it would have been called a roadhouse. Since it was technically within the town limits, the highway was well-ploughed and sanded. The snow had stopped earlier in the day and if the temperature went up a few degrees more, maybe the accumulation would melt. I hated it when the snow stayed on the ground this early in December. It made a long winter endless.

The neon letters and graphic of somebody's idea of a wing nut illuminated the parking lot, which wasn't as well-sanded as the highway. I really needed to start transporting my own bucket of Ice Melt. My boots skidded on the icy patches, but, lucky for me, about a dozen cars crowded the parking spots closest to the entrance. I used the vehicles for support and made it to within a few yards of the front door before my feet slid out from under me. I gripped the door handle of a nearby pickup truck and held on as the rest of my body disappeared under the vehicle. I looked up and read the sign on its door: DAVIDSON AND CUTLER SALVAGE.

Good. Fang was here. I could find out what he remembered about grad night. And, if it seemed appropriate, offer my condolences. I released the door handle, rolled over, and crawled out from under the truck. A tarp partially covered a glittery object in the bed of the truck. It beckoned me. I pushed back the tarp: a disco ball! Could this be the disco ball from the high school gym?

I touched the multi-faceted surface. It felt like glass, but was probably hard plastic. Big and shiny and tacky, it would look perfect hanging from the cathedral ceiling of the greenhouse during Glory's food benefit. I had to have it. I would have it.

I made it up the three steps and opened the front door of the Wing. I wasn't a fan of loud country-and-western music, but Monday night in these parts didn't afford much choice if one was looking for food, booze, or company.

Fang slumped against the bar with a younger man yattering in his ear. I slipped out of my faux-fox-fur coat and hoisted myself onto the empty stool on Fang's other side.

I ordered a glass of white wine and prodded Fang in the arm. "Hi."

He barely looked at me. "How you doing, Bliss?" In addition to other odd jobs, Fang delivered packages to the greenhouse and collected shipments for the Royal Mail and UPS. On Friday, he had been his usual easy-going self. Now, he stared into his beer as though it would really help him forget his problems. If he wanted forgetfulness, he should switch to tequila.

The other man leaned around Fang. "I'm Larry Cutler, Fang's cousin. You alone?"

Well, there it was. Not much of a pickup line, but now I could move on. "Hi, Larry. I'm Bliss. I went to school with Fang."

He looked disappointed. "Oh, I guess that means you're as old as Fang."

"Pretty close, Larry." I was three months older.

Larry went back to eating free peanuts and staring at the female bartender, forty if she was a day. But she did have an impressive rack.

Now that Fang was in my sights, I wasn't sure how to proceed. Did he suspect the skeleton he found was his twin sister? If not, I didn't want to be the one to break the news.

I tried for neutral. "It must have been awful, what you found in the old high school. Quite a shock."

I wasn't good at diplomacy, and Fang cut through my pitiful attempt. "It was Faith, you know."

I put my hand on his arm. "I guess you knew all along that something bad had happened to her."

"All this time, we thought she disappeared off the bus in Toronto. Turns out, whatever happened, happened right here in this sleepy little town."

"I know." For the life of me, I couldn't think of anything to say that wasn't a platitude, or just plain dumb. Time to move on.

"Um, I see you have the old high school disco ball in

the back of your truck. I could use it, you know, a kind of nostalgia thing. I'll give you twenty bucks for it."

"Nah."

"It's part of my personal history. How about thirty?"

"Nope."

Playing hardball, was he? "Okay. Forty. And that's my final offer." I could buy a new ball from an online party store for less. I wanted this one.

Fang sighed and ordered another beer. I didn't want to hassle him under the sad circumstances and decided to leave it for a while, then come back at him with an offer of forty-five dollars.

At the other end of the bar, a couple of familiar faces pressed together in a private conversation: Thea Vanderbloom and Dwayne Rundell. They weren't any more welcoming than Fang when I hopped up beside Thea. Good thing I wasn't sensitive.

I sipped my wine and beamed at them. Thea had on a long-sleeved black T-shirt and a silver lariat necklace. Dwayne wore a black western-style shirt. "Are you guys taking line-dancing lessons here? Are we going to see a demonstration by the fab duo of Dwayne and Thea?" I checked their boots for spurs.

"Hi, Moonbeam." Thea sat up straighter on her stool. A glass of icy pop snapped and crackled in front of her. Guess she was the designated driver tonight.

Dwayne looked over her head. "Well, look at you, all dressed up. She almost looks like a real girl, Thea."

"Oh, aren't you a clever boy?" I stuck three fingers into his beer and chucked him under the chin.

He grabbed a napkin and wiped his neck. "Thea!"

"Go to the restroom and wash your face, hon. I'll get you another beer." Thea shooed him off in the direction of the Gents, then shook her head at me. "I don't know why you can't be a bit more respectful."

"Me? He took the first shot."

"You call him *Duh*-wayne. That's not nice."

"Do I?" I was honestly surprised. "Sorry. I'll try to do better."

Thea threw me a suspicious look before taking the last mini-pretzel from the bowl in front of her and signalling the bartender to bring more.

I addressed Constable Crybaby when he returned. "I'll buy you another beer, Dwayne." There, that should make Thea happy.

It didn't. "Now you're saying *Dwa*-aayne."

"Maybe I have a speech impediment. Did you ever consider that?" I slid off my stool and looked around the room. In a far, dim corner I spotted the faint gleam of blond spikes. Redfern. The uniformed OPP officer must be the investigator. Both sat with their backs to the wall, cop-style. A third man with a thinning spot on the top of his head faced them.

Wineglass in hand, I sauntered over to their table. Redfern saw me coming but didn't give me a welcoming smile or wave me to come on over, dash it, and meet the boys.

Coffee cups and an empty carafe shared the tabletop with a basket of chicken bones.

Standing beside the balding man, I realized it was the doctor from the emergency room. My nose throbbed at the memory and I felt my lips. They were still swollen and I had used a lot of cover-up to hide the scratches on my face. But Dr. Doom was wrong about my eyes turning black without an immediate application of ice.

A folder lay open in front of the doctor. Redfern reached across the table and closed it, but not before I caught a glimpse of the photo.

I was tempted to go back to the bar and pick Larry up. Not for the night, but just to see Redfern's reaction. "Hi, Chief. How about introducing me to your friends?"

"This is Dr. Ed Reiner, our coroner."

"I met him this afternoon."

Dr. Reiner nodded and kept his hands pressed against the folder in case I ripped it away and ran out into the night with it.

"He's also a gynecologist," Redfern added. Maybe it was the light from the smudged overhead chandelier, but I'm sure I noticed a malicious gleam in his eye. Note to self: never tell your personal fears to your boyfriend. He may forget your birthday but never that you have an aversion to examining tables and stirrups.

I edged away from Dr. Reiner. The OPP investigator looked familiar but I couldn't place him at first. He was good-looking in an exotic, Mediterranean sort of way, with olive skin, black hair and eyes, and the longest lashes I'd ever seen. Well, except once on a camel at the Toronto Zoo. I knew him from somewhere. I usually let my sub-conscious do the memory work, and now it set to covering the face with stubble, growing the hair into long, greasy strands, dressing the body in dusty leathers ...

I had it. "Sn—"

"Tony!" Redfern snapped at me. "This is Sergeant

Tony Pinato. He's an OPP investigator and will be working on the case with me."

In a lower voice, he added, "Forget what you think you know, Cornwall. This is Tony."

Tony chuckled, a raspy, damaged sound I had grown so used to hearing last summer when I lived in fear for my life in Hemp Hollow. Tony had been an undercover cop but I didn't find that out until later. At the time, I thought he was a real biker, dangerous yet strangely attractive.

"You're looking good, Miss Bliss. I hope we'll have time to sit down and have a drink together before I leave town."

A long, thin scar ran up the side of his throat, ending somewhere under his chin. Now, I realized that gravelly voice was actually caused by an injury, maybe from a knife wound, rather than from years of smoking, as I had thought.

"That would be lovely, Tony." I aimed my best smile at him and ignored Redfern. Dr. Reiner's intense scrutiny made me squirm. I wondered if he was measuring me for a speculum. I pulled my pink sweatshirt firmly over the rump of my new, tight jeans and moved closer to Tony.

"Well, we won't keep you, Cornwall. I'm sure you have other friends at the bar to visit." Redfern sent me a wintry smile, one that didn't reach his eyes.

I pointed at the basket of bones. "What, you boys didn't have salad? Good nutrition helps the little grey cells work, you know." At least three chickens had given their lives for this meal.

Tony laughed and Redfern smouldered. What?

I yanked the folder out from under the doctor's hands. Before anyone could stop me, I opened it and tapped the top photo. Two cone-shaped objects with a numbered identification tag lay against a white background, a ruler beside them. They were six inches high. "I guess you boys know what these are?"

Nobody spoke.

I slapped the folder closed and slid it back to the doctor. Picking up my wine, I turned to leave, tossing my braid and throwing two words over my shoulder. "I do."

CHAPTER FIFTEEN

MY FAUX FUR LOOKED LIKE a mangy groundhog had crawled up onto the stool to die. I don't know what I had been thinking when I bought it. Fang slouched lower on the bar with half a glass of beer in front of him. I considered buying another white wine, but Dwayne's and Thea's presence convinced me one was enough. They were off-duty, but Dwayne undoubtedly carried a Breathalyzer *and* a radar gun in his private vehicle. Unless doing so would be *against regulations*, in which case he wouldn't dream of it.

The door opened and a couple swept in and paused for a moment on the threshold. When no one clapped or cheered, they let the door close and waited for the waitress to seat them at a table for two in the middle of the floor, where the overhead light shone the brightest. The Weasels visited local establishments once or twice a week. They liked to be seen spending money and enjoying the fine cuisine. The first Monday of the month must be Wing Nut night.

The waitress returned with glasses of red wine, took their orders, and bustled away. I picked up my almost-empty glass and moved in. On the way, I snagged an empty chair from a nearby table.

I plunked my glass on the table and sat down. "Good evening." I smiled pleasantly at one face, then the other.

They reared back. Andrea's throat made a strange clicking noise while the Weasel eyed me like I had a wart on the end of my nose. God, what was wrong with everyone tonight?

Andrea recovered first. "What do you want, Bliss?" She picked up her wine and sipped.

The Weasel's hard eyes narrowed and he swirled the wine in his glass like it was a rare vintage rather than the house plonk. I looked at his hand clenched around the stem. Geez, overreaction or what?

"I just wanted to say hello." I turned sideways at the little table and crossed my legs.

Andrea looked at my boots. "Prada?" Little lines appeared between her eyes. The last botox injection had worn off.

I turned my foot so she could see the gold-coloured, double-buckled skulls at the ankle. "Alexander McQueen."

She sucked in some more air. "That's ... they cost ..."

I waited, but Andrea went mute, so I volunteered. "About fifteen hundred." I looked at her black shear-ling-lined boots with the adjustable side straps. "Jimmy

Choo." It was a statement, not a question. I know my boots.

She nodded, and I confided to the Weasel, "A bargain at only twelve hundred. Or thereabouts."

He paled. "For one pair of boots?"

"They're Jimmy Choo, Mike," I told him, then turned back to Andrea. "I have a pair of Jimmy Choos, too. Last summer when I was knocked off my bike into a ditch full of water, my boots were ruined. So when you two kind people revisited my divorce settlement and came to the right decision, I bought a pair of Jimmy Choo biker boots. Just a little personal treat, you know, after living in a trailer park and almost starving for two years." Andrea had knocked me into that ditch, but her legal training prevented her from throwing herself at my feet and begging forgiveness.

Mike had gone ominously quiet and, to keep the conversation going — a conversation that had taken a different turn from what I had intended — I told him, "The biker boots are about twelve hundred as well. I really wanted the perforated suede pair, but I didn't think they would be practical for riding a motorcycle."

It seemed he didn't care about my boots. He couldn't take his eyes off his wife's pair. Just wait until he got her home. Andrea would feel the end of the cheapskate's tongue.

The waitress interrupted to lay a couple of salads on the table. Boring. I was a bit peckish myself, but figured I had mere minutes before one of the Weasels hailed the cops in the corner to throw me out.

"Is there something you wanted, Bliss?" Andrea

sprinkled a few drops of dressing onto her salad and moved the lettuce around with her fork.

"Not really. I just wanted to get Mike's take on the murders. He was part of the graduating class. Did you know that?"

"Of course I know. But that has nothing to do with Mike, with us. That happened a long time ago. You certainly live up to your own advertising, Bliss." She pointed to the words emblazoned in sequins on the front of my sweatshirt: PISSING OFF THE WHOLE PLANET, ONE PERSON AT A TIME.

"I do my best." I turned my back on her and addressed a future Prime Minister of this country, if you believed his publicity. "I guess you hope the murderer is found soon. The longer this drags on, the more likely it is that the media will find out about your involvement."

The Weasel slapped his fork onto the table. "Get one thing straight, Bliss. We are not having a repeat of last summer. You got your settlement and nothing you do or say will get you more. So, get lost!"

"Come, now. Take it easy. This has nothing to do with the settlement, although I think you got off easy. The point is, you had a fling with Sophie during senior year. Now, Sophie is dead."

He grabbed my wrist and squeezed. "That has nothing to do with me. Everybody had a crack at Sophie."

"Mike," Andrea warned.

I ignored her and let my wrist go limp. "So, what were you doing Saturday night? Can anyone verify your whereabouts? Except for your wife, I mean?"

"I don't answer to you." His hand tightened around my wrist.

"There are four cops in this room. Let go or I'll call for help." When his grip loosened, I pulled free and stood up. "I didn't mean to disturb your meal. Carry on."

My heart was thumping as I left the table, only partly from the adrenaline of battle. Mike was ambitious and had a ruthless streak, a bad combination. I believed he would commit a crime to bolster his political career — if he thought he could get away with it. Question: had he been this way in high school? I hadn't been on his radar back then, and didn't know the answer.

Outside, the glitter ball in Fang's truck refused to let me pass. I twitched the tarp aside and the ball sparkled under the neon lights, almost begging me not to leave it in the back of the dirty truck bed.

I opened the passenger door and laid two twenty dollar bills on the seat. After a moment's thought, I added another twenty, just in case Fang felt inclined to whine about the price. He was a businessman, of sorts. When he sobered up, he would be thrilled with the exchange.

The ball was lightweight, but too big to fit in my vehicle, even if the hatchback wasn't still crammed full of Christmas crap. Fortunately, the rolls of duct tape I had picked up at the checkout counter spilled out the top of the nearest bag. I ran back to borrow Fang's tarp.

By the time I had that sucker wrapped and taped to the top of my car, I was sweating buckets inside my furry coat. The temperature was definitely rising. I had to crawl through the front seat with the tape, throw the roll over the top of the ball, grab it, and crawl through the seat again. Multiple times. But my prize was secure.

It was nine o'clock when I finished. Closing time at the Wing Nut. The Weasels dribbled out, looked my way, then quickly got into their car and drove off. Next, Fang staggered down the steps, supported by cousin Larry. Redfern and his posse, including Thea and Dwayne, exited right behind them. I saw a Breathalyzer in Larry's near future.

As I pulled onto the highway, I looked in my rear-view mirror. Fang stumbled after me, arms waving, legs buckling. He fell to his knees, leaned forward and puked on the ice-covered parking lot.

Maybe Fang was more attached to the glitter ball than I realized.

CHAPTER
SIXTEEN

"SHUT UP," NEIL TOLD TONY. He had been listening to the gruff chuckling since he picked his friend up at the Super 8 Motel earlier that morning. After breakfast at the Mason Jar, they had proceeded to the first crime scene. Tony spent a few minutes silently gazing at the locker that had allegedly been a young girl's tomb for a decade and a half. This sobered him for a few minutes, until they were back in the 4 X 4 on their way to St. Paul's. He managed to keep his face straight while giving vent to explosive snorts of amusement.

He knuckled Neil on the shoulder. "I wish I'd thought to take a photo of Bliss racing out of the parking lot last night with Fang Davidson's big silver ball wrapped in a tarp and duct-taped to the top of her car." Tony gave up the battle and laughed out loud. "Are you going to arrest your little lady friend for theft?"

Neil pulled up in front of the church. "Not happening. Fang won't file a complaint. He knows if he did,

Bliss will have a logical explanation, even if she has to lie her head off."

"What's she going to do with that thing?"

"How should I know? I drove by her place this morning, and it's still sitting on the top of her car." The temperature had spiked a few degrees overnight and a foot of slush covered the streets. Neil gave the steering wheel a vicious twist as the vehicle edged toward the curb. *Where were the freaking ploughs?*

Tony slid his hand into the "holy shit" strap. "Ah, so the little spitfire spent the night alone? You mad at her, or the other way around?"

"Without a doubt, she's pissed at me again. I should have asked her to join us last night at the Wing Nut so she could help us with the case. That's what she thinks, I'm guessing."

"She has eyes on the whole town and could be a big help if you'd quit acting like such a tight-ass. There's something weird going on between you two. Is it about Debbie?"

Neil didn't want to talk about Debbie with Tony. He pulled to the curb in front of the church. "Have a look around, then we'll see if the husband is home and in better shape than yesterday."

The church was locked, and Neil used the key given to him by one of the church officials. Their boots clattered up the spiral wooden stairs to the choir loft. Tony leaned on the railing and looked down on the pews where Sophie's body had landed. The area remained taped off, but Neil planned to release the crime scene back to the church later today. If the OPP investigator agreed.

Tony lifted his head and sniffed. "Churches smell

funny, like rotting wood and judgment. Let's go find Kelly Quantz."

The manse stood directly behind the church, invisible from the street. A pleasant, round-faced woman in the kitchen told them that they could find "the grieving widower" in his studio. She seemed vague about its whereabouts and they went back outside and trudged half the perimeter of the rambling old house before finding a glassed-in area that looked more like a sunroom than an artist's workspace.

"I don't see any paintings," Tony observed as Neil rapped on the door. On the other side of the glass walls, Quantz hunched over a drafting table, one hand — the right — wielding a thick pencil, the other holding a tumbler of clear liquid to his lips.

"He's a graphic artist. Cartoons, comics? Looks like he's out of whisky and had to break out the vodka." Neil nodded to Kelly as the man looked up at them.

"Maybe that's water in the glass."

"Want to bet. Lunch?"

Tony watched the man lurch toward them. "Nope."

"Good afternoon, Mr. Quantz. Remember me, Neil Redfern, Chief of Police?" Neil had worn his cap today in deference to the milder temperature. He tucked it under his arm and held out his hand.

Kelly looked at the hand and reached for it but couldn't connect. He closed one eye. Neil captured the hand, more to steady the man than anything else. "This is Detective Sergeant Anthony Pinato with the Ontario Provincial Police."

Neil exchanged looks with Tony. Great, the man was still shit-faced. Fang's interview at the office yesterday afternoon had been a waste of time — he didn't remember any more than Cornwall did about grad night, and he couldn't add anything to his sister's missing person file. They didn't want to push Earl Archman until he recovered from his emergency room visit, and now this. Sober, healthy witnesses were thin on the ground.

"Just a few questions, Mr. Quantz. May we come in?"

"'Course. Sure." Kelly stepped back. The back of his knees hit the edge of his footstool and he toppled. Tony caught him before he fell over and helped him back into his chair. Then he seated himself on the footstool, leaving Neil to stand over the man. He disliked looming over someone like this, but the enclosure was so small he had no choice. He noticed two of the glass walls were lined waist-high with electronic audio equipment.

"Sorry to trouble you at a time like this, Mr. Quantz. You must have a lot of plans to make."

"Not busy. Can't make no ... uh, any plans. Don't know when Sophie's body will be released. That doctor, what's his name? Reener? He says he'll let me know when they're done and I can arrange the funeral." His lips quivered and he took another drink from his glass.

"I understand." Neil looked over at Kelly's drawing table and noticed a caricature of something half-woman, half ... was it a squirrel? He blinked a few times, but the figure still had ears and a bushy tail and a pair of improbably large breasts. Man, it was disturbing. He didn't want to take the chance of offending Quantz, so didn't mention it.

Tony, however, had no such reservation. He pointed at the drawing. "What the hell is that?"

The widower said proudly. "It's my new design. I've created a line of elemental avatars I'm hoping to sell to a gaming company. This is Amandaline."

Tony squinted at the drawing. "She's a squirrel?"

"No, she isn't! She belongs to the element of air. She can fly, catching the updrafts. And … and downdrafts."

Tony didn't let up. "I don't think she'll get through the liftoff part of flying, not with those, uh, boobs. And she has squirrel ears and a squirrel tail."

Quantz turned the drawing over. "Amandaline is not a squirrel." He finished off the contents of his glass and reached around the back of his chair for a bottle. Neil was right, it was vodka.

It was time to stop cosseting Quantz and question him before the man passed out. He leaned over and removed the bottle and glass from Quantz's hands.

"Hey! Give that back. You got no right …"

Tony glanced from the artist to the drawing. He picked it up and held it against the light of the glass wall.

Neil deposited bottle and glass well out of Quantz's reach. "You need to stop drinking long enough to answer some questions about your wife's death, Mr. Quantz. Sergeant Pinato will go to the kitchen and ask the nice lady who's washing your dishes to make some coffee."

He spent Tony's absence wandering around the studio, mentally estimating the value of the electronics and artist's paraphernalia. A laptop and colour printer sat on a small table, sharing shelf space with reams of copy paper, drawing pads, and jars of coloured pencils.

"Do you still work as a DJ, Mr. Quantz?"

"Not so much anymore." Quantz had adopted a sullen expression and stared out the window at the melting snow. "The kids want a young DJ with tight pants and a shaved head. I do some anniversary parties, stuff like that, in the summer. My equipment is outdated, too. Cost too much to replace."

"Do you remember the party in the gym of the old high school the year your wife graduated?"

Quantz's eyes filled with tears. "I DJed all the school dances back then. That's where I first fell in love with Sophie. I was twelve years older and didn't think I stood a chance."

"Yet you and she married, when? After she graduated from Divinity College?"

"That's right. The boys, they all took advantage of Sophie, but after she started trusting me in final year, she wouldn't have anything to do with them anymore. Even before she went off to university. I used to visit her on weekends, everything above board, mind you."

Tony returned with a cup steaming with black coffee. He handed it to Quantz, but took it back quickly after Quantz's shaking hands spilled a few drops onto the tiled floor.

Neil stepped back a pace. "About the graduation dance in 2000, Mr. Quantz. What do you remember about that night?"

"I don't remember anything unusual if that's what

you mean." He accepted the coffee cup from Tony again, holding it in both hands.

"Did you see Faith Davidson leave the gym?"

"Faith?" Quantz hooked his shaking fingers through the cup handle and brought the cup carefully to his lips. "That's the skeleton, right? Poor girl. Can't help you, though. I'm not sure I even remember what she looked like."

"What about Sophie? Did she leave with a group of friends?"

Quantz examined the ceiling, as though deep in thought. "I don't recall. It was a long time ago. All the kids were gone by the time I packed up my equipment, though." He used both hands to set his cup on a nearby table.

Neil glanced again at the electronics stacked neatly against the wall. "It's a shame you'll have to move."

"Eh?" Quantz bolted upright. "Move? From here?"

"Of course. I believe the house is owned by the Episcopal Church. Since your wife is no longer the incumbent priest, you'll have to move to make room for the new one. And Sophie's salary will stop. Where will you go, sir?"

Quantz sobered before their eyes. He looked around the room.

Neil and Tony waited while reality sank in.

Quantz looked up at them. "You're right. Now I'm homeless. And broke. What's going to happen to me?"

He slid from his chair to his knees. "Oh God. Why did this have to happen to Sophie? Now, I have nothing." Sobs ripped through his thin frame, and he bent forward until his forehead rested on the floor.

He moaned. "You don't know what it's like. To lose your wife like this. I didn't get the chance to say goodbye or tell her I love her."

Neil's breath caught in his chest. He pushed his black memories away and gestured Tony over. "If this is an act, he should win an Academy Award, but if it isn't, we can't leave him like this. Apparently, he won't talk to Victim Services."

The cold from the tile floor seeped through his boots. Tony threw a knit blanket over the prostrate man on the floor. "Do you have a psych ward at the hospital?"

"Are you kidding me? We have six beds, and they're usually full. But I was thinking more of a tag-team from the church. The ladies seem to be looking after his meals and cleaning. Maybe a few at a time can babysit him until he dries out."

It was mid-afternoon before they left Quantz in the capable hands of a committee of women who promised to keep an eye on him.

"You know, they'll smother him with kindness, and he'll keep hitting the bottle," Tony said, as they waited in the drive-through line at Timmy's.

Neil paid for their lunch. "He'll sober up pretty fast when he's sitting on the curb with his squirrel-girl drawings and his outdated audio equipment."

"Where are we going now?" Tony sunk his teeth into his honey-mustard chicken sandwich.

Neil drove with one hand on the wheel, while bolting down his BLT. "We're going to the Belcourt greenhouse.Cornwall will be there. You can ask her what those cone-shaped objects in the photo are. Because, fucked if I know."

CHAPTER
SEVENTEEN

NEIL GRUNTED IN SATISFACTION when they turned off Concession 10 into the greenhouse parking lot. "We're in luck. That's Fang Davidson's truck beside Cornwall's Matrix."

Tony set his feet carefully onto the slush-covered pavement. "There's nothing taped to her roof. Who's your money on if they're in there slugging it out for custody of that tacky mirror ball?"

"Cornwall, hands down. She won't be thwarted by an old classmate who's in legal possession of a sparkly object she covets."

The main greenhouse door opened into an anteroom, which, in turn, led into a foyer. The top of a marble table held one small blooming plant in a black pot. This was Rae Zaborski's desk when she worked as receptionist. Two dirt-filled, four-foot-high containers took pride of place in opposite corners.

Tony looked down at the label on one of the pots.

"*Titan arum*. What the hell's that? There's nothing in here. Big tub of dirt is all."

"They're dormant, or the seeds are growing, something like that. It's also known as a Corpse Flower, and we're lucky it isn't blooming. It flowered last summer and take my word for it, a five-day-old corpse smells better. One of these jungle plants stunk up the whole east end of town."

"Sorry I missed that," Tony said and a smile tugged at his lips. "Where is everybody?"

They moved forward into a corridor. One side looked out on a vista of rooms separated by transparent walls. In the distance, a worker operated a spraying machine while in another room two people wearing lab coats, hats, and masks bent over a bench. Sharp instruments hung from their gloved hands.

Neil noticed the red tendrils of hair spilling from the cap of the taller figure: Glory Yates. When Tony raised his hand to rap on the glass, Neil stopped him. "We need to find Fang and Cornwall. Let's try the offices along here."

"This place reminds me of a fuckin' funeral parlour, it's so quiet." Tony rolled his shoulders. "I can hear those friggin' plants growing. And are those crickets, or frogs?"

Neil listened. "Sounds like frogs, but I wouldn't bet on it around here. Come on."

A group of small office cubicles with opaque walls lined the far end of the corridor. In the middle office, Dougal Seabrook tapped frenetically on a laptop. A grey parrot perched on his shoulder, ribbiting like a pond full of bullfrogs. The bird turned its beady black eyes toward the two men in the doorway and croaked, "Boys, it's the fuzz. Hide the reefers!"

Seabrook had taught the bird to react at the sight of a uniform, any uniform, including the hydro meter reader and the UPS driver.

Tony's loud guffaw caused Seabrook to glance up, but his fingers remained on the keyboard. "Afternoon, Neil. If you're looking for Bliss, she's around somewhere."

According to Cornwall, her cousin was working on his second novel, another steamy mystery about murder with a nineteenth-century setting. Seabrook's gaze moved over Tony without curiosity and then dropped to his keyboard again. "Try the atrium. Unless she left. She works fewer hours than a banker."

"How can you tell an atrium from the rest of this place?" Tony asked, looking up at the vast, clear ceiling above their heads.

Neil shrugged, picking up the thick, heavy scent of wet earth. His nose itched.

"How come there are so many rooms?" Tony indicated the vista of plants. Every hue of the rainbow was represented in the blossoms, and every shade of green in the leaves and stems.

"Maybe some plants need more light and humidity than others," Neil guessed. He knew little about exotic plants, and cared even less. He sneezed. Fungi spores were airborne, weren't they? He picked up his pace but halted when he heard voices ahead.

Rain drummed on the panes and slid down the walls. The atrium dwarfed the rest of the structure.

The enclosure had glass walls and a door like the plant rooms, but lowered screens hid the interior from their view. The space stretched the length of the greenhouse.

"Just a little more, Fang. That's it, to the right, just a little. Now you're getting it," Cornwall's voice encouraged.

Male groaning accompanied Cornwall's urging. "Come on, Bliss. I can't stay in this position much longer. This thing is forty inches across."

Tony looked at Neil. "Man, are you sure you want to go in there?"

Neil pushed past his friend and opened the door.

Cornwall had her arms wrapped around the bottom supports of a twenty-foot stepladder while she strained her neck to look up.

Fang stood on the uppermost rung, reaching up with pliers in one hand and a roll of duct tape in the other.

They approached quietly, not wanting to startle Fang. "He's a dead man if he falls from that height," Tony mentioned casually.

Fang spotted them and called down, "Can you arrest her? I came to deliver some parcels, and Bliss acts like I'm her slave. She made me help her unload all the Christmas junk from her car, then I had to give her the motor and electrical cord she forgot to steal last night along with my ball and tarp. Now, I'm risking my life setting this up for her. She's bossier than my wife."

"He has four children," Cornwall called over her shoulder. "Isn't that careless of him?"

Neil pulled Tony aside. "Get Fang off that ladder. See

if you can get him talking about his sister's life before she disappeared. I'll take one for the team and ask Cornwall our burning question of the day."

Cornwall wanted assurances from Fang that the motor was rigged up before giving him permission to descend. She flicked the switch beside the door, to ensure the glitter ball revolved.

"It works!" Then her smile receded. "Wait a minute. What happened to the spotlight, Fang?"

"It didn't work, so I threw it out. Get Chico to donate a new light or, here's a thought, buy one."

"But you're still going to come back and take the ball down after the benefit, right? And hang it in my garage?"

Neil took Cornwall's hand and pulled her to one side, leaving Fang to Tony. "Never mind that right now. Tell me what those two cone-shaped objects are."

"First, tell me where you found them." Cornwall never played games, except sometimes in the bedroom. But blackmailing came as naturally to her as breathing, even if she considered it negotiating.

"I'm the one who asks the questions. You answer them. That's the way it works."

"Well, pardon me. How about this, then? I'll guess and you tell me if I'm right." She didn't wait for his agreement. "You found them in the locker room close to the body."

It took effort to keep his face neutral. She guessed again.

"Or else they were actually in the locker with Faith. Both of them."

He gritted his teeth before recalling his dentist's

advice about grinding and enamel loss. Relaxing his jaw, he looked down at Cornwall's head. "All right! They were in the locker with the bones. Now, what are they?"

She offered up a dazzling smile. "Six-inch cones. Imagine them wrapped with green tape. And filled with a lovely floral arrangement of red roses and babies' breath."

"Of course." Neil felt like slapping his own head. "All the girls had one. What about the boys? Were their boutonnieres inserted into a cone?"

Cornwall's look was disdainful. "That would be one heck of a boutonniere, wouldn't it? They had one rose wrapped with some leaves, then stuck through their lapels and pinned."

She lowered her voice. "So you found two cones in the locker. Somebody threw two graduation bouquets on top of Faith's body, closed the locker, and just walked away."

"But, why two?" Neil mused.

"If the murderer was one of the girls, she could have thrown her bouquet in as well as Faith's."

"Maybe."

The door behind them swung open, slamming him in the back.

Glory Yates entered, releasing her thick mane from her white cap. She still wore the lab coat and the face mask hung around her neck. Her houseboy, Pan, similarly attired, hovered behind his boss.

"Oh, hello, Neil. Excuse me. I need to speak with Bliss." She gave him a quick uplift of her lips. Glory was a member of the Police Services Board. He had never had any personal run-ins with her, but according to Cornwall she was the devil's mistress, prowling the graveyards at night, sipping blood from a crystal goblet while she waited for her Dark Lord.

She addressed Cornwall. "There you are, Bliss. Did you contact the list of delinquent clients I gave you this morning?"

At Cornwall's nod, she continued. "Good. I have another three names, and you might as well get to them before you leave today."

Bliss accepted the paper from the outstretched hand and stuffed it in her back pocket.

Glory's eyes scanned the mountain of Canadian Tire bags in one corner. "Oh, I see you're moving forward with your decorating tasks for our open house. Carry on then."

As she turned to leave, she hesitated and looked up at the glitter ball. It spun slowly, catching a few beams of light from the overcast sky. "Very nice. But it needs a spotlight. See to it. Fang, I hope Bliss isn't taking advantage of you again …"

Her words ended abruptly and her body became still. She found the one stranger among them. Her mouth formed a perfect *O*.

Tendrils of curls tumbled around her face, and her pale complexion turned pink. She floated forward, stopping a few feet from Tony. One hand twitched as though she wanted to reach out and touch him.

Tony blinked and cleared his throat. His olive skin never reddened. But something changed in his face. Black eyelashes swept his cheeks. His dark eyes opened wide and his gaze locked with hers. Neil had seen this reaction before.

GLORIA FERRIS

Tony's right hand reached for Glory's and, instead of a traditional handshake, their fingers intertwined.

Was it Neil's imagination, or did forked lightning flash in the darkened sky above the atrium?

He closed his eyes against the sight. "Ah, shit."

CHAPTER
EIGHTEEN

"YOU HAVE TO TALK TO TONY. He doesn't know what he's getting into." I scooped more chicken casserole onto my plate. Thinking Redfern looked somewhat peaked at the greenhouse, I cooked him dinner. And made a salad from ingredients I found in the fridge. It was almost magical, the way food periodically showed up in there. But really I was thankful Rae dragged groceries in from time to time.

Redfern shovelled in the food like he hadn't eaten all day, poor guy. "I thought you couldn't cook."

"I never said that. I just prefer not to." I pushed the salad bowl his way. "Load up. You probably need more fibre."

He pushed it back. "My fibre is fine. Don't worry about Tony. He can take care of himself. It's Glory I'm concerned about."

"Glory. Are you kidding me? She'll suck Tony dry and discard the shell."

He smiled, leaned back, and pushed his empty plate away. "Good dinner. I appreciate your efforts."

I put our plates in the sink and covered the leftovers. "Don't get used to it. Go to the living room and put your feet up. I'll be right there. Coffee? Beer?"

He got up, but narrowed his eyes. "What's up with you?"

I stood on tiptoes and gave him a quick kiss on his way past me. Honestly, I wasn't sure what was up with me.

Once the kitchen was tidied, I prepared a tray laden with our coffees and two servings of cheesecake. Redfern accepted my offering quickly, like I had a boa constrictor wound around my neck. Shoot it or run, his expression seemed to be debating.

I noticed the black notebook and pen in his hand. "Are we going to talk about the case?"

"Yes, we are. I've made three columns here. First column consists of names of people I intend to interview. Second column is for tick marks after the interviews. Guess what the third column is for."

"I have no idea, officer." I did, but wasn't a fan of lists, so decided not to participate in this line of questioning where I was being set up to be the big loser. And I think he was lying about the columns. No way could you get three on that ratty little notebook.

"The third column has Bliss Cornwall as a heading. Which of these people have you already interrogated? Let's see. Fang, Earl Archman, Charles Leeds, Mike Bains. Anyone else?"

"For your information, *Chief*, Fang was too drunk

and despondent last night at the Wing Nut to make any sense, and today he just complained — a lot — about the few simple tasks I asked him to perform. I meant to ask about grad night, but you and Tony came bursting in before I had a chance."

"Earl Archman—"

"… went on at great length about how the Class of 2000 was the worst he had the misfortune to teach. Your friend, the gynecologist, interrupted us before I could get any useful details from him."

Redfern looked up from his columns. "You need to get over this phobia about gynecologists. What do you propose to do when you get pregnant?"

"Uh, not get pregnant. Anyway, I've nothing against female gynecologists. But a man poking around a woman's nether parts for money is just wrong. I suspect his motives."

Redfern touched my knee. "You're very entertaining, Cornwall, but can we discuss Charles Leeds now? You hung out with him for most of yesterday. Don't tell me you didn't discuss the graduation party."

"Do I detect a pinch of jealousy?"

He snorted in a most unflattering way. "Hardly. He has three kids, remember. Talk."

"I didn't have that much time to get into anything with him. I went to Canadian Tire hoping to score some decorations for Glory's charity open house. I managed to obtain a few. Chico helped me out to the parking lot. We fell. Mr. Archman cracked his arm on the pavement when he slipped. And then the ambulance came. There you have it."

"You and Chico didn't discuss the deaths or grad night?"

"Not really. While we waited in the checkout line, I showed him the yearbook pictures. He had snapped most of them himself. We did take a short waltz down memory lane, but only about photography. I was bored to tears."

"You spent time in the emergency room. What did you talk about there?"

"Mostly, he was on the phone, instructing his minions to cover the parking lot with Ice Melt. Then his wife called and reamed him out for twenty minutes about Chucky Junior's hockey schedule and telling him why he should get it changed so she doesn't have to get up at 3:00 a.m. every Saturday morning. After he hung up, he explained why it wasn't his fault the parking lot was a death trap and he hoped Mr. Archman wouldn't sue him. Uh, let me see." I wracked my brain. "That's about it. He whined a lot. You came in with your henchman, Bernie, and this time I was rather happy to see you. That is, until you so rudely refused me a ride back to my car."

He put the notebook on the coffee table and pulled me onto his lap. "I'm sorry about that. I'm such a bastard. What about Mike Bains?"

Nuts, I had hoped he wouldn't bring that up. "I guess the discussion I had with Andrea about designer boots isn't relevant. No? Didn't think so. Okay, well. You may be interested to know the Weasel doesn't have an alibi for Saturday night or early Sunday morning when Sophie Quantz was killed."

"Say that again."

I prepared to comply but didn't get very far. Redfern went critical mass on me. I fell off his lap and onto the couch where I stayed until he ran out of steam. There was no point trying to establish a give-and-take partnership with him.

"You need to butt out of this investigation, Cornwall. Starting now!"

"All right!" I had a thought. "Where's Tony? You didn't say. Didn't he want to come for dinner?"

Redfern's complexion slowly returned to normal colour. "He said he needed an early night but wanted me to thank you for the invitation."

We looked at each other. "That doesn't sound like Tony, does it?" I picked up my cell.

Pan didn't answer until the third ring. "Hi, Pan. So, what were you doing at the greenhouse today?" I moved back over to sit on the arm of Redfern's chair. His arm curled around my waist. "Really? You're kidding."

I let Pan complain about the Bloody Baroness before giving Redfern the scoop. "Glory doesn't think Pan has enough to do at the house, so she's teaching him how to be productive at the greenhouse. Today he had a lesson in detecting mould."

It was time to interrupt Pan's whine-fest. "Yeah, that really sucks. I know how busy you are at home. Where is she now? ... Really? When is she coming back?"

Redfern moved his head against mine and tried to hear Pan's words. Did I have a speaker button on this phone? I should look into that.

Pan returned to the subject of his servitude to an

ungrateful mistress. I cut him off and put the phone down. "Did you hear that?"

"No. Did he say something about Tony?"

"Not directly. Glory left a few hours ago with an overnight bag. Since they're both MIA, what are chances they aren't together?"

Redfern stood up and began to pace.

I thought back over the past couple of years, since Glory's divorce from Dougal. That relationship seemed to have turned her off men for good, which made total sense, but I still figured Tony's soul hung in the balance.

I asked, "So, does Tony have a history of sudden attraction to She Devils?"

"He does. But keep that to yourself. Speaking of attractions, why don't you get your white thong and come back to the cabin with me?"

"How about you stay here tonight instead? I'm not going to your shack in the woods to freeze my ass off."

"You won't freeze anything. Guaranteed."

"Nope. Here's the deal. White thong here. Cabin, alone."

"Where's Rae?"

"I wondered when you'd remember Rae. Well, truthfully, she's in her room. She took her dinner in there to study, and so we could be alone. She thinks you don't like her."

"I like her just fine." He lowered his voice. "But she used to be a hooker."

Dramatically, I lowered by voice even more. "So let it go. She isn't one now. She was never charged, so you aren't compromising your integrity by being friendly."

"I can't sleep over in the same house. What if she goes back to the life? My career could be screwed."

"That's crazy. I'm not spending another night at the cabin. That's just the way it is."

"I'll put the pictures away. I know it upsets you."

"After, what, almost four years, you keep a picture of your deceased wife beside your bed. You can't honestly wonder why I don't want to spend the night there."

"Debbie will always be part of my life. That doesn't reflect on my feelings for you."

"It would have been better had you said Debbie will always be a part of your past. I'm giving you all the space you need, Redfern, but I can't be your solace while you continue to mourn indefinitely."

"Mourning is subjective. You can't put a time limit on it."

"Okay, got it. When you're here, I feel you're really with me, that's all I'm trying to say. At your cabin, you have pictures everywhere. You brought her with you from Toronto. It's your place and hers. I'm just a visitor. If you can't see that, then…." I ran out of words. I couldn't explain how I felt, and this wasn't the first discussion we'd had about Debbie. If she was an ex, I could deal with it, but it was hard to compete with a ghost.

His face took on a stubborn expression. "If you lived alone, there wouldn't be a problem."

"Back at you."

He grabbed his coat from the hook. "I'll talk to you tomorrow."

The door closed very quietly, and a minute later I heard his vehicle start up and drive away. It broke my heart, thinking of him heading back to his cold cabin. But it was his choice. I ate my cheesecake. Then I ate his.

I went to bed with an icepack over my eyes, although it was too late. Dr. Doom's prediction had come true. There wasn't enough makeup in the world to cover the purple-black smudges around both my eyes.

CHAPTER
NINETEEN

CORNWALL WAS RIGHT about one thing. The cabin was glacial. Neil kept his coat on while he performed his nightly rituals.

The cabin was heated by a propane gas fireplace and several strategically-placed electric heaters. The fireplace shut off automatically after a few hours, and he couldn't leave the heaters running while he was out. He came home, and woke up, to a chilly house. But only in the spring, winter, and fall. Summer was pleasant except for the blackflies, mosquitoes, and skunks that raised their families under the back steps.

He plugged in the heaters and reset the fireplace, remembering he hadn't ordered propane and the tank had to be nearing empty. He fell into an old armchair pulled close to the fireplace and rested his boots on the hearth.

He was frustrated at the length of time it was taking for the lab to confirm that the bones belonged to

Faith Davidson. The Davidson family didn't believe in routine x-rays. Since Faith, along with most of the clan, had been blessed with near-perfect teeth, there were no x-rays to help with ID. They would have to wait until DNA from the skeleton's teeth matched samples taken from Mr. and Mrs. Davidson to confirm identity. The shape of the teeth, strands of long, dark hair, and the timing of Faith's disappearance increased the odds that the remains were hers. Even the two tiny cones that once held celebration bouquets, and the decayed rose petals from the locker, pointed to Faith.

He had no choice but to proceed as though the girl was Faith Davidson. By his reaction at the scene, even Fang was certain he had found his twin sister when he opened the door of the locker.

So, if Faith never got on the bus to Toronto that night, who was the girl at the bus stop? Did she even exist? Earl Archman was the only witness to come forward at the time of Faith's disappearance to state he saw a young girl in a white dress at the bus stop the night of the grad party. The bus driver could neither corroborate nor contradict the statement. He had to interview Earl Archman tomorrow.

He reached into his jacket pocket and pulled his notebook out. One of the two female chaperones had passed away. He made a note to interview the other one tomorrow. It was too much of a coincidence that Sophie Quantz was killed less than twenty-four hours after the skeletal remains were discovered. There had to be a connection between the graduation party and both deaths. He would assign Thea the task of tracking down every other member of that graduating class.

He forced himself to his feet, put his notebook away, and walked into his cramped bedroom, carrying one of the electric space heaters. He plugged in the heater, undressed quickly, and slid between the cold sheets. They felt damp as well as icy. He tried to picture Bliss wearing her white thong, but he was too chilled to sustain even that image. He reached out and pulled the heater closer to the bed. One of these nights, the cabin was going to burn to the ground, and him with it. He couldn't blame Cornwall for avoiding this place.

He should find a warmer, more convenient place to live. Perhaps buy a house. But that would mean making a commitment to remain here.

Before turning off the lamp, he glanced, as always, at Debbie's picture. He made a point of putting the picture away before Bliss arrived. Except for that one time. She hadn't said anything, but she hadn't been back since.

When he first looked around for a place to rent, he was hesitant when the realtor brought him here. But it was the closest place he could find that was within quick response distance. Gradually he grew accustomed to the night noises and enjoyed the absence of sirens, gunshots, and the voices of people in pain or distress, although some of those voices were in his head forever.

The station received several calls a week from hysterical homeowners who spotted bears — or maybe just the same one — lurking around their properties. The kicker was, the police couldn't do a thing about it. You couldn't shoot a bear just because it was foraging for food. So, each complainant was told the same thing:

phone the Ministry of Natural Resources, number provided, and they will explain how to discourage bears from hanging about.

Neil had seen one a couple of months ago, lumbering around the side of the cabin as he drove up one evening. Thank God Bliss hadn't been with him. After that, he had started bringing his gun home with him instead of locking it up in the station like he insisted his officers do when they completed their shifts.

His mind refused to turn off and let him sleep. Far better to be pressed against Cornwall in her warm bed than shivering alone here. Maybe he should buy some flannel sheets. And flannel pyjamas. Just like his grandfather. No, strike that mental image. Maybe he should just move out and find a place with heat. Or, should he go back to Toronto?

An hour later, his eyes were still wide open. Debbie crept into his thoughts again. She was always home from work before him. Dinner was in the oven unless they decided to go to one of the little ethnic restaurants that peppered their downtown neighbourhood. She'd tell him about her day as administrative assistant to one of the city councillors. And he would give her an uncensored version of what happened during his shift. She listened and massaged the tension out of his shoulders, but didn't tell him what he should do.

Unbidden, that last night replayed itself in his mind. Holding Debbie's hand in the ambulance as it raced through the rain-slick streets toward Toronto General. Refusing to acknowledge that she and their unborn baby were already gone.

There was nothing he could have done, the doctors said after the autopsy. There was no way anyone could have known about her congenital heart defect. The pregnancy may have overtaxed her heart, but it could have happened anytime. Time bomb.

The next few months were a blur. When the fog lifted, he felt he had to get away from her family, his family and friends and, most of all, the memories. When he saw the Ontario Association of Chiefs of Police vacancy for Lockport, he applied. He had never heard of the place. Now, he visited family when he felt like it, but no one came hunting for him, especially from November to April when whiteouts could close the highway at any time. City people weren't up for it.

He ignored the scrabbling sounds outside his window, trusting it was a raccoon and not the town bear, which should be hibernating by now. His eyes closed.

CHAPTER TWENTY

DOUGAL DIDN'T LOOK UP as I passed him on the way to my tiny cubicle. He was immersed in another world — of murder and of conservatories full of lush, dripping flora. His first book, *Death in the Conservatory*, told the tale of a dashing gentleman in mid-1800s Toronto who discovers the body of a woman under a palm tree in the glasshouse of his luxurious city home. Of course this gentleman doesn't want his wife to find out the body used to be his mistress. I read the book and, holy geez, marble limbs and lustful loins abounded throughout each chapter. Since the mistress was from Montreal, Dougal threw in a handful of French phrases, like *tout nu* and *frisson*. But that, it appears, was exactly the attraction for readers and why Dougal's publisher wanted a sequel *tout de suite*. Now, the sequel, *Death in the Convent,* was almost ready for his editor, and he was being more of a jerk than usual, like the whole world should recognize his genius.

I introduced myself as Jenny Jolie to the first dead-beat customer and was totally reasonable with him. The gentleman from an area code I'd never heard of screamed in fractured English that he wasn't going to pay the $800 he owed Belcourt Nurseries for the forty *Calathea makoyana* plants he admitted receiving in good condition. I tactfully pointed out that their demise was because he planted them in full sun and neglected to mist them. The instructions were included with the plants in English, and if he couldn't read English, that also was his own fault. Next time he should buy the plants from Brazil where they originate if he wasn't happy with our product. Just cough up the money.

He responded with a high-decibel "Fluck you."

We had already established he didn't have a good grasp of the English language, so I yelled back, "Fluck you, too, buddy."

I wrote WHFO, which was my ranking code for When Hell Freezes Over, next to his name and prepared to call the second number on the list.

"Will you keep it down in here?" Dougal stuck his head in the doorway. "The racket is causing plants all over the greenhouse to wither and die." He frowned at me. "You really need to work on your customer relations interactions. We'll be hearing from the Minister of Foreign Affairs before day's end after that diatribe."

"I doubt it, but I'm pretty sure you can kiss that eight hundred dollars goodbye."

He scowled even harder and stepped into my cubicle. "It's your job to collect money from overdue customer accounts, not insult them and call it a day."

"Get lost. Of every ten calls I make, I close nine of them. You're lucky to have me and should give me a raise."

"And you should be locked up during daylight hours. But that's unlikely to happen either."

His dark hair and facial stubble were the same length and, frankly, it was not a good look. "I hope you're going to shave before Holly comes home. She prefers her men clean-shaven, as do I."

"You don't have anything in common with Hol, so don't give yourself airs. Just quit screaming at customers."

I motioned for him to come closer. "Do you think Glory went out with Tony last night?"

"Don't know and don't care."

"You should have seen the pheromones flying between Glory and Tony yesterday when they met. Actually, a really torrid affair could benefit all of us if it puts Satan's Chosen One in a better mood."

He planted his butt on the corner of my desk. "I don't think that will make any difference. Her personality was the same when we were married."

Before I could make the obvious comment that perhaps Dougal hadn't been up to the job in the lovemaking department, my cell rang.

"It's Pan," I said. I listened to him until he ran down. "No, she's here. Yeah, that's really interesting. I'm sure your job is safe. Keep me informed, will you?"

"What's got his apron in a twist?" Dougal asked.

"You won't believe this. Glory didn't go home last night." I leaned forward and lowered my voice. "At all. But her car is outside now, so she must have come straight to the greenhouse this morning from wherever she spent the night."

He got up. "I'm all for anything that keeps her away from here as much as possible. Just don't count on a big personality change."

"I think Redfern is a little worried about her. Funny ..."

"What I want to know is, do you call him Redfern when you're doing him? Seems kind of formal for the occasion."

"Mind your own business. Stick around and help me with my next call. It's to Dorval, Quebec. He owes six hundred and fifty dollars and will insist on speaking French ..."

"You don't speak French."

"Exactly." I picked up the phone. "So, this should be fun. I'll put him on speaker, if you show me how to do it, and you can learn some new French swear words to use in your books."

He declined to participate and went back to his own make-believe world. I called the Quebec number, switching my name to Angie Aniston. It turned out that the customer spoke perfect English, apologized for the omission, and promised to put the cheque in the mail. Right. Like I hadn't heard that before. I put PP next to his name — Promises, Promises.

The other two customers sounded just as sincerely sorry for their negligence and would rectify their over-sights immediately. I didn't believe a word either of them said. I assigned them MBIDI — Maybe But I Doubt It.

There was no fun to be had at the greenhouse this

morning so I called one of my own clients, Fern Brickle. Glory and Mrs. Brickle had been my original cleaning customers during the dark years I spent on poverty row, and both remained customers of Bliss This House.

Mrs. Brickle invited me to come right over for tea. I put on my taupe down-filled jacket and dropped my phone into my tote bag.

In deference to the driving sleet that showed no signs of letting up before spring, I had worn my black UGGs and was just stepping into them at the door when I heard my name screeched from one of the plant rooms. Before I had time to run for the parking lot, Glory steamed up to me and jabbed a clawed forefinger at my face.

"You! I want to talk to you." If she had spent the night in a tangled mess of sheets with Tony, lack of sleep didn't show on her face. Her hair tumbled as artfully as usual over her shoulders, and her makeup was flawless. She didn't even have bags under her eyes. On closer inspection I was concerned to see the whites of her eyes were tinged with pink. I stared at the wall.

"Here I am. What's up?"

"Please look at me when I'm speaking to you."

Please? I dared a glance at her face and realized she was unusually calm and her voice somewhat less than piercing. Maybe sex was working for her after all.

"Okay. If this is about the decorations for the food bank benefit, I have everything covered. And I'll have it all set up in time. Don't worry about it."

"This isn't about the decorations. Although, you're going to have to take over the advertising for the event.

Dougal says he has a deadline and can't spare the time to visit the newspaper office and printer. But right now I want to discuss your meddling into police investigations in this town."

"What meddling? *Moi?*"

"You do remember I'm on the Police Services Board, don't you."

"Um, sure." *Who cared?*

Glory looked at me like I should know what she was talking about. When I didn't answer — I had lost track of the question — she blew a stray wisp of hair away from her face.

"Don't you know anything about how this town runs? The board is comprised of myself, Bert Thiesson, Mayor Mike Bains, and Andrea Bains, who is the deputy mayor."

"Isn't Mr. Thiesson a hundred years old? And my condolences for having to interact with the Weasels on a board. Can't you resign?"

"Shut up and listen. Bert is eighty-four and, while very capable for his age, easily swayed. That means that, typically, it's me against the other three board members. So, if it comes to a vote about not renewing the chief of police's contract, guess what will happen?"

"What! They can't do that. Redfern is the best police chief this town has ever had. They can't fire him."

"You don't have to convince me that he's competent. But believe me, the Weas ... the Bainses ... will find a way to get rid of him. I heard what happened at the Wing Nut on Monday night."

"What? Redfern's job is in jeopardy because I pulled the Weasels' tails? I do that every chance I get."

"You pretty much accused him of murdering Faith Davidson and Sophie Quantz!"

"I certainly did not. I merely asked him if he had an alibi for the night Sophie died. And I was joking."

"Your humour leaves a lot of people cold. Especially Mike and Andrea. As long as you're dating Neil Redfern, you have to stay out of his investigations. You're making things very difficult for him."

"I was present at the old high school the night Faith died. How can I stay out of it?"

"You better find a way, or you'll be moving to Toronto with Neil. If he still wants you — and I wouldn't count on that."

"All right, I got it already."

"I hope so. We have an *in camera* board meeting tonight. I want to be able to assure the other members that there will be no outside interference from *anybody* for the duration of the investigations. Can I do that? That means you will desist discussing the case with other potential witnesses."

"Yes." Although, how the hell was I supposed to determine who was a potential witness? That Caribbean vacation looked better and better. With or without Redfern.

"Good. Maybe Mike and Andrea will back off. I'll do my best." She raised her finger and waved it back and forth in front of my face. "If minding your own business means you have more time on your hands, you can …"

I moved closer and peered up into her face.

"What are you looking at?"

"There's a really long hair sticking out between your

nose and upper lip. Hold still. I think I can grab it with my fingers."

I reached up. She clapped her hand over her mouth and backed away. Panic filled her eyes, and she turned and ran for the washroom.

Dougal's disembodied voice called out, "Nice going, Bliss. Now she thinks she had a hair sprouting from her face while she was out with the new boyfriend last night. It'll be a hard hat zone around here for the next week."

"I couldn't help myself. Sometimes, it's just too easy. Enjoy the rest of your day, sweetie."

"And you enjoy doing all my advertising work for her stupid charity benefit. You might want to get started on that. It takes time to design and print flyers. Then you have to post them all over town. Oh, and don't forget the newspaper ads …"

"I hate you." I slammed the door on his delighted sniggers.

The temperature had dropped, and a thick coating of ice covered my windshield. I turned on the heater to defrost mode. I couldn't find the scraper and had to chip at the ice with the roll of duct tape left over from the glitter ball liberation. Luckily the washer fluid *still* contained anti-freeze, since I couldn't recall switching over to regular last summer.

Between blasting the screen with heat from the inside, soaking the outside with anti-freeze, and turning the wipers to hyper drive, the ice melted in the middle of the windshield, giving me plenty of visibility.

The county plows hadn't made it through the side roads yet, and at least a foot of crusty snow overlaid

GLORIA FERRIS

Concession 10. I felt it scrape my undercarriage the few hundred yards to the highway. At the corner, I backed up and gunned it, back end fishtailing until my tires gripped the sand generously scattered on the highway by the Ministry of Transportation plows.

I passed the Wing Nut and noticed a police cruiser waiting to pull out. So what, this time I wasn't speeding at all. The cop car narrowed the gap between us to an unsafe distance. *Waaa-waaa-waaa.* Lights flashed on and off.

What the hell now? I sighed and pulled to the shoulder.

The squad car stopped behind mine. When Constable Dopey got out, I wanted to bash my head against the steering wheel.

CHAPTER
TWENTY-ONE

I ROLLED DOWN MY WINDOW. "Hi, Dwayne. What is it this time?" I made sure to say his name fast so he couldn't cry to Thea that I called him *Duh-wayne* or *Dwa-aayne* again.

"Licence and registration, please."

"What now? I wasn't speeding. And why were you having lunch at the Wing Nut so late?"

He pulled his summons book out. "Maybe you weren't speeding this time, but your hatchback window is covered with ice, obscuring your vision. Your windshield isn't so great, either. And none of your business when I have lunch."

The last sheet of ice slid down my windshield. "My windshield is fine, and as for the back, that's what side mirrors are for. Right?"

"Your backup lights are obscured by snow. That's a summons for you."

"Let me see that." The door hit him in the stomach when I got out.

"Wait. I didn't tell you to get out…. Return to your vehicle immediately."

I marched to the back of my Matrix and brushed the snow off my tail lights. For good measure, I cleaned my licence plate. "There. Are you happy now?"

"There's a thick coating of ice on the lights. You have to scrape that off."

"I don't have a scraper at the moment."

He flicked over a page in his book. "In that case, I'm sorry, but this time I can't let you off with a warning. Ice on your tail lights is a driving hazard."

"No problem. Give me a moment." I hiked up my jacket and set my butt against the first tail light. I squirmed against it and began to move in a rotating, grinding motion.

Dwayne looked around. "Stop that." He took a step back.

"Is the camera on your dashboard rolling, Dwayne?" I threw my arms in the air, bumping and grinding, tossing my head back and forth, eyes closed. "Oh, baby. I'm almost there. Getting hotter, hotter. Smoking hot. The ice is melting." Vehicles roared past, honking appreciatively. None of them moved over to the far lane as the law required when passing a parked police vehicle. Dwayne didn't seem to notice those transgressions.

He cast a wild glance back at his cruiser and moved in front of me. "Okay, stop. If you stop, I won't write you up."

I threw my whole body into it, shoulders rotating,

hips gyrating. "Can't stop. Almost there. Then I have to defrost the other one. I don't think you're supposed to block out the camera." An eighteen-wheeler roared toward us. The horn blared and I gave the driver a thumbs-up.

"Stop. Please!"

I stopped. The denim clung damply to my rear end.

"Boy, you are a piece of work, Bliss. Get lost."

He turned on his heel and stamped away. The back of his uniform was again covered in salt and sand from passing traffic. So was the side of my car, but it was worth it. I pouted and waved at the dashcam, then threw it a kiss. When I pulled away, I made sure to use my indicator light.

Mrs. Brickle had been one of the chaperones at grad night. Glory *and* Redfern might have a couple of wee fits when they learned I visited Mrs. Brickle. But she was a client, so to hell with them.

Mrs. Brickle lived on Sandpiper Street, about a block and a half from my parent's place. She was a childless widow in her eighties, although she looked much younger. And I hadn't thought of this before, but she had to have been retired when she chaperoned the grad dance. Odd. I'd ask her about that later. And maybe she would remember something useful. Again, to hell with Redfern. And Glory.

Two of my cleaning staff, Cora Wayne and Marjorie Hamdock, were just finishing up when I arrived. We stood chatting in the hallway while the two women put on their coats.

"Oh, Bliss?" Marjorie paused in the open doorway. "Can I take next Wednesday off? I need to take Storm to London for his orthodontist appointment. The braces are finally coming off."

"Sure." I typed a note into my phone. "I'll get someone to cover for you." *Who paid for orthodontic work for their pet?* "Uh, so how *is* your cat these days?"

"Derek? He's fine, for his age. Fifteen now, and fat as a coon. Thanks, Bliss."

Confused, I followed them outside. If I had kids someday, I was naming them John and Sarah. And if I ever got a cat, I'd call it Fluffy. "Can I speak to you for a minute, Cora?"

Cora waved to Marjorie to go ahead. "Sure, what's up, Bliss? I can clean Mrs. Brickle's place by myself next Wednesday if you want. It will just take a few hours longer."

"No, it isn't that. I'll get someone to help you. Do you still make costumes?"

"Sure. What do you need?"

I gave her a sketch I had drawn up and explained what fabric I wanted. Ten minutes later, I was seated opposite Mrs. Brickle in her living room. I placed a magazine under me so I wouldn't leave a wet butt mark on her sofa.

The house smelled faintly of vinegar and lemon. We used whatever products the client stocked. Mrs. Brickle preferred vinegar and water for most cleaning jobs, and a natural lemon-based spray for her furniture.

"Have some Earl Grey. Sugar? Now, tell me, what brings you here this afternoon?"

I smiled at her. "Can't I just visit my favourite customer?"

"I wish you would visit more often. But you have that determined look about you that means you have something on your mind."

A colourful scarf was wound around Mrs. Brickle's short white hair. Her fringed peacock-coloured tunic and wide-legged navy pants recalled the magical sixties. Maybe the sixties fashions were back in style and I was missing it: I was no fashionista. Well, except for boots. I loved boots.

"Bliss?"

"Oh, sorry, Mrs. B. I love your outfit. I couldn't put myself together like that on my best day."

"You always look nice. You're a lovely, smart young woman who has overcome some difficult obstacles in her life."

"I'm going to come back once a week for an infusion of self-esteem, Mrs. B. You could bottle and sell it!"

"Your visits are better than a tonic, Bliss. Have a cookie and tell me what's on your mind."

"Don't mind if I do." I bit into one of her homemade shortbreads. *Mm-mmm*, heavenly. "I'm sure you've heard about Faith and Sophie."

"Of course. The girls were talking about it." The "girls" were Cora and Marjorie. "Even though no one has come right out and said that the body found in the old high school is Faith, I don't think there's any doubt. And with Sophie being murdered right after she was found, the two deaths must be related."

"Exactly my thinking. They were both at the grad dance. And so were you and I."

"That's true. The school had difficulty obtaining chaperones. I had already been retired for several years, but they asked me if I wouldn't mind attending this one last event. I suppose the police are focussing on anyone who attended the graduation party who still lives in Lockport."

"There aren't that many, Mrs. B."

"No? Have another cookie."

I reached into my bag and pulled the yearbooks out. "There were thirteen graduates, one DJ, and three chaperones. Really, any of us could have killed Faith Davidson." I opened the yearbook to the graduate photos and pointed. "Five settled in the area — me, Mike Bains, Chico Leeds, Sophie Wingman, and Fang Davidson. We suspect Faith Davidson died that night and Sophie four nights ago. That leaves four — me, Mike, Chico, and Fang." I looked at Mrs. B. She nodded and ran her knobby, arthritic fingers over the young faces on the page.

I continued. "Of the three chaperones, two are still here — you and Mr. Archman." I didn't want to point out that the third was dead. "And the DJ, Kelly Quantz."

She summarized for me. "Seven suspects altogether. If you discount the two of us, we're left with Mike Bains, Chico Leeds, Fang Davidson, Kelly Quantz, and Earl Archman."

We locked eyes.

Mrs. B adjusted her headscarf with unsteady hands.

"Of course, one person may have killed Faith, and another is responsible for Sophie's death."

When I protested, Mrs. B shook her head. "I know, Bliss. I don't believe that either. How could both deaths not be related?"

"The discovery of Faith's bones could have been the trigger that led to Sophie's murder, Mrs. B. She must have known something."

"Have this last cookie, dear. If the old high school had been torn down years ago like it should have been, Faith's body would have been discovered then. I wonder if timing has anything to do with the second death."

"And I wonder if the police have the same list of suspects."

"Maybe you can liaise with your young man and make sure he's on the right track."

A spray of shortbread crumbs flew from my mouth and landed on Mrs. Brickle's newly-polished coffee table. I brushed them into my hand and glanced up at her. "My young man doesn't want my help. He demands I stay as far away from his investigation as possible."

"But you have a lot of information to share. You were there since the beginning, and you know all the suspects."

"Yeah, well, let's face it, Mrs. B. Like everyone else at the grad party except the chaperones, I was wasted. Tequila. Awful stuff. I can't stand even the smell of it now. Actually, I wouldn't have blamed the chaperones for taking a nip or two, just to get through the festivities. It must have been brutal for you."

Mrs. Brickle sat back. Maybe she hadn't realized the

students were drunk that night, and I had shocked her.

Not a chance. She laughed. "Bliss, I have a vivid recollection of you crouching under the refreshment table. One of the other grads would hand you a glass of punch or a pop can and you topped it up from a bottle — tequila, it seems. We discussed keeping you all in the gymnasium until collected by your parents, but Earl Archman said he was unlocking the doors at midnight and he didn't give a — well, never mind his exact words. Earl did take a few sips from his flask throughout the evening, as I recall. And you must remember Emily Czerneski. She was just a little bird of a woman, in her last year of teaching. She wouldn't have been much help in a scuffle. She passed only a few years ago, the dear soul. Anyway, Earl opened the doors to the parking lot and the three of us stood well back while you all stampeded out."

Her eyes took on a mistiness as she recalled the images from the past. "I never saw many of those students again."

"Mrs. B. Do you remember Faith leaving with the rest of the crowd? If so, she must have come back later."

Mrs. Brickle refocussed and looked at me. "I can't say I remember her movements specifically. There was just a rush of bodies through the doorway."

"Did anyone check the bathrooms closest to the gym? We had to go through the locker rooms to get to them."

She sipped her cooling tea. "If I'm not mistaken, Earl went to the doors of both locker rooms and called out. It's unlikely he would have gone into the girls' locker room."

"What happened next?"

"We waited while Kelly Quantz finished packing up his audio equipment. Then we turned off the lights in the gymnasium and Earl locked the doors behind us. No, wait!" She set her cup back in its saucer with a rattle. "He was going to lock the doors, but we remembered the decorating committee members were coming back in the morning to clean up and make sure the decorations were dropped off at the new school. That means ..."

"We know that didn't happen." No point mentioning I was part of the decorating committee. I thought about choices; choices and consequences. If I had gone back into the school the next morning before the workmen boarded it up, would I have needed to use the washroom? Almost certainly. My stomach had been touch and go for days after that night. If I saw blood on the floor of the locker room, what would I have done? Certainly not opened all the lockers, not unless a trail of blood led to one in particular ...

"Bliss. Are you feeling all right? Have some more tea, dear."

"No, I'm fine, Mrs. B. So, we don't know if Faith was killed and her body stuffed in the locker during the course of the evening or if she — and someone else— came back later."

"I'm sorry I can't remember more details." She shook her head. "I'll keep trying to recall more."

Death had not been invited to graduation. But it had been there all the same, hiding in a corner, waiting for Faith.

CHAPTER
TWENTY-TWO

A LIGHT KICK ON NEIL'S office door preceded Lavinia's entrance with a tray of coffee and doughnuts. She knew he liked the glazed ones, and had included two of them on a plate with a couple of crullers.

"Whew!" She waved her hand in the air. "Open a window for a few minutes, why don't you?" She slid the crime scene photos and reports to one side with an elbow and set the tray on Neil's desk. "Too much testosterone in here."

Neil pushed the plate toward Tony. He looked out his window. The snow had started up again, and the wind hurled sheets of it against the glass. "Maybe later. Thanks, you always know when I need coffee, Lavinia."

"I'll be out for a few minutes. We're out of milk." She gave them both a tolerant look and closed the door quietly behind her.

Tony snatched up both glazed doughnuts. "You got it made, man. Your own office, somebody to bring you coffee. The weather sucks here, but the snow must keep the crime statistics down."

"Not so you'd notice. Are you forgetting we have two murders to solve?"

"We should catch a break if there's only one killer involved." He finished the doughnuts in three or four bites and eyed the crullers. "I hate those twisty things. How come you don't have an investigator on the payroll? You're the first chief I've run into who has to do all his own investigating. And where are your sergeants?"

Neil pushed the coffee tray to one corner of his desk and fanned the photos back out. "One investigator retired the same time as the former chief, just before I took over, and the second one a few months after. The Police Board has been dragging its feet over approving the release of funds to hire more. I'm without a sergeant for the same reason. There were three — one of them retired and the others transferred to Waterloo Regional. The board keeps promising to cough up the money for replacements. Now, hoist your ass off that chair and write this down."

Tony sighed, but got to his feet and picked up a dry-erase marker. He flipped the whiteboard over to the blank side and waited.

"If we proceed on the assumption that we have one perpetrator, this is our list of suspects — Fang Davidson, Charles Leeds, Michael Bains, Earl Archman, Fern Brickle, Kelly Quantz. And Bliss Cornwall."

Tony paused after writing Quantz's name. "Are you serious? You want me to add Bliss's name to the list of suspects? Your Bliss?"

"Humour me. I don't consider Bliss a viable suspect, but we can't leave her name off. Like the other six, she was in the old high school the night Faith disappeared." When Tony opened his mouth, Neil added, "Let's assume Faith died that night."

Tony shrugged and wrote Bliss's name down.

A burst of raucous laughter reached them from the squad room. After it died away, Neil continued. "Sophie Quantz was killed because Faith died fifteen years ago. We need to find out what the connection is."

Tony helped himself to the last cruller. "All the kids were drunk and there are only two of the chaperones left: Archman and Brickle. Have you talked to either one?" He shoved the doughnut into his mouth and washed it down with coffee.

"Not yet." He didn't mention that Bliss had a conversation with Archman in the hospital. Tony already thought Bliss's involvement was hilarious.

"Who else on this list needs interviewing?"

Neil glanced at the whiteboard. "We talked to Fang and Kelly Quantz. We need to speak to Leeds, Bains, Archman, and Brickle. And we need to move on this fast."

"I have a dinner date, so I'll do one interview this afternoon. How about you take Archman while I pay Bains a visit at his office? Best if you stay away from him. Tomorrow we'll tackle the other two — Leeds and Brickle. I'll leave Miss Bliss to you." He snickered. "Unless you call for help."

"Fuck off, Tony. I can handle Cornwall."

Another round of laughter erupted from the other

side of the office door. This time it subsided only to surge into a wave of hooting and foot stamping.

Neil threw open his door and leaned out. Five officers — almost his entire day shift — surrounded a computer terminal. Only Thea and Dwayne hung back. Dwayne's face was an unflattering shade of mottled pink and red, while Thea stood stony-faced with arms crossed.

Bernie spotted Neil and his hand moved.

"Don't touch that mouse, Bernie." Four officers moved aside to let Neil shoulder his way in. "Run that video from the beginning."

"Yeah, Chief, you might not want to …"

"From the beginning, Bernie." Tony hung over his shoulder, anxious to be let in on the joke.

The video from the dashcam showed Dwayne. And Cornwall. Neil's eyes narrowed as he watched. He tried to keep his face immobile, calling on his drug squad experience to keep the emotions from his expression. He didn't know whether to laugh or have that stroke he was expecting.

At the conclusion of the video, some of his officers tried to sidle away. He fixed them with his eyes. "Nobody move."

"Again," he told Bernie. The room was so still, he could hear the rumble of somebody's stomach. "In my office, Dwayne. The rest of you, get back to work. I want the house-to-house reports within the hour. I hope I don't need to mention that this video is proprietary, so if it gets out to the public, or appears on YouTube, some-one's head will roll."

He shut his door on Tony's amused face and rounded on Dwayne. "What the hell were you thinking, Dwayne?"

Dwayne swallowed audibly. "I can't help it, Chief. She aggravates me every opportunity she gets. Her lights and windows were obscured by snow and ice. It wasn't safe, and I had to pull her over."

"How many other motorists did you pull over today for obscured lights?"

"Well, Bliss was the only one today. I was busy with the house-to-house inquiries, then I went for lunch. She was the first driver I saw when I pulled out of the Wing Nut."

"I know she pushes your buttons deliberately, Dwayne. But here's a tip. Don't engage her unless you see her committing an armed robbery or assaulting someone. It's just not worth it."

"But, Chief ..."

"This isn't up for debate. Now get back to work."

"But ... her attitude ..."

"We can't charge her for having a bad attitude."

Dwayne's shoulders slumped. Before Neil could say anything more, another round of laughter, this time accompanied by clapping and cheering, rattled the door. He could hear Tony's hoarse chuckle underlying the other sounds. His right eye began to throb and, with a fatalistic shrug, he opened his door to usher Dwayne out.

This was not a good day. Cornwall stood in the middle of the squad room. His officers applauded and high-fived her. She looked perplexed, then Thea said something to her and her face lit up with understanding.

"Oh, that. Glad I gave you guys a laugh today. I know how stressful your work can be."

She caught sight of Neil in the doorway with Dwayne. Her smile widened. Her expressive eyes, enhanced with makeup, sparkled at him. "Uh, got a minute, Chief? I might have some information on our murders."

CHAPTER
TWENTY-THREE

TONY SHOVED IN BEHIND ME and flipped over the whiteboard. Redfern shuffled the crime scene photos together, then sat on the edge of his desk with his arms folded. I glanced from one to the other.

"You're not as fast as you think you are, Tony. I saw my name on your suspect list." I crossed my arms as well and waited for Redfern to explain himself.

It turned into a staring contest. I won, because I can go for ten minutes without blinking if I want. After only three, Redfern's eyes watered and he looked away. "Hah." I turned to Tony. "Who put my name on that list? Is this a joke or something?"

"Well, it wasn't my idea, Miss Bliss. You know how by-the-book our chief here is."

Redfern gave Tony a disgusted look. "You'd throw your own dog into a cat fight, wouldn't you, Pinato?"

"Hey, man, I'm not taking this lady on. I heard what

you said to Dwayne." At Redfern's surprised expression, he said, "Your voice carries."

At the mention of Dwayne's name, I forgot about Redfern's suspect list. "How about that idiot? Do you know what he stopped me for today?"

"He told me about it. And the entire station saw the video."

"Well, then, you know how ridiculous he is. His actions are bordering on police harassment."

"If you followed the rules, you wouldn't find yourself under his scrutiny so often."

"Hey, Bliss." Tony stepped between us and pushed me away from Redfern. "Where did you learn those moves? Pretty sexy. I especially loved that little pouty wave and air kiss at the end. Too bad we don't have audio."

"I'm a porn pro. Just call me Peaches. Can I see the video?" I hadn't taken my eyes off Redfern's face.

His fair skin began to turn a telltale red-brick colour. "No. You can't."

"Why not?"

"Because I said so. And because it would be against regulations."

"What regulations?" All men have a screw loose, and some have looser screws than others. I opened my mouth to tell Redfern what I thought about his stupid regulations, which I followed most of the time anyway, but Tony butted in again.

"God, you two act like a couple of teenagers. Do you fight about everything? Is it some kind of weird foreplay? If so, Neil ..."

Redfern turned on Tony and said, "Mind your own business," at the same time I said, "It's not foreplay, you horse's ass." Let them wonder who the horse's ass was.

"Neil, you know Bliss pisses in the eye of authority, so quit making it so easy for her. And Bliss, cut Neil some slack and show a little respect for his job at least."

"Thank you, Dr. Phil." I clomped toward the door, making sure my heels hit the old wooden floor as heavily as I could manage. Redfern hated it when I did that. Unfortunately, UGGs don't make much of a noise statement.

"Wait a minute," Redfern called after me. "Why are you here? You said you had some information."

I didn't. I only said that because every eye in the outer office was on me when I came in. I dropped in to see how things were going and to ask what plans Redfern had for dinner. Now I didn't give a shit.

"Never mind. From here on in, you needn't worry about me interfering with your investigations. Since you so clearly find me a nuisance, I'll just keep anything I learn to myself. You won't have Bliss Moonbeam Cornwall to insult any longer."

"Before you stomp away, may I ask if you have the yearbooks in that bag?" Redfern's voice dripped icicles. Freaking control freak.

I yanked the yearbooks out of my tote. I knew he expected me to pitch them at his head, so I placed them carefully on the desk and lined them up precisely square to the outer edges.

I left the office door open, nodded at the cops in the squad room, and took my time making a grand exit.

Grand until the wind flung snow in my face, causing me to miss the last step onto the sidewalk. I landed on my ass in a pile of slush.

"Fucking boots!" That's the last time I wear flat heels.

∎

Fang hadn't answered my calls or returned my messages. That's the only reason I was looking for Dogtown. I hadn't been there since the infamous grad party night, or morning rather, when I woke up in the back of his truck. I had been in a coma on the way in and my eyes had been closed the whole trip out. I had never been back. Hence, I wasn't exactly sure where to find Dogtown.

It was somewhere farther north of the town's limits than Hemp Hollow, where I spent two of the most unpleasant years of my life, but west of the highway. Maybe. It's not like there's a sign pointing the way to Dogtown. It wasn't even a real town. But it bordered Ghost Swamp — so-called because the mist rising from its odoriferous waters resembled spirits.

I made a left turn off the highway, then alternated left and right. When I estimated I had gone too far, I backtracked. The snow fell faster, making visibility a challenge. Within minutes, the daylight disappeared behind a maple forest stripped of leaves.

If I hadn't been so pissed at Redfern, I would have gone home and looked for Fang tomorrow. Now, I had no idea where the highway was. I needed to buy a GPS.

The snow was at least twenty centimetres deep on the road. And there were no tire tracks to lead me to safety. A swamp lurked somewhere around here and it would be just my luck to drive right into it. I stopped the car and pulled my phone out. I hesitated.

If I called Redfern, he would search for me. Hell, he would have the whole force search for me. Then I would have to listen to a lecture about ... well, so many things. I wasn't up for it, definitely not desperate enough yet. I opened the window and stuck my head out. I sniffed. Putrefied vegetation with a touch of dead animal odour. I had to be close to the swamp. It hadn't frozen over yet. Therefore, Dogtown was nearby ...

Not twenty-five metres beyond the side of my car, I saw lights shimmer through a gap in the treeline. I shut off my car and started walking. The lights danced crazily in the wind, appearing and disappearing. The snow covered my ankles, packing into my boots. I heard voices, or was that the howling of wolves? I'd take swamp ghosts over wolves any day.

I stopped at a high chain-link gate — thrown open, thank God. I trudged through the gateposts. Strings of coloured lights hung between trailer homes. Flames from a bonfire defied the snow and soared skyward. Packs of children and a few dogs ran between the trailers. The sounds of a crackling fire, screaming children, and barking dogs never sounded better. I wasn't alone in the storm!

Several of the dogs — they looked more like coyotes — faced me and growled low in their throats. One of the wee sprites caught sight of me and screamed in fright. Another shouted, "Papa, Papa, come quick. It's a witch!" Another shouted, "Monster! Monster!"

Kind of rude. "Excuse me, sweetie. Can you tell me where this is? I'm lost." Several more mutts joined the growling pack and soon they all snarled and gnashed their fangs at me. Chances were pretty good this was Dogtown, but confirmation would be useful.

A man's figure materialized beside me. As he came closer, I saw he was carrying an armful of logs. "Never mind, Chevy. It's just a lady, not a witch or monster. Go back to playing, but mind the fire."

The kids ran off, but the dogs stayed.

I couldn't make out the man's features. They were hidden behind a beard that seemed to have no end. A Toronto Maple Leafs toque hid his eyebrows.

"You lost, young lady?"

"Is this Dog…, uh, yes, I'm lost."

"This is Dogtown. Where are you headed?"

"Well, Dogtown."

"So, you found it. You can't be lost."

"I don't know how I got here, or how to get back to the highway."

"Young lady, you're confusing me. Why are you here?"

"I'm looking for F…, uh, Rupert Davidson."

"Fang? I'm his dad. What do you want with Fang? You don't have a bun in the oven, do you? Hope not. You're, what, barely five feet tall? You'd shorten our gene pool considerably." He chortled and threw a log into the fire.

"No bun. And I'm five foot two. Fang isn't answering his phone, and I want him to look at my eavestrough. Parts of it are coming loose from the house." Boy, this

GARY PUBLIC LIBRARY

had been such a bad idea. "I'm really sorry about Faith, Mr. Davidson. She was a nice person, and smart. Is there going to be a service?"

He peered into my face. "Say, you're that little girl Fang brought home in the back of his truck one time, aren't you? You were wrapped up in a rug and I had to drive you home."

"Yes, I was only seventeen then."

"I guess you were at that. That was the night Faith disappeared, though it was a couple of days before we knew she wasn't at my sister's in Toronto. After a while we sensed she wasn't coming back, but we never thought she was so close by." He lifted his face to the falling snow. "It's warming up. We'll have rain by morning."

Right. Like it was going to rain before next April. Maybe May. "I can't imagine why anyone would want to harm Faith."

"There was something on her mind that weekend. But she wouldn't say. Now I wonder if it had anything to do with ... well, with what happened to her. I wish we'd tried harder to find out what was troubling her." Another log flew into the flames and he shouted over my head, "Edsel Margaret Davidson! I told you to mind the fire. Get home now!"

"I'm sure if she was ready to tell you, she would have, Mr. Davidson."

"Nice of you to say that, young lady, but we'll never know, not now. They haven't said for sure it's Faith — took some DNA from me and her mother. But we already know. Once they get their testing done, we can have a funeral and bring her home." He gestured with his head to an area beyond the trailers. "We have our own family cemetery. We'll put Faith there. Maybe in the spring."

"Have you told the police that something was bothering Faith that weekend?"

"I told them. Say, you sure you're not after Fang for yourself? You used to pal around with him, I remember. He's got a wife and four children now, you know."

"So I hear. I'm not after him, honestly. I didn't realize how hard it is to find Dogtown in a snowstorm."

The remaining logs tumbled into the fire. "All right, then. He's not home right now. He says you're a pain in the ass. That's why he won't answer, but I'll give him the message and make sure he calls you back."

"Okay. Can you give me directions back to the highway?"

Mr. Davidson walked me to the gate. "Your car is pointed east. Keep going and take the first right and it will take you to the highway. Mind the swamp. Turn right again to get back to town."

"Thanks. How come you don't have your gate closed? I thought you like to keep strangers out?" I slipped in the deep snow, and Mr. Davidson grabbed me by my scarf and pulled me upright.

"Probably wouldn't have kept you out, would it? We only close it on Sundays, to slow down the Jehovah Witnesses. It's hard to discourage them, believe it or not. They seem to think we're a pack of heathens in here." He tightened his grip on my scarf and hauled me across the road to my car. I put my fingers under the knot to loosen it.

"Oh, that's easy, Mr. Davidson. Just tell them you're Wiccans. It works for me." He opened my door and I climbed in. Sheets of snow slid onto my seat and floorboards.

"Huh. Wiccans, eh? I'll try it. I don't suppose you have anything for the Mormons?"

"Tell them you're Jehovah's Witnesses. That should do it."

"Thank you kindly, young lady. I'll tell Fang to call you tomorrow. You drive safely now." White, even teeth gleamed through the dark moustache and beard.

I pulled my foot into the car a millisecond before he slammed the door. Wet snow filled my beloved black UGGs with the Swarovski crystal button closure. If they were ruined, I would never be able to replace them. I'd have to buy new ones, in a different style.

Did Mr. Davidson instruct me to take the first left, or the first right?

CHAPTER
TWENTY-FOUR

A CALL TO THE HIGH SCHOOL verified that Earl Archman was at home, recuperating from his fall in the Canadian Tire parking lot. His admin assistant expressed some concern and asked Neil to call her back if Earl needed her help with anything.

His phone rang as he pulled up in front of Archman's house, a small, neat bungalow with no distinguishing features except a life-sized stuffed Grinch sitting on a rocking chair on the porch. "Ed. What's up?"

"Have you talked to Earl Archman yet?"

"I'm just about to. I'm in front of his house now."

"Glad I caught you, then. I remembered something I meant to tell you on Monday when he had his accident. I forgot, sorry. I've delivered three babies since then."

"Forgot what, Ed?"

"He didn't break his arm when he fell on the ice on Monday morning."

"What? The guy got hauled into the ER on a

stretcher. Cornwall and the manager of the store saw him fall." Had they watched the man actually fall? Or did they just notice him lying on the ground?

"I'm not saying he didn't fall. But the x-ray showed the break was just starting to heal, and inflammation was too pronounced for an hour-old injury. He had some other bruises that were a day or two old. He said he took a spill on his front walk the day before, Sunday, but didn't realize he had broken a bone until he slipped again on Monday and was in too much pain to get up."

"Is that possible, Ed? Can you fracture a bone and not realize it?"

"Sure. Especially when you carry as much weight as this man. I x-rayed his feet while he was in the hospital in case he had stress fractures there."

"What are you saying? He's overweight?" Neil thought of the photo in the yearbook, a young man who looked to be thirty or so, good-looking, slim …

"Morbidly obese. He's only mid-forties, but I doubt he'll see fifty. And I told him so. No point pulling your punches with people in that stage of denial. Anyway, I just thought you should know."

Sitting across from the man in his living room, Neil was glad of Ed's heads-up. His right arm was encased in plaster. The furniture was shabby, the type of furniture a single man kept because he never actually looked at his surroundings. A fine coating of dust covered the surfaces of the tables, and piles of magazines dedicated to hunting and the gun enthusiast littered the bare hardwood floor.

The man's eyes were almost fully hidden by folds of flesh and Neil couldn't tell their colour. His hair was plentiful and dark brown, with no hint of grey. Mounds of flesh overflowed the flowered armchair, and Neil struggled not to let the unexpected wave of compassion he felt for this hulk of a man show.

"Sorry to bother you, sir. I know you need your rest, but I'm hoping you can help us in our investigation."

"Let's see if I can save us both some time, Chief Redfern. I knew both the victims, Faith Davidson and Sophie Wingman, or Sophie Quantz. The girls were students of mine many years ago."

Archman shifted uncomfortably and took a drink of water from a plastic bottle he held in his left hand.

"Do you remember anything about the victims that might shed some light on what happened to them?"

"Well, now, Chief, that's a broad question. Faith was a good student, excellent in math. She applied to, and was accepted at, Ryerson in Toronto. I can't remember what she was studying, but whatever it was, she would have done well. Life really is a bitch sometimes, because that girl had potential.

"Sophie? Now, Sophie was a good student as well, but her focus was more on screwing every boy in her class, even the ones with steady girlfriends. But she did a complete turnaround after high school graduation, if I heard correctly. Went on to Divinity College, then returned as an Episcopal priest. Surprised everyone. Married Kelly Quantz, who had been lusting after her since she was fifteen. As far as I know, he worshipped from afar and never stepped over the line into sex with an underage girl."

He paused for another sip of water and to catch his

breath. He slipped an inhaler out of his shirt pocket and took several puffs.

"Asthma," he explained. "My own fault. I should have given up smoking when I was twenty-five, instead of waiting until I was forty-five. Last month."

"Both girls were murdered," Neil pointed out.

"I realize that," Archman snapped. "What else do you want to know?"

"Tell me about the rest of the class."

"You mean, the few that are still here?" He indicated the 2000 yearbook resting on the coffee table between them. "I refreshed my memory. Not that I really needed to. That class was unforgettable, and not in a good way. There are only four that still live here, four that are still alive, I should say."

"And they are?"

"Come off it, Chief. You know who they are as well as I do. Fang Davidson, Charles Leeds, Michael Bains, and your own Bliss Moonbeam Cornwall."

Neil winced. Talk about a conflict of interest. "Let's start with Fang. What was he like in high school?"

"As you know, Fang lives in Dogtown. There was a certain mystique surrounding students from Dogtown back then, and there still is. A collection of mobile homes outside of town, a closed family unit. We've had a lot of kids in our schools over the years from Dogtown, and, on the surface, it's hard to tell them from any of the others."

"On the surface?"

"Not as many go to university or college. But they're just as smart. Our best mechanics, hairstylists, clerks, snowplow drivers, caterers, landscapers — they all come from Dogtown. They keep Bruce County running. And the teeth! My God, I never met a kid from Dogtown who didn't have naturally perfect teeth. A geneticist would have a field day testing those families."

Neil pictured the finely formed teeth in the skull found in the locker. "So, no trouble with Fang?"

"Just the usual pranks. Nothing malicious. Played well with others, as they say. Well-liked." Archman shrugged. "Nothing special comes to mind."

"How about Charles Leeds?"

"Again, nothing special. A good enough student, but not interested in a career other than taking over the Canadian Tire franchise from his grandfather. Earned a business degree. He was under the thumb of a girl a year behind him, Tabby, or Kitty, or some such stupid name. He was part of Bliss's posse. She led him around by the nose, and I think he had a crush on her, but like I said, his girlfriend kept him on a pretty short lead. A regular kid. Got kids of his own now, I hear."

"Three of them," Neil answered. "And Mike Bains?"

Archman paused for more water and another puff of asthma inhalant. "Ah, Michael. A cut above the rest, that boy. A bit of a sociopath."

Neil nearly dropped his pen. From what Cornwall recounted of her conversation with Archman, the sun shone out of Mike Bains's ass. "Sociopath? Why do you say that?"

"He analyzed people and stored the information until he could find a way to manipulate them with it. He knew where he wanted to go and didn't care who he stepped on to get there. He knew even in high school that he was going to become a lawyer first, then go into politics. He's always had his eye on the prime minister's job. Would he resort to murder to achieve his goals? I can't say, but then, I'm not an expert on personality disorders."

Neil thought for a moment. "I don't suppose you remember who was dating whom their final semester?"

Archman laughed, and this turned into a coughing fit. His face turned an alarming purple colour. Neil was ready to pound the man's back or call for an ambulance.

When the coughing subsided, Archman continued. "You must be joking. I had that class for forty minutes per day. I couldn't begin to keep their liaisons straight. I heard rumours that Sophie *dated* a lot of the boys briefly. Charles was as good as married already to his grade-eleven charmer. Mike ..."

He paused. "...Mike was more discreet about his dating. Too bad Bliss didn't realize he was a selfish, spoiled little prick."

Neil started. "Bliss? I thought she and Bains didn't date until university."

"That's true, but she mooned over him in high school like all the other girls. A shame, too. Guess he realized she was his best bet for a meal ticket, somebody to help him pay for law school. Pretty, loyal, smart, but not twisted enough to figure him out. She never did see him for what he is, not until he abandoned her when someone with political influence came along. And, to think, Andrea Whitmore was Bliss's lawyer during the divorce proceedings. Bent the law and got away with it.

But Bliss is well out of it. Andrea and Michael deserve each other."

He fixed Neil with his eyes. "I hope you're being good to Bliss, Chief. She's a smartass, and her attitude used to give me migraines, but she has a good heart. I'd like to see her find someone who appreciates her."

The skin on Neil's face heated up. "Does anything come to mind about the grad night that might hint at what happened to Faith, now that we suspect she never left on that bus?"

"Between you and me, I had a wee bit of Johnny Walker in my pocket flask. I was drafted for the chaperone duty and it was as heinous an experience as I expected. The kids were all shit-faced but I couldn't catch them at it. They were running all over the school, shrieking and spilling food on the floor. And the fucking music blasted my eardrums out, so I mostly stayed out of the line of fire and waited for the worst night, or my life, to end. And I didn't care which, not at that point. At midnight I unlocked the doors and they left. That's it."

"Did you check the school for loiterers before you and the other chaperones left?"

"There were no loiterers. They were all pounding on the gym doors by eleven forty-five, but since the program said midnight, I made the little shitheads wait until midnight. That being said, I didn't count them as they escaped. Once they were gone, I helped Kelly pack up his equipment. He left, I checked the boys' locker room, called into the girls', ushered the lady chaperones out, turned off the lights, and we left. Thus ended one spectacularly loathsome night."

"But you locked the doors?"

"No, I did not. The decorating committee was supposed to come back the next morning and clean up. The school was abandoned already. Why lock the doors? Although the front doors had been locked all evening, to keep the kids in."

Neil waited while the man caught his breath. "We found a dead girl in one of the lockers. Chances are good it's Faith Davidson."

"I know that!" Archman looked like he wanted to spring out of his chair, if only he wasn't weighted down by a hundred excess pounds. "Ever since I heard her body was found, I haven't thought of anything else. What if she wasn't dead? What if I could have saved her if I'd gone right into the locker room or asked one of the ladies to do it?"

"I don't think she was still alive, sir." Not with that hole in her skull. "But then you reported you saw her later at the bus stop."

"That's what I thought. When she was reported missing and the police investigated, I told them I saw a young girl in a white dress with long dark hair waiting at the bus stop. At the time, we thought Faith disappeared at the other end. In Toronto. Now we know it wasn't her at all."

Archman pressed his left hand against his temple. "Plenty of remorse and guilt for this boy, whichever way you look at it."

Neil wanted to believe him. But some people were just born liars.

Neil stood up. "Thank you for your time, Mr.

Archman. I may have to talk to you again. Here's my card. Please call me if anything occurs to you, no matter how minor you think it is. How long will you be off work?"

"I'm taking the next semester off. That doctor in ER made me realize I'm a dead man walking. It took ten years after my wife and I split up for me to get into this condition. But I don't have ten years to get back in shape. I have to do it quickly or I won't make it, and I realize I don't want to die. I just hope it's not too late."

"I don't think it's ever too late," Neil told him. "Dr. Reiner mentioned you broke your arm earlier than Monday morning."

"Okay. Let's clear this up once and for all. I fell outside my front steps on Sunday morning. Several of my neighbours saw me and ran over. They had to help me up, which was embarrassing to say the least. My arm hurt, but then so did a lot of other things. I was barely able to drive and decided to see my doctor before going to work on Monday. I stopped at Canadian Tire first to pick up some furnace filters and fell because that idiot Leeds boy didn't de-ice his parking lot. Again, my right arm took my weight, which as you can see is considerable. I knew there was something seriously wrong."

Neil nodded. "Is there anyone I can call for you? A relative or friend. Maybe someone at work?" He was thinking of the concerned admin assistant.

Archman waved him away. "Thank you. I'm okay on my own. I'll call if I think of anything helpful."

"Just a couple more questions, Mr. Archman. Are you right- or left-handed?"

"Left."

"Do you own any firearms?"

"I have a Ruger Mark II for target shooting. Although I haven't been to the range for several years. I do have a Possession and Acquisition Licence for it."

"The Ruger uses .22 calibre ammunition, I believe." Neil didn't take his eyes off Archman's face. "Is that all you have?"

"That's it." Beads of sweat popped out along his forehead, but he didn't move to wipe them away.

"And can you account for your time Sunday morning from midnight to 6:00 a.m.?"

The man looked around at the barren room and laughed.

CHAPTER
TWENTY-FIVE

AFTER THREE HOURS at the greenhouse tuning up negligent customers and updating my business timesheets, I returned home to a foot-deep flood on the street in front of my house. It took me twenty minutes to shovel the mush away from the storm grates to drain the water.

I wore a yellow slicker over my coat, and a matching sou'wester hat to prevent my hair from kinking any tighter. I was overdressed, and opened the raincoat to let some steam escape.

Fang's truck shuddered to a stop in my driveway as I was putting the shovel back in the garage. "I'm not repairing your eavestrough for free." He jammed his hands into the pockets of his quilted jacket and mumbled around the cigarette in his mouth.

"I don't expect you to do it for free. When did I say that?"

We stood under the overhang of my open garage door, meagre shelter from the pelting rain. The temperature had risen overnight and through the morning, turning the snow into piles of dirty slush. Mr. Davidson had been right.

Fang turned his head and said something I pretended not to hear.

"Just give me a price and get at it."

"I wouldn't even be here except Lester made me come. I'm not working on your roof in the rain."

"Lester who?"

"Lester, my dad. For some reason, he likes you. Beats me why. Anyway, you better get that wet snow off your roof pronto. It's sliding into the troughs, and you'll end up with a worse problem than you have now."

I handed Fang a shovel and pointed to the ladder.

Since I'm not one to ask people to do something I wouldn't do myself, I joined Fang on the roof with a second shovel. We worked productively for a while. The scrape of metal on shingles and the plopping sound of rain on my vinyl hat were quite soothing.

Fang sent me dark looks I ignored. Up and down Morningside Drive, my neighbours had the same concern for the snow load on their roofs and had taken the day off work. Some of them had cases of beer and sandwiches with them. Others dragged up boxes of Christmas decorations. We all waved. Rain and slippery roofs never stopped Lockportals from getting the job done. Most of the houses on this street were bungalows and the worst you could expect from a tumble into the shrubs was a scratched face and a spilled beer.

Fang broke his silence. "You remind me of Donald Duck in that getup. You remember the cartoon where he's on a sinking ship?"

"If that's a metaphor for something deep, Fang, good one. Hurry up. Chico should be here soon. I asked him to bring some food and coffee with him."

Fang perked up, and then his face fell again. "Look at this." He indicated a strip of eavestrough that had ripped away from the house.

"No problem. I have a hammer and some roofing nails. You can fix it temporarily, then come back tomorrow and do the rest. Oh, I think that's Chico's truck coming down the street."

"I can't do this for you tomorrow. I have a lot of other jobs ahead of you, not to mention deliveries. And salvaging."

"Give me a price." He pulled a figure out of his ass, and I said, "I'll add 15 percent if you place me at the head of the line." The money wasn't coming out of my pocket. I was just the tenant. Sort of. By renting a room to Rae — for a modest amount — I actually made a few bucks every month.

Fang agreed so readily, I suspected his initial figure was a little high. But better to pay extra now rather than chance the roof collapsing and the eavestrough falling onto the driveway.

My feet began to slide and I gripped the chimney. "I'll finish here if you go over the peak and do the other side." Watching him scramble over the top of the house, I felt some concern for his safety. I'd better check the homeowner's insurance policy to make sure my dad was covered if Fang missed the shrubs and hit the patio in the backyard.

I leaned my shovel against the chimney and sat on the edge of the roof with my feet planted firmly on the top rung of the ladder. Chico's vehicle splashed through the melting snow and parked in the driveway behind Fang's truck. He got out, his arms filled with paper bags of fast food.

"Come on up, Chico," I called. "We can have a picnic. Fang is on the other side, but he should be finished there soon."

"I'm not dressed for it, Bliss. You come down."

Chico wore his Canadian Tire parka and a matching toque. "You're dressed perfectly. How's the tread on your boots? That looks good. Come up."

Fang struggled back over the top of the roof. He looked like a wet dog, and kind of smelled like one as he accepted a Styrofoam container of chili from Chico.

"Why did you call me, Bliss?" Chico hadn't opened his chili, but if he gripped the container any tighter, the lid was going to fly off and take his eye out. It occurred to me that not everyone was comfortable sitting on a slick roof.

To repress the simmering mutiny I sensed in my motley crew, I started talking. "Okay. The three of us are on the suspect list for two murders. Sorry, Fang, but that includes Faith. Just because you're her brother, doesn't mean the police won't be considering you."

"What can we do about it?" Chico still hadn't opened his chili. "My only alibi for Sophie's murder is my wife. Same probably for you, Fang. And we know the cops don't believe family. All we can do is hope they find the real killer before one of us goes down for it." After one look at my black eyes, Chico talked over my head to Fang.

"One of you two," I clarified. "Chief Redfern doesn't really think I did it, but he doesn't know you both like I do, so he has to suspect you." No point mentioning that I had the best alibi ever for Sophie's murder — I was in bed all night with a cop.

"Like the man said, what can we do?" Fang had finished off his chili and eyed Chico's. Chico silently handed over his container.

"The other four suspects are the Weasel, Mrs. Brickle, Kelly Quantz, and Mr. Archman. It wasn't one of us, or Mrs. Brickle either. That leaves the Weasel, Kelly, and Mr. Archman." I carefully opened the tab on my coffee and sipped. Good old Hortons. Their coffee was still scalding despite the trip in Chico's truck and the rooftop airing.

Chico shifted his bony butt on the ledge. "Who's the weasel?"

"That's Mike Bains," Fang answered for me. "I don't like thinking about anyone killing Faith, but if it was Mike, he needs to pay for it."

"I don't know," Chico said. "Mr. Archman was pretty mean back then. Remember all the detentions he gave us?"

I snorted. "Grow up. We were rotten kids. It's a wonder any of us managed to graduate. I would hate to find out that I was married to a murderer for eight years, and I can't think of a reason for the Weasel *or* Mr. Archman

BRUNSWICK

to kill Faith. And the discovery of Faith's body has to be tied in with Sophie's murder. It's a mess."

Chico was sitting above the damaged trough, gripping the metal. If he fell, he was taking the whole length of it with him. Fang would charge me extra, plus 15 percent.

"Why are we up here, anyway?" Chico asked. "We can talk inside, or in your garage."

"Fresh air, privacy. Relax. Just don't look down. In any case, let's go with the idea that the perpetrator is Mr. Archman or Kelly Quantz. Or the Weasel."

"Go where? You're no Miss Marple, and we're not Cagney and Lacey. What if we stir something up, and the murderer strikes again?"

Obviously, Chico didn't remember that Cagney and Lacey were women. "We won't stir anything up. We need to piece together grad night. One of you may have seen something you've forgotten. Maybe Faith argued with someone, or maybe she was followed into the locker room."

"You're saying you don't remember that night either? Any of it?" Fang crushed his empty coffee cup and stuffed it into one of the dripping paper bags. "We were pretty blitzed."

"Give me a break. I don't even remember leaving." I could almost taste the tequila. A wave of nausea hit me, and I guessed it wasn't entirely from the chili.

"They locked us in." Chico straightened and I grabbed his arm to stop him from toppling over. "That's against the Fire Code."

Fang lay back against the shingles, one arm

cushioning his head, letting the cold rain wash over his face. You can't get any wetter than soaked. "I remember bits and pieces. But nothing about Faith especially." He closed his eyes. "I drove my truck.... Where did we end up?"

"In a field. We built a fire." Images flashed through my mind, but they disappeared so suddenly, I couldn't be sure they were my memories or dreams. Maybe even movies I had seen. "I woke up in the back of Fang's truck. Do you remember driving home, Fang?"

"Shit, no. It's a miracle I didn't drive right into Ghost Swamp and sink without a trace. Then my parents would have lost both of us that night."

"I would have gone down with you," I said, morosely. Looking back on our teenaged years, it was a miracle we survived to adulthood.

"Tyger graduated the next year, and they didn't hold a party after the ceremony. There hasn't been one since ours." Chico leaned against the chimney and sniffed his coffee. If he poked his tongue through the tab hole and got stuck, I was going to have to laugh.

Tyger was Chico's wife's real name. She had been the girlfriend who had bossed him around through four years of high school. "Chico, you told me the other day in your store that you took a lot of pictures that night. What happened to them?"

"I had a Nikon and a Polaroid. The photos from the Nikon are the ones that ended up in the next year's yearbook. I know I took some Polaroids because I didn't have any film left, but who the hell knows where they went."

Fang took out a battered cigarette and lit it. "What about the pictures that didn't make it into the yearbook? Maybe we can look through those."

"Tyger threw them out years ago. And the negatives." He looked across at Fang. "Is that weed?"

"Yeah, but it won't stay lit in this fucking rain."

Chico's head swivelled to a spot down the street. "Bliss, isn't that Chief Redfern's Cherokee? Hell and damnations."

"He isn't stopping. But if he asks later, tell him we were just reminiscing about old times … no, wait, don't say that. We were discussing the food bank benefit."

"Sure, I'll lie to the cops for you. No problem. Whatever you say, as usual." Fang gave up on his joint and stuck it back in his pocket. "I'm leaving. Not that this hasn't been a blast, but next time, haul up a case of beer. I can smell your neighbour's Bud Light from here."

Whoa, didn't that give me an idea. A really good idea. "We need to conduct an experiment," I said. "Both of you be back here at eight o'clock tonight. Dress for the weather. And bring flashlights."

CHAPTER
TWENTY-SIX

"WHAT'S GOING ON HERE? People are sitting on their roofs." Tony rolled down the passenger window and stuck his head out. "They have shovels and cases of beer. I love this town!"

After Tony interviewed Mike Bains, he insisted on accompanying Neil to talk to Mrs. Brickle. "I want to see the mastermind behind the senior citizen marijuana dessert ring you busted last summer," was how he put it. They had finished up at her house on Sandpiper Street a block over and were headed back to the station via Morningside Drive.

"They're shovelling the wet snow off so their roofs don't collapse. It's quite a social affair in this town." He slowed so Tony had a better view.

"Geez. It's been raining all day. Look at that trio. Two drowned crows and a duck."

"That's Cornwall's house."

"Slow down, man. So, that little yellow one in the

middle is Bliss?" He craned his neck. "That looks like Fang Davidson. I wonder who the other guy is."

Neil put his foot on the brake and looked across the street. "Charles Leeds."

"Almost half of our suspects on one roof. A cop's dream. Let's get out and shake them up."

Neil pulled away from the curb. "I have a better idea. Let's get some coffee and discuss today's interviews."

Tony reluctantly closed the window. "Aren't you anxious about your lady sitting on a roof with two men? Either one of them could be our killer."

"Nothing I say will have any effect on Cornwall's course of action. On anything."

He felt Tony's eyes appraising him, and waited for it …

"Hell, why don't you just marry Bliss and be done with it? Then you two can duke it out in one room where you can't hide or run away from each other."

"It's not that simple, Tony. Both of us have … issues."

Tony snorted and turned down the heat. "I forgot. You're already married."

Neil's fingers tightened on the wheel. "Look who's giving marital advice — a man who's been married three times."

As he hoped, this distracted his friend. "Stop exaggerating. I've been married twice. I don't count the Vegas wedding. It wasn't legal because Tiffany was already married. And we were stinkin' trashed the whole weekend."

"Sure."

"And don't mention ex-wives in front of Glory."

Neil turned his head. "She doesn't know your

marital track record? I told you, Tony, it's not right to blow into a town, sweep a lonely woman off her feet, and then blow out again with the next wind. Glory Yates is a decent person and deserves better."

"Keep your shirt on, dude. I've been honest with Glory. We really connected. I don't plan to do anything to hurt her."

"Who do you think you're talking to? You've left a string of broken-hearted ex-girlfriends all over the province."

"Well now, just maybe I've turned over a new leaf. You'll just have to wait and see." Tony spied the Tim Hortons sign coming up. "Swing in here. I need a double-double fix and a couple of Boston creams."

While they waited for their drive-through order, Neil tried one more time. "Just keep two things in mind, will you?"

"I didn't know you could count that high, but go ahead."

"First, before you do something stupid, remember Glory is on the Police Services Board. And right now she's my only ally. Mike and Andrea Bains are gunning for me because of my relationship with Cornwall. And the fourth member will vote any way the mayor wants as long as his driveway is cleared of snow for free."

"Noted, bud." A Boston cream doughnut disappeared into Tony's mouth. He offered the second to Neil, who shook his head. "Still won't eat doughnuts in public? You are one weird copper. A disgrace to the uniform. So, what's the second thing, as if I need to hear it again?"

"Just be careful where you lay your head while you're in Lockport."

Except for Lavinia, the station was empty. "Everybody's out on patrol, Chief. I left the house-to-house reports on your desk, but I read them myself. Nobody in the area saw or heard anything unusual Saturday night to early Sunday morning when Sophie Quantz died. Zilch."

"Okay, thanks, Lavinia." In his office, he and Tony took off their coats and opened their coffees. "Let's hear what Mike Bains had to say."

"In a word: nothing. He didn't notice Faith in particular at the graduation affair. According to him, he spent the evening chatting with the chaperones, most particularly Miss Emily Czerneski, who is conveniently dead. According to this paragon, he didn't imbibe a drop of liquor or engage in salacious behaviour of any kind. He didn't see anything unusual except his classmates acting like a bunch of jungle apes."

Neil laughed. "Are those his exact words?"

"No, I'm paraphrasing. He didn't say this either, but he doesn't like you one little bit." Tony pulled his notebook out of his pocket and opened his laptop. "I'll type this up while I remember every useless word the phony little bastard uttered."

"Did you run into the formidable Mrs. Bains?"

"She was present while I interviewed her husband, reminding me that she is his lawyer. Confirmed he was with her in bed during the time Sophie Quantz was shot in the head at the church."

Neil read through the pages of house-to-house interviews. Lavinia was right. Four reports of nothing. "Did he admit dating either Faith or Sophie?"

"Sophie. Briefly, just before spring break in March. He was very careful not to besmirch Sophie by saying she was available to everyone, especially in front of his wife, but he managed to get the point across."

Neil turned on his laptop. "While you're documenting the Bains interview, I'll do the Brickle one."

"Not much for us there, either. Another suspect with no useful information, and no alibi for early Sunday morning. Lives alone. No one to corroborate she stayed in all night." Tony looked up. "Did you see Mrs. Brickle's hands? They're so twisted with arthritis, I doubt she could hold a gun, never mind affect a perfect head shot."

"I agree. She goes to the bottom of the list."

Tony looked up. "We have seven suspects for Sophie Quantz's murder — as long as you insist on including Bliss — and not one of them has an alibi worth shit. Davidson, Leeds, and Bains are all alibied by their wives. Archman, Brickle, Quantz, and Bliss don't even have that."

"Well, Cornwall does, as a matter of fact …"

Tony's eyes fastened on him, and he elaborated. "We were together. All night."

"So, you're Bliss's alibi. Are you prepared to swear in court that she was with you the entire night? She couldn't have skipped out, shot Sophie Quantz at St. Paul's, then returned to bed without you noticing?"

"Not unless she drugged me. So far, motive eludes us and we have no murder weapons. Faith was struck on the head. Sophie was shot, likely with a .32 handgun. One thing: Faith was struck on the left side of her head, near the front, indicating a right-handed assailant. Earl Archman is left-handed. So he says, and we'll check that. I can't see a man in his physical condition hoofing it around the block, climbing the stairs to the choir loft to shoot Sophie. He'd go to the bottom of the list except he's nervous about something." Neil clicked the Save option with his mouse. "The other five suspects are right-handed."

"We got fuck-all," Tony observed. "On anybody."

Neil's phone rang. "Reiner," he mouthed to Tony. After the first few words, he pressed a button. "You're on speaker, Ed. Tony Pinato is with me."

"I just got a call from the Forensic Pathology Unit about the bones. I didn't expect to hear anything for months, but this …"

They listened without interrupting.

"… this is something they thought important enough to let me know — they found fetal remains among the bones."

Neil's fingers tightened on his cell. "Any chance of a DNA match?"

"They're faxing an interim report on the findings. A DNA match is possible regarding the fetus, once the lab confirms the skeleton is Faith Davidson and we provide them with DNA from the father. I'm sorry I missed it when I packed up the bones for transport."

"Not your fault, Ed. Thanks for letting us know."

He disconnected and looked at Tony. "We probably just narrowed our suspects down to the five men on our list."

CHAPTER
TWENTY-SEVEN

WE MET AT MY HOUSE at eight o'clock sharp. After one look at Rae in her pink T-shirt and yoga pants, Chico and Fang tried to talk her into coming with us. I ixnayed that. "She was only in grade school when we graduated, so she has no part in this." Rae was twenty-six and they needed to keep in mind they were both married with ten or twelve children between them.

We headed out in separate vehicles and, at eight-twenty, stood in the barren wasteland that used to be the student parking lot behind the gymnasium of the old high school. The rain had changed to sleet, which coated the cracked asphalt with a thin slick of ice. I stood well away from Chico.

Police tape whipped in a wind that couldn't make up its mind whether to blow west off the lake or south from the U.S., where a major winter storm was brewing. Neither choice boded well for a town caught in the crosshairs.

"Somebody broke through the tape." I had wanted to do it myself.

"That was me." Fang took a final drag off his cigarette and threw it away. "The cops released the scene a few days ago, so me and Larry carried out anything worth a few bucks. There wasn't much. Better turn on your flashlights."

He pulled on the metal door of the gym and it swung open on creaking hinges. Inside, the darkness was absolute. We aimed our beams straight ahead but they illuminated nothing but an expanse of dusty flooring and a few trash bins.

"I took out the folding tables and chairs." Fang lit up another, not so legal, cigarette. He took a couple of drags, then handed it to Chico, but when he in turn offered it to me, I passed. My two experiences with the stuff last summer — inadvertent and not my fault — convinced me I was allergic to the stuff.

"Hold your lights on me." I tipped over a trash bin and jumped back as paper plates, napkins, plastic utensils, and something with a long tail skittered across the floor.

The noise was deafening in the empty space as the metal bin rolled out of sight.

"What are you doing?" Fang shouted. "Somebody will hear."

"Nobody is around to hear." I dumped the other two bins, then kicked aside the garbage. It was so old, it didn't even smell. "I'm looking for clues. I don't see anything, though."

"I think the cops would have checked through the trash, Bliss."

"Look," I said to Fang, "before we continue with our experiment, I want to go into the locker room where Faith was found. I'm not doing it out of morbid curiosity. I must have gone in there at some point during the three hours we were held prisoner that night. Maybe if I see it again, something will come back to me. You guys can wait here."

"I'll come with you." Chico's voice was a little shaky, but I appreciated the support. "We were all running back and forth between the girls' and boys' locker rooms."

"Call me when you're done." Fang's footsteps echoed on the wooden floor. "I'll be in the parking lot."

Chico walked so closely behind me, I had to jab him in the stomach with my elbow. The exit door to the hallway stuck and it took our combined strength to force it open. By now, I was sure my idea was a foolish one. How could I summon up memories from that crazy, noisy party? Now the school was cold, dark, and empty. All life had departed long ago.

The door to the girls' locker room was propped open. We stood shoulder to shoulder in the middle of the cracked tile floor. Silence surrounded us. One of the items *not* on my bucket list is an hour in a sensory deprivation tank, and this place fit the bill. Chico sucked on the joint and the smell of weed added to my stomach jitters.

The beam from my flashlight swept across scarred benches and lingered on the dreaded common shower stall. I spent many a self-conscious moment in that shower, hoping the other girls wouldn't make jokes about my inadequate boobs. Yeah, lots of opportunities for traumatic high school reminiscences here, but nothing from grad night.

My flashlight dimmed as I turned it toward the bank of lockers to our left. Chico's elbow brushed against my shoulder and he added his powerful torchlight to my feeble one. Naturally, he had the biggest, heaviest, brightest flashlight Canadian Tire could provide. Side by side, we inched closer.

Fifteen four-foot lockers comprised the row. I couldn't remember which had been mine. Every door hung open. Fang and Larry would have begun their search for booty at the lockers closest to the door, and stopped when they found Faith. The police completed the search.

We stopped about midway along the row. Only a small dark stain on the floor distinguished the locker from the others. Inside, the same stain covered the bottom. I knew where it came from, but refused to think what it had looked like through fifteen years of changing temperatures, insects, and rotting flesh. And the roses that had wilted then became part of Faith.

"That's not right." Chico's voice startled me. "Faith was a nice girl. She shouldn't have been killed and left in there all these years." He threw the roach to the floor and crushed it under his heel.

"No, it isn't. Somebody we know threw two bouquets of roses on top of her body, slammed the door closed, and hoped she'd never be discovered." I was never going to forget this place. I would always think of it like it was now, as Faith's tomb. Even demolition wouldn't banish the bad energy. When I got old, I had to make sure I didn't end up living in the retirement home planned for this site.

"Come on, Bliss. Let's get out of here. I won't remember anything now, not after seeing this."

In the gym, I called out to Fang, and he reappeared from the parking lot, a fresh doobie dangling from his lips.

I dropped my tote and whipped out a blanket, candles, a bottle of tequila, and three plastic glasses.

Chico shuffled in place. "I'm not drinking that stuff. Did you bring any beer?"

"No beer. And you don't have to drink the tequila." I borrowed Fang's lighter and set out a dozen tealights in a wide circle. In the centre I spread the blanket. "Sit."

"You better not be summoning up any demons," Fang chortled nervously. "I have to be home by eleven or Leanne will hang my balls on the Christmas tree."

"Charming image." I lit a large pillar candle and placed it in the middle of the blanket, then poured an inch of tequila into three glasses. "Everyone knows that the sense of smell is directly connected to the memory synapses of the brain. Pick up a glass. We'll close our eyes and inhale. Remember we're in the gym on the night of our high school graduation …"

"I think she's bat-shit nuts," Chico whispered to Fang, accepting a drag of the joint. But he sounded more relaxed than in the locker room, so maybe the weed was a good idea.

"*Shhttt.*" I closed my eyes and inhaled. Nothing

magical happened. I waited. Still nothing. I opened them again, disappointed that my experiment wasn't working. Backlit by the surrounding candles and illuminated from the front by the larger central candle, my companions looked far different than the seventeen-year-olds who were so eager to leave their childhoods behind.

I had sat like this, yoga-style, under a table, with two bottles — or was it three — of tequila, tipping the liquid into proffered pop cans and punch glasses. The music thumped, the other eleven grads — since Lionel Petty refused to come home from Victoria — milled around, their feet and legs passing back and forth …

Shitballs on a cracker. No wonder I couldn't recall any details from that night. It wasn't that I was plowed on tequila — okay, I was — but I couldn't see anything from under the table. Crap. I could sniff all the tequila I wanted. It wouldn't help. And maybe I didn't even go to the bathroom.

"Anything?" I asked my companions. By candlelight, they looked more relaxed, considering we were sitting on a frigid wooden floor in the dark, in an abandoned building. Chico aimed his flashlight at the ceiling. "Didn't we have a glitter ball?"

"Bliss has it. She stole it from me." Fang took a long drag and stuck his nose back into his tequila. He must have forgotten his aversion, and downed the entire glassful, which was a smidge more than a shot.

The sounds of his choking and spitting resounded from the empty spaces around us. "God damn, that's awful." He spat some more.

"I told you to smell it, not drink it, idiot." I poured a drop more into his glass.

"I don't need to smell any more. I don't remember anything out of the ordinary."

I jumped on that. "So, memories of that night are coming back to you?"

"Yeah, I guess. The music, the fucking disco ball flashing and spiralling. It turned my stomach. I thought I was going to puke and went to the bathroom in the locker room."

"Did you see anyone coming or going?"

"Everybody was in and out of the locker room. Even some of the girls came in with us. Big joke, girls in the boys' locker room. There were probably boys in the girls' locker room. At one point, Mrs. Czerneski came in and made us all go back to the gym."

I thought about that. "Not Mr. Archman?"

"Not that I know of. I think he was trashed, too. He spent the whole night watching the clocks over the basketball hoops and taking nips from his flask. Hope it was something better than tequila." He spat again.

"Stop spitting! Do you remember Mr. Archman talking to anyone in particular?"

"How should I know? I wouldn't have noticed him at all except I was watching the clock, too. God, what an endless night. Too bad I can't remember if I enjoyed myself after that."

This was a waste of time.

"What about Kelly Quantz?"

"What about him? He never took his eyes off Sophie, as usual. He was so pathetic. In love with a girl who dated everyone except him. He finally got her, though." Fang re-lit the joint, then passed it to Chico. "For a while, at least. This whole thing sucks."

Chico played his flashlight aimlessly across the ceiling. "So, where's the disco ball now?" He spoke quite proficiently around the joint hanging from his lip. I sensed he was no stranger to the demon weed.

"It's in the greenhouse. You'll see it on the fourteenth of this month. Don't forget that date. Now, can we focus, gentlemen?"

"My ass is frozen numb," Chico complained. "I can't remember anything except something to do with the disco ball. Let's get out of here."

"Not yet," I snapped. "Keep sniffing, both of you. Chico, you keep mentioning the disco ball. What about it?"

"Hey." Fang sat up straight. "Chico was on a stepladder. Mr. Archman made him get down. I remember him yelling. The ladder was over against the wall, and me and Larry salvaged it. It's a twelve-footer, good quality ..."

The double doors at the far end of the gym swung wide, sending a current of cold air across the floor. The garbage fluttered and scattered into the shadows. Footsteps hit the floor with a heavy cadence. Beyond the pale flickering of the candles, the darkness shrouded the intruder's approach. The deliberate footfalls were familiar, and awareness of his identity touched me seconds before he reached the light.

In those few seconds, I snatched the joint from Chico's mouth, squeezed the end to extinguish it, and tossed it over my shoulder, where, I hoped, a drug-savvy cop wouldn't bother to look for it to test for DNA.

The candlelight framed blond spikes, like the crest on Beelzebub's head. Hands resting on his gun holster, he asked, so mildly the blood froze in my veins, "What the *fucking hell* are you three up to now?"

CHAPTER
TWENTY-EIGHT

AS MORGUES GO, this one wouldn't make Neil's nightmare list. No dissecting tables, no layered drawers held bodies, no trays of bone saws or other sinister instruments. It was just a room in the basement of the hospital where a body waited until the family arranged for the funeral home to pick it up.

Neil looked around. There was no sheet-covered corpse tonight. Ed had asked him and Tony to meet him here at 10:00 p.m. He'd had to rush off to deliver a baby and didn't have time to explain why.

Yawning so hard his jaw cracked, Neil leaned his head back and listened to Tony crunch potato chips and gulp from a litre bottle of orange juice.

It had been his misfortune to drive by the abandoned high school earlier and see three vehicles parked haphazardly in the parking lot — Cornwall's Matrix, Davidson's old Ford pickup, and a van which turned out to belong to Chico Leeds.

He had smelled the weed as soon as he opened the door. For one dizzying moment, he thought they were holding a drug-fuelled séance. Candles set out in a circle, with one big one in the centre, and the trio sitting cross-legged on the floor — it never occurred to him they were conducting an odour-to-memory test.

Cornwall had a hypersensitive sense of smell and couldn't understand that other people didn't. He smiled to himself, picturing the three of them holding tequila up to their noses and trying to summon fifteen-year-old memories. It was a harmless stunt, as long as the killer didn't turn out to be Davidson or Leeds.

The men were half-stoned, but Neil didn't see any pot on them — and he wasn't interested in body searches. First of all, he'd have had to peel Cornwall off his back, literally, and secondly, he'd have to listen to her complain about draconian marijuana laws regarding consenting adults for, well, the rest of his life. He knew Cornwall never touched the stuff herself, but that wouldn't stop her from defending her friends. It wasn't worth it.

He waited while they blew out the candles and gathered up the trappings of the experiment. He stopped Cornwall from throwing the half-full bottle of tequila into the trash can. "Some kids might find it before this place is torn down."

Neither of the men would touch it, so Cornwall tucked it into her huge purse. He opened his mouth, but shut it again, just in time. Reminding her to transport the bag in the rear of her hatchback, out of reach, would just earn him one of her snarly looks.

He followed them into the parking lot and watched Davidson and Leeds sprint across the slick pavement to their vehicles. By the time he turned back to Cornwall, she was in her car and peeling after them. Her purse was undoubtedly beside her in the passenger seat. At least Dwayne wasn't on duty to impose the full force of the "no alcohol within reach" law.

He bolted upright in his chair at the sound of a gunshot. His hand flew to his belt.

"Have a nice nap, princess?" Tony laughed and waved the potato chip bag he had blown up and burst.

Before Neil could slow his heart rate to normal, the door flew open and Ed Reiner surged into the room. "Sorry to keep you waiting. Difficult delivery. All fine now, though."

It wasn't easy to find a place to meet on a December weeknight in this town. The restaurants closed by eight, and the bars were too noisy and public. Monday night at the Wing Nut was a case in point. Tony's room at the Super 8 was an option, as was the station, but the hospital morgue was handier for an overworked obstetrician. While they waited for Ed, Neil had told Tony about Cornwall and her homeys at the old high school. Typically, Tony considered the account amusing, but unimportant. He was likely right, except for the amusing part.

Ed carried a file, which he slapped down on a desk old enough to have seen action during the Second World War. "As promised, the Forensic Pathology Unit faxed over the report on the fetal bones. I really wish I'd thought to separate and count the bones before I shipped them to Toronto."

"Nobody expected you to, man. You were focussing on the head wound. I'm just surprised we got a report so soon." Tony glanced at his watch, clearly anxious to get out of there. Back to Glory, most likely.

Neil was certain he wouldn't be welcome in Cornwall's bed tonight. "Yeah, Ed, it's not your fault. What does the report say?"

"Okay. It's approximately a sixteen-week fetus."

"When we take DNA samples from the four male suspects, the results will tell us who fathered Faith's baby, but not necessarily who killed her," Neil said.

Tony swallowed the last of his orange juice and pitched the empty container into a nearby waste basket. "We aren't even sure we're looking for a male killer. This case is so freaking screwed up — two deaths separated by fifteen years. The first victim's pregnancy may not even be important."

"Possible," Ed said. "Faith left Lockport right after school ended and never returned until the night of the graduation party. Maybe she had a boyfriend in Toronto. If she met someone shortly after moving there and was intimate with him, the pregnancy might have nothing to do with her death."

Neil struggled to recall information he read in the missing person report. "That's unlikely. She stayed with an aunt in Toronto. The aunt was an emergency room nurse who worked the three-to-eleven shift. Faith paid for her room and board by rushing home from class and looking after her two cousins, ages eight and eleven. Apparently, she didn't have time for a social life. Looks like someone fathered that baby right here before she left in June."

"Poor kid." Tony struggled into his uniform parka. "In that case, my money is on the little bastard who knocked her up. When she came back for graduation, she told him and he lashed out, killing her. Then he stuffed her into the locker and threw her bouquet in after her. He walked away and never looked back. We're going to hunt him down and make sure he pays for what he did to her. I don't care how young he was at the time, he better not get off with a slap on the wrist."

Neil stood up. "Let's keep in mind there were two grown men at the graduation party — Earl Archman and Kelly Quantz. And two bouquets were tossed into the locker on top of Faith. That suggests a girl was involved.

"Valid points, bud." Tony stopped in the doorway and looked back. "Only two girls involved — Sophie Quantz and Miss Bliss. Sophie is dead, and I hope you aren't raising your lady to the head of the suspect list. Even I wouldn't buy that, and I always suspect everyone."

Neil ignored the reference to Cornwall. "I'm betting there were two people present when Faith died. And Sophie was one of them."

Ed took off his glasses and rubbed his eyes until the whites reddened. "Have you accounted for all the girls in the class?"

"There were seven altogether, including Cornwall, Faith, and Sophie. We've contacted the other four. None of them remembered anything helpful. We'll check to make sure they weren't in Lockport when Sophie died, but it looks like they're in the clear."

Tony eyed the door. "Fine. The second bouquet belonged to Sophie. Let's go with that. She was there when Faith was killed, knew who did it, and died because she knew. Let's go with that, too. The question is, why didn't she tell someone at the time, or in the years since?"

"There are several reasons why she wouldn't speak up when it happened. Complicity. Maybe fear. Perhaps she was able to block the incident out of her mind until Faith's body was discovered."

Ed thumped the scarred desktop with his fist. "She became a priest, didn't she? She turned her life around, perhaps trying to make up for her part in Faith's death. What if she decided it was time to tell the truth? What if she contacted whoever else was present in the locker room and told him she was going to the police …?"

"That person would most likely need to shut her up," Neil finished.

"Let's go with that," Tony responded. He ambled to the exit.

CHAPTER
TWENTY-NINE

THROBBING TEMPLES WOKE ME on Friday morning. I couldn't breathe through my nose even though the swelling in my face had all but disappeared and the bruises had faded to yellow. I didn't have time for a cold, damn it.

Breathing in the humid air at the greenhouse didn't appeal to me, so I ran the payroll for Bliss This House from my laptop on my kitchen table and did some rescheduling. Marjorie needed Wednesday off to take her son, Storm, to the orthodontist. No problem there. One of the subs could help Cora at Mrs. Brickle's. Done with a phone call and a click.

Next, Rae needed the same day off so she could write her registered massage therapy final exam in Kitchener. Since she put in eight hours at Glory's on Wednesdays, I needed to find someone to fill in for her who could work a full day. And I had to pick her replacement carefully. It had taken Glory months to get used to Rae after I moved from slave labour to management of my own cleaning company. I don't know which she regretted more — losing my cleaning skills or being forced to pay decent wages. Now I was going to ask her to change cleaners again. I'd better wear my motorcycle helmet when I broke the news to her. Or, better yet, do it by phone.

I called the greenhouse to speak with the Madam. Rae answered and put me through to Dougal before I could stop her. He screamed at me to get my lazy ass in to work and start on the long list of delinquent accounts. When pressed, he admitted only two names graced the current naughty list. Then he reminded me to get on the promotional tour bus for Glory's food benefit since any dereliction on my part would reflect badly on him. And no, Glory hadn't come in either. He was in sole charge of the greenhouse and how was he supposed to get the first draft of his third novel started if he had to run the place? He had a life, too, and was leaving town to join Holly in Toronto the minute the food benefit was over. Oh, and I better get started on putting the decorations up because the Canadian Tire bags were littering the break room …

I hung up; not that he'd notice for another five minutes. I sneezed three times, signalling the start of the runny stage of a head cold. Just in case it was the flu, I figured I should get my work done before I collapsed and perhaps died of complications from pneumonia. Then a lot of people would be sorry. Before I left the house, I sent an email to my staff with the revised schedule and took a cold tablet to dry up the snot tsunami.

The pill hadn't kicked in by the time I got to the

Lockport Sentinel office on Commercial Crescent, just south of the Wing Nut. It took considerable pleading, and several bouts of uncontrollable sneezing, before the editor agreed to place a four-by-six ad for the food drive benefit in the next issue of the weekly newspaper. I thanked him but he turned his back and pulled out a container of anti-bacterial wipes. Next stop, the printers.

Zeus Printing occupied the ground floor of a mid-rise modern building (hereabouts that meant a three-storey structure built in the eighties) conveniently located next door to the newspaper office. Since the pill had started to work by this time and I couldn't sneeze on the owner, I had to go from pleading to full-out begging to get posters printed *gratis*. So humiliating.

Eventually, the tightwad loosened his death grip on his cash register. We settled on a dozen twelve-by-fourteen posters in exchange for his business name on a sponsor's sign above the food donation bin. He would provide the sign. I agreed, hoping the sign would fit through the door.

I remembered promising Chico a couple of thank-you signs and figured I could make them up myself using bristol board and permanent markers. Then I'd duct-tape one to a tree outside the greenhouse, and the other to the door of the men's room.

The floor above the printers' housed the legal office of Bains and Bains. How cute was that? I had an idea. Glory had demanded I stay away from the Weasels for Redfern's sake. Redfern demanded I stay away from them — why? I couldn't remember, but how about if I just smoothed the waters and, at the same time, picked the Weasel's brain about grad night? Surely, nobody could complain about that.

I took the elevator and exited into a sparse reception area. So far, so good. The receptionist was AWOL, either in the bathroom or on maternity leave. The comfy chairs in the waiting area were also empty. I strolled down a short hall and stopped outside a partially open door. The Weasel's voice soothed a client with promises of a hefty settlement before the court date. Since there was no second voice, the Weasel was phone-billing, a practice I remembered well. When Mike first set up his office, I did the reception work, sent out the monthly billings, and handled disgruntled clients. Perfect training for my current jobs.

I pushed the door open and walked in. Ignoring the surprise and anger on Mike's attractive features, I plopped into his visitor's chair with a sigh of relief. Those cold tablets sure knocked you on your ass.

Mike concluded his call and started right in. "What the hell do you want?"

I unbuttoned my coat and slid my arms out like I intended to stay a while. "I want to apologize for upsetting you the other night at the Wing Nut. I hope you didn't think I was accusing you of murdering Faith and Sophie."

"That's what it sounded like to me. And I don't believe you came here to apologize. I'm quite sure you don't know how to do that."

"I had a lot of practice when we were married,

remember? Everything was my fault. Even when I was right, I was wrong, so I spent a lot of time apologizing." Not in the door two minutes, and I was off track.

I stopped and tried to breathe deeply, but broke into a coughing fit. By the time I recovered my breath, I had also recovered some focus. "Anyway, I thought if we put our heads together, we might come up with something helpful about grad night."

"Helpful to whom? You? The police? I've talked to the OPP investigator and I'm not talking to you."

"Don't you care what happened to Faith and Sophie? They were our friends."

"Faith was a long time ago, and I haven't talked to Sophie since that night, either. We don't attend St. Paul's Church."

Little snippets of memories sometimes pop up when you least expect them. "I know you went out with Sophie. But didn't you date Faith as well? Toward the end of the school year?" That had been an unlikely pairing. Shy, introspective Faith Davidson. Ambitious, controlling Mike Bains. "Did you see her over the summer?"

"Not that it's any of your business, but no. I spent the summer as a counsellor at Silver Birch Camp the other side of Mount Forest. And I didn't date her."

"Okay. You must have talked to her at grad night in October, though."

"So what if I did? I talked to a lot of people that night. I told the OPP sergeant all this and I'm not repeating it to you."

"Okay. I'm guessing you didn't see Faith head to the locker room or notice her leaving at midnight with the rest of us?"

His mouth pursed into a tight oval. "I think you should get out before I call your boyfriend and insist he charge you with obstruction."

"How about you ..." I burst into a sneezing fit, and when I was done Andrea stood in the doorway.

"What's going on? Why is she here?" Her designer business suit and Louis Vuitton shoes matched perfectly. Brown and more brown. Andrea was about thirty-seven, five years older than Mike, and, while not unattractive in a horsey sort of way, she could use a few fashion tips. Maybe a new hairdo, some makeup, a personality transplant ...

"Don't worry about it, Andrea. She's playing at being a detective. Guess her boyfriend is out of his depth investigating murders. She's just leaving."

I blew my nose and threw the tissue into the wastebasket beside the desk. Both Weasels watched me with disgust. "Actually, I'm glad you're both here. What's this I hear about you threatening to terminate Chief Redfern's contract because of his relationship with me?" What was I saying? I had to be allergic to the active ingredient in cold tablets.

Andrea looked down at me like I was an earwig begging to be squashed. "That's not your concern, Bliss. The Police Services Board will proceed as it sees fit ..."

The Weasel interrupted. "Redfern's contract is up in six months. We will revisit the issue then. Whether we renew the contract or not depends on many factors. Only one concerns his relationship with you, and whether he can control you. We won't allow you to continue blundering around in police matters, as you're doing right now."

Control me? "You know he's a damned good chief. I bet you were one of his biggest fans until we started dating." *Dating? Was that what we were doing?* God, my head was spinning.

Andrea crossed her arms and took a step closer. "You should be committed to a secure facility. Are you accusing my husband of caring whom you sleep with?"

"Sounds crazy when you put it like that," I admitted. "So, why do you really want to get rid of him?" I looked from one to the other. "Whatever the reason, you better knock it off."

"Or what?" Mike sneered. "Are you threatening to blackmail me again?"

"Me? Blackmail you? What a silly accusation."

"You promised you didn't keep a copy of that picture!" He stood up and leaned over the desk. Now I had both of them looming over me. "Did you lie about that?"

"Are you talking about the picture of you smoking a joint in university? Well, I kind of did lie about that. I have several copies. See, you promised to be faithful until death, and Andrea promised to represent my best interests during our divorce proceedings. Face it. We're a pack of liars. We should form a club — the Lockport Liars."

"I won't be blackmailed again by you." Mike spoke softly and distinctly.

"Did I say anything about blackmail? You need to get a grip."

"Why are you really here?" Andrea's voice matched the Weasel's in chilling quietude.

"I came to ask Mike if he remembered anything about grad night. I thought together we might come up with something to help with the investigation. That's all."

"Get out." Andrea stood aside as I got to my feet.

I stopped in the doorway and looked back. "Congratulations on winning the Liberal nomination for this riding, Mike. Guess you're getting ready for the federal election whenever the present government implodes through its own corruption and greed."

"We're ready now," Andrea said. "There's nothing you can do to stop us."

"I wouldn't dream of interfering. In the meantime, don't underestimate me. And don't mess with Redfern."

CHAPTER
THIRTY

LUNCHTIME AT TIMMY'S is a free-for-all. First, you have to fight your way to the counter, then you've got to balance a tray while you shove through the crowd to grab a seat before Grandma or Uncle Barney body-checks you into the potted plants.

Against all odds, I snagged a window table, chicken soup and roll in hand. Sniffling and sneezing has its advantages because the tables near me remained clear while I ate. I couldn't taste or smell the soup, but assumed it was delicious. That gave me an idea. Man, I was full of ideas today.

I ordered another chicken soup lunch and a couple of coffees — to go — and borrowed an old-fashioned phonebook from the kind, matronly lady at the counter. She used the doughnut tongs to push the items across the counter to me. I looked up Earl Archman's address and picked up my order. By the look on the counter lady's face, she was going to drop the phonebook straight into the trash. People are so nervous around a few germs these days.

Before getting out of my vehicle in front of Mr. Archman's bungalow on Balmoral Crescent, I studied my face in the visor mirror. Yikes. My cover-up had failed and the yellow skin around my eyes made me look like I had Hep A, or even B. My nose and upper lip had reddened from all the blowing. I needed to stay away from Redfern for a few days. If I wanted to force him to his knees and elicit apologies for his asshole behaviour, he shouldn't see me like this.

My face was good enough for my former math teacher, though.

I noticed that Mr. Archman's backyard butted up to the rear of the St. Paul's manse. The stone tower of St. Paul's Church loomed over the rooftop of the house. *Creepy.* While Sophie was being killed, Mr. Archman — and his neighbours, to be fair — were within a couple of hundred metres. It would have been possible for him to shinny over the fence to do the deed — if he didn't weigh three hundred pounds.

I realized I was leaning toward Mr. Archman being the killer. That would simplify things a lot. I had second thoughts about confronting him alone, in his home. On the plus side, I could outrun him. So, as long as I didn't stand within striking distance, he couldn't club me or strangle me. I brought my own coffee so he couldn't slip me poison. As long as he didn't pull out a gun, things should work out in my favour.

I rang the doorbell while admiring the giant Grinch on the rocking chair. Now, that was my idea of the Christmas spirit. The doorbell worked because I heard it when I pressed my ear against the curtained glass in the door. He should be home. The town grapevine reported he was taking sick leave for the rest of the school year. I pushed the button twice more before the door flew open.

"Oh, for God's sake! What the hell are you doing at my door, Miss Cornwall? Can't a sick man get any peace? What do you want?"

A lot of women seem to like that three-days-growth-of-beard look. I find it a total turn-off and told Redfern early on in our relationship that stubble was grounds for immediate dismissal. He took that to heart because I've never felt the slightest bristling during our close encounters.

I digress wildly, but my point is that stubble was especially unattractive on Mr. Archman. Between that and his soiled grey sweat suit, the man was, frankly, a mess. I felt much better about my own appearance.

"Hi, Mr. Archman." I smiled brightly, cracking the chapped skin around my lips. "I brought you some lunch."

"I'm on a diet. Go away." The door began to close. I thought of shoving my foot in like they do in the movies, but given the difference between his weight and mine, that may have been a bad idea.

"Oh, come on now. You could use a little chicken soup, couldn't you? And some coffee? It's from Timmy's."

He hesitated, and that was all the advantage I needed. I pushed on the door and managed to squeeze in the crack before he slammed it shut behind me. I skipped a few metres down the hallway, mindful of the striking distance I vowed to avoid.

On the right was the living room. I set the cardboard tray on the coffee table but stayed on my feet. He glared at me, and I pretended great interest in the room, which was, honestly, a disaster.

When his wife left, she must have taken most of the furniture, forcing Mr. Archman to scavenge from the landfill or from curbside during the municipality's annual discarded furniture and appliance pickup day. Our entry into the room caused a few dust bunnies to hop off the furniture and join the rest of the gang on the floor. And, bugger ... the magazines and books scattered around all featured guns and archery.

I wrenched my attention back to the murdering SOB, while he collapsed into an armchair that faced a flat-screen TV. Remember Martin's duct-taped armchair on *Frasier*? This one would have benefited from a couple of rolls. I rummaged through my tote bag before remembering I'd left my supply at the greenhouse.

"Why must you torment me, Miss Cornwall? Can't you see I want to be alone, to die without witnesses and be found months from now, mummified or otherwise ready for burial?" He rested his plaster-encased right arm in his lap.

I contemplated him in astonishment and, forgetting to stay well away, I crept to within a few feet of his chair. "Good one, Mr. Archman. But I don't think the police are going to let you go softly into that good night, not quite yet. Not while the killer of Faith and Sophie is at large."

I glanced out the dining room window. I didn't see a gate in the wooden fence separating the backyard from the manse. Plus, it was at least eight feet high. So, if Mr. Archman killed Sophie, he must have walked around the crescent to the other side.

"You'll feel better with some hot soup inside you. Here, I'll leave the bowl in the tray and open your coffee. Do you take milk and sugar?"

He finally gave in. While he ate, I chatted about nothing in particular, ignoring his eye rolls.

At one point, he interrupted: "I see you didn't bring a can of paint for my bathroom. I'm partial to yellow, but I wouldn't mind looking at a few colour chips. And I'll pay for the paint."

Okay, no more kid gloves. "I don't paint. I have my own cleaning business. How about we put our heads together about the grad party in the gym, Mr. A? See if we can't come up with something to help the police. You tell me what you remember, and I'll compare it to my recollection. More and more details are coming back to me every day."

"Nice try, Miss Cornwall. You were in no condition to remember anything, and I've already told your boyfriend everything I recall. And it seems to me we had a discussion at the hospital when I was in too much pain to toss you out." A noodle hung from the hairs on his chin, but I wasn't going near it.

"How about you call me Bliss? And can I call you Earl?"

"No. As I told your boyfriend, I regret inadvertently leaving Faith's body in the locker room, even though I had no way of knowing it was there, and I regret mistaking some other young woman for Faith at the bus stop later that night. What's done is done. Now, if you don't mind...."

I erupted in a violent, wet sneezing fit. While I mopped up, Mr. A heaved himself out of his chair and tottered out of the room. In case he came back with a gun, I looked around for my purse and prepared to flee, but I wasn't fast enough.

Aerosol can held high, he sprayed around the room. My nose was too congested to smell it. "Stop it! That's toxic." Hell, it could be roach spray.

"Calm down, Miss Cornwall. It's only Lysol. I'm hoping it will kill the virulent germs you're spreading around my home."

"Yeah, you need more than that. No offence, Mr. A., but this place needs a good cleaning. Are you perhaps a hoarder?" I drew a happy face in the dust covering his coffee table.

He looked around. "What do you mean? It's a little messy, maybe ..."

"Sit down and relax. I have a proposal for you." Geez, that didn't come out exactly like I intended. "I mean, I have a proposition." Shit, I should just spit it out.

He sat, but kept his trigger finger on the nozzle of the can.

I took out a brochure and a price list from my purse. "You may have heard of my cleaning company, Bliss This House? No? What I propose is that I send in a team for a full day to give this whole house a good going over. Here, this is my price."

When I saw his mouth open to protest, I said, "No, wait, since you and I go way back" — *gag me* — "I'll knock 20 percent off the price. Then, a team of two will come in every other week for four hours to do the routine cleaning. Laundry and windows are extra."

His chin sank onto his chest and he peered through the layers of flesh surrounding his eyes. "I may have fallen into bad housekeeping habits lately. But I'm not a healthy man. I may well die before long, so I don't think ..."

"Okay, Earl, what's all this shit about dying? You need to lose a few pounds — okay, maybe a couple hundred pounds — and you have sleep apnea, undoubtedly a little high blood pressure, but you're not that old. You have time to get your body back into a less lethal condition."

He lifted his head. "Thank God you never went into the healing arts. Your bedside manner stinks. Now that I think of it, you were never even a hall monitor, were you?"

"I volunteered, but they wouldn't have me."

"Thank God," he said again. He was getting on my nerves.

I sneezed and was rewarded with another spritz from the Lysol can. I grabbed a World War Two weapons' magazine and fanned the air. "Do you by any chance belong to a gun club? You seem to be fascinated with deadly weapons, and you have, like, a hundred *Lock and Load* magazines sitting around."

"As a matter of fact, my great-uncle left me an extensive collection of souvenir pistols from the war. He taught me to shoot when I was a boy, and I did join the gun club later. I have a target pistol, legally registered. But you don't need to tell your boyfriend about the souvenirs. City cops don't understand our ways."

"Tell me about it." Did everyone refer to Redfern as my "boyfriend?" If we split up, would he henceforth be referred to as my "ex-boyfriend?"

"You were just leaving, Miss Cornwall."

"In a minute. Tell me what you're dying of.

He sighed. "If it will get rid of you. I need to lose a hundred pounds. My blood pressure is off the charts." From the cluttered table by his chair, he picked up a pill bottle and shook it. "I have to go to a sleep clinic and get fitted for one of those horrendous masks for sleeping. As far as I know, my valves are running clear, but I need to be checked by a heart specialist to make sure." He sighed again.

"Only a hundred pounds? That's not bad. Once you lose the weight, the other problems will resolve themselves. Do you want to know what I think?" By his expression, he didn't, but I told him anyway, "I believe you're suffering from depression. Maybe you should see a doctor, other than Dr. Who's-it at the hospital. He's a gynecologist, you know."

"And a very capable ER doctor. I have an appointment with my own doctor tomorrow. He'll set me up with all the pertinent specialists."

"Fine. I can send a team in next Friday. Is that good for you?" Damned if I was leaving here without information about grad night *and* without new business.

"If I say yes, will you leave?"

"Of course, you just have to ask." I stood up and zipped my coat. "If you think of anything regarding the graduation party, will you let me know? Here's my business card. Or, you can contact my *boyfriend* instead, if you'd rather."

"Goodbye, Miss Cornwall."

He shuffled to the door behind me. I wanted to invite him to Glory's charity benefit, thinking it might cheer him up. But when I sneezed — only once this time — he slammed the door shut.

I trudged to my car, wiping my nose and searching my pockets for the blister pack of cold pills. I still hoped Mr. Archman was the killer, but not as much as before.

CHAPTER
THIRTY-ONE

THE STATION HAD one interview room, barely enough space for a perp and his lawyer and two cops. Neil took a seat and waited while Thea, Dwayne, and Bernie pulled their chairs into alignment with the whiteboard. Tony picked up a marker and drew a line down the centre of the board.

"Okay, boys and girls. We've hit a brick wall regarding Faith Davidson's death. Looks like homicide, smells like homicide, most likely *is* homicide. She was sixteen weeks pregnant when she died, and we don't know who the father was yet. He may have been very unhappy over hearing about the pregnancy, and that, my kiddies, would be a motive. Are we looking for a male perpetrator? Looks like it, but he may have had a female accomplice." He pointed at the list of seven names on the left side of the board. "In my humble opinion, we could strike off Miss Bliss Moonbeam Cornwall's name. But the chief here insists she's a contender, so her name stays."

Bernie sniggered while Dwayne snorted. Thea rolled her eyes and jabbed Dwayne in the arm with her elbow. Neil stirred in his chair and quelled his staff with a look.

"So," Tony continued, throwing the marker in the air and catching it, "let's focus on Reverend Sophie Quantz. I don't think we can discount her husband. Kelly Quantz has been drunk since his wife's death and I'd bet he's been best friends with the booze before that. He could have followed his wife into the church and shot her. So far, we haven't found a motive."

"Do you think he could have killed Faith Davidson, too?" Thea asked.

"Don't know. He could have. He was on the scene," Tony responded. He turned and wrote *PAL?* at the top of the board over the first column. "Do any of our suspects have a Possession and Acquisition Licence?"

Thea opened the folder on her lap. "First of all, the casing we found in St. Paul's choir loft is a .32 ACP. Next, I checked with the RCMP, and six people on that list have a PAL for a target pistol and ammo. Also an Authorization to Transport for each of them."

Neil stood up and squared his taut shoulder muscles. "All six belong to a gun club of some sort. Any .32s, Thea?"

"No, Chief. All own Rugers, mostly Mark I's. They all use .22 calibre ammo."

"Even Fern Brickle?" Neil was surprised she owned a target pistol, given her advanced arthritis.

Thea consulted her file again. "Her PAL is about to expire. The RCMP has sent out her ninety-day reminder."

Tony tapped the end of his marker on the board,

leaving a grouping of little black dots. "I don't know about the rest of you coppers, but I'm dying to know who doesn't have a PAL."

Thea smiled. "I didn't say the seventh person doesn't have a PAL. Fang Davidson has a licence for two long guns, both older shotguns, neither take .32s."

Tony placed a tick mark against each name under the PAL column. Beside the word *PAL*, he wrote *No .32s*. "So all our suspects have experience with handguns. Except Fang, but I'm assuming he'd be able to hit the broad side of a barn if you placed a pistol in his hand. We can't rule any of them out." He threw an evil smirk at Neil.

Bernie cleared his throat. "There's one thing we should remember." At Neil's nod of encouragement, he continued. "There may be hundreds of Second World War souvenir guns tucked away in attics and garages. Most of them unregistered."

The idea of all those unlicensed weapons made the skin on the back of Neil's neck tighten. "Local gun owners have had ample opportunity to come forward and register their arms." Shit, he sounded like he had a stick up his ass.

"I'm just saying, Chief, if you could compare the RCMP Firearm Centre's list of licences against actual guns, you'd come up way short on licences. And some of the souvenir handguns use .32 ammo. Just a thought." Bernie folded his arms and closed his eyes, indicating the end to his contribution.

Neil dropped into his chair and stretched out his legs. "This just keeps getting better and better. We'd have a hell of a time getting warrants to search random premises for unregistered handguns. Looks like we'll have to come at this another way. What else have you got, Tony?"

Tony wrote *ALIBIS* above the second column. "Nobody has an alibi for early Sunday morning. Spouses and significant others don't count." He avoided looking at Neil, and drew an *X* under each name.

He studied the names for a minute. "I'm inclined to drop the two females from the suspect list. Fern Brickle can't hold a gun, let alone shoot one and hit her target. And Bliss Cornwall? Can't even pretend to come up with a motive for her." He stroked off Bliss's and Fern Brickle's names. "That leaves us with the five men: Archman, Bains, Leeds, Davidson, and Quantz."

One thing Neil knew for certain: If Cornwall was inclined to shoot someone, her ex-husband wouldn't still be top side of the turf. But he found it strange that she never mentioned owning a target pistol.

He dismissed the constables and closed the door behind them. "You made a good point, bud."

"Which one was that? All my points are good." Tony laughed, and his hand went automatically to his shirt pocket, feeling for the long-absent cigarettes. "Does Lavinia have any doughnuts out there?"

"No. And I mean about Kelly Quantz. Maybe we're wrong about the motive for Sophie's death. If Kelly killed her, the timing could just be coincidence."

"Yeah, I was sort of kidding. Why would he kill her? The life insurance policy issued by the diocese will barely pay for her burial plot and headstone. And without her,

Kelly is out on the street. By the looks of him, he won't be too good at surviving in the real world."

Neil stuck his head into the squad room and called Thea back. "Find out if Kelly Quantz is the beneficiary of any life insurance policy other than through the Episcopal Church. Check deeper into Sophie's assets and investments. And look into Kelly's personal relationships: girlfriend, boyfriend, enemies."

Tony pulled on his heavy coat. "Nothing more to be done today, bro. I'm taking Glory out to dinner, if I can find a nice place in this backwater town of yours. You need to get your ass over to Miss Bliss's and beg forgiveness for whatever stupid things you've done recently. Pick one and go with it. Maybe she'll forget all the others."

Neil stopped him before he reached the door. "Since you mentioned Glory.... Headquarters isn't going to let you stay on here indefinitely. If we don't make progress soon, they'll pull you. I don't like repeating myself, but have you given any thought to how your leaving will affect Glory?"

Tony placed his hat rakishly off-centre and nodded. "What happens, happens. Maybe I'm just a quick roll in the hay for Ms. Yates. She's out of my league, in case you haven't noticed. We're having fun, one day at a time. You go clear up your own issues with your pretty little rebel before preaching to me." With a final, deep chuckle, Tony shut the door behind him.

CHAPTER
THIRTY-TWO

I WENT STRAIGHT HOME from Earl's and took two more daytime cold pills. I stripped down, took a long, hot shower, and pulled on a sports bra and yoga shorts. I wrapped myself in a fleece robe and fuzzy slippers. With my hair skinned back in a ponytail and the yellow skin around my eyes glowing like the noonday sun, I looked like ... well, like nothing you'd want to date.

Rae came into the kitchen while I was foraging in the fridge. The shelves were bare except for a pre-packaged salad, which didn't appeal to me. I needed some comfort food. Somebody better go grocery shopping, and soon.

Discouraged, I slammed the door closed.

Rae said, "Bliss, there's a stir-fry in the pan on the stove. I'll heat it up for you." She scooped a man-sized portion into a bowl, nuked it, and set it before me with cutlery, while balancing a ten-pound anatomy textbook in her left hand.

"Bliss. I've been thinking about your hair …"

I held up one hand in a "stop" motion and talked around a mouthful of rice. "No more colours, Rae. I want my natural colour back. When I look in the mirror, which I'm avoiding these days, I don't even recognize myself." I sniffed wetly.

Rae stepped back a few feet. "That's just what I was going to suggest. I think we should strip out every colour, return it to a warm, light brown, and add a few lighter highlights. It will look awesome." Rae is the only person I know who can say "awesome" without sounding like an eleven-year-old Justin Bieber groupie.

"That's the way it was before you added every colour of the rainbow. People are giving me strange looks." I scrubbed at my nose with a tissue.

"That would be due to your yellow eyes and red nose. So we'll tackle your hair later tonight?"

"It's a date. And thanks for the food. I'm going to the garage for a while."

"What for? It's cold and dirty in there."

"I have to think. And I need to visit with my motorcycle to remind myself that spring is only four or five months away."

I scored a bag of cheese puffs from the pantry, which cheered me up no end. A bottle of orange juice was the perfect accompanying beverage. It's a known fact that orange foods are packed with vitamins.

With these items under my arm, I snatched up a pair of old runners and entered the garage. I turned the space heater to its highest setting and, while waiting for the place to warm up, pulled the cover off my

Suzuki Savage. I ran my hands over the polished front fender and threw my leg over the seat. I wrapped my fingers around the handlebars for a moment and closed my eyes, imagining a soft wind blowing against my face, wheels flying over the pavement …

Sighing, I got off the bike and, with a clean rag, rubbed a few smudges from the gleaming metal. I whispered, "Only a few more months, then we're free again."

Redfern's big-boy Gold Wing was parked near the Savage. It was so like him — solid, reliable, and built for endurance. I snorted at my flight of fancy and gave the Gold Wing a pat through the vinyl cover.

My dad's massive first-generation treadmill took up an entire corner of the garage. It faced a dated twenty-one-inch TV with the dusty remote sitting on top. To my surprise, the TV lit up without hesitation. Saggy couch, heater, TV, treadmill. This was Dad's retreat when Blyth had one of her hormonal teenage fits and chased me out of her room with manicure scissors. True story; she did it all the time.

I stepped onto the treadmill and pushed the start button. It creaked and jerked and emitted a smell like burning dust. Great, my nose was working again.

As the machine started, I poked at the up arrow and took off running.

The orange juice was almost gone, and most of the cheese puffs, when I heard the door from the kitchen open. Redfern plunked himself down on the couch. He could move quickly and quietly for a guy his size. He didn't mention my appearance, which boded well for his short-term survival.

He looked around and sniffed. "I smell hot electrical wiring. How long since that treadmill's been used?"

"Don't know. First time for me." I pressed the up arrow again and trotted faster. At least the snot production was slowing down. "How did you know I was in here?"

"Rae told me. She said you looked quite nostalgic and planned to eat a whole bag of cheese puffs."

I held up the bag and offered him the last one. He declined. "So, you actually talked to Rae. Wow."

"She warmed up her chicken stir-fry for me."

"Wow," I said again. "If you're looking for a girlfriend who cooks, cleans, and is skilled in the mechanics of sex, you could do worse."

"Funny. Other than the cooking, you do okay. Can we talk about something else?"

I thought about that for a minute. I took the last swig of juice. And the final cheese puff. "I got nothing else. What's on your mind?"

"You never told me you could shoot."

"You never asked. I haven't told you I can do back flips around the yard and hold a headstand for thirty minutes either."

"Now, that I can believe. Where's your target pistol now?"

I looked at him and turned my speed up another notch even though I was already panting. I pulled my sports bra out, then let it snap back against my dripping skin. "I didn't take it with me when I left the spousal home. The Weasel can't sell it without my signature, so unless he tossed it, he must still have it. Hey, isn't it illegal to store a gun for someone else?"

Redfern took out his notebook and wrote something in it. Good, maybe he could charge the Weasel for a gun violation. That would be fun for me.

"How long have you been on that treadmill?" He reached over and pressed the down arrow a bunch of times.

I looked at my watch. "About forty-five minutes. I feel like I could run forever, which is funny because I have this horrible, drippy head cold."

My pack of cold tablets had fallen out of the pocket of my robe. He picked it up and read the tiny print on the side of the box. "How many of these have you taken?"

"Two. Well, maybe six if you count the ones I took this morning and afternoon. I think I've finally dried up, though."

He waved the package in front of my nose. "These expired four years ago."

"That explains why I had to take so many. Hey, quit turning my speed down. I'm sweating the cold out of my system." Bloody hell. I was walking so slowly a turtle could have passed me.

He pressed stop and yanked me off the treadmill. "Put your robe on while I get you some water." He stuck my cold tablets in his pocket.

When he returned, he handed the water over at arm's length. I sprawled on the couch and waited while he turned over an empty plastic box and sat down three feet away near his Gold Wing.

"Do you know anyone who owns a pistol that chambers .32s?"

My heart was hammering in my ears, and my legs twitched like I was on amphetamines. "So, Sophie Quantz was shot with a .32? A .32 ACP?"

"Keep that to yourself, okay?"

"Of course. You know how discreet I am. Well, now, if you're looking for a gun that uses .32 ammo, you have your work cut out for you. Bruce County has thousands."

"I heard hundreds, but go on. Tell me about your personal experience with guns."

"I know zilch about modern guns. I used to go with my grandpa every Saturday to the target range at the club-house. He and his cronies brought the guns they liberated from the enemy during the war. They'd sit and clean them and hand them around for the other guys to admire. They told whoppers about how they acquired a particular weapon. They fed us kids chocolate bars and pop. It was great. That's how I know so much about old guns."

"What kinds, exactly?"

"Specifically, semi-automatic pistols that use .32 cali-bre cartridges. Well, the most common was the Mauser HSc. I remember four or five of them. My grandpa also had a Dreyse and a Sauer 38H. I really liked that little Sauer. Grandpa taught me to shoot with it."

"Those are all prohibited weapons."

"My goodness, who knew? But I'm not done. There were Lugers, a couple of Walthers, even an Astra. I think they took 9x19-millimetre Parabellum rounds, though." Actually, I *knew* they took 9x19s, but nobody likes a smarty-pants. I picked up the remote and turned up the volume.

Redfern pulled the remote out of my hand and

stared at the screen. "What the hell are you watching?"

"It's a *Duck Dynasty* marathon. See, these rednecks in Louisiana struck it rich with a duck call their father invented. His name is Phil and he's married to Miss Kay ..."

Redfern hit the off button. "Can you concentrate for a minute?" He had moved off his box and onto the old couch beside me. Either my knowledge of guns had impressed him, or my looks were improving.

"I thought I was."

"I'm trying to get my head around the fact that prohibited weapons may be scattered all over the county."

"There's no *may be* about it. You have no idea, and best you don't go poking around in attics or basements."

"Or garages." Redfern made a point of scanning his surroundings. Blue plastic tote boxes were stacked against one wall, piled three high, none labelled. A man's dream of a toolbox on wheels held a tantalizing selection of drawers that might open to reveal a screwdriver collection. Or guns. Cardboard file boxes held documents — or perhaps guns. A tall tarp-covered case in the back corner might harbour a cherished hockey stick collection — or four or five long guns, never registered or licensed.

"Where is your grandfather's gun collection now?"

I deliberately kept my eyes front. "Who knows? Am I still on your suspect list?"

"Tony tried removing you, but officially you're still on the list because you're one of the few grad students left in town. I don't think you killed anybody. Yet."

"You're too kind." I truly could not understand

the man's logic. I shouldn't even try. My fingers inched toward the remote.

He moved it out of my reach. "Who else attended these clubhouse meetings?"

"Uh, I'm not sure I remember." Fucked if I was going to rat anyone out. To give my hands something to do, I picked up a bottle of gun oil and opened it. I breathed in the tangy aroma.

Immediately, the smell transported me back more than twenty years to the clubhouse. I was nine again, sitting at the table with the old men while they gossiped and cleaned their guns. Grandpa sometimes let me hold one, but he had to help me. They weren't very heavy, unloaded, but cumbersome for little fingers. Grandpa told me repeatedly never to point a gun, even one I was sure wasn't loaded, at anyone.

Redfern nudged me. "Come on, Cornwall. I could use your help on this. Chances are good that the gun that killed Sophie Quantz was at that clubhouse. If we find her killer, we may solve Faith's murder, too."

I put the cap back on the gun oil. He was right. I had been hiding from the fact that someone I knew, and knew all my life, was a murderer.

"Did you just ask for my help, Redfern?"

"Are you going to make me pay for that scene in my office this afternoon?"

"What do you think? But first we find the killer."

He flinched at the "we," but nodded. "So, where is this clubhouse?"

"Back then, Lockport didn't have an official Canadian Legion branch, so the vets took over an old shed south of town and set up some tables, an old refrigerator, and an outhouse. That outhouse was scary. There were spiders as big as your head in there. The boys were lucky. They could just duck behind a tree."

"Right, Cornwall, boys have it made. We can pee on the ground or in a bottle if required. Is the building still there?"

"It is. It's now the Bruce County Regional Prohibited Weapon and Target Shooting Club. I hear they even installed an indoor toilet."

"You made up that name."

"Maybe, but it's something like that. The country club has a range, too. That's where I shot when I was married to the Weasel. My point is, a lot of people enjoy target shooting as a hobby around here. But I'm guessing you already know all this. You can't have been Chief of Police for three years without learning a thing or two about our culture."

He just smiled. "Right. Who were the other kids you played with at the clubhouse?"

I opened the gun oil and took another sniff. I felt like a traitor. "I remember Chico was there, so his grandfather must have been one of the old guys." I named a few other kids who were now long gone from Lockport, coming home to visit family once in a while.

"What about Fang's grandfather?"

"He wasn't one of the group. But seriously, Redfern, I'm sure Dogtown has an entire driving shed full of shotguns and hunting rifles. Hunting is a religion to them and, from what I've heard, they eat stuff they kill." That reminded me. I snatched the remote and turned it back on, but kept the volume off. I wanted to see if the Robertsons were eating squirrel for dinner. Or frogs, Jase's favourite food. "If you're going to Dogtown with a search warrant, better take your squad with you. If they don't shoot you, they'll keep you for breeding stock. I hear they're looking for tall blondes."

Redfern didn't look worried. He stood up and dropped his police-issue coat. It *was* warming up nicely in the garage. I wiggled out of my robe.

He ran his eyes up my sweaty togs. "Sexy. What did you do today?"

I shrugged. "The usual. Then I spoke to a potential new customer." That should cover me if he found out I visited Earl Archman. Should I risk telling Redfern that Earl inherited his great-uncle's Second World War weapons stash? Maybe, but I decided to wait. Should I confess to visiting with the Weasels again? Possibly, but not right away. I had to watch my mouth. For some reason, I was curiously chatty today.

He put his arm around my shoulders. "Who else attended these Saturday socials and taught their grandchildren about guns?"

"Well, the Weasel's grandfather. The Weasel never came, but his grandfather did."

"I suppose you were too young to remember what specific guns each man had?"

On the screen, Jase and Jep were pulling another prank on poor Willie. Dragging my attention back to Redfern, I replied, "Other than my grandfather, no. I was nine, for heaven's sake."

"When did you stop going with your grandfather to the clubhouse?"

"I only went for a year or so. I started f-bombing the other kids at school and pointing my trigger finger at them, so my parents wouldn't let me go anymore. Have you got anything to share with me?"

"Like my interviews with suspects? No."

I sighed. "That's what I figured. It's all one way with you, Redfern. You take and take, but you give nothing back."

"Are we still talking about the investigation? If the subject is more personal, I'd like a chance at rebuttal."

"I'm not up for another fight. It's been a long day and I think my UGGs are ruined."

He opened his mouth, then promptly closed it again. "That's that, then. Guess I'll be on my way. Back to my lonely cabin in the woods." He removed his arm and stood up.

"Don't let the bears bite."

I waited until I heard him drive away before switching off the TV and heater. I dragged a ten-foot ladder to the centre of the garage and propped it against the centre beam. I climbed to the second last step.

I reached over my head and searched around until my fingers touched a large black metal box. After Grandpa passed away, Dad set the box up here. I used to climb up and open it once in a while, just to feel close to my grandpa again. If it ever became my decision to make, I didn't know how I would dispose of them.

I climbed another step. The first gun I unwrapped was the Walther. I leaned over and put my nose close to it. I did the same to the other three — the Dreyse, the Sauer, and the Mauser. I picked up the Sauer and turned it in my hands, feeling the weight, remembering.

The guns weren't mine, so I should leave them where they were and forget about them for now. I wrapped the oil-stained cloth around the Sauer and put it back with the others.

My left foot rolled off the rung and I clutched at the beam to steady myself. My elbow dislodged an object resting about four feet from the gun box. It fell to the cement floor with a dull thud.

I clambered down the ladder and poked at the bundle with my toe. It was long, wrapped in a dirty blue towel, and secured with duct tape. It had missed my Savage's back fender by inches.

I found an old box cutter in the toolbox to cut through the duct tape, and unrolled the towel.

A dagger, about fifteen inches long, gleamed dully against the fabric. I brought it closer to my eyes and made out a tiny eagle and a string of worn letters and numbers, starting with a *W*. A groove ran along the flat edge of the wood handle. The handle was meant to slide into a rifle socket. I dropped it back onto the towel and leaned away.

It was a Second World War German bayonet. How the hell had Grandpa smuggled this back from Europe?

I sat on the cold cement floor for a few minutes, thinking. I tested the blade edges. Not sharp enough to cut on contact, and you'd have to poke someone pretty hard with the point to pierce the skin.

I wrapped the soiled towel around the bayonet, threw the cover over the bike, and switched off the garage lights.

In my bedroom, I shoved the bayonet under the bed. When I stood up, Rae was standing beside me, her arms filled with bottles of hair-dyeing chemicals.

CHAPTER
THIRTY-THREE

MY HEART RATE had slowed to *trip trip trip* from *boom boom boom*. It was a good thing Redfern had shut the treadmill off or I might still be draped over it, dead, my heart stopped by an overdose of cold medication. One piece of good news, though. My sinuses were completely clear, although my respiration was rapid and shallow, as they say in the ER where I would be had I taken one more of those tablets.

Rain beat at the windows and the refrigerator hummed in the kitchen. Somewhere a faucet dripped, one drop every five seconds. Who could sleep with all that noise? I punched my pillow and squinted at the digital clock. Already 2:48 a.m. In another five hours, the alarm would beep.

Should I get up and make a cup of herbal tea? Or decaffeinated coffee? And some cheese puffs? I felt like shit if I didn't get eight hours. An idea blossomed.

I could turn the alarm off, why the hell not? But first, I should turn off my phone so Dougal couldn't call and ask me why my ass wasn't at work. Screw him. Arm-twisting deadbeat customers could wait another day.

I rolled onto my side and reached for my cellphone, but froze when I heard a sound outside the window. I told myself it was a raccoon raiding my garbage can. The noise continued, followed by foot treads on the deck. Definitely too heavy for a coon.

Bear! The town bear was right outside my bedroom window. No point calling the police night dispatcher. He would recite the Ministry of Natural Resource's phone number and hang up. This wasn't good.

I slid off the bed and crept over to the window. I looked to the right and saw a shadow disappear around the corner toward the front of the house. I yanked my phone from the charger and raced down the hall, throwing open Rae's door. I jumped on her bed and shook her. "Rae! Get up. A bear is trying to get into the house. Wake up!"

"Go away, Bliss. Bears are in hibernation. Go back to sleep." She turned over and pressed her pillow over her head.

I bounced up and down on my knees. "I'm telling you, a bear is casing the house, trying to find a way in. Get up. You might have to chase it away."

Rae pulled on a robe and followed me into the living room, complaining with every step. I had left the drapes open, but the streetlights allowed very little illumination into the house. All was silent outside. Still, the hair on my arms stood up and my hyper-vigilant brain sensed human, not animal presence. Someone was lurking outside....

I jumped away from the window. A framed print fell to the floor with a crash as I flattened myself against the narrow wall between the big picture window and the door. My phone fell and skittered off into the shadows. Rae clutched my arm and I shook her off. "Run back to your room and call 911. We have a two-legged intruder."

Usually I lock my doors, but tonight — over-medicated and stupid — I hadn't. The sound of the knob turning almost stopped my heart. Fucking hell! I needed a weapon and there wasn't as much as a vase within reach. The door opened an inch and I threw my weight against it. As it slammed shut, I turned the lock.

I ran to the front window and looked around the drapes. A shape darker than the night stood on the flag-stone walkway. Damn! I needed to turn on the outside lights. I pulled my head back and reached out to feel for the light switch beside the door. An explosion shattered the window, right where my head had been a second ago. Shards of glass shot across the hardwood floor. I collapsed and rolled into a ball, hands over my ears. I knew a gunshot when I heard one.

When no second blast came, I scampered on all fours across the living room, oblivious to the fragments of glass cutting into my hands, knees, and toes. In my bedroom, I ran into Rae's legs. I dove under my bed and dragged out Grandpa's bayonet. We locked ourselves in my ensuite and waited for the cops.

Ten minutes after Rae's call to report an intruder,

two cruisers blocked both ends of the street while a third parked on the sidewalk in front of my house: pretty good response time for the middle of the night. Flashing lights allowed the nosy neighbours to watch one officer busily run yellow tape over and around trees and bushes.

Inside, Bernie and Dwayne hovered over Rae, ostensibly taking her statement, but in my opinion it was just a ruse to get close to the shapely young blonde. Rae had her bunny slippers on to protect her feet from the glass-strewn floor. She clutched her pink, fuzzy robe tightly to her throat.

Nobody took my statement or seemed to care that it was my head that almost got blown off. I dabbed at the cuts on my feet and knees and wrapped paper towels around my bleeding hands. Thea took pictures of the shot-out window, stopping to make an occasional entry in her notebook. She frowned in concentration and ignored me as diligently as the men.

"You guys should look on the front stoop for a shell casing," I volunteered.

She gave me a cool, professional smile. "Thanks, we got this."

"The perp touched the door handle on the outside. He probably wore gloves but you should dust for fingerprints just in case he didn't."

"We did. Thanks, though."

"Doesn't anybody want to hear what happened? Shouldn't somebody be making me a cup of tea or driving me to the ER to get the glass picked out of my skin?"

"The Chief wants to inter— question you himself.

He'll be along any minute."

"Really? Well, guess I'll go make some coffee or something. Or, I know, I'll just stab myself with a fork, how's that?" No one paid any attention to me as I went to my bedroom and pushed the bayonet farther under the bed. I didn't want to sidetrack Redfern with unrelated details.

I pulled the curtains completely closed and made my bed neatly. I dressed in loose track pants that were cheap to replace if I bled to death on them. The area around my eyes was almost back to normal and it took minimal makeup to create a face that looked like it had had eight hours sleep instead of nada. I rewrapped my hands in toilet paper. Somehow my fingertips had escaped shredding.

I plunked down on my bed to wait for the big chief. It didn't take a genius, or a cop, to figure out that someone wanted me dead. Had I struck a nerve with the person who killed Faith and Sophie? Redfern was going to deduce that I had poked the wrong alligator in my quest to unearth the truth. Although, he wouldn't put it that way. *Meddling* would be his verb of choice. I tried to quell the tremors that wracked my body.

It didn't seem fair that I had been shot at and still didn't have a frigging clue why, or who the bad guy was. And where the hell was my phone? I wanted to text my parents. This time I would tell them what a horrible time I was going through. Maybe they would invite me to visit them in their hippie haven on Vancouver Island. Man, I'd be on the next plane out of Pearson Airport in Toronto.

I wrapped myself in an afghan and tried to cry. A

good restorative howl would do me good. But fuck it! I never was much for the waterworks. I reached for the TV remote. Maybe the Shopping Channel had something I needed.

I rocked back and forth in the middle of the bed, my fingers feverishly punching the buttons on the remote.

CHAPTER
THIRTY-FOUR

IT SEEMED NEIL was asleep for mere minutes when the night dispatcher called. Cornwall's front window had been shot out. No injuries were reported, and the entire night shift had already been dispatched to the scene, along with the on-call SOCOs.

Neil immediately contacted off-duty staff and sent them to the Davidson, Leeds, Brickle, and Quantz residences. Tony took the Bainses and Neil reserved Earl Archman for himself.

Archman answered his door wearing a tent-like bathrobe, his thick brown hair hanging like wiry strips of rope. Winter boots stood on a rubber tray by the door and several coats hung on a hook. None showed signs of the rain that continued to fall unabated. Archman seemed appropriately disoriented, and when Neil told him why he was there, the man turned a disturbing shade of purple. Neil helped him to his recliner and located the asthma inhaler. With the man's permission, he ran upstairs and took a quick glance at the unmade bed and discarded clothing. The pant hems were dry.

In the living room, Archman's skin colour had faded to his normal greyish-white. Neil suggested he not open his door to anyone other than the police, keep his drapes closed, and call if he noticed anything suspicious.

As Neil was climbing back into his car, dispatch reported that no one was answering the door at the St. Paul's manse. Kelly Quantz was either passed out inside or not there at all. Neil ordered an Alert out on the man and asked for a warrant to be initiated to enter the residence.

On Cornwall's front lawn, a constable handed Neil a plastic evidence bag containing a shell casing. He reported they had found footprints around the back, side, and front of the house and were attempting to take casts, but the rain filled the depressions and blurred the edges. They would keep trying, but photographs might be all they could salvage. No prints on the front door handle.

Inside the house, the collection team was finishing up. A bullet had been dug out of the wall facing the front window. The intruder hadn't gained access to the house, so taking fingerprints was unnecessary.

To the east, the sky brightened almost imperceptibly. Neil dismissed everyone except Bernie. The sounds of clattering china came from the kitchen.

"Miss Zaborsky is making tea for Bliss," Bernie explained.

"Stay in the house with them until you're relieved. I'll send someone from day shift as soon as possible. Now, where is Ms. Cornwall?"

Bernie pointed down the hall. "In her bedroom."

"When the stores open, will you contact someone to replace the window? Thanks, Bernie."

He had to stop himself from running down the hall. He threw the door open without knocking first. When he saw Cornwall rocking in the middle of her bed with a green knitted blanket wrapped around her body, he nearly lost it.

Neil shut the door and with two steps he dropped to the floor beside her and pulled her into his arms. She started to cry. Her body shook, and he held her tighter. She stopped crying and squeaked. He realized he was squeezing too tightly and eased off.

"Where were you?" Her voice rose, but at least the tears had stopped. "I needed you."

"I'm sorry. I had to ensure our suspects were paid an official visit as soon as possible. Once I knew you weren't hurt, I made a call myself."

"Apology accepted." She forced a smile. "So, who did you see?"

Neil took a closer look at her hands and feet. Bloody lengths of toilet paper trailed from her fingers. "Are you in much pain? Why didn't you tell Thea?"

"She was busy with cop stuff. They're only scratches."

Neil searched through her medicine cabinet in the ensuite. "Where's your first aid-stuff?"

"Under the sink."

He had to rummage behind an assortment of feminine-hygiene products and hair rollers before he found the right container. While he applied antibiotic ointment and Band-Aids to her cuts, he tried to sound offhand as he asked, "Where were you standing when the window was blown out?"

"Right in front of it. If I hadn't moved to turn on the outside lights, my brains would be splattered all over the room." Her bottom lip trembled and she bit down on it. Tears pooled in her eyes again.

There was a soft rap on the door. Rae stood on the other side, a tray balanced in one arm. Neil took it from her and shoved the door closed with his foot. He poured tea into a cup and added some milk before holding the cup to her lips. He noticed her hair was different again. This time there were only a couple of colours in the mix.

She took a slurp of tea, choked, and spat it out over the front of his shirt. "Shit. Hot. Sorry." Her little hand reached out to wipe the tea off his chest.

He gently covered her hand with his. "Don't get your Band-Aids wet."

"You never told me which suspect you visited. Is it me? Am I being interrogated without counsel?" Her mouth turned up at the corners.

Thank God the shock was wearing off. He wrapped her a little tighter in the blanket and held the cooling tea to her lips again. "Careful. Just a sip. I sent teams to talk to Davidson, Leeds, Brickle, and Quantz. Tony is interviewing the Bainses."

"I hope Tony gets out alive. So, by process of elimination, you must have gone to Earl Archman's house. By yourself?"

An expression he had seen before flitted across her face. What was it? "Why not by myself? I'm a big boy." Guilt. That was it. She had been up to something. Wasn't it just yesterday that he told her to stay out of the investigation? Did she ...?

"You talked to Earl Archman, didn't you?"

"I told you last night that I spoke to a potential new client."

Neil closed his eyes, trying to calm himself. No way in *hell* would Cornwall ever stay out of police business if she decided she had something to contribute. Either he had to accept her relentless interference, or one of them had to leave town.

He opened his eyes to find her watching him with a calculated expression on her face. "Well, got something to say, Cornwall?"

"I guess. But tell me this first. Did Thea dig a .32 calibre slug out of my wall?"

"We found a bullet, but we don't know what it is yet. We also found a casing outside your living room window, a small one."

She inspected her fingernails, painted a dark blue, but chipped and ragged now. "Earl may have divulged that he has some Second World War pistols, from his great-uncle, I think he said."

"Why didn't you tell me this immediately?" This should be good. Her stories always were.

"Well, he asked me not to. I didn't like to break a confidence."

"Really, Cornwall? I understand you've been through an ordeal, but I expected a better excuse from you. This one is hardly up to your standard."

Her eyes sparked fire and she threw back the blanket revealing an orange sweatshirt with the words "No,

I'm Not Deaf, I'm Ignoring You" stamped across the front. Inexplicably, she had managed to put makeup on. Her lips glistened with pink gloss. Hopping off the bed, she put her wrists on her hips and leaned toward him. "I guess you've used up your weekly quota of sympathy. Let me know when you get another delivery and I'll be sure to invite you over."

"Don't take that tone with me, Cornwall. You screwed up again and you know it. You should have told me right away about Archman's guns. What if he shot me? How would you feel about betraying a confidence then?"

Shit, now he'd done it. She threw herself back on the bed. Her body shuddered as she buried her face in a pillow. He didn't know whether to administer an official reprimand or take her into his arms again.

Before he could reach for her, she whirled around, leaped up, and threw her arms around his neck. "I'm so, so sorry, Redfern. I could have sent you into a fatal trap. I'm pretty sure all your suspects have souvenir pistols or hunting guns, but I should have told you about Earl's guns anyway."

Neil pulled her in closer and pressed her head against his chest. This was the first time she had ever apologized to him. She could have been killed tonight. And that would have destroyed him. He couldn't take another loss in his life.

When she raised her head and looked at him, he bent and placed his lips on hers. His phone emitted its text ring. He took it out of his pocket. It was Bernie from the living room:

Need to speak.

Neil wiped Cornwall's lip gloss off his mouth before leaving the room. She followed him.

Bernie gestured him into a corner, away from Cornwall. "Dispatch got a call from one of the Dogtown Davidsons. He was driving on a side road bordering Ghost Swamp. Saw something on the shoulder. Thought it might be roadkill, but it wasn't."

As was often the case, Neil wanted to throttle Bernie. "What was it?"

"Body ..." He paused. "Of a man."

If Bernie asked "Guess whose body it is?" Neil wouldn't be able to control himself.

Bernie skipped that step. "It's Kelly Quantz. Shot through the head."

CHAPTER
THIRTY-FIVE

KELLY QUANTZ'S BODY lay crumpled on the muddy shoulder of Sideroad 15. The cold rain fell into his wide-open eyes and had washed clean the small hole in his forehead. Poor, stupid bastard.

The passenger-side tires of an old Dodge truck settled into the mud forty metres in front of the body. Someone was running the plates, but Neil recalled seeing the truck in the manse driveway when he interviewed Quantz. Dwayne Rundell and Margo Philmore searched the steep bank leading down to the edge of an adjacent swamp. All he could see were their heads and hear an occasional obscenity when one of them got a soaker from the icy, stagnant water.

He had already sent two officers to St. Paul's manse to secure the premises and conduct a search. Something in the house might suggest a reason for Quantz's presence on this county back road.

He sniffed. "God, that reeks. What is that?" He'd

come across a week-old corpse once in a derelict rooming house, and this was similar. But Quantz hadn't been lying by the side of the road for more than a few hours, or one of the Davidsons would have spotted him before now. According to Lester Davidson, who had found the body, Dogtown residents used Sideroad 15 regularly to access the highway.

Thea pulled her mask down long enough to reply, "Stagnant water, rotting vegetation, maybe a dead animal or two — just your usual swamp stink."

Tony balanced precariously against the side of the 4 X 4 while donning shoe coverings. "Guess we're just a couple of city boys, dude."

"You're late again," Neil said. "My SOCOs are almost finished here."

"The party ain't over 'til I say it's over." Tony pulled his hood up. "I don't see any other tire tracks along here. Think he offed himself?"

"He's been despondent since his wife's death, and drinking heavily. But from here I can see the bullet hole in his forehead and no gun in the vicinity. So, I'd say it's another homicide."

"Agreed." Tony trudged over to the body and squatted to speak to Ed Reiner, who was on his knees in the mud.

Ed had beat Neil to the scene and had scarcely looked up from the body. He turned the head to one side and looked under the sodden clothing. The hands were bagged to preserve any evidence of defensive wounds or material under the nails. Now, Tony helped him roll the body over onto a piece of heavy plastic to avoid contaminating the front of the body by contact with the gravel. The coroner parted the hair and fingered the scalp of the dead man.

The text tone on Neil's phone sounded. Cornwall.

WH DD? BRN WNT SY

It took him a minute. He hesitated before replying:

LATER

Good for Bernie, but it was only a matter of time before somebody called Cornwall or Rae with the news that would be all over town soon.

He called Bernie. "Sorry I can't send anyone to relieve you for a while yet. Are you okay with some overtime?" Bernie was always okay with overtime, especially if he didn't have to stand around in the cold. Or heat, or when Detroit was playing Edmonton, or when it was a fine day for golfing.

"No problem." Bernie's voice lowered to a whisper. "Although Bliss keeps threatening to leave the house claiming unlawful confinement, individual rights, and we can just kiss her ass, you know…"

"Tell her to stay put, or you will, on my instructions, place her in protective custody — in a cell. She can pick which one. Keep her in your sight at all times, Bernie. Someone tried to kill her once, and we have to assume he'll try again."

"I'll do my best."

Thea waved a small plastic bag in front of him. "Cartridge casing. Looks like a .32 calibre, same as the one from the church, and the one we found on Bliss's front lawn earlier."

"Let's see if the perp was careless and left us a print

this time," Neil said. The rain stung his face and the temperature was plummeting. In a few hours, this crime scene could be knee deep in snow.

"Any footprints?"

"Nope. The shooter must have stood on the pavement." Thea stowed the casing in her evidence bag. "All we got is a body and a casing. I printed the inside of the truck and I'll look for hair and fibres, but unless the perp sat inside with Quantz, I doubt we'll find anything useful."

Ed tossed a tarp over the body and plodded over to Neil. "Why can't we have one of those portable tents to cover the scene like they have on crime shows? So I could examine the body without freezing my balls off."

"If I'd known we were going to have a crime wave, Ed, I'd have requisitioned one for you. Notice anything odd from your cursory inspection?"

"The bullet went through his forehead an inch above the left eyebrow. Sound familiar? Except Reverend Quantz fell from the choir loft after she was shot, while her husband merely dropped in his tracks."

Ed stripped off his gear and threw it into a plastic-lined container. "Again, the bullet is still inside the cranium. No stippling around the wound, meaning another distance shot."

"A good marksman. But that doesn't point to any suspect in particular. They all belong, or belonged, to gun clubs. Except Fang Davidson. And I'm sure he learned to shoot before he started kindergarten." He was policing a town of "fuck the gun laws" dissidents. Neil asked the obvious question. "Any ideas about time of death?"

"What? You think this is an episode of *CSI*?" Ed looked at his watch. "Lividity is well-established. I can tell you he wasn't moved, or wasn't moved far, after death. Rigor mortis isn't complete. Although a liver temperature is unreliable in this cold weather, I'm guessing Mr. Quantz has been dead between eight and ten hours."

Neil looked at his watch: 9:47 a.m. "So, somewhere between midnight last night and 2:00 a.m." Rae Zaborski's 911 call had been logged at 3:02 a.m. It appeared Quantz was killed first, then the perp drove back to town and tried to kill Cornwall. The killer was either getting desperate or cocky.

He said to Ed, "Lester Davidson was the last to return to Dogtown last night. He returned around 11:00 p.m. and closed the compound gate. His route brought him down this side road, but he didn't see a truck or a body."

"Death occurred no earlier than midnight." Ed pulled his black toque over his ears and used the end of his scarf to swipe at the steam on his glasses.

"We're done here," Tony called. "Okay for the EMTs to take the body now?"

Neil looked at Ed, who nodded and remarked, "I hope we don't see any more of these for a while."

"That makes two of us." Neil lifted the crime scene tape to allow the EMTs access to the body.

A shout from the ditch turned all heads. Dwayne clambered up the bank, swinging an object from the end of a stick. But his feet failed to find solid ground on the slippery shoulder and he flung his prize at the road before sliding back downhill, disappearing from sight.

The object skipped across the slick surface and stopped within a metre of Neil's boots.

It was a pistol. An old one.

"It's the fucking murder weapon!" Tony grabbed Thea and swung her off her feet. He dropped her when she elbowed him in the neck. "Sorry, babe. Forgot myself."

"We *hope* it's the murder weapon," Neil cautioned.

Thea unpacked the Nikon, and Neil took a few photos with his phone. Even the EMTs abandoned Kelly Quantz's body to join the cops and coroner regarding the pistol with satisfaction and something like wonder.

"Can this be it?" Ed queried. "With all the muck and sludge, this is a lucky find."

"Fuck!" Neil rubbed the back of his neck. "Quantz died around midnight, several hours before Ms. Cornwall was attacked. So, unless the perp killed Quantz, drove to town, tried to shoot Cornwall, then drove back here to drop the gun in the ditch, we have a second gun in play."

"Yeah, but why?" Tony's initial excitement had waned. "Why not shoot Quantz, then shoot Cornwall — sorry, man," he looked apologetically at Neil, "— with the same gun, then get rid of it?"

"It doesn't make sense," Neil agreed. He turned to Thea. "Bag it up, and run prints when you get it out of the rain. And check the gun registry. Chances are slim it's registered, but worth a look. Good job, Dwayne."

He looked around. Where was Dwayne?

Two filthy, dripping arms appeared over the crest of the ditch. Dwayne's mud-covered head followed. "Yeah, thanks for your help, everybody. Appreciate your concern. I'll need a tetanus shot after that swamp bath."

Neil said to no one in particular, "Don't let him get into one of our cars without spreading a tarp first."

He turned and headed for his Cherokee. "My presence is requested at a Police Services Board meeting this evening." He smiled at Tony without humour. "And so is yours, pal."

CHAPTER
THIRTY-SIX

The battle of the board game raged on the coffee table. Maybe "raged" was an overstatement. Bernie was *the* slowest Scrabble player on planet Earth, but if I didn't get some good tiles soon, he would win his third straight game. To accommodate Scrabble novice Rae, we had agreed to bend the rules and allow proper nouns. But it was Bernie who had just spelled out *Zamboni* and happily taken the 50-point bonus.

While Rae pondered her rack intently, a text came in from Dougal.

ARE YOU OK?

Like he ever cared before.

FNE. SHKN & FW CTS

Unlike Redfern, Dougal understood my texts perfectly.

GOOD. THEN GET YOUR ASS OVER TO MY HOUSE

I tossed my phone on the couch. Telling Dougal to

fuck off would be a waste of time. He considered it a term of endearment.

Rae nibbled her lip and scrunched up her nose. She had overrun her sixty-second time limit, but Bernie seemed in no hurry to point this out to her, so I headed for the kitchen. It was noon; time for some refreshment. The cheese puffs were long gone, as were the potato chips, and blue tortilla chips. If I was going to be held hostage much longer, somebody was going to have to bring in provisions.

I came back with a can of ginger ale, two wine glasses, and a bottle of red. I tossed a bag of baby carrots at Rae so she could stop chewing her own lip. Bernie eyed the wine with his big, sad eyes, but I handed him the pop. I didn't want his aim thrown off by alcohol if another attempt was made on my life. I could probably shoot straighter than him, but he had the gun and was paid to protect me.

My phone beeped. Another text from Dougal:
WHAT ABOUT RAE? I NEED SOMEBODY!!!
I called him. "What is your problem?"
"I need either you or Rae to come to my house."
"Why?"
His voice was so low I could barely make out his words. "It's complicated."
"I'm going to hang up."
"No, don't! Okay. It's Glory. She came over with Pan and is telling me personal things about her and Pinato."
"Really? You mean, like really personal? As in what they do in bed?"

Bernie and Rae stopped contemplating the board and stared at me. I walked over to the window. The broken part was covered with cardboard and a cold wind rattled through the cracks.

Dougal breathed heavily into his phone. "No, that I could stand. Barely. She wants to talk about *feelings*. Apparently it's my fault she couldn't open up during our marriage, and she wants me to understand how different things are with the Italian stallion. He's making a new woman of her."

"What's wrong with that? You were a crashing failure of a husband, everyone knows that. Why's she bringing all that up now?"

"I'm not interested in her reasons. I have a deadline coming up and can't listen to her yammer any more. One of you needs to get over here and take her away."

"Glory speaks fluent French, doesn't she? Maybe she can come up with phrases for your new novel. No. Wait, I know. Write a sex scene and ask her to transcribe it into French. That should keep her mind off her feelings."

There was silence for a few seconds, and I took the opportunity to pour myself another glass of wine. Then, he found his voice. "Does that mean you're not coming over? What about Rae?"

I hung up on him. If I parted with Rae, I'd have to feed Bernie. That would mean cooking. I glanced out the unbroken section of the window. Bernie looked up from the board and drawled, "Step away from the window."

"There's a truck in the driveway. Moffitt Glass."

A knock on the door threw Bernie into guard-dog mode. Gun in hand, he peered through the peephole.

Satisfied last night's gunman hadn't returned to finish me off, he let in two young men. According to the name tags on their coats, one was Brad, and the other was Ivan.

With dubious glances at Bernie's gun and dishevelled uniform, and the food scraps from our long morning's Scrabble games, Brad and Ivan set to work measuring the broken panes.

While they busied themselves, I set my glass aside, and closed my eyes. I must have dozed off. When I opened them again, the front window was intact, Brad and Ivan were gone, and Thea sat in Bernie's place. I smelled cheese.

Thea got up and pulled the drapes across the window to close off the darkening afternoon. I picked up my cell to check my phone messages. Twelve messages, two from Dougal, begging for help. Glory had already consumed one full bottle of his best Riesling and was hinting about a second. Pan had made himself coffee and broken out the potato chips. It looked like they were going to make an evening of it. Worse, Glory had stopped referring to him as "the worm" and showed signs of nostalgia, dredging up horrible (according to him) memories of their honeymoon. Pan sat in a chair behind Glory and rolled his eyes at every intimate detail. Would somebody help him?

Not me. The other ten messages were in response to an email blitz I had launched earlier in the day requesting information on the latest shooting victim. They confirmed that Kelly Quantz was the unlucky winner.

And then there were five — me, Chico, Fang, the

Weasel, and Mr. Archman. Six if you counted Mrs. Brickle. When my head stopped spinning from the possibilities, I was left with the usual impasse. I didn't for a second consider Mrs. Brickle a suspect. Fang and Chico were out of the question, too. And it couldn't be the Weasel, for all his weasely qualities. I had been married to him for eight years. I would have known if he was capable of homicide. And Mr. Archman? Three hundred pounds of gasping, lumbering sarcasm, waving a gun in one hand and an inhaler in the other, running through the streets, evading police? I couldn't fathom it.

That left me. There was no other possibility. I was the killer.

The hell with it. I vowed to leave the whole investigative mess for Redfern and Tony to figure out. Rae brought in plates of homemade macaroni and cheese, with mushrooms, spinach, and red peppers mixed in. I poured another glass of wine, ignoring Thea's frown of disapproval. What? People in the witness protection program weren't allowed alcohol?

"So, why are you on guard duty?" I asked her. "Weren't you working the crime scene this morning?"

"I was. The evidence is on its way to Toronto, and my report is done. There was nobody else available, and the Chief is worried about you. So, here I am." She looked exhausted and not thrilled with her present lot in life.

"Did you find a .32 calibre shell casing at the scene?"

"You know I can't tell you anything about that, Moonbeam. You'll find out the same time the details are released to the public."

"Right you are, Constable. Who's going to be on

night duty?" If it was Dwayne, I'd just save everyone a heap of trouble and shoot myself.

"The Chief. After the emergency Police Services Board meeting tonight, he's going to swing by his cabin and pick up some clothes, then bunk in here with you till we find the killer ..."

"Uh?"

"... so I suggest you lay off the wine and take a bubble bath. You look like you've been on a three-day bender. Maybe you could brush your hair for a start."

"Did you say there was a Police Services Board meeting? Tonight? It's Saturday."

"I said it was an emergency meeting. And don't bother to ask what it's about. I don't know. The mayor called it. Sergeant Pinato is attending, too."

Oh boy. While I was in confessing mode with Redfern, I should have told him I went to the Weasel's law office yesterday and really pissed him and the missus off. I picked at the Band-Aids on my hands and thought furiously. Was Redfern being called on the carpet? If so, it was my fault. Well, not *totally* my fault. I had been under the influence of outdated cold medication. That was the truth. But it wasn't enough. I was a selfish bitch, and my actions could cost Redfern his job.

I poured more wine into my glass. Thea reached over and took the bottle away. Ha. The joke was on her. The bottle was empty. There was something Glory said, about a contract. Yeah, they couldn't get rid of Redfern until his contract was up. Then, they could choose not to renew it. I wasn't going to let that happen. The solution was obvious. Somehow I had to get rid of the Weasel before he could get rid of Redfern.

Okay then, I had a goal. Now, I just had to formulate a plan to accomplish that goal. Stick with what you know, that was always a good start. I had used blackmail successfully last summer to squeeze my share of our marital assets out of the Weasel. Perfect. Blackmail was on the table.

I smiled at Thea and Rae. "Okay, girlfriends, let's party down. Rae, fetch your nail polish collection. We're going to paint our toes and giggle until it hurts."

CHAPTER
THIRTY-SEVEN

NEIL WOLFED DOWN a cheeseburger at the Mason Jar, then returned to his office to sift through the photos and reports from the second Quantz murder investigation. A message from Ed reiterated that he couldn't narrow the time of death further. Midnight to 2:00 a.m. this morning. The body had been transferred to London for autopsy.

After leaving the crime scene, Tony had gone to St. Paul's manse to assist the officers already there. They were searching through the dead man's effects. Neil had checked in with them several times, but nothing of importance had been found.

He looked at the old schoolroom clock hanging on the wall beside the door. Half an hour until the start of the board meeting. It wasn't unusual for a mayor to call a meeting with the police chief to update the board during a serious investigation. The difficult part would be preventing the suspicion and dislike he felt for Mike

Bains from showing. Tony would make a good buffer, if he showed up.

He called Tony's cell.

His friend answered on the first ring with a gruff "What's up?" After listening, he said, "Are you afraid I'm not going to make it in time to hold your hand at the meeting?"

"Something like that. We have twenty minutes until showtime. Get your lazy ass over here."

"If you insist. I wouldn't pass up a chance to see my sweetie being cute and official.... And I don't mean you."

"Quit fucking around, Tony. What's your ETA?"

"How about now?" He walked through the door and threw his coat at the rack. He stuffed his phone into his pocket and tried to smooth down his unruly black hair. "I have something special for my comrade-in-arms. We found it in Mr. Quantz's lair, less than an hour ago. I wanted to surprise you."

Neil's exhaustion lifted. "Better make it quick. Ten minutes and counting."

"I knew I'd see this lady again." Tony slapped a large baggie on the desk. Inside was Quantz's drawing of the squirrel-girl with the huge hooters. What was her name? Amandaline? Almandine? He turned it over.

A sentence had been written and scratched out. A second sentence had a line drawn through it, but it was still legible: "You have to pay for what you did to Faith and Sophie."

Neil looked up and saw the excitement in Tony's face. "Quantz knew who killed his wife and Faith Davidson. Sophie must have told him who she was meeting at the church. He tried to blackmail the perp, and got a bullet for his efforts."

Tony nodded. "The fucker burned some paper in his wastebasket, most likely his practice pages, but we found this one under his ratty chair. Wonder what made him try it?"

"After it hit home that he had to leave the manse with no resources and no means of supporting himself, he must have resorted to blackmail."

Tony flipped the baggie over to stare at Almandine. "We didn't find a cellphone on his body or in his house. I'm guessing the perp either took it or threw it into the swamp with the gun. Just his bad luck the gun fell short. It'll take time to get Quantz's phone and email records, but considering this practice blackmail note, he either mailed his demand or dropped it off."

"In his desperate state, I can't see him waiting four, five days for the Royal Snail to deliver it. I'm betting he delivered it personally, left it in a mailbox maybe." Neil swept the bagged blackmail note into his desk drawer and locked it.

He said to Tony, "I've got some news for you, too. Thea lifted a partial thumbprint from the barrel of the Mauser. The rest was wiped clean. Might be the break we need."

"Best news I've heard since I landed in Crazytown. Now, all you need is the thumb to match."

"Let's go. The meeting was supposed to start five minutes ago."

Tony rose slowly and made no attempt to straighten his rumpled uniform. "So, we're fashionably late." He reached for his coat. "Where's the town hall in this village of the damned?"

"Follow me. The Municipal Chambers are up one flight and along a dingy hall."

Their boots clattered up the wooden staircase, and the sound echoed through the empty corridors. They passed darkened rooms and paused before a closed door. A strip of light shone on the linoleum floor at their feet.

"Shit. What happened? Did your real town hall burn down? This is a dump." Tony put his hand on Neil's arm to delay him. "Are you going to mention the latest victim's blackmail scheme?"

"Nope. Bains is still a suspect. We're not telling him anything we wouldn't say to a newspaper reporter."

The Bainses, Glory Yates, and Bert Thiessen had taken seats facing the door. Glory had left an empty chair between herself and the other three. Neil and Tony sat down side by side with the old wooden conference table separating them from the board members.

Andrea Bains looked at her watch. Tony smiled at her politely while Neil ignored her gesture.

The mayor said, "I call this meeting to order. Let's get down to business so we can all get out of here and go home. It *is* Saturday." Bains tapped his manicured fingers on a thin folder lying on the table in front of him.

Tony leaned back slightly and crossed his arms. Neil waited quietly and set his expression to neutral. His eyes scanned three of the faces across the table, dismissing Bert Thiesson from the upcoming discussion. This was a situation that could implode or fizzle. The previous mayor had hired Neil, or he wouldn't be sitting here now. Even before he met Cornwall, he had heard rumours of how ruthless Mike Bains could be.

The board could only fire him now if they had cause. Neil remembered Earl Archman telling him that Bains was a sociopath. The restrained rage in the man's eyes reinforced in Neil's mind that he must tread very carefully here tonight.

"We've had two murders in this town in the space of a week. Chief Redfern, I have yet to receive a report from you regarding progress on the investigations. It shouldn't be necessary for me to call a special meeting to learn the facts that you and our OPP investigator have uncovered, but in the absence of your courtesy — and responsibility — in this matter, here we are."

"Is there any coffee?" Bert opened the Timmy's bag in front of him and pulled out a bagel. He leaned forward and looked across the Bainses at Glory. "How about it, dearie? Where's the coffee?"

Glory put her fingers to her temples as though she had a headache. "There's no coffee, Bert. Please, just pay attention to the discussion."

Neil had been concerned about having Glory and Tony in the same room during a professional discussion. So far, they had avoided eye contact with each other and kept their hormonal surges under control. He didn't think the Bainses were aware of the sizzling relationship between their fellow board member and the OPP investigator, and he didn't want them to figure it out tonight.

"With all due respect, Mr. Mayor, if I spent time at my computer, typing up preliminary reports for you, who would be assisting our OPP liaison investigator with our murder inquiries? As you know, a town this size should have two investigators on the payroll. We have none."

Andrea Bains refused to be distracted. She fingered the plain gold chain around her neck. "Perhaps, Chief Redfern, your personal relationships are interfering with your duties."

Here we go. Neil sensed Tony stirring beside him and shot him a warning glance. "What relationships would you be referring to, Mrs. Bains?"

A pair of glasses lay on the table in front of Andrea. She put them on and peered at him as if he were a specimen under a microscope. "To start with, it has come to our attention that you and Sergeant Pinato are personal friends. It may be advantageous if we had someone more ... well, shall we say, more impartial, to lead the investigations. We have no choice but to request alternate and additional resources from the OPP."

Neil and Tony glanced at each other and smiled.

"And," she continued, "I dislike mentioning this, Chief Redfern, but we also have to consider your relationship with Bliss Cornwall ..."

Tony interrupted. "Bliss *Moonbeam* Cornwall."

Andrea drew back and stared across the table as though the chair had spoken out of turn. "She has been interfering with these investigations, and you, Chief Redfern, have allowed it to continue. She even accused my husband of murder."

Bains nodded approval at this wife's summation. "As a courtesy, we want to officially inform you of our decision to contact the OPP and request a replacement for Sergeant Pinato."

There was that word *courtesy* again. Neil had had enough of this crap. Before he could fire off a response, Glory beat him to it.

"Just a minute, Mr. Mayor. You told me you were calling this meeting so the board could ask the chief and Sergeant Pinato to update us about the deaths. There has been no prior discussion about the other matters Mrs. Bains has raised tonight. I believe you are both out of order."

"What's going on?" Bert asked, shaking his empty bag. "Did I miss a vote?"

Neil stood up. "I agree with Ms. Yates. Let's all calm down and discuss these murders."

He stared down at Bains. "You mentioned two murders? We have three. Don't forget Faith Davidson. The discovery of her remains is connected with the two more recent murders. Bliss Cornwall was present at the grad party and was one of the last people to see Faith before she disappeared. As were you, Mayor Bains. Ms. Cornwall knows all the suspects, as do you. If you believe I have been sharing confidential information with her, then by all means report me to the relevant authorities. Don't forget to explain that, since you are one of the suspects, I felt it prudent not to share all aspects of this ongoing investigation with you."

Bains clenched his fists on top of the folder, and his mottled complexion left no doubt how he viewed Neil's comment. Andrea patted her husband's arm, but he jerked away from her touch.

Neil put his hands on the table and leaned forward. "Just to make myself clear — you, Mr. Mayor, are a suspect in three homicides, and that status trumps any updates you feel you are privy to as head of the Police Services Board."

He walked over to stand beside the door, arms folded.

Tony got to his feet. He slid a card across the table to the mayor. "Here's my boss's contact information. Feel free to call him if you want to lodge a complaint about me, or ask for a replacement. Good luck with that."

He turned his attention to Andrea Bains. "Madam, Chief Redfern and I have worked several investigations together. During that time, we have developed a bond. If you can prove this murder investigation has been negatively affected by our relationship, then you, too, are welcome to call my boss."

In the doorway, he turned. His glance swept over the mayor and his wife. "As far as I'm concerned, my part in this witch hunt is over."

Glory pulled her eyes away from Tony and pushed her chair back. "I propose we adjourn this meeting. There won't be a vote taken here tonight." She hurried out of the room, closely followed by Neil and Tony.

Neil closed the door without looking back.

CHAPTER
THIRTY-EIGHT

"YOU KNOW RAE is here, right? She's not leaving," I called out to Redfern who had just dumped a sports bag on my bedroom floor and unceremoniously shoved my clothes aside in the tiny closet to hang up a garment bag of uniforms. He beetled into the bathroom without even stopping to kiss me.

The shower stopped. "What?"

"Rae. She stays."

"I'm not asking her to leave." He came out rubbing his wet hair with a towel. The rest of him was moist and pink from the hot water. I envied him — all men, in fact. No matter what they have to offer, they're proud of it, and show it off at every opportunity. In Redfern's case, his pride was justified. Flat stomach, rippling muscles, but not overdone. He belonged to a men's soccer league and they played all year round, our small town boasting an indoor field, and he had the thighs and calves to prove it.

"Like what you see?" He threw his towel into the bathroom and slid into bed. "I'll have to ask you to keep your hands off me tonight. I haven't slept in days."

"Get over yourself. Except for a few minutes during the changing of the guard this afternoon, I haven't slept for days, either. And I'm traumatized from the attempt on my life. If you lay a finger on me tonight, you'll lose it."

"You never were easy, Cornwall. It took me nearly four months to get you into bed."

"You should have tried a little harder. You'd have gotten laid a lot sooner."

"You're a cruel woman, telling me that now. Wait, I forgot. Shows how tired I am." He got out of bed and went to the closet, scrabbling around on the floor. He came back with his gun and placed it on the bedside table, barrel facing away from his head. Always the safety nut.

"Don't touch it. We need to get a safe in this house to stow my gun in when I'm here."

"Yeah, that's what I need. A gun safe. I'm sure you wouldn't even tell me the code."

"You got it." He turned off the lamp and rolled away, facing his gun.

I poked him.

"Cut it out. I told you, I'm too tired."

"Tell me what happened at the board meeting and I'll leave you alone. What did the Weasel say?"

He groaned and turned onto his back. "Nothing much. He threatened to have me and Tony replaced as investigators. Tony told him to bring it on. I mentioned I couldn't share details of the investigations since he was on the suspect list. That didn't go down well, so short meeting. Glory was supportive and ended the meeting before there was bloodshed. But she looked like she had a headache or wasn't feeling well."

"A hangover, trust me. She spent the afternoon at Dougal's house, drinking white wine and explaining why it was his fault she used to be an emotional ice queen. I'm surprised she was useful at all. Did they threaten to fire you?"

"They did, in a roundabout way. Will you move back to Toronto with me?"

"Probably not. Did they mention me?"

"They mentioned you at great length, with fire heating up their cold blue eyes."

"Aw, what a poetic turn of phrase. Have you noticed their eyes are the same colour? Spooky." Dead silence was the only response. I digested what he had told me. I poked him again.

"What!"

"What did they say about me? Specifically."

"Specifically, the charming Andrea is incensed because you accused her husband of murder. Whose murder she didn't really say. Maybe Faith's, maybe all three. And word is out about your playing detective."

"Well, shit." I mused on that for a bit. "Kelly wasn't dead when … I last conversed with the Weasels. She exaggerates." Whew. My visit to the law office of Bains and Mrs. Bains on Friday morning hadn't been mentioned at the meeting. Guess I caught a break there.

Redfern didn't snore, a big plus in a bedmate. He just went into a coma when he slept, but could wake up in an instant. I prodded him in the back.

"Jeezuz, Cornwall!"

"I'm too tired to sleep. Do you want to look at my toenails? I have Azure Waters on one foot and Irish Mist on the other."

"What are you talking about? I'll pass on the toes, but if you want, I'll rub your back. Roll over."

That felt so good. I sighed with pleasure and began to drift off.

Redfern tapped my shoulder. "Okay, maybe I'm not too tired. Just don't expect anything fancy."

I

Redfern put on his tie in front of the bathroom window. "Do you have an iron?"

I thought about that for a minute. "I don't think they make irons anymore."

"What about a steamer?"

"Get real, Redfern. There isn't a wrinkle on you."

"I'm thinking about tomorrow. My shirts are creased from hanging in the garment bag."

"I'll ask Rae. Maybe she has an iron." From his comment, Redfern planned to stick around for a while. Well, we'd take that one day at a time.

His equipment belt hung over the bedpost, gun safely holstered. I reached out a finger to the Taser holster.

"Don't touch that!" He yanked the belt away and strapped it on. "Never touch my belt."

I rolled over on my back. "You're the first man who's ever said that to me."

"You should get dressed." He fastened his Kevlar vest.

"No, I shouldn't. It's Sunday."

"You can't stay here alone. I haven't anyone available to watch you today. We're stretched too thin as it is."

"I have Rae."

"I've already talked to Rae. She's spending the day at Glory's. Something about plucking, or waxing. How long does that take?" His face reflected the confusion most men feel over beauty treatment regimes.

"Longer than you'd think when Glory is involved. I'm not going to waste a day at her house of horrors. She'd make me clean her windows or dust for cobwebs. I never saw a house so prone to cobwebs. It must have something to do with her undead status. And she goes ballistic when she sees one. Nope, not going there."

"How about Dougal? I'm dropping you off some-where, so pick a place and stay there until I come for you. And there'll be an Alert out on you, so if any of my officers spot you, they have orders to bring you in. We'll see how you like spending a snowy Sunday in one of our deluxe cells."

"You only have four cells, and they all smell like human body fluids. No need to go all caveman on me, Redfern. Last night's performance wasn't that stellar."

"Don't make my job harder than it is, Cornwall. Please. Give me one less thing to worry about. And, for the record, you weren't complaining last night about my performance."

"I slept through most of it. Okay. Drop me off at Dougal's. Although, I can't guarantee he won't throw me out as soon as you leave."

He sat on the bed and pulled me upright beside him. "One thing before we leave. I'm going to show you something. This needs to stay between us, so no sharing with Rae. Okay?"

"Sure."

"What do you make of this?" He handed me his cell.

"That's a Mauser." I enlarged the picture. "An HSc model, I think. See the low positioning of the grip screw? This would be an early model, most likely from the 1940s. My grandpa has ... had one like it. An expert can tell you the age for sure by checking the serial number and looking for an eagle imprint somewhere near the trigger guard. That's about all I remember. Oh, the early ones also had a wooden grip." I handed the phone back. "Whose gun is it?"

"We found it near Kelly Quantz's body yesterday."

"So, it's probably the same gun that killed Sophie last week? Do you think the murderer dropped it accidentally?"

"Maybe, but could be he didn't want it to be found in his possession, or on his property. It's unlicensed, or he wouldn't be so cavalier about leaving it at the scene."

I went into the bathroom to get dressed. Unlike Redfern, I wasn't comfortable prancing around naked.

I called out to him, "Did you, uh ..." How could I put this. "Did you search Mr. Archman's house for weapons?"

"We're trying to get a search warrant, but it doesn't look good. We only have your word that he possesses them. He didn't say they were in the house, did he?"

"Nope. They could be in a storage locker or a bank

deposit box, I guess. And he wouldn't likely talk about his souvenirs if he used one to kill Sophie and planned to kill Kelly. I wonder why Kelly was killed?"

"I can't share that information. Come on, let's go. You can eat at Dougal's."

I brightened at that suggestion. Dougal's house-keeper, Mrs. Boudreau, was a fantastic cook, better even than Rae, and she always left him casseroles and pasta dishes for the weekends.

Redfern accompanied me to Dougal's door and handed me off like a UPS package. He pushed me inside and closed the door with Dougal on the wrong side. They were on the doorstep for a few minutes, Dougal shivering in the cold. The fresh air would do him good.

When my crazy cousin was finally released from police custody, the expression on his face was too precious for words. You'd think he'd just watched a cockroach crawl out of his pillowcase. I took a picture and emailed it to his girlfriend, Holly.

The day passed pleasantly enough. At least for me. Dougal didn't speak — bonus — and stayed in his study labouring over his latest romance, although he preferred to call them "historical suspense novels." The only suspense in his last novel consisted of which chambermaid the master was going to screw first, before Lady La-Di-Da turned him into a faithful, doting husband. As if. Mind you, this latest tome takes place in a convent, so the master might have his hands full.

Mrs. Boudreau had indeed left delicious meals in the fridge. I locked Simon, the profane parrot, in the solarium so I wouldn't have to listen to his salacious invitations, and had the rest of the house to myself. Plate of lasagna in hand, I wandered through the spacious rooms, even Dougal's bedroom, gathering decorating ideas to avoid when I had my own house.

The disturbing reading material on Dougal's bed-side table turned me off snooping. Man, I hoped Holly was on board with Dougal's tastes. I ate a bag of potato chips — no cheese puffs in this house — in front of the bay window in the living room, forgetting for the moment that I was a target.

A white Land Rover skidded to a stop at the curb, sending a wave of dirty slush across the sidewalk. Glory jumped out of the driver's seat wearing a knee-length white faux fur coat and matching hat. She steamrollered up the walkway carrying a bottle of white wine in each fist. Rae and Pan followed behind like stray puppies. Pan carried her purse.

I raced to the study and rapped on the door. "Are you in there, buttercup?"

"Fuck off."

"You have company, sweetie."

"Tell them to go away. I'm busy."

Goddamn. This day might yet be saved. "I'm not supposed to answer the door, remember?"

He shoved past me and made for the front hall.

I flapped my hands and followed him. "Shit, Dougal, when's the last time you took a shower?" By the time he flung the door open, I had my phone out.

Dougal's face when he saw his ex-wife on his door-step again? Priceless.

CHAPTER
THIRTY-NINE

THE REST OF THE WEEK wasn't nearly as much fun. The days fell into a deadly routine: Redfern dropped me and Rae at the greenhouse in the mornings, and Dougal drove us home at five o'clock. I'd love to know what Redfern said to make my self-centred cousin stick to me like a burrito fart at a poker game. Dougal even dragged himself away from his laptop long enough to pick up the flyers at the fundraiser and plaster them around town.

A junior constable waited with us at my house until Redfern got in, usually after 9:00 p.m. I was getting used to having him around nights, and I don't think he missed his cabin. He swung by there every day to pick something up, things like his iron. Yeah, I'm serious. The guy has his own iron.

Every time my mind strayed to the murders, and my close encounter with the Grim Reaper, I steered it deliberately away. All the possibilities — Fang, Chico, the Weasel, Mr. Archman — seemed preposterous. I was beginning to think we had it all wrong. Somebody else's name should be on the list. Whose, I hadn't a clue, but maybe my subconscious would work it out.

Sophie's funeral took place on Friday. Her family didn't feel it necessary to wait until Kelly's body was released for burial, so husband and wife could be interred together. That made me wonder if anyone would even claim Kelly's body. Sad, but maybe the Episcopal Church would step up and pay the funeral costs.

Rae wanted me to go with her to the service at St. Paul's, but I pleaded a mild form of theophobia and, while she looked that up on her laptop, phoned a skiving customer in Fukushima. The man wanted to pay his overdue bill in yen, but I didn't have a monetary conversion chart and had no idea what he was talking about. By the time I straightened him out and he agreed to pay in Canadian dollars, Rae had driven away in her ancient Echo.

During my formative years, my family didn't belong to any religious denomination and my parents were fond of dragging me and my sister, Blyth, to a different church every Sunday to broaden our worldview perspective. Or, so my dad said. As a result of this early church-hopping, I had only a passing acquaintance with religious ritual. If I went to Sophie's funeral at St. Paul's, I wouldn't know whether to genuflect or slap a yarmulke on my head. Even worse, some of those places passed a contribution bucket along the pews and I never knew if toonies and loonies were acceptable, or if they expected bills. To seal the deal on my non-appearance at Sophie's funeral, I would have needed a police escort, and they were all busy.

By Friday, though, I was ready to chew my own leg off to escape captivity. The decorations for Saturday were in place, including a couple of spotlights kindly donated by Chico. It only took two phone calls and a barrage of emails before he relented. Fang brought them over and installed them with no more than a token complaint or two, although his flawless white teeth gnashed audibly. He stayed and helped me string hundreds of white lights near the apex of the ceiling. Then he draped tinsel over the cords. It was gorgeous. Too bad Fang had to come back after New Year's and take it all down again. I kept forgetting I wasn't supposed to stand near windows.

I couldn't leave the greenhouse to visit my Bliss This House clients, and this reminded me that I had promised Earl Archman I'd bring a cleaning crew over on Friday. No way would he let the crew in without me there to ease the way. It occurred to me that he might not let me in, ever, but new clients weren't easy to come by, so I meant to try.

I planted myself beside Dougal's desk and waited politely for him to notice me. It took a while.

"Fuck off."

I needed to humour him. "What's the setting of your new book? *Death in the Convent*, is it?"

He looked at me briefly. "Surprise. The setting is a convent. In Old Quebec."

"You've never even been to New Quebec."

"Holly and I are spending Christmas at the Château Frontenac. I'm leaving to join her in Toronto right after this stupid fundraiser is over tomorrow. We leave for Quebec City on Monday. We have a whole week to explore, and I can come back and add details to the manuscript. Then, it's back to work on the outline of my third, as yet unnamed, novel. Anything else you want to know?"

"Well, I hope you two have a wonderful time. Um, the thing is, I need a favour."

"No. Fuck off."

"Come on, Dougal. I just need you to drive me into town to pick up my costume for tomorrow. A half-hour, tops. I'll buy you a takeout lunch from any fast food place you want." That should do it. He thrived on junk food.

"Anyplace? Come back in an hour. Wait, I can't. I'm not supposed to let you out."

"Redfern meant I wasn't to go out *alone*. You'll be with me, so it's fine."

I spent the hour arranging for Cora Wayne and two other off-duty cleaners to meet me at Earl Archman's. All three were pleased to be offered an extra shift so close to Christmas. I reminded myself to pick up small gifts to go with the bonuses I planned to give my staff.

Dougal smelled okay in the close proximity of his vehicle. He remained unbathed and unshaven only on the weekends, and only when Holly was out of town. He bitched the whole way in, though. Under normal circumstances, I would be worried he'd leave me stranded by the side of the highway. But Redfern must have really put the frighteners on because when I directed him to Earl's house, he simply told me to be quick and pulled out a French-English phrase book.

Cora and the other two were already on the sidewalk. I paid Cora and placed the costume gently on the back seat of Dougal's vehicle. He set his book down and reached for the ignition, and I said, "Just a minute, okay? I'll be right back."

I explained to my staff that we had a difficult client on our hands. He might be a hoarder. Definitely, he was cranky, and he had Olympic-level sarcasm skills. They should stand well back until I deemed it was safe for them to enter.

Mr. Archman opened the door on the third ring. I was ready this time and hurled myself through the opening before he could slam it shut. He looked from me to the three women waiting on his porch. "What's this, Miss Cornwall? Another intervention?"

"Call me Bliss. Can I call you Earl? Remember, it's cleaning day. My staff is here to help you get organized, tidy up, and … and… get clean!"

"I suppose there's no point in asking you to leave and never come back?" The poor man looked so defeated, I felt sorry for him. Glancing at my staff, I could see they felt the same way. He would be in good hands.

"No point whatsoever. Step aside, Earl, and let the professionals get at it. We've brought our own supplies." I took a closer look at him. "I believe you're thinner already, Earl. Good for you! But surely those aren't the same track pants you had on the last time I was here? How's your arm coming along?"

"Can it, Miss Cornwall. Stop calling me Earl. Do what you have to do and get out."

"If only I had a loonie for every time I heard that, and usually the *f*-verb is involved." I ushered the ladies in. Dougal beeped his horn, and I gave him a wave before closing the door on the relentless snow and the annoying moron at the curb.

I stood in the hall with Earl — Mr. Archman — and looked around to make sure the others were out of earshot. "Listen, I'm sorry if I got you into trouble with the police. I know you told me about your Second World War guns in confidence. But when I heard that … my boyfriend came to your house after Kelly Quantz was killed, I just blurted it out. I hope they didn't ransack your house looking for weapons." I glanced into the living room, which did, indeed, look like a platoon of ransackers had swept through, scattering paper, upturning cushions, and finishing with an extra-thick coating of dust.

"They haven't been by so far, and I don't care if they do come. You don't think I'm stupid enough to keep guns here in the house, do you? Especially unregistered firearms."

"Well, good. I hear you. We can carry on, then?" A *beep beep* sounded from outside.

"Do I have a choice, Miss Cornwall? I suppose I have no say in this matter. These ladies will poke through my belongings at will. I have no dignity or privacy left."

"Give it a rest, Mr. A. They will only organize what's out in the open. Your drawers are sacrosanct, haha. Park your pride for the afternoon, and you'll have a whole new perspective on life."

"I perused the advertising material you left me last time, Miss Cornwall, and I saw nothing about parking or perspectives. Still, I will retire to the basement and await my transformation. Send me your bill, but it better be the sum we agreed upon."

"Remember to drink lots of water," I called over my shoulder as he edged me onto the porch and slammed the door.

Dougal was enraged. Apparently the phrase book lacked engaging characterization, and the plot needed fine-tuning. Even after I bought him a Triple-Bypass Burger with a side order of poutine, he whined all the way back to the greenhouse. I glanced into the back seat at my costume.

I was going to knock them dead in that outfit.

CHAPTER
FORTY

"GOT SOME BAD NEWS for you, bud." Tony threw himself into the visitor's chair. Melting snow from his boots formed a growing pool on the floor.

"If you tell me you're dumping Glory, I'll have to shoot you."

"Nah. The babe and I are tighter than ever. You should be more concerned about me ending up with a broken heart than her. She's got money, and class. Can't see her settling for a working dude like me. Low pay, long hours." He sighed and stared out the window at the grey sky.

"What's the bad news, then?" Neil had a good idea, but hoped he was wrong.

"HQ is pulling me. I've been here, what, two weeks? They figure if we haven't found the dirtbag by now, it ain't gonna happen. I have to report this afternoon to London base, and spend the next few days finalizing my report. You should get a copy in a week or so."

"This is Friday. Do they want you to work the weekend?"

"Nope. I'm off the clock. Glory and I are meeting up in Toronto after this charity bash tomorrow at the greenhouse. We'll spend the rest of the weekend at some fancy hotel she booked." Tony looked gloomier than ever at the thought. "Good thing, I guess. She wouldn't be happy at my place."

He was right. Glory had been born into privilege. She wouldn't want to spend the night at a cramped city bedsit where sirens wailed by night and horns blared endlessly by day. Neil had seen Tony's London apartment.

"Sorry to lose you. I'll tell Cornwall you said goodbye."

Tony's rough laugh erupted. "I was hoping before I left, you and Miss Bliss would be on first name terms. Never saw an odder couple."

"It's her way of keeping me at a distance. When she's ready, she'll let me know."

Tony laughed longer and louder. "Most people use first names before doing the horizontal hula. Maybe you need to resolve the Debbie thing before Bliss starts calling you *Chief* Redfern and kicks you out of bed."

"That could happen. I'm working on my issues."

"Just a suggestion, bud, but maybe work faster? Have you told Bliss you love her?"

Neil's ears burned. "What's wrong with you, Tony? When did you get so touchy-feely? Have you been through sensitivity training or something? Not that you didn't need it, but I think they overdid it."

"Just saying. Nothing wrong with the L-word. I'm fond of the little lady, and if you weren't my friend, and if I weren't attached at the moment, I'd take a run at her myself."

"She's attached at the moment, too, so fuck off."

Tony shrugged. "Just don't wait too long, that's all I'm saying."

What was up with all this personal shit? What happened to the deep undercover copper who had to be dragged back, kicking and complaining bitterly, from the biker subculture? It was almost like he had been reprogrammed and his button reset to "ordinary."

"Look, Tony, I appreciate your help. Too bad we didn't get the perp, but I'll keep at it." He regarded the whiteboard. "I hate that fucking thing."

Tony stood up and flipped it around. "What are you sayin', man? I wish I had one of my own. Look here. It self-erases if I turn this knob!"

"Don't erase it yet. With Quantz dead, we're down to four male names if we accept that Faith Davidson's pregnancy was responsible for her death. Then, we further surmise that Sophie Quantz's death occurred because she was present and threatened to expose Faith's killer. Kelly Quantz died because he tried to blackmail the killer. And why was Cornwall targeted? We don't know the answer to that. All this shit is conjecture at this point."

He walked over to the whiteboard, picked up a marker, and stroked through the names Fang Davidson and Chico Leeds. "I can't see Fang being responsible either for his sister's pregnancy, or her death. As far as

I know, Dogtown residents do not engage in rampant incest or inbreeding. They're just a group of people who want to live in the country and enjoy family life without nosy neighbours. I have no sense that Fang is a deviant. And Chico can't even stand up to Cornwall. I can't find one person who links him to Faith back in high school."

"That's just your gut talking," Tony said. "Not saying you're wrong, but if you ain't, we're left with Earl Archman and Mike Bains. Fang could have lost his temper and offed his sister because she brought disgrace on the family. And nobody can stand up to Miss Bliss. Well, you come close. Maybe that's why she puts up with you."

When Neil was sure Tony was finished talking, he said, "Even if we get a DNA match from the fetal bones, we can't prove the sperm donor killed Faith. I've felt all along we have to focus on Sophie, and now Kelly."

Tony dropped into his chair again. "We have been. The Mauser's a bust unless we get a match on that partial. It could be anybody's. Nobody's got an alibi. I hate leaving you with this mess, Neil, but I'll stay in touch and let you know if I come up with any ideas. In any case, I'll come back in the summer and we'll take a trip on our bikes. As long as you get rid of that sissy Gold Wing and get yourself a man's ride."

Neil ignored his jab. "What if we add a new name to our suspect list?"

"Who you got in mind?"

Neil wrote the name on the board. From it, he drew two lines to Sophie's and Kelly Quantz's names. Then, without hesitation, he drew a line from one of the original suspects to Faith Davidson. "It would explain the attack on Cornwall, as well."

Tony went silent. He tilted his head against the back of his chair and closed his eyes.

Neil watched his friend. Was he on the right track, finally?

Tony's eyes snapped open and in their dark depths Neil recognized a flicker of hope and a reflection of his own frustration.

With one swift motion, Tony jumped to his feet and pounded Neil on the back. "I should turn in my badge and take a job as a security guard. You're just as bad, pal. Why the fucking hell didn't we see this before?"

CHAPTER
FORTY-ONE

WHEN DOUGAL AND I returned to the greenhouse from Mr. Archman's, the walls resounded with unearthly but familiar screams. I breathed a sigh of relief. Glory was back to normal. We encountered a befuddled Pan in the centre of the anteroom, one hand clutching an aerosol bottle, and the other a wad of paper towel.

"What are you doing, Pan?" I asked. Dougal kept walking.

Pan's black-agate gaze swept the expanse of glass walls and ceiling. "Her Holiness instructed me to clean the glass in here. I don't clean, you know that, Bliss. Now that you're back, you can do it. Here." He tried to pass over the symbols of his servitude, but I backed away.

"You'll do fine, Pan. It's easy. First of all, put that hornet spray back where you got it. Find the spray bottle containing the vinegar and water solution. It has a pump handle. Point the nozzle away from you, at the glass, and pump twice. Then use the paper towel to dry the spot.

Do a few panes at a time; that way you'll keep track of your progress. I repeat, put the insecticide away and use glass cleaner."

"After this, she wants me to clean the atrium, where the fundraiser is being held. It's bigger!"

"Much bigger," I agreed.

"I have to do the whole thing. How am I supposed to reach higher than the end of my arm?"

"Easy. There's a stepladder you can use. Ivy Belcourt had it custom-made for the greenhouse. You still won't be able to reach the apex of the ceiling, but just do your best."

Pan shook his head, and his stumpy black ponytail jiggled in agitation. "I didn't sign on for this. I'm going to quit my job and go back to Vancouver."

"Isn't there an arrest warrant out for you in Vancouver?"

"Just for possession of marijuana. A measly half an ounce, for personal use. I'm sure the statute of limitations has kicked in by now."

"Better stay right here where you are, but I'd avoid Chief Redfern if I were you. He's not fond of drugs. Who's Glory screeching at, anyway?"

"She's on the phone to the Royal York Hotel. They screwed up her reservation and don't have a suite available."

"What reservation? Is she leaving? Will she be gone long?"

"Haven't you heard, Bliss ..." He pointed the bottle at the closest pane. I pushed his arm down and a spray of waspicide hit the floor.

I covered my nose with my sleeve. "Heard what?"

"Well," he stepped in closer. "Sergeant Pinato had to go back to … wherever he came from. She's leaving to meet him in Toronto tomorrow night after the benefit, and coming back Monday. After that, I don't know. She's in such *le desespoir*."

"You've been hanging around Dougal too long, my friend. She's just in a plain snit." The caterwauling reached a crescendo, then dipped and faded into a gurgle. Either the crisis was over, or she had overheated and passed out.

I spun Pan around and sent him back to the supply closet, then stopped in the foyer at Rae's desk. She hung up the phone and pushed her blonde hair away from her face. "You wouldn't believe the calls I'm getting from people who want to know if the food drive benefit is still on for tomorrow. We should have quite a crowd."

"Why wouldn't it still be on?"

"A really bad storm is supposed to blow in tonight and continue through tomorrow. I guess people thought we might cancel. But Glory says it's happening no matter what."

"Did the funeral go okay?"

Rae must have swallowed the "theophobia" excuse because she didn't ask why I hadn't shown up. "I only stayed for the service. The interment was just for the family. It was so sad, Bliss. Reverend Quantz had her grandmother and a few cousins in the front row, that's all. The guild ladies held a tea in the manse, but they didn't need my help and I wasn't up for making small talk. I've heard people whispering about Reverend Quantz's past. You know, how *available* she was when she was a teenager. As if that should matter now, after all the good things she's done since she became a priest."

"You're right, Rae. Sophie's past shouldn't matter. And it doesn't." Nothing mattered to Sophie now. I knew Rae was thinking about her own not-too-distant past as a hooker in Hemp Hollow.

Through the layers of glass walls, I spotted Redfern's Cherokee pull into the parking lot and stop beside Dougal's Lexus. The snow fell fast and horizontally, and his hair and shoulders collected a thick white coating in the few steps from his vehicle to the front door.

In the anteroom, he brushed the snow off and nodded at Pan before continuing into the foyer.

"Afternoon, ladies. I thought I'd pick you up early and drive you home." He turned his head and looked back. "What's wrong with Pan? His shirt is wet and he smells like vinegar."

"Good, he has the right bottle this time. Get your coat and purse, Rae. We're outta here."

The phone rang and Rae told another caller that, yes, the food drive benefit was going ahead at one o'clock tomorrow afternoon. When she hung up, she said, "Listen, you two go ahead without me. The phones are crazy busy, and I'll get a lift with Dougal or Glory. There's a chicken casserole in the fridge. Just heat it at three-fifty for thirty minutes."

"Is that after pre-heating?" I asked, then chortled at her expression. Even I knew you had to pre-heat. "Come on, Redfern, let's get out of here before the Hive Queen makes me mop up the snow you tracked in."

"Why do you have your coat and boots on?"

I pretended I didn't hear him and raced to Dougal's Lexus to transfer my costume to Redfern's back seat.

"I need to stop at the cabin and pick up a few things," Redfern said.

There was a stop sign at the corner of Concession Road 10 and Highway 21, but he barely yielded before pulling onto the highway. If I'd done that, Dwayne would have chased me down and tried to give me a ticket.

Redfern's cabin wasn't far from the greenhouse — just on the other side of the highway, down a tree-lined side road, and the first left along a path now almost impassable with snow drifts. Perfect for a hermit, or a city cop who didn't know any better.

"I'll wait for you here," I told him when he stopped in front of the tiny cottage.

He went around and opened my door. "I don't think so. Come in with me."

"Really, I'm okay out here. I'll just send a few texts, maybe phone my sister. Take your time."

"Out. You're in protective custody, remember?" He pulled me out. My utilitarian Cougars never hit the snow as he hauled me into his cold, damp cave.

He flipped on the light and I clutched his arm in shock. Somebody, or something, had tossed the place. From the front door, the entire living quarters, except the bedroom and bathroom, were visible. The kitchen area had taken the worst hit. Redfern didn't keep much food around, but the cupboard doors — there were only two of them — hung open. Snow blew in the small sliding window over the sink.

A sound from the bedroom brought Redfern's gun

out of the holster and into his hand. "Squat down behind the sofa and stay there," he ordered, and circled the living area, hugging the wall.

See, this is what happens on TV. The innocent bystander is told to stay back, then gets killed while the other guy runs off on his own and doesn't die because he has the gun.

I followed close behind Redfern as he approached the open bedroom door.

"Will you ever listen to me?" His voice held no hope of that happening in his lifetime. He was learning.

"That's what my parents used to ask. What have we got?" I already had a good idea what we'd find. I had seen the piles of poop scattered over the counter and the floor.

Sitting in the middle of Redfern's bed was a raccoon. Not one of your overweight, citified raccoons. This was a Bruce County raccoon — lean, mean, and arrogant as hell.

It looked at us and chittered.

"It's mad because you don't have any food in your cupboards. Shoot it," I said to Redfern.

He put his gun away and stared at the raccoon. It stared back. "How am I going to get you out of here?" he asked it.

"Uh, shoot it."

"I'm not going to shoot it."

"Right. That would make a big mess on the bed. Good point. How about you Taser him? You need the practice anyway, right?"

He reached forward slowly and grasped a corner of the bedspread. "Get the other side. We'll wrap it up and let it go outside."

Did the man know nothing about raccoons? Or me? "I haven't had a rabies shot. No shit, Redfern, shoot it or Taser it, your choice, but don't go all nature-nut on me."

Redfern held up the bedspread and leaped toward the raccoon, but missed by a mile. I jumped out of the way and let the beast tear past me. We chased after it and were just in time to see it disappear through the kitchen window, chattering angrily. Redfern closed the window.

"I meant to fix that lock. I have some plywood and a nail gun. You stand here for a minute in case it comes back."

Sure, no problem. While Redfern rummaged in a small storage room beside the fireplace, I searched the kitchen drawer for a weapon. I found a corkscrew, a good one. Redfern didn't drink anything with a cork. Ergo, it was mine, left behind on one of my few visits to the cabin of carnal delights.

I stood ready with the corkscrew, but the raccoon stayed gone. When Redfern returned, I cleaned the poop and spilled cereal off the floor and wiped the table and counters with a disinfectant. "If you want, you can bring your bedding to my house and use my washer and dryer."

"Okay. Thanks." He took off his coat and set to work, every movement quick and efficient. He wasn't even upset about the raccoon. Good-looking, smart, brave, even-tempered, good with tools. What more could a girl ask for? Someone not quite so arrogant, or burdened with heavy baggage, perhaps? Nobody's perfect.

I sat in a kitchen chair and watched him. "I see the raccoon took a few of your things."

"What's that?" Knees planted on either side of the

sink, he fitted the sheet of plywood across the wooden window frame and picked up the nail gun. I think I would have installed it on the outside of the window, but what do I know?

"Your wife's pictures. The one beside your bed is missing. So are the ones in here."

He went still but didn't turn around. "I put them away."

"When?"

"A couple of days ago when I came by to pick up some uniforms."

"Why?"

The nails *kee-cheeked* through the wood. "It was time. Now, we can work on our relationship. Isn't that what you wanted? Or were you just using Debbie as an excuse to keep me at a distance?"

Kee-cheek, kee-cheek.

Was I? I didn't think so but I didn't have to take a blood oath either way right now, did I? "Putting those pictures away is an important first step, and I know it was hard for you. So, now I'll take one."

He jumped down from the sink and set the nail gun on the table. "I'm intrigued. Go on."

"From this moment forward, I'm going to call you Neil. You don't have to call me Bliss until you're ready. Okay ... Neil?" God, that sounded so weird. Neil, Neil, Neil. I wasn't sure I could pull it off. Maybe we only worked as Cornwall and Redfern.

He knelt beside me and took my hand. "I think I can manage a second step ... Bliss."

We looked at each other for a long moment, then

burst out laughing. I picked up the corkscrew again. "This is a celebratory moment. Got any wine, Neil?"

"You know better, Bliss. I have a bottle of whisky in the cupboard, if the raccoon didn't drink it."

"Pass."

"Let's go to your place and celebrate. I'll get my stuff and be right with you."

I followed him back to the bedroom while he packed jeans, sweatshirts, and runners. How long did he plan to stay? If he started throwing in shorts and flip-flops, I would be forced to ask that very question. I opened his top drawer.

"What are you doing?"

"You sure have a lot of Jockeys for a guy." They weren't exactly colour-coordinated but they were folded and arranged more neatly than my unmentionables. "Do you have an underwear fetish?"

"For white thongs, maybe, and only when you're wearing one."

"So sweet, Neil. Is there anything in these other drawers you don't want me to see?"

"Go ahead and look, but don't blame me if a snake is hibernating in one of my socks."

"Okay, I'm done helping." I slammed the top drawer closed and leaned against the wall. When I tired of watching him fold every item neatly before stashing it into the sports bag, I went into the living room.

My hand reached out to the nail gun sitting on the kitchen table. I wanted to nail something. Just once. I picked it up.

I knew better than to point it at my face or any other

body part. I aimed it at the floor. I just had to pull this trigger here ...

Ka-tick. Nothing happened. I was sure Neil had pulled this trigger thing. Spreading my legs and using both hands like I was going to fire a pistol, I pulled.

Another *ka-tick*, but no nail shot into the floor. Maybe it was out of ammo. The walls in this rustic paradise were wood panelling and could use some anchoring. I'd try once more, then put it down before Neil came out and had a male fit because I was touching one of his tools.

With my free hand, I felt the panelling. Yup, a little loose right here. Neil had pushed the gun closer to the surface ...

Kee-cheek!

I screamed and tried to pull my left hand away from the wall. My sleeve was pinned firmly to the wood. In my panic, I pulled the trigger twice more. *Kee-cheek. Kee-cheek.* I screamed again. My fingers wouldn't let go of the thing, or stop pressing the trigger.

Redfern ... Neil ... ran into the room with gun drawn. When he saw what was happening, he shouted, "Drop it! Drop it!"

I tried. I couldn't. He came up behind me and grabbed my hand. "Let go!"

It fired a few more times before he finally pried my finger off the hair-trigger. The sucker fell to the floor and lay still. He kicked it away from me and, thank God, his gun was back in its holster.

I tried a cute smile on him. "Now you know better than to leave me alone with a power tool. Ha." The smile and comment fell flat. His face looked just the same as it did the time I puked on his shoes. That wasn't my fault, either.

"It's not a power tool. It's spring-loaded and has to touch the surface before it fires a nail."

"You should have explained that to me earlier." I nudged him. "So, we're still using first names, right? Neil?" He hadn't even warned me not to touch the damn thing.

"I'll get a claw hammer to pull the nails out. Wait right here."

Despite his expression, he probably thought his instruction humorous since the sleeve of my coat was pinned to the wall by at least four nails. I had no problem slipping out of the coat. I examined my wrist. Not a scratch!

Once we were in his vehicle, he began the slow process of backing down the drive without sliding into the ditch. The second we turned onto the highway, he said, "You never did tell me why you had your coat and boots on when I got to the greenhouse."

"Uh … well …"

"Before you come out with some convoluted lie, keep in mind you were standing in a pool of melted snow."

CHAPTER
FORTY-TWO

NEIL'S HEART RATE didn't return to normal until he turned into Cornwall's ... Bliss's ... driveway. When he had heard her scream from the front room, he thought ... well, he didn't know what he thought. He just reacted, pulling his Glock and racing to protect her. The sight of the nail gun firing into the wall beside her hand was almost as chilling as confronting an armed intruder. He couldn't wait to tell Tony. He always appreciated a good Bliss story.

She was skilled at diversionary tactics; he'd say that for her. It wasn't until they were on the snow-packed highway that he remembered to ask her again why she had on her outdoor clothes when he arrived at the greenhouse earlier.

He listened to her explanation without comment. At least she told the plain truth this time, with no excuses. He wasn't surprised she had slipped her leash, only surprised it hadn't happened before today. She'd been cooperative all week about remaining under someone's eye, even cousin Dougal's, who was unfortunately subject to bribery and distraction.

Earl Archman had slid down a few rungs on the suspect list since Kelly Quantz's murder. Bliss was safe enough with him, especially if some of her staff were around. But she was still a target, and would remain one until he caught the killer.

He looked over at her profile. At least she didn't jump out of the vehicle as soon as it stopped in front of her house.

Gun ready, he stood in the driveway, listening and watching. Satisfied, he opened Bliss's door and hustled her into the house. Her docility disturbed him. Maybe she was already regretting their first-name decision.

The smell of cooking food reminded him he hadn't eaten since breakfast. Two place settings waited on the kitchen table, and included a wineglass and a beer glass.

"There you two are. I've eaten already. The casserole is in the oven, still hot, and there's a salad in the fridge." Rae looked from one to the other. "I'm going to the gym for an hour or two. Chief, I'm parked on the street, so no need to move for me. Bye."

Snatching her coat and purse off a hook by the door, she fled.

"You could try to put her at ease, Neil." Bliss said this absently, like she had something else on her mind. She poured a glass of wine and sat down.

Neil took the casserole out of the oven and set the salad on the table. She stared into her glass but didn't drink. He filled a plate for her and pushed it in front of her.

Bliss took a mouthful, swallowed, and looked at him. The area around her eyes was no longer discoloured and she hadn't put the Egyptian-style makeup on today. Her eyes slanted the same way as her cousin's, but while his were blue, hers were whisky-coloured. Under the harsh kitchen lights, gold flecks appeared in the irises. A casual observer would call them brown, but that didn't come close.

"Anything to share on the investigation? Anything new?"

"We may have a few more leads." He watched her fingers play with the stem of her glass. The cuts on her hands from the broken glass had healed except for one inflamed area on her right index finger. The light purple polish on her nails was chipped at the edges.

"Kelly Quantz was killed before I was attacked, right? You found the gun at the scene. So, the killer threw away the gun he used on both Quantzes, and used a second one on me. What calibre bullet was it?"

"We don't have a ballistics report back yet, but it looks like another .32."

He watched her face and suspected her brain was sorting the information stored deep in her memory.

"None of the suspects are licensed for a .32, right? He could be using a second souvenir Mauser. The only other Second World War pistol I remember that used a .32 is a Sauer 38H."

"Your favourite."

"Yes. Small enough for a child to use, lethal enough to kill."

"Do you recall how many Sauers were passed back

and forth at the clubhouse?"

She carefully turned over a lettuce leaf on her plate like she expected to find something moving. "A couple. I can't remember who else had one."

"Eat up and let's get to bed. You have a big day tomorrow at the greenhouse."

She looked straight at him. "You're holding something back. How can I help if you aren't honest with me? Don't forget I'm involved, too."

He made a decision. "I will tell you, but this is not for sharing. Got it? I mean it, Bliss. Don't tell Dougal, or Rae, or dash off to Earl Archman and run it by him. That goes for Fern Brickle."

"I got it already, Neil. Geez, have a little trust."

"The Mauser that Dwayne found in the swamp has a partial thumbprint on the grip. Enough points that we can likely match it up if we get a comparison."

He thought she'd be excited. Instead, she got up and dumped her food in the garbage can under the sink. "You should compare it to Desperado Dwayne's thumb."

"It's not his." He didn't mention that checking the print against Dwayne's was the first thing Thea did. "I wish you'd try harder to get along with Dwayne."

"I'd get along with him fine if he didn't try to charge my ass every time he saw me behind the wheel. Have you asked the suspects to come in voluntarily and have their prints taken for elimination purposes?"

He kept forgetting she used to be married to a lawyer and knew more about the law than the average citizen. "We did. Three of them came willingly, the fourth declined."

"Don't tell me. The lawyer refused because he wasn't legally required to cooperate. He was above suspicion, et cetera, et cetera. All huffy and superior."

"Pretty much."

"So, were you able to eliminate anyone?" She did her best to sound off-hand, but he knew she was concerned about her friends.

"The thumbprint doesn't belong to Fang, Chico, or Earl Archman. That's all we can determine at this point."

Bliss was silent for a minute. "Is it possible someone else is involved? Someone who isn't on the suspect list?"

Neil started. *How did she get there?* Maybe she just didn't want to believe Bains was a murderer. Nobody wanted to find out they had been married to a killer. "Do you have a name in mind?"

"Not yet. I'm setting my subconscious to work, though. It's smarter than my conscious. I should have an answer for you by morning." Her cheeky smile appeared for a brief second.

"Then I'll sleep easy. Which reminds me, isn't it past our bedtime?"

"Patience, Neil. You have to wait up for Rae, then check all the doors and windows are locked. Doesn't mean we can't get started, I guess."

As he dropped into bed, Neil had to admit sleeping in Bliss's warm house beat his shack in the woods. He groaned, reflecting that he would now have to pull several dozen nails from the plywood around the window and repair the lock.

He didn't mean to ask her this, but the words fell out of his mouth before he could stop them. "Did you go out with Fang in high school?"

Her eyes barely flickered. "I told you we hung out." She turned out her light.

"Did you date him?"

"Who's asking, my boyfriend or a cop?"

"Boyfriend."

"None of your business."

"Now, I'm asking as a cop."

She laughed and pummelled him with a pillow. "Same answer. Not relevant to the investigation. Turn your light off."

Neil rolled over to comply, but as he reached for the switch, he caught a glimpse of something under the bed, just at the edge. His fingers closed over cold metal. What the hell? He pulled it out.

A sword? Dagger? He examined it more closely. The edges of the blade weren't sharp enough to cut through skin. The shaft on the end would fit onto a rifle. A bayonet.

He held it aloft. Was she keeping it under the bed for protection? Was it Grandpa's?

Bliss's eyes followed the length of steel to its tip. He could see her weighing her options. Disclaim any knowledge, or own up? He should have known she'd produce a third choice.

She threw herself on top of him, and he swung the bayonet away from their bodies.

"Oh, mighty Odin! Before you march into battle and smite thine enemy with this enchanted sword, pray satisfy this lady's lust. Take me now!"

CHAPTER
FORTY-THREE

THE INSTANT RAE AND I entered the greenhouse, Glory hit us with her long and detailed clipboard job list. I had a feeling a lot of pain was going down before we worked our way through even half of it.

"You, Bliss. Don't bother to take off your coat. We want our visitors to come through the back door directly into the atrium, so you need to shovel a path from the parking lot. When that's done, nail up a couple of signs to direct people. Chico donated some tacky outdoor candy canes, didn't he? Line the pathway from the parking lot with them. That way people can't get lost. When that's done, come and find me. There's plenty more to do. Any questions?"

"Why do I have to shovel? What's Dougal doing?"

"The useless worm is bringing the plants out to the tables. I'll arrange them according to price." Behind Glory, Dougal pushed a trolley laden with colourful flowers. He smirked and waved.

"What about Pan?" At least he could do something useful and make up the signs.

"Pan has a touch of flu and had to stay home."

Pan either had a touch of insecticide-poisoning, or he was lying to get out of work. I didn't care which; I was going to get even with that lazy little screw-up.

"What's that?" Glory pointed a claw at the hockey bag I had dragged in.

"My costume and stuff." It was my dad's and didn't smell minty fresh, but finding something long enough to transport a bayonet had proven a challenge. I knew perfectly well no law forbade the carrying of a knife or sword, as long as it isn't a switchblade, but I needed to hide it from Glory since, law or no law, she would take it away from me. Once it was on my person as part of my costume, she'd have to chase me down to get it.

Neil had given me the flint eye when I told him what I was going to do with the bayonet. I could tell he was wondering what other treasures my house held for an officer of the law. That worried me a lot. If he became a permanent fixture at the house, he was bound to poke around and find my cache. Even though the guns weren't mine, technically-speaking, somebody would go down for illegal possession of prohibited weapons, and I was the one with legal tenancy to the premises.

"Bliss, did you hear me? And before I forget, you can take those four boxes of cheap china back to Canadian Tire, or else store them in your own basement. Just get them out of here. Seasons Repast indeed! Now, Rae, you set up the boxes for the food donations. Make sure they're covered in tasteful holiday paper and place them on either side of the door in the atrium. The donated baked goods for the refreshment tables were dropped off earlier. And thank you for that, Rae. You did a good job. When Bliss is finished shovelling, she can help you set out the food and prepare the coffee and tea urns." She snapped her fingers. "Let's go now, people."

"Where's the damn shovel?" I asked, earning myself an exasperated sigh.

"How should I know?" She waved her arm vaguely in the direction of the four winds. "Look for it and make it snappy."

The shovel handle protruded from a snowbank at the far end of the parking lot. I had to dig it out with my hands, then empty the snow out of my boots. By the time I cleared the last foot of walkway to the back door, the first part had drifted in again. I know when I'm beat. Sticking the half-dozen candy canes on the piles of snow I had just created, I declared that job done. If the snow continued to swirl in this frenzied dance of blinding whiteness, no one would show up anyway.

Just when I thought I was finished and could get out of the cold, I remembered the signs. Not only did I have to direct non-existent visitors to the back, I had promised Chico I would advertise his generosity. The printer guy was bringing his own. I had Chico's signs made up already and just had to stick one to — something outside. The other would go on the men's room door as promised. Armed with a hammer and a few nails tucked into my pockets, I ventured out again. I could really use Neil's nail gun … now that I knew how to use it.

The sign was printed on bristol board, and I hadn't

much hope that it would last long in this wind. I selected a tough-looking pine and hammered in two nails. Did trees feel pain? I hoped not. I had nothing against trees.

Glory must have arranged with our private snow-plough company to clear out the parking lot before the party. A pickup with a plough affixed to the front drove straight at me. I threw myself into the nearest snowbank. Was the killer having another go at me, this time using a snowplow instead of a gun? It was a crazy thought, and it didn't last long. The driver swerved at the last minute. As he passed, he threw back his head and his mouth opened in a soundless laugh. Fang! He opened the window and yelled back to me, "Nice jump. See you later, Bliss!"

I was going to kill *him*.

Inside, things seemed to be humming along. It was noon and, *screw Glory*, I was getting into my costume. After I ate a couple of the lemon squares that had been laid out on the refreshment table, that is.

Glory's stilettos pounded along the hall outside the atrium, coming closer. I ducked behind the food donation box that Rae had tastefully covered in holi-day wrapping. The twelve-foot, pre-lit tree stood in stately winking splendour close by. I held my breath as the door opened. Glory mumbled to herself, then withdrew and clacked away. I waited until I heard her berating Dougal for mixing up the colours of the Hoyas — didn't he know anything about floral design? She should have known he didn't, having been married to him for the worst five years of her life (according to Dougal, it seemed twice that long.) Nice to see things were back to normal between those two. I raced to the ladies' room.

The Belcourts had anticipated their greenhouse becoming a tourist attraction once the atrium was transformed into a reptile and insect sanctuary, a.k.a. tropical garden. To that end, two lovely washrooms, one for men, one for women, adjoined the atrium, one on either side of the hallway. I can't describe the men's room, but the ladies' boasted three stalls with toilets that flushed automatically if you sat there too long. At least the doors didn't fly open at the same time. Dad's hockey bag waited in front of the triple sinks.

There was little chance Glory would intrude, as she had commandeered the manager's office during Ivy Belcourt's Arizona sojourn. The office had a private bathroom … or so I'd heard, since I was never invited on a tour.

Rae came in, already in her costume. The dress and her hair reminded me of something, but I couldn't place it.

"Who are you, again? Barbie?"

"No." She turned from the mirror and looked at me reproachfully. "I'm a Disney princess. Guess which one?"

I hated guessing. I studied the long, puffy-skirted dress. It was blue, with a darker blue bodice. She had pulled her blonde hair back into an elegant chignon. "Snow White? Ariel? No, wait. Who's that other one — Jasmine?"

"Cinderella!"

"Right, right. You make a perfect Cinderella, Rae. Did you bring the face paint, like I asked?"

"I have it right here. Do you want to paint some flowers on your face?"

"I want *you* to paint some *things* on my face. I have a drawing."

I tore off my clothes, right down to my black thong. My costume comprised many pieces, all black. By the time I wiggled into them all, Rae's face wore an expression of disbelief. I flatter myself that a trace of horror tinged her wide, blinking eyes.

"Oh, no, Bliss. Wow. Glory will be too pissed to even pee her pants!"

"I think she's too posh to pee anywhere, ever." We giggled like fools, then froze when someone knocked on the door. Glory!

I dove for the nearest cubicle but stopped when Dougal called out "You girls decent?" He walked in without waiting for an answer. "Chico is here and wants to know where to set up his cameras." He backed away when he caught sight of me. "What are you supposed to be? Never mind, Glory will spontaneously shatter into a million ice shards and that's good enough for me."

"Forget about my costume." I pointed at him. "That's not cool. Why are you dressed like Adolf Hitler?"

CHAPTER
FORTY-FOUR

DOUGAL CARRIED A BLACK BOWLER. He set it on his head and said, "I'm Charlie Chaplin!"

"You don't have enough room between the end of your nose and your upper lip for a square moustache. You look like Hitler trying to pass as Charlie Chaplin to escape the Red Army. Better do something before Glory and the customers see you."

He looked at himself in the mirror. "Fuck it. It's good enough. Nobody will show up in this storm, anyway. I just hope the greenhouse doesn't blow down."

We stood silently and listened to the howling of the west wind as it swept off Lake Huron, picking up moisture and turning it to snow. If the greenhouse survived its first winter, it would stand for a few more. With any luck, the ominous moaning overhead came from the pines surrounding the parking lot, and not the steel structure buckling. Or the glass cracking.

I shoved Dougal toward the door. "Tell Chico to set

up in the corner opposite the refreshment table. I'll be out as soon as Rae paints my face."

Muttering "This should be good," he straightened his hat and left. Rae set to work with her paints. We jumped at a single high-pitched shriek. Glory must have caught sight of Adolf Chaplin.

Twenty minutes later, it was my turn to face the Gilded Gorgon. In the atrium, Chico stood behind his tripod and aimed practice shots at the six-foot Bambi standing in the corner. The plastic abomination was surrounded by a dozen red-and-green plaster elves cavorting in a woodland scene. The woodland consisted of a set of three plastic pre-lit palm trees with painted coconuts hanging from the foliage. *Très* tacky. I had outdone myself and created the perfect Christmas hell.

I had my cell ready, and when Chico looked up from his camera and spotted me, I took a shot of his face.

"Holy moly, Bliss. You're going to scare the crap out of the kids."

Without warning, Glory came up behind me and spun me around. "What is this? Start talking. No, go change immediately!"

I reached down and tore a few small holes in my glittery tights.

It was the perfect, finishing touch to the rest of my costume: black satin skirt with uneven hem, a separate, sleeveless bustier that didn't quite meet the waistline of the skirt, and fingerless gloves that reached my elbows. My fingernails and toenails were matte black, and Rae had painted a reptile crawling up my throat — I had wanted a dragon, but she didn't know how to draw one.

The lizard's claws reached up over the edge of my face and Rae had used the cleft in my chin to place the creature's red forked tongue. Heavy black eyeliner, dark red lipstick, and a few hideous creatures leering from behind my ears completed the look. Instead of jewellery, which would have sent the outfit over the top, I had hung the bayonet through the loop of a plain black leather belt. My hair was gelled and sprayed into a wild halo around my face. Black glitter drifted to the floor when I moved my head and I reminded myself not to inhale it. The best part? A set of black tattered wings moved when I pulled a black cord on the bustier.

"I'm the Black Christmas Angel," I announced.

"You look more like the Angel of Doom! Get your clothes back on. People will be here any minute!" Glory's eyes were tinged with pink, coordinating nicely with her blush-coloured silk palazzo pants and matching tunic. With three-inch gold pumps, she towered half a foot over me, and I was wearing four-inch black leather gladiator sandals.

"Where's your costume?" I asked, moving to stand behind Chico. He took one look at Glory's eyes and wrapped his arms protectively around his photography gear. Silly boy, he knew nothing of her powers or he would have abandoned his expensive equipment and run into the storm.

"I don't have to wear a costume. I'm running this benefit and am dressed accordingly."

"In case you haven't looked outside lately, there's a blizzard bearing down on us. It may be our annual storm of the century. Nobody's going to show up." I was standing up to her pretty well. The costume must be giving me extra courage. I waggled my wings at her.

The outside door opened and Fang walked in, followed by a gaggle of children, at least a dozen. More folk streamed in. From the beards and plaid coats the men wore, they had to hail from Dogtown. The women were smartly turned out and everyone over four feet tall carried a grocery bag of food for the needy.

Glory turned her attention from my costume to the growing puddles on the floor. What did she think was going to happen when people tracked in snow? If she was half as smart as she claimed to be, she would have taken out an insurance policy in case someone slipped and broke a leg.

Before she could chastise Fang and his family, the door opened again to admit more snow-covered guests. Within minutes, the room began to fill up. Some of them wore snowmobile gear, dropping their outerwear and helmets in a pile near the door. That brought back some memories. The Weasel had a Yamaha Viper, and I had my own Arctic Cat Crossfire. We often went on day-long excursions with other members of the country club. It had been one of the few activities with him that I enjoyed back then. Well, that and target shooting.

Glory transformed herself into the perfect hostess, greeting each person by name, showing them where to deposit their food contributions, directing them to the plant tables. Dougal — his moustache now thinned out — presided over the colourful blooms, pointing out the best specimens to weather the trip across the parking lot to their cars. After that, they weren't his responsibility. They would all be dead by New Year's anyway.

Chico stared fixedly up at the disco ball, revolving and glittering above his head. I poked him in the arm to focus his attention. "Get ready, Chico."

"For what? You just told me to bring a camera and tripod."

I captured Rae and pulled her into the huddle. "Pictures of the kiddies with Bambi here, taken by a professional photographer, are five dollars each. I'll get a container for the money. Rae, use Glory's clipboard." I flipped to an empty page. "Write down email information and particulars about each kid. Chico will take the list home, download the pictures, then email the photos. Simple. Any questions?"

The plan worked well, with one tiny ripple. As Chico ran back and forth, moving Bambi to the right spot, taking some practice shots, a little girl ran up to him. Even before she whined, "Daddy, daddy!" I knew she was Chico's daughter. The black curly hair and glasses were a dead giveaway and weren't the problem. Unfortunately, she had inherited her mother's red-faced scowl and Yoda ears. I'm not joking; this was the ugliest kid I'd ever seen.

Tyger stood behind her daughter and looked pointedly at my chest. "Did you get implants, Bliss? I don't remember those." Two older kids rubbed their snotty noses on the sleeves of their sweaters.

I adjusted my girls. "It's all in the presentation, Tyger." The bustier had thrown my barely Bs into va-voom Cs.

"Daddy, take my picture," the sprite shrilled, pulling on his shirt. "Now!" After puberty, she'd give Glory a run for the Shrew of the Year title.

"Okay, Esmeralda, just hop up there beside Bambi and smile."

"Not Bambi," Esmeralda said, twisting her lips into an epic pout. "Her!" She pointed at me. "The witch with the wings."

"Hey, I'm the Black Christmas Angel!"

"Please, Bliss." Chico pleaded. His glance darted to Tyger, and a line of sweat broke out on his brow. Man, he was even more whipped than in high school.

"Oh, all right." I stood in front of the largest fake palm tree, with Esmeralda leaning against me. When she smiled, she didn't look so bad, except for the ears, but those can be fixed nowadays.

I'm pretty sure Esmeralda never paid her five bucks, but before I had a chance to mention it, the other two Leeds kids — twin boys as it happened — wanted a photo with the witch, too.

That was the beginning of a trend. Every kid in the room between the ages of three and fourteen lined up behind Rae for a chance to get their picture taken with the scary black angel. Or witch, whatever. Money is money. I fluttered my wings at each of them before Chico took the shot, and they screamed in joyful terror. The noise was giving me a headache.

Between each customer, I noticed Chico would glance up at the disco ball and open his mouth to say something. Another kid diverted his attention every time.

Most of the dads lined up, too, and the bucket overflowed. I wasn't worried about ending up on YouTube or Facebook. No one would recognize my paint-covered face or believe these were my boobs. Poor Bambi went completely unnoticed.

Old Bert Thiesson caused me a moment's discomfort when his hand wandered too far down my back and I had to jab him in the ribs. He was definitely frisky for someone a hundred and ten. I was glad to see Mr. Archman made it. He hobbled in, arm still in a cast. He gave Chico the snake eye but consented to a photo, sighing dramatically and throwing ten bucks in the bucket. He definitely looked thinner.

"This will be your *before* picture, Mr. A. Next year, after you've lost the hundred pounds, we'll take an *after* picture!"

He shook his head. "Maybe you can enlarge this one and prop it beside my casket. But promise me you won't deliver my eulogy, Miss Cornwall? It might be difficult, but I'd roll in my grave."

"Oh, Mr. A — can I call you Earl? — none of that talk, now. I'm going to come over and visit you again. I need some advice on storing, um, Second World War *souvenirs*, if you get my meaning."

He gave me a signature eye roll and stumped quickly away without warning me not to call him Earl. I was serious. I had to remove Grandpa's weapons from my garage before somebody in my family was charged. Maybe me and Earl could store our guns together.

Fang brought his four kids over and introduced them as Edsel, Chevy, Nash, and Hudson.

"Are you naming the next one Studebaker?" I asked him.

"We're thinking maybe Packard."

They all had Fang's sharp, dark eyes and straight, white teeth, which showed up nicely in the picture. One was a little girl about five, and it crossed my mind that Faith could have looked very much like her when she was this age. Fang threw five dollars in the pail. I should have told Rae it was five bucks *per kid*.

Even Fern Brickle stopped by to chat and admire my outfit. She contributed twenty dollars and gamely put her arm around my waist for a photo. We were making money hand over fist. Glory cast me a baleful glare once in a while, but stayed away. Too bad. I so wanted a picture of the two of us together. It might go viral. The Ice Queen and the Black Angel. A new Christmas classic.

The Weasels arrived by snowmobile, smiling and waving like they were starring in a Viagra commercial. Andrea would be driving my Crossfire. Neither wanted a photo with the busty black angel, apparently. They avoided eye contact with me, and I saw panic in their faces as the crowd continued to swell and push them ever closer to the forest tableau. Andrea had on her Jimmy Choos, and I just barely held back a snort of derision. Who wears Jimmy Choos on a snowmobile? I said to Chico, "If the Weasel gets within shutter range, get a shot of us." That might give me more blackmail material should I again need it someday.

"Listen, Bliss," Chico called back. "I remembered what happened to the Polaroid shots from grad night." He raised his eyes to the disco ball.

"What?" I looked up. The spotlights caught the silvery facets of the ball as it gently revolved above our heads.

"I got a ladder and used my jackknife to slice it open near the top. I slid about a dozen pictures in, one by one. A kind of time capsule. Then Mr. Archman made me get down."

"Do you think they're still viewable?" From what I remembered of Polaroid pictures, they faded after a time, faces first and the brighter colours last.

"Not likely. Alternating cold and heat wouldn't do them any good. But we should look. Maybe we'll see something that might help the police figure out ... you know."

"Come over tomorrow, okay, and we'll cut the ball open." The memento I had worked so hard to acquire would be destroyed, but what if Faith's yellow dress showed up? And somebody else was in a picture with her? It was a long shot, but we had to look.

Before he could acquiesce, Dwayne Rundell cut through the crowd and stood in front of me, hands on belt. He had his official face on, meaning he just looked dumber than usual.

"What now, Dwayne? I haven't driven my car in a week, so whatever your problem is, it can't be related to anything I've done."

"You can't walk around with that dagger hanging off your belt."

I had completely forgotten the bayonet. I put my hand over the hilt ... handle. "What are you talking about?" I refrained from adding *idiot*, so I can't be blamed for what followed.

"It's a prohibited weapon. Hand it over." He was attracting an audience of ear-flapping, nosy eavesdroppers.

"It is *not* a prohibited weapon! It's part of my costume. You need to look up the regulations on prohibited weapons because, clearly, you're an idiot." Heat surged through my body and moisture collected in my cleavage. This was harassment. I didn't care what Neil called it.

Dwayne reached over and pulled the bayonet out of my belt. He raised it over his head, out of my reach. If he thought I was going to jump for it, he was wrong. I tried to breathe, but nothing happened. Sweat trickled down my back, under my wings. I drew my foot back and prepared to kneecap him.

Neil was suddenly there between us. My sandal connected with his shin. He grunted and closed his hand over my bicep. He nudged Dwayne ahead of him. "Both of you. In the hall. Now!"

In the hallway, he pulled us along until we were out of sight and earshot of the crowd in the atrium. He stopped in front of one of the plant rooms.

He looked from Dwayne to me, then back again. "This stops now. Hear me? Dwayne, a bayonet is not listed as a prohibited weapon. The legality is in the intent. She's not using it as a weapon of defence or with intent to harm. Carrying a bayonet as part of a costume is not illegal. To charge Ms. Cornwall under these circumstances will most likely earn you a reprimand from a judge for wasting his time."

He looked at the bayonet. "Take that and put it in

the back of my Cherokee." Dwayne trudged away without one word out of his stupid mouth.

When Redfern turned back to me, his voice was taut with anger. "Will there ever come a time when you treat an officer — any officer — with respect? And not make a public scene?"

When I opened my mouth, he overrode me. "Well, Bliss? Is expecting you to conduct yourself with even a modicum of decorum a hopeless objective?"

What an arrogant asshole! My head was going to explode with rage. I held my index finger under his nose. "We already had a discussion about the bayonet, remember? Now, instead of sticking up for me, you side with your half-witted constable. Again. But that's fine, okay? You don't need to have my back. From now on, I rely on myself and nobody else. And another thing, don't call me Bliss anymore, okay, *Redfern*!"

I whirled away, but turned back. "Just bite me! Okay, *Redfern*?"

I stomped back to the atrium. People stared at me but I didn't care. Chico took a few more pictures of me with kids and dads, but it was clear the party was winding down. Redfern returned and called for attention.

"Folks, the weather has worsened. I've been in touch with the OPP, and they're planning to close Highway 21 shortly. Within the next few minutes, I suggest that everyone make their way to their vehicles and head back to town. Drive slowly and you should be fine. We have a snowplow waiting at the corner to lead the way. Thank you." His face was brick red and I suspect my own displayed a similar shade of anger.

I gathered up the money while Chico packed up his gear. People didn't exactly stampede through the exit, but there were one or two body jams and more than a few exotic plants crushed before they even left the atrium.

CHAPTER
FORTY-FIVE

GLORY THRUST A FREE yellow-blossomed plant into a customer's arms and ushered him out the door.

"Thank God that's the last one," she said, pushing her red curls away from her flushed face. It wasn't clear whether she meant the last plant or the last customer. It was true either way. The plant table was bare, and we were alone at last. The storm had picked up strength and hurled curtains of sleet at the glass, rattling the panes as if trying to find a way inside.

"Let's get out of here, too," I said. "We have to drive on the highway for a half-mile before we get to the town limits, and if the OPP closes it, we could be stuck here for days. Can one of you drop me and Rae off? Where is she, anyway?"

"Rae went home with some fat guy with a broken arm." Dougal looked at me as though I should have known this. "She left about a half-hour ago."

"Rae left with Mr. Archman? Why didn't she wait

for me?"

"That's Mr. Archman, our math teacher from high school? The dude has seriously let himself go."

"But Rae ...?"

"She didn't have her car and he offered her a ride. Guess she figured you'd get home okay. You have the whole police force in your back pocket."

"Not so much as you'd think. Well, doesn't matter. You can drive me home."

"I'm meeting Holly in Toronto, remember? I got dropped off here this morning with my bag. I hired a car and driver for the trip and he should be here any minute. So, sorry, can't help you."

I looked at Glory. She was surveying the chaos around us with narrowed eyes.

"What about you, Glory. Are you going home before you meet Tony?"

"No, sorry. I have my weekend bag in my office. I'm getting out of here now. If I can't outrun the OPP closures on the highway, I'll have to take the back roads. Luckily my Land Rover has winter tires and an excellent navigation system."

Dougal's phone dinged, and as he answered, I said to Glory, "So, both of you are going to leave me here alone?" This was not a good idea.

"Phone Neil. He'll come back for you or send someone. Don't be such a baby. You won't be here for long."

No way would Redfern come back to get me. No way would I ask him to. I could be storm-stayed in this house of breakable glass for days.

Dougal shouted into his phone, "What! I already

paid you. I don't care about a refund. I need to get to Toronto tonight. Get here in twenty minutes ..." His blue eyes were slits in his face as he pounded the end key.

He looked at Glory. "My cowardly driver isn't coming. He's afraid of the storm. Can I ride shotgun for you? I'll get a taxi from your hotel to Holly's condo."

Say no, say no, I silently pleaded. Even Dougal was better than nobody if I had to spend the night at the greenhouse.

I really thought she'd tell him to drop dead. She wouldn't be able to tolerate his company for however many hours it would take to drive out of Bruce County's snowbelt and into the so-called civilization of Toronto.

She prodded him in the chest. "Two conditions. You take a tranquilizer before we leave. And you don't make a sound. I don't care if we slide through a guard rail into a river, you are not to whine, scream, or worse, babble. One word and I'll leave you by the side of whichever godforsaken road we end up on. Got it?"

He nodded vigorously ... and silently.

They rushed for the door and raced into the hallway to gather their bags. I stood in the middle of the atrium.

What the hell?

Glory turned back. "Bliss, since you'll be here for a while yet, gather all the garbage into bags and set them by the door. But don't put them outside. We don't want to attract animals. Tidy up a bit, and mop the floor in here. You can even make a start on packing up the decorations. If something happens and neither one of us returns by late Monday, turn the misters on in Plant Rooms A through D. For five minutes only, got that?

Don't worry if there's a power failure. The generators will come on and provide heat and light to the plant rooms. If it gets cool in here or the office areas, you may have to wait with the plants. But don't touch any of them."

What the fuck is happening?

Dougal stuck his head back in. "Almost forgot. Bliss, the lights are on a timer. They're programmed to switch off at seven o'clock. The plant room lights stay on, of course. You'll be out of here before then, though. I'll say hi to Holly for you."

"It's already six o'clock," I called after them. "How do I bypass the off-switch?" But they were already running for their luggage. Glory didn't even change out of her silk outfit.

They ignored my pleas and, in less than a minute, raced out to the parking lot, where Glory warmed up her vehicle while Dougal used his hands to sweep the snow from the windows. Then they were gone, fishtailing out of sight. The snow was falling so fast and thick that I caught only a glimpse of the red tail lights as they disappeared onto Concession Road 10.

I looked at my watch. Only fifty-five minutes before the lights went out. I located the light timer in Glory's … Ivy Belcourt's office. But I had no clue how to bypass it. I was afraid if I messed with it, the lights would go off right now.

I called Rae. She answered on the first ring. "Bliss! Where are you? I was getting worried."

"Well, don't stop. Worrying, I mean. I'm still at the greenhouse. Alone. Glory and Dougal are trying to get to Toronto."

"Chief Redfern is coming back for you, isn't he?"

"We had a fight, a bad one, and I think we broke up. So, nobody's coming back to get me. I just wanted to let you know what's happened in case my dead, dehydrated body is found a week or two from now when the roads are open again."

"Bliss, you're not supposed to be by yourself until the murderer is caught!"

I hung up on her. It was her fault I was alone. And it hadn't occurred to me until she mentioned it that I was in protective custody. Really? I looked around. Alone!

Everyone on the suspect list, past and present, had been here this afternoon. And all had followed the plow home. I had to surmise that only a totally unhinged psychopath would venture back out. Luckily, only my insane cousin, my so-called friend, and the Royal Pain knew I was here alone.

I looked at my watch again. If the lights in the plant rooms stayed on, I could find my way through the hall. It wouldn't be dead dark anywhere in the greenhouse. One thing about thick, falling snow. It turned the black of night into the white of — night. I could sleep under a desk with my coat wrapped around me, and if the power failed, I could crawl into one of the plant rooms and cozy up to something tall, damp, and green.

I had a plan and I would survive. I wasn't Bliss Moonbeam Cornwall for nothing.

First, I should go back to the atrium and forage for any leftover food. And Glory could kiss my heinie before I'd clean up the place.

The coffee and hot water urns hadn't been unplugged. I shook the coffee urn. Maybe a third full. The other one, maybe half. Good, at least I could drink coffee and make myself tea until they ran dry. A few drying cookies and date squares remained on the trays.

A stray, unwelcome thought flitted through my mind. I could call Redfern. He wouldn't leave me stranded. I quickly banished the idea. I'd rather be stranded. Another thing about Bliss Moonbeam Cornwall? I'm "cut off her nose to spite her face" stubborn. Even if it killed me.

Now that the body heat projected by dozens of people had dissipated, I was chilly, especially my chest. I rubbed my bare arms and decided to change into my civvies before the lights went out.

A faint scraping sound came from somewhere, outside I thought. I went still and listened. There it was again. While the outside door of the atrium was solid, the walls were glass — fortified glass, I trusted, although I had never cared enough to ask.

A large shadow moved along the path, close to the greenhouse walls. Where did it come from? If it came from the parking lot, it could be human, either my salvation or my death. If the figure had slogged through the line of pines outside the atrium, it could have originated in the forest on the other side of River Road. In that case, I had a bear outside. It was strong enough to swipe its paw through the glass and gain entrance. The fucker should be hibernating, but hell, this was Bruce County. Enough said.

I had nothing to protect myself with. Redfern had taken my bayonet. Hornet spray could work, but Pan had returned it to the storage room at the end of the long hallway. Hot water from the urn? These paltry defence options whizzed through my mind, but were all rejected as ineffectual to a determined predator, whether human or animal. I could run, but could I hide well enough to elude whatever was outside? I wasn't going quietly, or easily, that's all I knew.

A fist pounded on the door. "Bliss? Open this door, damn it. I saw you through the window."

CHAPTER
FORTY-SIX

THE OPP HAD CLOSED Highway 21 at 17:00 hours. The barriers had been placed on either end of the town limits so nobody was coming into, or leaving, Lockport. Locals could still traverse the main street and access businesses and stores, or reach their homes. Or the hospital, if necessary. The wind continued to blow the snow into whiteouts, reducing visibility to zero at times. A minivan exiting the Wing Nut had lost control and slid across both lanes of the highway, initiating a twelve-vehicle accident.

There were no serious injuries, but some of the motorists were furious, and a few fights had broken out. Neil was called to the scene from the greenhouse and stayed to help sort out the mess. Two squad cars, lights whirling to warn oncoming traffic, defined the perimeter. Dwayne had made at least half a dozen trips in the 4 X 4, shuttling passengers and children home while the drivers waited to be processed. Like vultures, tow trucks belched exhaust into the air and waited for the go-ahead to hook up a disabled vehicle and drag it away for costly repairs.

This was Neil's third winter in Lockport, and he was used to civilians refusing to stay home when the weather was bad. They thought winter tires or four-wheel drive should get them through anything. He whirled around as another snowmobile crossed not ten metres from where he was standing in the centre of the road. What was with these people? You couldn't see a metre in front of your face, yet they jumped on their sleds and roared all over the side roads. If another one crossed close to this scene, he was going to ticket their ass.

He called Thea over. "Were you able to get a discarded cup at the greenhouse this afternoon? From either of the subjects?" He had to shout to make himself heard over the howl of the wind.

"I got two coffee cups, one from each. Dutifully bagged and labelled. Now locked up at the station and ready for me to compare prints to the partial thumb from the Mauser we found at the swamp. Chain of evidence guaranteed."

"Good job, Thea. Excellent."

Her cell rang and she excused herself to dig it out of her heavy nylon coat. She listened for a minute. "Are you sure? Okay, I'll tell him. Thanks for letting me know, Rae."

"Rae Zaborski," she told Neil. "She got a ride home earlier, thinking Dougal or Glory would give Bliss a lift. However, Dougal and Ms. Yates have scarpered away to Toronto, apparently, trying to drive out of the storm, I guess, using the back roads. In any case, Bliss is alone at the greenhouse."

Neil's first thought was that Bliss would be extremely pissed at him. He had placed her under guard, refusing to let her drive her own car. Now she had no protection, and no way to get home. The only consolation was the weather. To reach the greenhouse, anyone who meant her harm would have to edge around the OPP barrier and drive on a closed highway. And the killer had no way of knowing she was there alone.

She would be safe, but she might be terrified, alone in a glass building with the wind buffeting the panes and the snow obscuring anything beyond its walls.

Had she broken up with him? Her parting remark of "Bite me" had been shouted at full volume. Everyone in the atrium must have heard her. Shit. She might be loud and obstinate, but she had a point to her anger — this time. She had been patient with his issues concerning Debbie, and yet he took Dwayne's side when it was apparent Dwayne was wrong. He knew she had problems of her own — trust and abandonment, mostly. Her husband left her for another woman, and her parents seemed too busy with their lives to keep in touch. She had bounced back from that, and yet he didn't even support her on a simple legal issue. She must consider him no better than her ex-husband. Yeah, he was pretty sure she had dumped him.

Maybe it wasn't too late. He should drive over there and get her. They were just about done here anyway. He was about to wave Thea over when he heard a metallic crash. Peering through the whiteout, he spotted a new vehicle added to the pileup: a large SUV. It had exited the Wing Nut parking lot. Hadn't the fool seen the collection of dented vehicles in front of him?

"What the hell." Thea ran up to Neil.

"Get the Breathalyzer for this one," he told her. "I'll be with you in a minute."

Dwayne sat in the cruiser, ostensibly using the radio to call dispatch, but more likely warming up. Who the fuck wasn't cold? Neil wrenched open the door.

He thrust the keys to the 4 X 4 into Dwayne's hands. "Go back to the greenhouse and pick Bliss up. Take her home and wait with her until I get there. All night if necessary."

Dwayne's eyes slid to the left, then forward again. "But Chief, what if she won't come with me?" He climbed slowly out of the cruiser.

"I'm quite certain she'll be ready to leave with anyone, even you. She may harangue you on the trip out, in which case suck it up. Don't answer back, and don't threaten to arrest her. In other words, don't piss her off. Got it, Dwayne?"

"Got it, Chief. Uh, you know I'll have to drive around the OPP barrier."

"That's why you're taking the 4 X 4, Dwayne. Take it easy and you'll do fine. Wait; give me the keys to the cruiser."

He tried to call Bliss, but she didn't, or more likely wouldn't, answer. He walked over to help Thea administer the Breathalyzer to the clearly inebriated driver who had just rear-ended the pileup. There must be a full moon up there behind the falling snow.

CHAPTER
FORTY-SEVEN

"**GET THE LEAD OUT, BLISS.** The entrance to the parking lot is drifting over and I don't want to get stuck trying to get out."

The flaps of Dwayne's hat dangled beside his ears, but I had no desire to laugh. I was actually glad to see Constable Fuckup. "What are you doing back here?"

"Not my idea. The Chief sent me to get you."

"Why didn't he come himself?"

"He's tied up at a multiple-vehicle pileup on the highway in front of the Wing Nut. Let's go. It's not getting any better out there. I don't want to spend the night here with you."

"Right you are, Dwayne. You'll need to unhook my wings so I can put my coat on. There are two little clips …"

He backed away. "I'm not touching you. The Chief would kill me if he finds out. As it is, he's giving me an oral quiz in two weeks on Prohibited Weapons. I'm going to have to study the Criminal Code, Section 84, Firearms and Other Weapons. All because of you."

I managed not to laugh. "Well, it's only one section, right? It's not like you have to memorize the Firearms Act." Redfern knew all along Dwayne was wrong. Redfern was even more wrong when he tried to blame me. He'd pay for that. "One's got nothing to do with the other. Unhook me so we can get out of here."

His radio squawked and Dwayne turned away like I was a terrorist with a wiretap on his shoulder radio. "Yeah, Chief? Yes, I have her. We're leaving momentarily. She wants me to unclip her wings, but I didn't touch her. Roger that."

I couldn't hear Redfern's words, but the intent came through loud and clear. I'd been at the end of that tone a time or two myself.

"Okay, Chief. Roger."

Dwayne came at me with steely determination in his eyes. "Hold still. The Chief says it's okay for me to do this."

I turned my back to him and rolled my eyes. "Well, as long as it's okay with the Chief." While his cold fingers fumbled at my bare back, I glanced at the ceiling. The disco ball turned slowly, catching the light with each spin.

"Here." Dwayne thrust the wings into my hands. "Now get your coat and let's go. Make sure you tell the Chief I didn't take any liberties with your body."

"Roger that." I tossed the wings on the table near the coffee urn. "There's a ladder lying against the wall under the table, Dwayne. Get it out. We have to take the disco ball with us."

He looked up. "No way. What's wrong with you?"

"It's evidence. There could be some pictures in there that might explain what happened to Faith Davidson. I don't want to leave it here in case the murderer gets his hands on it."

"You're loony, Bliss." But he crawled under the table and dragged the ladder out. He set it up, then stood looking at me. "You do know the ball won't fit in the back of the 4 X 4?"

"Okay, we'll remove the contents and leave the rest. Give me your penknife. I need to cut the cable." Wait. That sounded wrong, even to me. There was some electricity going to the motor that turned the ball, or it wouldn't revolve, right?

Dwayne and I stared at each other. I looked at my watch. Ten minutes left until the lights went out. I didn't want to take the chance of cutting a live electrical cord in the dark. I knew as much about electricity as I did about spring-loaded nail guns.

I climbed the first few rungs. "Let's have that blade, Dwayne. I'll slice through the ball without cutting the cord."

"I can't let you have my knife. It's against regulations to let a civilian touch police-issued equipment."

That suited me fine. "Then you go up, Dwayne. Don't try to save the ball. Just hack through it and rip it apart. Anything inside will fall out onto the floor."

I saw by the expression on his face that he wasn't going to do it.

"Did I mention that the lights are on a timer and will cut out at seven o'clock? That's six minutes from now."

Dwayne unsnapped his coat and threw it to me. Holding the blade in front of him and spouting profanity unbefitting an officer of the law, he ran up the ladder. He stabbed the disco ball once, then again and again. Each time he had to withdraw the blade from the revolving sphere before he overbalanced.

"Slice, slice!" I yelled. "Stab and slice." Damn it. If I had my bayonet, that ball would be split and gutted by now. I dropped his coat on top of my wings.

Three minutes to go. He climbed another rung and wrapped his arms around the ball. The motor grinded in protest. "Ouch, ouch, this thing is made of glass! I'm getting shredded."

What a drama queen. "It's plastic, Dwayne. Put your knife away and pull the edges apart."

"These twinkle lights are burning my neck." He dropped his knife, just missing my head.

"I doubt it. They're LED. The spotlights might get a little warm, though. About sixty seconds left, Dwayne."

The motor squealed as the disco ball disgorged its fifteen-year-old secret. A dozen squares of heavy paper dropped to the floor. I ran around picking them up. There wasn't time to take a close look, but other than a few smudges of colour, the surfaces seemed to be mainly white. Since my chest was mostly bare cleavage, I had no handy spot for storage. I lifted my skirt and thrust the Polaroids down the front of my tights.

The disco ball began to turn again, its tattered and torn facets still sparkling and glinting under the spotlights. No time to mourn. I called up to Dwayne, "You can come down now. The lights will go off any second. I'll grab my coat and we can …"

"*Shhh*. Somebody's out there." He descended two rungs at a time. "A snowmobile stopped on River Road and I saw the driver head into the trees outside."

His hand went to his gun. "It may be someone wanting to get out of the storm, but get into the hall, fast …"

A helmet-clad form suddenly appeared at the glass, raised the face shield, and peered in at us. Just as the lights went out, I saw the figure take a step back and raise one arm. There was a deafening explosion as glass shattered and flew inward.

Beside me, Dwayne cried out and slumped to his knees.

CHAPTER
FORTY-EIGHT

"DWAYNE! ARE YOU OKAY? Get up!"

"Can't breathe — got hit in the vest. Open ... door to the hallway. Need ... to find cover."

I did as he asked, and helped drag him out of the atrium. Faint alien light shone from the plant rooms, turning the corridor a sickly green. Dwayne crawled toward the closest doorway — the women's washroom. The sound of smashing glass from the atrium sent my heart rate into triple digits.

"No! We'll be trapped." The washrooms had solid walls.

I flung open the door to Plant Room F. We were assaulted by warm, humid air that smelled of earth and vegetation. The ventilation system whirred and the lighting tracks hummed, helping to mask our movements. I hoped. Chest-high, broad-leafed plants filled the space, and there were narrow paths between them for the workers to walk along. Tables lined the room, with more plants standing against them.

The intruder had a gun. I had ... what? A bottle of herbicide spray? I needed to find a weapon, but I saw nothing else other than flower pots, bags of earth, and a few hand trowels.

"Get under this table closest to the door," Dwayne gasped. "The door opens against it. It's my best chance of taking the guy down."

Was he nuts? I pushed aside some plants and helped Dwayne crawl under the table. I followed him, then pulled the pots back into place. There wasn't much light under the table, but I tried to get a closer look at Dwayne.

He wasn't bleeding, but he held his right arm at an awkward angle. "The bullet is stuck in your vest, Dwayne."

He looked down and groaned. "The impact may have broken some ribs. Radio.... My coat is in the atrium." He managed to pull his gun out but couldn't lift his arm.

Where the hell was my cell? My costume had no pockets ... it was in my tote in the washroom. Shit! "Dwayne. Do you have your cell on you?"

He felt around with his left hand and pulled it out. I snatched it from him. "What's your security code? Type it in!" I whispered. I tapped the texting app. "What's Redfern under?"

"I don't text him. Let me have it. I'll phone him."

Thank God, Redfern answered right away. "Chief, there's an intruder at the greenhouse. I've been shot. We're in the plant room nearest the women's washroom.

Under a table."

I could hear Redfern shouting at him. I removed my high-heeled sandals.

"She's okay, but I don't know if I can use my gun. I'll try. Hurry."

"Okay. Let me have it back. I have to turn off the sound now." I'd almost come to grief once before when my cell rang at an inopportune moment, and it wasn't going to happen again tonight.

He slumped onto the floor, his eyes fluttering. He was going into shock.

Shit!

I shook his shoulder. "Give me your gun. It's our only chance."

His eyes opened. "No. I'll lose my job. An officer never gives up his gun. Never."

His hand wrapped around the Glock's hand grip, but loosely. His index finger had fallen away from the trigger. I pulled the barrel away from his body. His fingers twitched but he couldn't reach out.

"Bliss … You can't …"

"Quiet!"

The door opened. I tried to remember facts I'd heard from Redfern and other cops, but never paid attention to. The Glock was a .40-calibre semi-automatic pistol. No safety, so it was ready to go. One pull on the trigger produced one bullet. The magazine contained fifteen rounds. It had been more than three years since I'd held a gun and aimed at a paper target. Would I be able to shoot a human being? I guess I'd find out.

I put one hand on Dwayne to quiet him. A pair of

boots halted not eighteen inches from our hiding spot. I put my hand over my mouth to stifle the cry of surprise. *Jimmy Choos!* Suddenly everything made sense. I wanted to punch myself for not understanding sooner. The Weasel wasn't getting his own hands dirty.

I scampered through the warren of table legs, depending on the overhead humming and whirring to mask the sound of my movements. I hoped that the tropical potted plants lined up in front of the tables prevented Andrea from catching sight of me. I prayed that Dwayne didn't cry out in pain and give his position away. I had no doubt Andrea would shoot him again. No time to think about Redfern or where he might be. I couldn't count on anyone else to save me. At that moment, I knew I could put a bullet in her chest to save my life, or Dwayne's. No more doubts.

"*Bli-iss?*" Andrea was clearly trying to pinpoint my position. "You know I'm going to kill you and your uniformed minder. Two more deaths don't matter to me. I heard you talking about the photos hidden in the glitter ball. I came back for them. Finding you here is just a bonus. Saves me time. Since the ball has been sliced open, you must have the pictures on you."

I was under a table directly opposite the door — opposite Andrea and her gun. My hands, as I held Dwayne's Glock, were becoming slick with sweat. "Why kill Sophie and Kelly Quantz?"

As I spoke, I crawled forward. Just in time, it turned out, as a bullet hit the tropical plants directly in front of the spot I had just vacated. That made two bullets she'd used. It didn't matter whether she had a second Mauser

GLORIA FERRIS

or a Sauer. Both chambered eight rounds. Six more to go. If she had another pistol that chambered more than eight, I was beyond screwed.

"After that girl's body was found in the locker, Sophie was going to tell the authorities." Andrea snorted derisively. "She was there when Michael accidentally knocked the girl down. At the time, Sophie promised not to say anything. She knew Michael didn't do it on purpose, and it would destroy his future if people knew. She should have kept her promise. I met her in the church instead of Michael. It was so easy. Same with her drunkard husband. He tried to blackmail Michael. I met him at the swamp and took care of him. Even easier. I thought that was the end of it, so I threw the Mauser away. I didn't want it found in my possession. Not registered, you see, so can't be traced back to us. It was my grandfather's, but I had no choice."

So far, Andrea hadn't moved from the doorway. I could see the lower part of her body weaving from side to side as she talked. She was trying to pinpoint my location. The next time I spoke, she would know I was making my way toward her, toward the door.

"What about me, Andrea?" As soon as the words were out of my mouth, I doubled back, toward Dwayne.

Her third and fourth bullets would have hit me had I stayed where I was. Every inch of my skin poured sweat and I was sure the Glock was going to slide right out of my grip when I finally pointed it at her.

"You've been making trouble for Michael since he threw you out like the piece of trash you are. You were there the night that girl died, and your snooping has

374

caused us trouble ever since. As long as you're around, our political career is in jeopardy. I decided to kill you after Kelly Quantz turned out to be so easy. I just ran home and got another gun. It was my grandfather's, too. So fortunate that it uses the same ammunition." She laughed, almost gaily. "I'll throw this one away as well. After. Then your boyfriend won't be able to connect us to either gun."

Andrea's chattiness dwindled into silence. I tried desperately to think of something else to say. "Why did Mike argue with Faith?"

This time, I fast-crawled in the opposite direction until I was close to the door, on the opposite side of the room from Dwayne.

Two bullets smashed into the row of pots. Several exploded, throwing plants and earth under the table. A pain shot across my calf and I stifled a yelp. Did a piece of flying clay hit me? How many bullets was that? Six?

Andrea spat with contempt. "She was pregnant. Can you imagine? The slut was pregnant. She wanted Michael to help support her bastard."

I heard what she said, but the information didn't shock me. What now? She had at least two bullets left. I could shoot her legs from under the table. Yes. That's what I'd do. But I preferred to wait until she was out of bullets.

"I want the pictures. And I *am* going to kill you."

Dwayne groaned, and I watched her body swing away from me, toward the corner table. She couldn't see him yet, but in just a few precious seconds, she would find him.

Still, she stood in the doorway. I watched her Jimmy

Choos pivot in the direction of Dwayne's hiding spot and she took a step. With one foot, she shoved a couple of pots aside. From across the room, I saw Dwayne's hand move limply. She saw it, too.

I didn't make a conscious decision. I wasn't even sure the damn Glock would fire when I pulled the trigger. Maybe Redfern didn't allow Dwayne to carry a loaded gun. Maybe I was going to fucking dine with my ancestors tonight. But I crawled out from under the table and stood up. Somebody screamed, "Drop the weapon." I thought for an instant that it was coming from me.

Right, I was a fucking Dirty Harry. Make my day. She spun around and we both fired.

I missed. She didn't.

CHAPTER
FORTY-NINE

DWAYNE HAD TAKEN the 4 X 4. No way would a cruiser get through the heavy drifts covering the highway. The concession road was sure to be worse, and the end of the greenhouse driveway into the parking lot — impassable.

Neil spotted a massive municipal snowplow idling in front of the Wing Nut. He ran toward it, shouting for Thea and Bernie to follow him. He banged on the door of the truck. When the window lowered, he recognized Fang Davidson.

He looked up into the bearded face. "I need to get to the greenhouse, now! Dwayne and Bliss are there with the killer. Dwayne's been shot. Drive us."

"Man, I don't think I should do that," Fang began. "I'm municipal, not authorized to drive on the highway past the town limits…"

"Did you not hear me? This is an emergency situation. I'll take responsibility."

"Jump in, and let's ride! Nobody threatens our Bliss and gets away with it."

Fang agreed so readily, Neil figured he was up for it all along, even eager. He called another officer over. "Get an ambulance over to the Belcourt Greenhouse. I don't care how they do it. Get another plough if you have to. We have an officer down. Maybe more. And get as much backup over there as possible."

The front seat of the behemoth was wide enough to fit the four of them comfortably, albeit without seatbelts. Fang swung around the accident vehicles still waiting to be processed. A hundred metres farther, he manoeuvred the truck around the highway barrier.

Once past the barrier, Fang lowered the plough and hit the gas. Snow flew to the side of the highway. Industrial windshield wipers scraped the curtains of falling snow aside almost before they hit the window. Fang took his foot off the gas to round the corner onto Concession 10, then sped up again.

Neil turned to Bernie and Thea. "Go in with your weapons ready. I'll try to take him out with the Taser. If I can't … I'll get out of your way."

Fang looked away from the road long enough to catch Neil's eye. "If this is the guy who killed Faith, shoot the bastard. Never mind your sissy-ass Taser!"

On one level, Neil agreed, but he wanted the suspect alive. There were too many unanswered questions about all three deaths. If Dwayne and Bliss were dead, all bets were off. He shook off the cold paralysis of fear that threatened to shut down his ability to make the correct decision. He needed to remain clear-headed. Bliss couldn't be dead.

"Did you raise Dwayne on the radio, Chief?" Thea's voice was steady, but Neil knew she had to be sick with worry for Dwayne. He should have brought someone else with him, but Thea — and Bernie — were his two most experienced officers at the accident scene.

"No. He called me on his cell instead of the radio. I don't want to chance using it now. It might put them in more danger."

Fang gave the steering wheel a hard yank to the right. The plough hit the eight-foot snow drift that covered the entrance to the greenhouse parking lot. It cut through without hesitation, throwing snow fifteen feet sideways. Fang stood on the brakes and the truck shuddered to a stop.

The iron light standards surrounding the parking area were dark. The front of the greenhouse where the foyer and offices were situated was cloaked in darkness. A faint greenish light emanated from the interior of the greenhouse, reflecting up through the high glass roofs. On a clear night, the glow could be seen for miles, but tonight's heavy snowfall absorbed it like a white shroud.

"Stay here," Neil ordered Fang. To the others, he said, "We don't want to announce ourselves by breaking in through the front entrance. We'll go around back to the atrium."

The path to the back door of the atrium was completely covered over with snow, heavy as sand. They slogged through it, with every nerve in Neil's body screaming for speed. Fear gripped his heart.

The atrium door was locked, but a section of glass wall had been smashed in, the opening large enough for them to squeeze through. "Quiet now. Weapons ready."

Was he making a mistake carrying a Taser in his hand instead of his Glock? Both Thea and Bernie were good shots — on the practice range. Neither of them had used their guns on a person. Neither had he.

They ran silently across the atrium. As Neil's eyes adjusted to the dark, he saw a helmet and a parka by the door. Not Cornwall's or Dwayne's. Good. Maybe he'd have a chance with the Taser. He peered into the hallway. A woman's voice. *Not Bliss.* "Subject is female. Sounds like Andrea Bains. She may have killed two people. Consider her dangerous," he whispered.

He ran into the corridor, Thea and Bernie on either side.

He reached the open doorway to the first plant room. If Andrea Bains glanced up, she would see the three cops bearing down on her. But she was looking at her feet, pointing a gun at something on the floor. No, not the floor, she was aiming under the table.

Before he could shout a warning, Bliss crawled out from beneath another table, directly behind Andrea. She held a Glock in her hand. He readied the Taser and sensed Bernie and Thea fan out on either side.

He yelled "Drop the weapon," but didn't wait for compliance. He threw himself into the plant room and hit the floor. Bernie and Thea crouched on either side of the doorway, taking aim. He pulled the trigger the same instant Andrea whirled on Bliss and they both fired.

Bliss's bullet crashed through the glass over their heads. Then she fell.

CHAPTER
FIFTY

THE BITCH HAD SHOT ME TWICE. Or, more accurately, she had *winged* me twice. If the medics don't have to dig a bullet out of you, you're winged, not shot. That's what the intern told me when the ambulance dropped me off. He slapped a couple of dressings on and said I'd have to wait to have my shoulder stitched up and my calf treated. They had to look after the cop first. Then they shoved me into a cubicle with a curtain around me, alone. I couldn't stop shaking and I was so cold. What I wouldn't give for my jeans, sweatshirt, and a heavy blanket.

The injury to my calf hadn't been caused by a piece of flower pot after all. That's how close the bitch's bullet came. I still buzzed with adrenaline, and replayed again and again the sight of Andrea's body jerking when Redfern zapped her with the Taser. Then Bernie handcuffed her while she was still vibrating. Excellent! I think she might have peed her pants. I was only sorry I didn't have video.

I heard a moan, close by and familiar. Wrapping the thin cotton blanket around me, I slid off the bed and peeked around the curtain. Across the room was another curtain, another bed. I scuttled over the cold tile in my bare feet. My calf hardly hurt.

"Hey, Dwayne! How goes it, buddy? What's the damage?"

Dwayne lay propped against a nest of pillows. While I had to wait for medical treatment, they had rushed him into x-ray, then wrapped his chest with bandages. Oh, to be a cop.

His face twisted in pain. "Three broken ribs. They taped me up. But you'd think they'd give a guy something for the pain. I feel like my lung is punctured. What about you? You're bleeding."

"Yep. Shot twice! And not even stitched yet."

"You look pretty bad. But if I were you, I'd lie down and try to bleed a bit more. When the Chief gets back, we're in for a world of trouble. You might want to wash your face, too. Maybe take a weed-whacker to your hair."

"In trouble for what? Almost being killed?"

"For you taking my gun. They can charge you with lots of things. Like assault with a weapon, possession of weapons dangerous to the public, careless use of a firearm. Me? I gave up my firearm and I think that's a hanging offence. This might even mean my badge."

I leaned out to make sure no ears were in flapping distance. "That's bullshit. But here's what we're going to do." I couldn't believe how sharp my mind was, considering the past few hours. "We're going to tell Redfern that you were unconscious and I took your gun to defend our lives. If I get charged with anything, bring it!" I was a pro at doing forlorn and pathetic. The judge would give me a medal. Maybe ask me to marry him.

He mulled that over, then said, "I'll go for that. I lost consciousness due to the pain of my injury. You tried to save us both. Too bad you aren't a better shot, Bliss. If the others hadn't arrived in the nick of time, we would both be dead now."

I heard voices in the hall, getting louder. I pointed at Dwayne and said, "Remember, zip it. Volunteer nothing."

I was back on my bed by the time Redfern pulled back the curtain. I took one look at his face and burst into tears. Again. Crap, this had to stop. I hadn't seen him since the bitch shot me. Suddenly, Redfern had been there by my side, touching me, brushing my hair back from my face. Then the EMTs arrived and scooped me up with Dwayne and transported us to the hospital where I had been waiting for hours by myself. I cried harder. Oh, man, I hated myself. I was turning into a wimp.

He went into the bathroom and returned with a warm, damp washcloth. "Come on, now, Bliss. Everything's fine. You have a few little injuries, nothing a couple of stitches won't cure. We have Andrea Bains in custody. She's being processed right now."

I wiped my cheeks and was horrified at the mess on the cloth. I had forgotten the face paint. God, I hope no one took pictures. "She told me she killed Sophie because Sophie was going to come forward and tell you that Mike killed Faith. She said it was 'accidental'. Then she shot Kelly Quantz because he tried to blackmail Mike."

"That's about what we figured. Did she happen to mention why she was after you?"

"I threatened Mike's political career or something equally lame. Do you know about the Polaroids in the glitter ball?" I wiped the makeup off my eyes.

"Uh, no." Redfern disappeared again and returned with another damp cloth. He scrubbed at my chin. "Sorry to wipe off the lizard tongue. It was kind of hot."

I told him what Chico had done on grad night and just remembered today. "Andrea heard Chico tell me during the fundraiser this afternoon. That's the main reason she came back. Finding me there was just a bonus, she said. And Dwayne wasn't important." I stopped and we listened to the loud groaning from the other side of the room.

I'd like to say I have a flair for the dramatic, but the truth is, I just remembered the Polaroids because they were scratching my sensitive parts. I reached into my tights and withdrew them, one at a time, enjoying the expression on Redfern's face. "How many is that? Ten? I thought there were more." I fished around and, sure enough, two more had slid down, almost to my knees.

"I didn't have a chance to look at them. Do they show anything helpful?"

He looked at each one in turn, before passing them back to me. "Maybe a photography expert could raise some images, but I doubt anything will show up clearly, even if we get the funds for it. Unless one of them showed Mike Bains actually shoving Faith Davidson into the bathroom sink, they wouldn't help in court anyway."

"I was married to a murderer for eight years. Thank

God he traded down for an older model. I may be scarred for life, though."

Redfern actually smiled. "I doubt it. But you will have two new physical scars to add to the one you got last summer saving my life." He ran his fingers along the still-sensitive area on my forearm.

"You saved mine tonight, Redfern. Guess that makes us even."

He took my hand. "I'm sorry I left you here so long by yourself. I wanted to call on Mr. Bains and tell him the news about his wife's arrest for two murders and two attempted murders. He's admitting nothing, and I doubt his wife will confess he was aware of her actions. Their residence is being searched right now in case there are more prohibited weapons. If so, we have him on that anyway."

"But she told me he was responsible for Faith's death! Can't you arrest him for that?"

"I need some evidence, something more than hearsay and speculation. I'll speak to the Crown Attorney in the morning. We'll decide how to proceed. In any case, I'm quite sure his political career is over."

"That's not enough."

"Agreed. But the truth is, we cops bag 'em, we don't convict 'em. All I can do is present the Crown with as much evidence as possible. The rest is up to the prosecutor."

I remembered something else Andrea had said, something that had barely registered at the time. "Faith was pregnant. With Mike's child. That's why he killed her. I don't believe it was an accident."

Redfern didn't look surprised at this news bulletin.

What else did he know that I didn't? "We'll never know for sure, but would Sophie lie for Mike all these years if she watched him cold-bloodedly murder her classmate?"

I threw myself back onto my pillow. "You're right. We'll never know the facts, will we? Never."

"I have one question for you." His navy eyes were serious.

"Yes?" *Shit, what now?*

"Have we reverted to using each other's last names? I only ask because I don't want to get into trouble again."

I thought about that. "What do we care what other people think? We're comfortable using last names, right? It's natural for us. It doesn't mean we're putting up emotional barriers. When I say 'Neil', I'm thinking 'Redfern' anyway."

"Okay by me. You'll always be my Cornwall."

I reached up and ran my hands through his spikes. They looked sharp, but were anything but. Our lips touched and heat surged through my chilled and battered body. I really think somebody should write a research paper on the effects of adrenaline on sexual arousal. I'd sign up for that study.

There was the sound of a throat being cleared, and when we looked up, a figure stood on our side of the curtain. It was Dr. Fingers, and he looked official. Gloved, gowned, and — no way was he touching me. I pulled the skimpy hospital blanket over my chest.

"Sorry to keep you waiting, Bliss. I was in the OR with an emergency C-section. Just a few stitches in that arm, and I'll have a look at your leg. Then you can get out of here."

"Hi Ed," Redfern said. "Have you heard? We found our killer. Killers, I should say, but only one of them may be convicted."

"I was talking to Thea in the waiting room. She told me. Glad you were on hand to save your young lady, here." His eyes twinkled icily at me through his sparkly clean glasses. I restrained myself from reaching up and placing a thumbprint on each lens.

Instead, I squeezed Redfern's arm. "Get me a real doctor!"

He and the quack exchanged amused glances. That really ticked me off.

I grabbed Redfern's tie and yanked his face down until it was inches from my own. "He's a fucking *gynecologist!*"

CHAPTER
FIFTY-ONE

THE BONES OF FAITH and her child were laid to rest in a private glade that could only be reached by taking a well-trodden path through a dense hardwood forest. Early May sunshine streamed through the budding trees, and carpets of tiny violets spread between the graves.

There was no church service, and I was the only outsider invited to the interment. At least fifty people, including dozens of children, surrounded the open grave. One by one, a relative stepped forward and read a poem, or shared a story of Faith's childhood. Lester opened a tattered bible and recited Psalm 23, the old version. A modest tombstone rested against a nearby birch tree, ready to set into a cement base once the soil on the grave had settled. Faith's name and dates of birth and death were etched into the stone. And underneath: "Forever 17." In tiny letters near the bottom, the words "and babe" were inscribed.

I pulled my sunglasses from my head and covered my eyes with them. If I had been a better friend to Faith, maybe she would have shared her secret with me, and this day would not end with her in the ground. I know I wouldn't have married the man who impregnated her, then killed her and left her body to rot in an abandoned building. Choices, right?

The heartfelt eulogies ended. Before leaving the family to say their final goodbyes, I reached down and set a bouquet of yellow roses on the coffin. Yellow had been Faith's favourite colour. I looked the meaning up online, and the gift of yellow roses meant friendship and caring. *Goodbye, Faith. I hope you landed in a safe and happy place.*

I took my time on the path, enjoying the bird sounds and smells of early spring. Hey, I didn't hate all nature, just the parts that bite, sting, or growl. Trees were very cool, water was great, even rocks had a certain beauty as long as you didn't turn one over. And I loved flowers, even the kinds that grew in a greenhouse.

A lot had happened since Andrea Bains was arrested before Christmas. Her trial was set for September, and I tried not to worry about testifying. As long as I didn't call the defence attorney a dickhead or refer to his client as "Mrs. Weasel," I should get through it without being thrown into the big house myself.

Andrea's thumbprint was on the Mauser used to kill Kelly Quantz. They had her on that one, and for the attempted murder of me and Dwayne. The gun she used in the greenhouse was indeed a Sauer, the model I learned to shoot as a child. I no longer thought of it as a cute firearm. As we suspected, when it came to her husband, Andrea clammed up and wouldn't incriminate him.

"Michael" dearest hadn't been charged and was still free. I recounted to Redfern and the Crown, maybe even the RCMP and CSIS, what Andrea told me in the greenhouse — Mike caused Faith's death. But Andrea said I was lying, and apparently the defence could drag up my past and paint me as the deserted, bitter first wife with an axe to grind. The Weasel might yet be charged, but chances aren't good he'll be convicted — of anything. I don't kid myself. Justice is not only blind; it's often deaf and dumb as well.

The Weasel was asked not to leave town, but as time passes and he isn't charged, the restriction will almost certainly be lifted. The Davidsons won't like that. It's possible Fang or Lester might take a run at the Weasel in their pickup truck some dark night. It's what I'd do.

One rather amusing note: Glory gathered the town councillors and staged a political coup the day she returned from her dirty weekend in Toronto with Tony. The councillors stripped the Weasel of his mayoral powers, and Glory installed herself as interim mayor. The municipal elections will take place in October and she's everyone's favourite to permanently seize the sceptre of power. On second thought, having the Glorious One as mayor might not turn out to be at all funny.

The scorching hot romance between Tony and Glory shows no sign of fizzling out. Tony spends all his free time at Glory's luxurious mansion, and he's trying to get a transfer to a nearby OPP detachment. Stay tuned to see how long their inferno of lust will endure with so much togetherness.

And Redfern and me? Well, he never left. The lease on his cabin expired and, without fuss or fanfare, he moved the rest of his stuff into my parents' house. As far as I know, he has yet to find Grandpa's weapons hoard in the garage. I need to do something about that soon.

He talks about buying a house together. That might happen. I want something modern, with a waterfront view. And if Rae doesn't come with us, Redfern will have to learn to cook.

The sun touched my face as I walked out of the burial ground. I felt lucky to be alive. Even though it was Friday, Dogtown's gates were closed in deference to Faith's burial. I climbed over and started across the road to my bike, parked in front of Redfern's red Gold Wing. He kicked his tires and rubbed a smudge off the chrome fender. He looked plenty sexy in a black leather jacket, dangling his red helmet by the strap. This would be our first ride of the season, and I looked forward to blowing the sludge out of the carburetor and feeling the wind whip some colour into my cheeks. A week on the Mayan Riviera in February hadn't completely eliminated the memories of the night in the greenhouse when I wasn't sure I was going to survive.

Redfern looked up as the heels of my new Balenciaga ankle boots hit the pavement. I couldn't see his eyes through his shades, but the corners of his mouth quirked up.

"How did it go, Cornwall?"

"Sad, but okay." I turned the key and adjusted my

sunglasses. Then I plunked on my helmet and set the bike to a fast idle.

"I packed us a picnic lunch to cheer you up. Roast beef sandwiches from the deli, sweet cider, cheese puffs. All your favourites." He threw his leg over the seat.

"No wine?"

He laughed at the very notion. "Maybe later. When we get hungry, we'll find a secluded spot in the forest where we won't be disturbed. Who knows how the afternoon will end?" He revved his engine at me.

I flipped the kickstand up and eased the Savage onto the pavement. Settling into the leather seat, I turned the throttle and called over my shoulder, "You'll have to catch me first, copper."

ACKNOWLEDGEMENTS

TO MY BETA READERS: Many thanks to Alyssa Ferris, Donna Houghton, and Lara Inneo. Without your valuable input and suggestions, *Shroud of Roses* wouldn't be the awesome story it turned into.

To Donna Warner, travelling buddy and frontline editor, thanks for meeting every deadline with me and spurring me on when I flagged. Every author needs a friend like you.

To Russ Ferris, my go-to guy for information on weapons. Thank you for researching Second World War firearms for me. I may need your help with the next book, too.

To Cheryl Courville, thank you, my friend, for helping me with Bliss's motorcycle. Quite a coincidence that you rode a red Suzuki Savage back in the day.

To Allison Hirst, my ever-organized editor at

ACKNOWLEDGEMENTS

Dundurn. Thank you once again for polishing *Shroud of Roses* into a worthy sequel to *Corpse Flower*. Fortunately, we appear to have the same sense of humour.

A special thanks to Toby H. Rose, M.D., FRCPC, deputy chief forensic pathologist at the Ontario Forensic Pathology Service in Toronto. Dr. Rose generously ensured that my description of the first body was forensically probable. Then again, what real-life solver of mysteries — and reader of fictional ones — could resist the lure of an old skeleton? It need hardly be mentioned that any errors are mine alone.

And finally, much gratitude goes to Police Chief Dan Rivett of the Saugeen Shores Police Services, who patiently answered my many, many questions about small-town policing, procedure, firearms, crime scenes, and a whole lot more. The tour of the police offices was an eye-opener and I'll make sure that the Lockport Police Services steps up to match the modern efficiency of Saugeen Shores. Again, any mistakes are on me — I'll just try not to be a repeat offender.

ALSO BY GLORIA FERRIS

Corpse Flower
A Cornwall and Redfern Mystery

Winner of the Unhanged Arthur Award for Best Unpublished First Crime Novel, 2010

Swindled out of a fair divorce settlement, former socialite Bliss Moonbeam Cornwall works a number of part-time jobs to pay the rent on a rundown trailer and keep her motorcycle on the road. House cleaner, yoga teacher, library assistant, cemetery groundskeeper, and drudge for her agoraphobic cousin — the work never ends. But Bliss still can't save enough money for what she really wants — another day in court. So, when her cousin offers her a generous fee to find a pollinating mate for his giant jungle plant, she agrees to help. How hard could it be?

That's when she discovers that her neighbours, employers, and even her cousin are involved in a string of illegal activities — including grow-ops, prostitution, and perhaps even murder. And on top of all that, Police Chief Neil Redfern's persistent scrutiny is interfering with her plans for revenge. With no one to back her up, Bliss must make a decision: she can give up on her dreams, or she can start fighting dirty.

MORE GREAT FICTION FROM DUNDURN

Pizza 911
A Mister Jinnah Mystery
Donald J. Hauka

The Tribune's editor-in-chief can kiss Hakeem Jinnah's ass goodbye! His bags are packed and he's off to Africa as king of his own Burger Palace. That is, until a charred, dismembered body is discovered in a pizza oven. The lure of one last front-page byline is too much for Jinnah to resist … even if it turns out to be his own obituary.

Pizza 911 puts the perpetually puffing, politically incorrect Jinnah on the trail of a vicious killer in a chase that takes him from Vancouver to Tanzania. Negotiating a deadly labyrinth of deceit, betrayal, and long-kept secrets, the neurotic newsman has to use his entire reporting repertoire — and then some — to get to the truth. Bikers, drugs lords, shadowy assassins, and a mysterious beautiful woman are all pieces in a complex puzzle that Jinnah must put together before it's too late for him, his family, and even his newspaper.

Based on the Gemini Award-nominated *Movie of the Week*, Pizza 911 delivers.

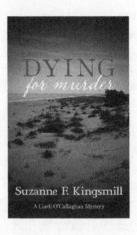

Dying for Murder
A Cordi O'Callaghan Mystery
Suzanne F. Kingsmill

Cordi O'Callaghan is trapped on a remote island research station and in way over her head. While a hurricane rages, Cordi stalks a murderer — or is it the other way around?

Zoologist Cordi O'Callaghan thinks she's in for a relaxing birdsong study at a research station on Spaniel Island, off the coast of South Carolina. But, as usual, she can't escape the chaos that follows her everywhere she goes. As a hurricane rages, trapping her and the rest of the researchers, the director of the station is found dead under troubling circumstances.

Unable to resist a mystery, Cordi sets out to investigate, and ends up getting a crash course on the life habits of bats, sea turtles, and rattlesnakes — and a refresher on attempted murder.

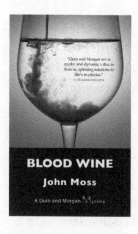

Blood Wine
A Quin and Morgan Mystery
John Moss

Detective Miranda Quin is not only fighting crime, she's fighting for her life.

The summer before 9/11, Toronto homicide detective Miranda Quin wakes up to find her lover dead beside her, yet has no memory of going to bed with him. Horrified by the result of the forensic investigation, the normally feisty Miranda moves through events in a daze while her partner, Detective David Morgan, offers support.

Because Miranda is the prime suspect, neither she nor Morgan is able to pursue the case officially, freeing them from jurisdictional constraints. They find it impossible to avoid being pulled into the rush of events that follow, from one mysterious death to another in a quirky narrative that brings in a New York policeman who reads Thoreau and a beautiful and dangerous European wine expert who is not what she appears to be. As the plot moves from Toronto to New York and London, a deadly fraud leads to explosive revelations of drug smuggling as a cover for international terrorism.

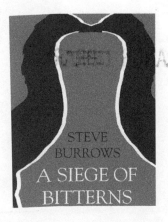

A Siege of Bitterns
A Birder Murder Mystery
Steve Burrows

***GLOBE AND MAIL* 100:**
BEST BOOKS OF 2014

Inspector Domenic Jejeune's success has made him a poster boy for the U.K. police service. The problem is Jejeune doesn't really want to be a detective at all; he much prefers watching birds Recently reassigned to the small Norfolk town of Saltmarsh, located in the heart of Britain's premier birding country, Jejeune's two worlds collide when he investigates the grisly murder of a prominent ecological activist. His ambitious police superintendent foresees a blaze of welcome publicity, but she begins to have her doubts when Jejeune's most promising theory involves a feud over birdwatching lists. A second murder only complicates matters.

To unravel this mystery, Jejeune must deal with unwelcome public acclaim, the mistrust of colleagues, and his own insecurities. In the case of the Saltmarsh murders, the victims may not be the only casualties.

X FERR 2015
Ferris, Gloria, 194?-,
Shroud of roses

GARY PUBLIC LIBRA

SEP 2 9 2015

KENNEDY BRANCH LIBRARY

Available at your favourite bookseller

DUNDURN

VISIT US AT

Dundurn.com
@dundurnpress
Facebook.com/dundurnpress
Pinterest.com/dundurnpress